CURSE OF
THE GORGON

What Reviewers Say About Tanai Walker's Work

Rise of the Gorgon

"*Rise of the Gorgon* by Tanai Walker is a fast-paced suspense about two women who uncover two different truths: one uncovers a terrifying conspiracy, and the other (the Gorgon) discovers free will. ...If you like fast-paced suspense with a complex storyline, a bit of romance, and a lot of ass-kicking, you will like this story. This is also a story about breaking free, finding free-will, and letting love lead to something more."
—*Lesbian Review*

Sacred Fire

"Walker crafts a fantastic tale incorporating mythological figures in contemporary settings. It's not every day you read a novel with a Black lesbian interacting with a Slavic forest spirit in an after-hours spot featuring scantily clad dancing women. She builds the tension with creative turns of phrases as she details how Swan is drawn deeper into the web woven by a goddess thousands of years ago. ...*Sacred Fire* is not your typical novel, but it's worthy of a read because of the author's ability to take an unlikely combination of situations and make them entertaining."—*Black Lesbian Literary Collective*

"Tanai Walker's *Sacred Fire* is the epitome of a paranormal novel. ...Walker is capable of beautifully describing actions and scenery. From the images on the postcards to having tea in an antique shop, it's all lovely to visualize."—*Rainbow Round Table*

Visit us at www.boldstrokesbooks.com

By the Author

Sacred Fire

Rise of the Gorgon

Curse of the Gorgon

CURSE OF THE GORGON

by

Tanai Walker

2023

CURSE OF THE GORGON

ISBN 13: 978-1-63679-395-5

This Trade Paperback Original Is Published By
Bold Strokes Books, Inc.
P.O. Box 249
Valley Falls, NY 12185

First Edition: April 2023

Credits
Editor: Cindy Cresap
Production Design: Susan Ramundo
Cover Design By Tammy Seidick

Acknowledgments

Dad, thanks for always asking about my book.

Gina and Jeraine, thanks for sharing your paradise while I powered through the end of this book.

Liz, thanks for lending out your expertise to beta read.

Dedication

To my amazing wife, Janette,
because she keeps my feet on the ground.

PROLOGUE

Indian Ocean
Western Sumatra

The sun and the sea. In the arms of a gorgeous, mysterious woman. Elle wanted to say so much as the waves rocked the small yacht, lulling the two of them after a session of afternoon lovemaking. Along with the steady gusts of salty wind, sadness stirred the tranquility around them. She lay next to Cass and tried to convince herself to get over the feelings that swelled inside her.

So much had happened since the death of Robert Loera, a troubled veteran Elle helped after interviewing him for a series. They'd become friends and he seemed to be adjusting. Then, one morning he came to her office and ended his life after making some cryptic statements about hurting people in the desert. Elle's questions into his death led her to Ziggurat, a company that hired discharged veterans as security personnel.

She'd gone to Kuwait not knowing that she had stumbled on to a mind control experiment gone awry. The perpetrators, Olympicorp, a shadowy conglomerate of subsidiaries, a cover for their crimes against humanity. Elle's investigations put her on their radar and sent Cass to sabotage her findings.

It had nearly been a year since their adventures in Kuwait; several days on the run from Cass's handler, as well as a horde of locals and personnel of Ziggurat poisoned by an experimental psychotropic bioweapon—a hive mind controlled by another deranged ex-soldier, his brain mutated by mind-altering experiments performed by Ziggurat.

Elle and Cass had barely escaped with their lives and decided for their own safety to put Kuwait behind them, including the inexplicable bond that drove them into each other's arms.

She did her best to return to her life as normal, despite the unanswered questions that had brought her to Kuwait in the first place, despite her worry for Cass, for whom she knew life was far from normal.

Then, months later came the invitation to Indonesia from Cass for a rendezvous in a tropical paradise. Upon recognizing the contents of the package, two plane tickets on a bed of flowers, Elle knew she would go wherever Cass was, no matter the risk. This realization both terrified and thrilled her. Still, she picked up her phone with trembling hands and began to clear her calendar.

Elle found herself on high alert throughout her journey. In hindsight, she should have listened to the nagging paranoia that indifferent eyes were watching her every move. Cass walked right up to her as she stumbled around the airport. She looked like a tourist in shades, shorts, and a T-shirt. She was tan, as if she had been out in the sun for a few days. She had a boat for them, and they sailed along the coast. They mixed with the tourists on shore, but mostly stayed close to the boat, swimming, paddle-boarding, fishing, and making love. It was as if Kuwait never happened.

Cass made it all look so easy, even the acceptance of a fate she did not deserve, how she insisted on going underground to keep Elle safe. Still, she had put them at risk by arranging the trip, proving that not even her steel resolve could keep them apart.

She looked to Cass and saw that she was not snoozing, but awake and watching her through partially closed eyes. Elle smiled at her and she smiled back. Cass turned over on her side and reached for her hand. Their fingers intertwined. Elle felt the warmth of her skin. Neither of them spoke a word. With so much to be said, it felt frivolous to spend their time in silence, smiling at each other in the sunshine.

A surge of wind turned the slightly choppy water into bucking waves. Cass's arms latched around her as the boat rose with such violence it tilted nearly onto its side. They lost their footing and were nearly tossed overboard. A torrent of salt water drenched Elle as she scrambled against the side railing. She felt Cass's arms clutch her waist as the boat bucked and reared. For a few terrifying moments, they were at the mercy of the sea.

The force loosened Cass's grip and Elle was airborne. She hit the back railing and nearly went over onto the swim platform. The world blurred for a moment, black and gray and blue sky. She opened her eyes. She was on her back looking up at the astonishingly blue sky, free of the storm Elle realized had caused the sudden violence.

She heard her name and craned her neck to see Cass clinging to the outboard. She propelled herself forward across the wet deck, unperturbed by the violent rocking of the boat, her eyes locked on Elle.

She managed to slide close enough for their reaching hands to touch.

The boat bucked with a force that flung Cass several feet into the air. She fell hard on her side and rolled into Elle who clung to her hoping she had not been knocked unconscious. Both stunned by the impact of their bodies, they rode out the storm.

The tempest calmed, and the boat bobbed on the choppy water that remained.

Cass raised her head and wrapped her hands around Elle's upper arm. "Are you okay?"

Before she could answer, a mechanical roar rumbled at the front of the boat. They looked up at the sky over the cabin to see a sheet of water that raged from the sea, bringing with it a flying craft that resembled a black helicopter without rotor blades. It hovered above the boat dripping curtains of water and jets of spray that reflected the sun into a multitude of ghostly rainbows. Two wings, hooked at the ends like blades, extended from the craft's sides. From the bottom, a hatch opened, and black cords fell and dangled just inches above the deck. Five men in black tactical gear slid down the cords, their faces covered with black helmets with black visors. They landed and began to advance through the sheets of water toward Cass and Elle.

"Stay here, and don't move even if they come for you," she said and guided Elle's arms around the railing.

Elle understood the gravity of her instructions, to not go down without a fight.

Cass moved toward the black visors, her wet hair loose and whipping in the wind. The five men paused for a few seconds and then advanced as one, carefully. They knew the danger of the woman facing them down on the deck.

Cass stooped quickly and picked up a broken fishing rod.

One of the five produced a wide circular device with a glowing light and lined with what looked to be jagged teeth. Another commanded Cass to go with them and no one would get hurt.

"Who sent you?" she asked.

In answer, they repeated the command, go with them and no one would get hurt.

Cass looked over her shoulder at Elle. The expression on her face was heartbreaking. She turned back to the men in black, and the strange craft floating above them.

"I can't go with you, not willingly."

They came at her at once. Cass brought the rod down on one of their shoulders and it snapped in half. She jabbed what remained into the visor on the helmet of another. One of them grabbed Cass's rod-wielding arm. She tried to twist away, but another of the men restrained her free arm. A booted foot slammed over one of her bare feet. Cass's face twisted in pain and she wrenched out of their collective grip. Still clutching the piece of rod, she drove it into the thigh of one of the men who'd tried to restrain her.

Behind Cass, another of the men brandished a stun gun. Elle shouted out a warning, but it was too late. She heard the two cracks like miniature lightning bolts and saw Cass fall to her knees. The attacker with the cracked visor tried to quickly wrap the strange round device around her neck. Elle realized the purpose of the thing and felt shock and revulsion. She saw that Cass had lifted her hand to keep the thing from being secured. Her wrist caught between the spikes.

Elle heard the stun gun repeatedly. The men in black bore down on her. One held the device around Cass's neck, the others took turns meting out punishment, one with the stun gun, another kicking, another punching. Cass bent forward, her strength fading in the fray, but she did not seem to lose consciousness. She kept her arm up inside the collar.

Elle noticed one of the men had broken off from the fray with Cass and was marching her way. She felt a scream escape her as he neared. She peered past him to see Cass upright despite the abuse hurled onto her.

Suddenly, the man in black forcing the collar flew backward with a force that slammed him into the side railings of the boat. Cass was able to disengage from the device which clattered to the deck and slid backward. She stood on shaking legs, then collapsed.

Elle tried to run for her, but the man in black blocked her path. She tried to fight back, but he grabbed her in a bear hug, lifted her squirming body, and carried her toward the cabin.

She lost sight of Cass then. Elle screamed her name as the men in black bore her, kicking and thrashing, to the front of the boat where they dropped her like a sack of potatoes.

She rolled over and saw the opening of the hatch and the black cords dangling down. Something large fell over the lip and landed a few feet away from her in a jangly metallic clatter. She looked up to see a narrow cage of black metal bars, chains, and panels. One of the men in black hoisted Elle to her feet and into the cage. The contraption lifted from the deck. Elle screamed at them as the cage lurched higher into the air toward the strange craft. When she was high enough, she could look over the cabin to see the men standing over Cass's prone body.

The hatch of the strange craft obstructed her view and she tried to stoop, praying not to hear a gunshot. The cage jangled and shook as she ascended into the dim hatch as if she were on some dilapidated ride at a roadside carnival. Once the ride stopped, she was shoved into a corner. Wild-eyed, she watched as the remaining men in black climbed into the craft. They did not bring Cass with them.

She heard a hiss and a *thunk* as the hatch door closed leaving them in complete darkness for a few seconds. Several interior lights blinked on as did panels of buttons and controls.

"Where is Cass?" Elle asked. "What have you done with her?"

None of them answered.

A sense of dread claimed her, and she felt tears gathering in her eyes. "What have you done with Cass?"

None of them spoke a word or even looked her way.

"You know it's illegal to detain me without letting me know why."

Still, there was no answer.

She looked around at her present company. They stared ahead, packed in with mere inches between them. Even inside the strange craft, they wore their visored helmets, which could not have been comfortable to wear in such a closed-in space. Elle let out an ear-piercing scream and a few of them flinched. One of them turned her way but quickly looked away.

"Where is Cass?" she asked.

They returned to their task of ignoring her. The tears came then. She crouched down as best she could inside the narrow cage. The craft went on and on for what seemed to be hours. Her stomach growled and her bladder began to sting. She prayed Cass fared better, but doubt coupled with dread had settled in to stay.

A thrumming beneath her feet woke her. The craft bounced and she heard a whoosh like air decompressing. She groaned, aware that she was still in an upright position, the muscles in her legs ached and her skin was covered in bruises earned from being tossed around the boat and her struggle with the men in black. She still smelled of the sea. Her clothes, shorts, and a T-shirt as well as her bikini underneath, were stiff from dried salt water. She was barefoot.

The hatch opened flooding the space with light. Through her tear-blurred eyes she saw the men in black gear file in. As her eyes cleared, she saw the silhouettes of two men in dark suits. They released the mechanisms to open the cage and half-carried her out of the craft and onto a gated blacktop.

She glanced around her for landmarks, signs, anything that could identify her location. She saw mountains in the distance, and even closer a large, dilapidated hangar. She spotted a helicopter and some cars parked close by.

They had taken her to an airstrip.

She found her footing as they led her across the cracked blacktop toward the hangar. As her eyes continued to adjust to the light, she looked around for flags or any other insignia to identify who had her. Finding no clues, she found herself wondering what was worse, being caught up in any given world government's net or Olympicorp, an organization that played by its own rules.

Inside the hangar, a small sleek jet waited. Otherwise, the place was empty save for a flock of birds flying between the high rust-colored rafters. The men in black escorted her past the jet and to a flight of metal stairs. At the top of the stairs was a doorless frame. On the other side, a few people milled around in suits. None of them looked her way or spoke.

They took her to a closet-like room with a foldout table and a wooden bench. They sat her there and left. She heard the click of a lock as they secured the door behind them. Elle looked around the tiny space and saw a camera mounted in the corner. Someone was watching her. She turned away and tucked her legs beneath her. The wood gleamed as if recently polished, and was slightly concaved like a church pew. It seemed out of place there in the drab little room. She had sat in many pews when she was younger. Her father would take her to speaking engagements around Atlanta at various churches. They would go out to dinner together afterward and talk about everything. By high school, she began to develop her own ideas about life. She was bitten by the writing bug, and her favorite subject was certainly not the Bible.

She stopped going to her father's speaking engagements and sitting in those pews waiting for him. She felt tears threaten her eyes. She quickly wiped at her face. She was uncertain of what the next person would say or do to her, but she could give them hell. She could fight. For herself and Cass.

The door handle turned, and the door opened.

"I know my rights," she shouted. "Someone needs to tell me why I am being detained."

A middle-aged woman with a mass of black frizzy hair entered. In her arms she cradled two lidded Styrofoam cups with straws, a brown paper sack, and several file folders.

"Ms. Pharell," she said and actually smiled.

Elle aped the expression wanly.

There was a man there as well, of average height with a wiry frame. Black. His head cleanshaven. He unbuttoned his suit coat and sat in a chair just outside the door.

The woman moved closer and placed the paper bag on the table. Elle tried not to concentrate on the smells coming from the bag—bread, meat, potatoes, spice, and grease. The cups rattled with melting ice. Elle's stomach reminded her that she had not eaten since she was dragged off the boat.

"Who are you?" Elle asked.

"Tamara Savrasov. I am an agent of the Foreign Intelligence Service," she said.

Russia.

Elle steeled herself. For what it counted, she was an American citizen. "You had no right to abduct me while I was on vacation in a complete ambush. Where is my friend Cassandra Hunt?"

"Russia had no hand in apprehending you and your friend," Savrasov said. "Perhaps you are not aware that your friend is wanted for questioning by several entities around the world."

Elle felt anger flare and she took a moment to temper herself. She knew the woman would not ask questions about things she did not already know.

"I'm sure you know the whole story, or else someone wouldn't have sent a UFO and armed men to take her alive."

Savrasov pursed her lips. She did not look to be the type to deter easily.

"And who is he?" Elle asked, pointing to the man at the door. He was looking at his phone as if he were not aware of Elle or Savrasov.

"I will allow him to introduce himself," she said. "Shall we proceed, Ms. Pharell?"

She turned her head away. Refused to speak. In her periphery, she saw Savrasov glance at her watch. "What brought you to Indonesia?"

"I was on vacation," Elle told her without turning to face her. "I just told you that."

"Yes, that is what you have told your family and friends, co-workers. Anne Humphries, your co-partner at the Green Patriot."

Elle did not answer.

"You called Hunt your friend. Is that the extent of your relationship? If you two are lovers, it is hardly of any consequence. You don't have to feel embarrassed about becoming entangled with someone like Hunt."

Annoyed, Elle turned to look at her. "Wow, a sympathetic Russian. I'm glad we could sit down and have this talk, Ms. Savrasov, I really am."

The woman searched her pile of folders and removed one. She opened it and perused the contents leisurely. One of the cups shifted as the melting ice resettled. Elle flinched. The woman casually slid one of the cups across the table.

Elle took the cup in her trembling hands and sipped. It was cola, cool bubbly, slightly watered down, but still refreshing. She drank more, but not too much.

"This Cassandra Hunt, you met her in Kuwait when you were investigating the suicide of a US Army soldier?"

"Yes," Elle said simply.

"You hired a team, and she came on as the interpreter."

Elle nodded.

She tilted her head and seemed distracted by the file again. "Before these past few days, when was the last time you saw this person Cassandra Hunt?"

"The last day we spent together in Kuwait City."

"Did you keep in touch?"

"No," Elle said.

"Did you exchange information? Phone number? Email? Address?"

"No," Elle said. "Nothing of the sort."

"Did the two of you run into some trouble in Kuwait? This was during the time of the Bedouin Revolt, an uprising of organized peasants who stormed the city."

That was what the media called it. Elle had watched the cover-up unfold on the way home from Kuwait. Of course, there was speculation from the world at large, and conspiracy theories abounded. Elle knew the truth. She had seen the people Ziggurat poisoned, a village abandoned in the desert with no clue of what happened to its inhabitants. Elle had seen the violent horde that included Ziggurat employees and tribal people.

"Yes, we were there," Elle countered. "But you know all about that."

"I don't." Savrasov's eyes widened in halfhearted disbelief. "Not even officials there know exactly what is going on, or they are pretending not to. No one seems to have any answers, except perhaps the conspiracy theorists such as your friend Tammy Crockett. They believe it was a cover-up."

"You know you're going to have to come at me with something more solid than some conspiracy theories. Tammy is a dear friend of mine, but she preempts all her stories with disclaimers."

She only downplayed Tammy to throw Savrasov off. She was quite brilliant and had used hotel footage to make a photographic connection between Cass and her connection to a daring robbery in Prague.

"Surely you had a run-in with the alleged rebels. A large group of them gathered at the hotel where you and Hunt stayed. There was also a traffic accident on a road you traveled."

"They were all over," Elle said. "Allegedly."

"Over four thousand," she said, sifting through the files. She slid a photo across the table. It was an aerial view of a mob of ragged, filthy people. Elle remembered the collective smell of them and turned her face away. Savrasov covered the photo with another, not to save her from reliving the trauma, the photo was of Cass in front of a row of shops. She wore a black coat and a black beanie on her head. She held a cup of coffee as she spoke with a brown-skinned man with a beard.

"The man in this photo is known to traffic in bio-warfare chemicals," Savrasov said, pointing with her pinky at the man in the photo. "Your friend gave him instructions to create a devastating gas. Luckily, we were watching him, and nothing came of his plans to use the weapon on the New Year's Eve crowd that gathered in Red Square."

Elle felt a shiver start to rise from deep within which she stifled, determined not to show the Russian woman that the thought of Cass rubbing elbows with terrorists made her nervous.

"The suspect could give us no information on this woman," she continued. "He called her a ghost. I have my doubts. You see, ghosts cannot be photographed. We used facial recognition, and nothing happened for a few years. Then, there was this robbery at a bank in Prague. Documents were taken from a scientist's safety deposit box. A few months later, she turned up in Kuwait in the middle of a revolt."

Elle tried to wipe any trace of emotion from her face. The Russians had made the same connections Tammy did. Her silence was enough, as Savrasov continued.

"You say you did not exchange any information with Cassandra Hunt, yet she managed to contact you? What form of communication did she use?"

"A courier brought a package," Elle said. That man still waited by the door, staring at his phone casually, seemingly apathetic to their conversation. "There were plane tickets inside for a specific date."

"Was there anything else? Instructions?"

"She said if I could make it, to come," Elle said.

"You decided to go."

"Why not? I needed a getaway," Elle snapped.

"Ms. Pharell, do you believe in psi powers of the mind?"

Her first thought was of the ridiculousness of the question and her second astonishment as she knew exactly what Savrasov wanted to talk about.

"I would not have before meeting Cass," Elle said slowly. What would it hurt to unpack some of the crazy on Savrasov? Maybe they would think she was completely insane, take pity, and send her home. Something told Elle that they would believe her completely.

"She told me that she has been under someone else's control. For how long? She doesn't remember because her memory is constantly being erased. She doesn't know where she came from, or if she has a family. Has she ever been cared for or lived like a normal human being? She doesn't remember Prague or anything before being assigned the task of infiltrating my team."

Savrasov stared at her for a moment. "You want to know what I think?" she asked. "I think she's a terrorist with some kind of Bond complex. She attached herself to a well-known reporter with a mother who is an American government official. She took you on an adventure, made you think you were through the looking glass, gave you all the answers you could ever want. She disguised her crimes by feeding you this story about not being in control over herself. You gave her your empathy, trust, and more."

She handed over the bag. Elle did not touch it, out of pride and because simply, she'd lost her appetite. The narrative Savrasov had painted was not what her question about psi powers of the mind alluded to. Even before when she'd made empathetic noises. Elle was not some naive reporter duped into the schemes of a terrorist.

"Where is Cass?" Elle asked.

"It is not my clearance level to know. I am to trust that she will pay for her crimes against Russia, as well as anyone involved in obstructing information."

Savrasov began to regather her documents and photographs.

"She's not a bad person," Elle insisted. "Cass was forced to do those things. Look into Olympicorp, investigate Ziggurat. Kuwait was going to happen whether we were there or not."

The woman stood and spoke in Russian. The man behind her looked up from his phone and gave an answer. Whatever that reply, Savrasov did not like it. Her face did not reveal any emotion. She only stared at Elle for a moment before pursing her lips.

"Enjoy your lunch, Ms. Pharell," she said and turned to leave. She paused and gave the man a nod of her head. He said something in Russian and Savrasov was gone. He stood and stretched, then looked around the tiny room before his eyes settled on Elle.

"Hello, Elle, I'm Carl Fletcher." His accent was American, and she felt relieved.

"Can you please tell me what is going on? Why am I being held here?"

"Go ahead and eat your lunch," he said. "It's getting cold."

She took the bag cautiously, opened it, and saw the outline of a sandwich covered in a white wrapper stained with grease. There were some rough-cut fries and a small Styrofoam container with a plastic lid.

"Where am I?" she asked.

"It's best we keep that to ourselves," he said. "The less you know, the better."

"Ignorance is not a comfort to me, Mr. Fletcher."

"I didn't think so," he said. "You're in Kazakhstan."

"Who do you work for?"

"The Security Defense Collective. A group of concerned nations has pooled their intelligence resources."

"I've never heard of that agency before," she said.

"Go ahead and eat your food."

She did. There was a loose meat sandwich. The potatoes were cold. Inside the Styrofoam container was a reddish soup with onions and spices. She looked back up at Fletcher who was back to looking at his phone.

"What are you going to ask me?" she asked.

He glanced away from the screen meeting her eyes only briefly. "Pardon?"

"You're obviously going to ask me some questions that will hopefully resolve what's going on here."

"So, you're not hungry?" he asked.

"I'll eat later. I want to know where you took Cass."

He glanced back at his phone before tucking it inside his jacket pocket. "You're not a prisoner of war or an enemy of the state. If you have something to say that could give us more information about the woman you call Cassandra Hunt, great, if you don't, you'll be returned to the United States with at worst, a travel restriction."

Elle was not appeased. "A travel restriction mandated by who?"

"Homeland Security, for your own safety."

"I'm a journalist," she said. "I suspect you know how important it is for me to be able to travel freely."

"Did I mention that it's for your own safety?"

"And Cass? What are you going to do with her? What about her due process?"

"She gets none. Her fate depends on her cooperation with the SDC. I will extend an offer of safety, but once again, it depends."

"It's not fair that she should be punished for things that were not in her control."

"I agree," Fletcher said with finality.

"I saw it all with my own eyes," Elle said. "I saw people in an underground facility in the desert, not just locals, people who worked there under the name Ziggurat, a company owned by Olympicorp. They used ex-US military to round up rural folk to experiment on, they doused them with psychotropic biochemicals. One of the soldiers, Lyles, he was another experiment. He could control anyone who came in contact with the gas. I think there was a leak, or he poisoned the entire facility, and they all became part of a hive mind. They came after us."

"I know your story," he said. "I know about Mount Olympus and the conglomerate of companies they hide behind called Olympicorp."

She jerked her thumb toward the door. "Savrasov asked about psi powers of the mind."

He smiled. "The Gorgon is too big a collar for the Russians, a peon like Savrasov."

The Gorgon. It was some moniker Cass carried. A codename? Elle did not care to consider that part of Cass, a tool of Olympicorp.

"Her name is Cassandra Hunt," Elle said.

Another smile as if he were chatting good-naturedly with a child about the existence of the Easter Bunny. "Is that her name? Because I don't have anything to match her with that name. No passport, no birth certificate with a country of origin."

"She was never allowed to know her country of origin."

"She *told* you she doesn't know," he said. "Having worked in this field, documenting the advancements in mind control, I doubt that all of one's memories can be completely wiped."

"Is that what you are after? Her memories?"

"Anything that she can tell us to get us closer to Mount Olympus would be helpful. As I said before, depending on her level of cooperation."

"And by level of cooperation you mean as Cassandra Hunt or the Gorgon?"

"You're a clever woman, Elle. You've seen things, understand what the average citizen doesn't want or care to see. Even before Kuwait. We need you to be realistic about this."

"I am being realistic. Are you recruiting her into the SDC or do you want her to be a mindless monster at your beck and call?"

Elle did not doubt Cass's ability to kill. She had seen it firsthand in Kuwait. She felt that it should have bothered her that the woman she had taken as a lover had blood on her hands, that she was a dangerous enemy of various countries. Yet whenever her thoughts of sympathy for Cass's alleged victims surfaced, Elle saw only her, the sadness in her eyes when she told of her life as an operative for a shadowy organization.

"I can't answer that question. It's going to be up to her," he said. "Maybe she's not as averse to that title you're so scared of saying aloud. Maybe she knows in this game the biggest monsters get the spoils."

"She's not a killer, not by choice."

"She killed to protect you. To save herself. She used skills she learned under strict conditions, in and out of a deprivation pod for days and weeks at a time. It turns the brain to mush. Like your friends from the desert."

"Is that what you're going to do to her?"

"Do you believe your Cassandra is a mindless zombie with a brain of atrophied mush? I spoke with her briefly before my rendezvous here. She's scared for you, and she is sharp."

Elle found herself split between relief and suspicion. According to Fletcher, Cass was still alive.

"Right now, we are making an attempt to inhibit her use of the sonic weapon implanted in her brain," he said.

"More torture," Elle said indignantly. "I won't let you do this to her. Not again."

"What are your plans to stop me? Will you go home and make Cass your next big story? Parade her around the media outlets until she puts a gun to her head?"

A jibe about Loera. A victim of Ziggurat. He had been part of the crews rounding up villagers stunned by poisonous gas. He suffered from PTSD from combat in Afghanistan, and the job he took with Ziggurat for contract soldiers exacerbated his symptoms to the point of psychosis. He was not the same when he returned and turned to a veterans' group. Elle met him while doing a story on the group and their struggles with mental health issues. Her interview with Loera went viral which presented resources to help him find a steady job and housing, as well as much-needed therapy. She interviewed him a few more times and the two of them became friends. He'd seemed to be doing well, until he came to her office at the Green Patriot and shot himself.

"It was people like you who broke Loera. If he hadn't been experimented on, he and a lot more people would be alive today."

Fletcher relented. "I don't doubt your intentions with Hunt or Loera. I do doubt your ability to know when the scope of what you offer as help, your platform. It does more harm than help."

"I have more than the Green Patriot, Mr. Fletcher. I have other resources."

"Do you mean your mother's Washington connections? That will definitely be good for her poll numbers. You've gotten yourself mixed up with a bad element in pursuit of a story linked to the mysterious Bedouin Revolt."

"You sound like Savrasov."

"I gave her that narrative to chew on. She likes it. People always like the sensational stuff. Reporter becomes a part of the news."

He was threatening her reputation, her mother's and family's name that they worked so hard to achieve.

"You're lucky to have your mother," he said. "She works hard. She deserves that senate seat she'd been aiming for. A scandal could put a kink in her plans."

"A woman's life is more valuable than an election. My mother would agree on that."

"A woman she doesn't know? A woman who is a known terrorist."

His cruel words gave her pause. Her mother had worked all her life for the upcoming primary. Under the circumstances, would she risk everything for a stranger like Cass?

"Go home, take your lumps and forget about this whole series of events, the raid, your little vacation. Forget Kuwait, forget Lyles and Loera," he said.

"I won't sweep this under the rug, and I can never forget about Cass. I'll wait until the whole damned election is over with and then I am going to find out what happened to her."

"Your mother said you're tough," he said. "She claims to be the only one who can talk you out of this whole crusade."

Elle straightened in her chair. "You talked to my mother."

"Yeah," Fletcher said wearily. He removed a small notepad from his jacket pocket, slim and bound in red leather. He placed it on the table open-faced. Among the pages filled with what she presumed to be his tight scrawling were two that were blank. Fletcher sat down in front of her.

"Well?" Elle asked. "What the hell did you tell my mother?"

"That you have gotten yourself in trouble, and I am advising you, helping you avoid trouble and get home."

Elle shook her head. "My mother is anything but naive."

Fletcher produced a pen, ballpoint, tinted plastic with red trim to indicate that the ink would be red. He placed the pen to paper and began to draw several conjoined angles which turned out to be a regular five-pointed star like the kind her first grade teacher used to draw on her A-plus spelling test. Except unlike Ms. Brown, he continued to trace over the star again and again. She watched him for a moment, puzzled. Had the bastard taken a break to doodle?

"You know, Elle," he said. "Deep down you want to let all this go away. What obligations do you have to this Cass person?"

All the while, he continued to trace that star, over and over. He was making an indentation in the paper, scratchy ink marks. What the hell was he talking about? She wanted to ask him, but her eyes were fixed on the star and how the tip of the pen hit the five corners perfectly, never over-drawing. The lines thickened where Fletcher traced.

"Cass is going to be fine, she's on the right side with us. Did you ever think that she would jump at the chance to take down Mount Olympus?"

His drawing did not bother her, and when he spoke again, she did not hear. She thought of Cass just hours ago, pressed against her, pretending to snooze. It was to be their final good-bye, and it was hard to face.

The whisper of pages and the star was gone. She looked at Fletcher. Watched him tuck the notebook into his jacket again.

"Let's get you home," he said.

Elle had never been so happy to hear those words in her life.

CHAPTER ONE

Security Defense Collective Headquarters
Almaty, Kazakhstan

The darkness of complete stasis. To Cass's body and brain, it was more familiar than sleep. Inside the upright pod, she floated, suspended in a metallic gel that kept her body at perfect temperature, a buffer between her body and any stray stimuli. Black tape covered her eyes for good measure. Various tubes snaked through openings bringing her oxygen via a mask that covered her nose and mouth. Those tubes brought nutrients along with a cocktail of sedatives, and psychoactive drugs went directly into her veins.

In the pod, her consciousness folded in on itself, an Ouroboros feeding on the fuel of its own destruction while simultaneously existing to feed. In theory, there was to be no coherent brain activity. In theory. She suspected that they knew she had learned to beat the process. She would have never been able to betray Thora and escape Olympicorp if she had not been able to break the thrall. She would have never been able to slip the yoke and switch sides if her mind had not been able to hold on to something to sustain it in the raging darkness. That something was the one sole determination that had not been programmed into her mind by Thora or anyone else, and that was getting back to Elle.

Elle.

The few memories she had of her burned intact with such permanence that nothing could ever swallow them up. She had favorites of course— Elle in that black bikini pressed close to her, smelling of salty sea air, murmuring sleepily into her ear. Her laughter as they sipped forbidden alcohol prohibited in Kuwait. There were memories of Elle that broke her heart, like the night on that Kuwaiti airstrip after escaping the madman Lyles, neither of them able to comprehend why it was so hard to part ways.

The memories that pained Cass the most were the final glimpses of Elle as they fought off the men in black tactical gear.

That had been over a year ago.

Her memories of Elle, besides the ones of this awful place, were the only ones she owned. They brought her comfort as she struggled with the SDC agents whose task it was to sedate her and prop her up on the platform base of the pod. It was Elle's face she thought of when she succumbed to the drugs as the agents sealed the pod. Elle's touch she imagined in the close-to-panic moments when the metallic gel filled the pod. As the prop sank away to leave her floating. It was Elle's voice that echoed in her head long after the darkness had taken over.

Those memories allowed her to hold on to a shred of her consciousness until the moment the prop rose from the platform hooking under her armpits like crutches to hold her upright.

She could feel her mind returning as she felt blood returning to her tingling limbs. Now that it was exposed to the air, the gel cooled and clung to her like a fatty carapace causing her skin beneath to prickle.

She heard the door of the pod slide open. Someone removed the tape from her eyes and she squinted as the overhead lights burned as bright as torches through her closed lids. She heard their buzzing hum exaggerated by the drugs that lingered in her system.

As usual, the agents handled her with a clinical disdain if not rougher than usual. She could hear the soles of their shoes on the concrete floor as they moved about removing the tubes and finally the face mask. She breathed in the chilly air of the lab but continued to keep her eyes shut from the stinging light.

"Are you with us?"

Over the too-loud buzz of the lights, she recognized the voice of the agent, a greasy-haired weasel who wore a smart pair of round spectacles. Ingman. He saw to her entombment into the pod, as well as her release with the aid of two to three other SDC agents.

"She was off the rails when they brought her in," a second agent said and let out a snigger that bounced around her. "Fought like a bitch about getting back into the pod."

"She fought sedation the entire ride back from Jove Island," said a third agent. "But we managed to keep her under."

At the mention of the island, she felt a flash of light behind her eyes as if someone had stuck her finger into an electrical socket. The jolt of memory hit her like high voltage and her eyes snapped open, tearing instantly from the light.

"Charybdis," she said, her voice hoarse from disuse.

She remembered the rocky island called Jove, and the events that had taken place, and the journey back to SDC headquarters. She'd still had blood on her hands as they dragged her from the helicopter. Fletcher had been waiting on the landing pad, black shades covering his eyes. His attempts to calm her only infuriated her more. She'd wanted to see Elle. He had promised her that much.

Fletcher and his games.

They'd had to tie her down to prepare her for the pod after she kicked Ingman in the groin, and he had lost his cool and removed his Glock, threatened to kill her. She'd only grinned. Now, she lay limply on the prop hooked beneath her arms, squinting in the swirling glare of the fluorescent lights. She had just enough strength to lift her head.

How long had she been in the tank? Three days? Five days? Fletcher never kept her in for longer than a few days. Then again, he had not been pleased that she and the team had come back from Jove Island empty-handed and light a few members.

Through the fog that covered her eyes, she saw one of the agents step close. She felt the prick of a needle in her neck, the burn of the injection. Immediately, her heart began to accelerate. Her body seized, shaking the prop, her feet slipping in gel.

"Awake now?" Ingman asked. He wore a red tie, its color bled up past his collar to his chin, staining his lips, his teeth, and down the front of his chest like a wound, dripping toward his crotch.

That snigger again, this time it sounded more like the bubbling bark of a hyena.

"She's tripping balls."

A hand appeared under her nose, and she felt a burst of some aerosol mist burn her nostrils. She tossed her head and Ingman grabbed her chin while speaking in a mock comforting tone. He shoved a suctioning hose down her throat to clear her airway of any of the gel. It tasted of pennies and lemons.

She gagged out a roar as he pulled the tube away. Her eyes adjusted to the light, and she saw the three of them clearer. One she recognized but could not recall his name. The other she had never seen before.

"Behave yourself," he said as the prop began to sink into the platform lowering her to the floor into a crouch. She tried to stand too soon on her unsteady legs. She slipped of course, falling in slow-motion, then landing on her ass and tipping backward over the platform. She plopped on the concrete floor in a puddle of gel.

Ingman laughed. "Like a little baby deer," he said to the other two agents. "She never waits for the meds to wear off. Be careful. Sometimes she strikes out in fear."

"Fear you?" she managed through trembling lips and coughed up a gob of gel which she spat at his feet.

The three chuckled. She heard the click of a bullet being loaded into the chamber of a pistol and she knew they were ready. He liked to show off for the new agents. He was ready to use force if she made an aggressive move and seemed to be waiting in anticipation for the opportunity to put a bullet in her head.

She felt another jolt behind her eyes. She closed them and saw Charybdis, pale skin, graying black hair, and steely eyes, with a hard, lean face. She would have killed her because that was what she had been programmed to do, protect the island against invaders, and to kill the Gorgon should she ever return.

A towel fell over her shoulders, and they gave her some space to collect herself. She recalled that she only wore underwear and a bra and wrapped herself in the towel.

Midway across the room, she saw a utility shower with tinted glass to shield her near nakedness and knew that there would be another towel on the rack when she was done. Certain that her legs were not steady enough to carry her the short distance, she began to crawl, the towel draped across her back, over the cold tiled floor toward the promise of warmth and some dignity.

There were several dark panes of glass panels in the walls, around the room which from her experience meant more than one observation room. Ingman and his cronies were not the only ones watching her make the journey across the cement floor.

She made it to the shower floor, a steep slope of rough, uneven concrete slab surrounded by more yellowing broken tile. She found the handle without looking and turned it to the desired setting. The water came, cool at first, further chilling her core, and then building to a near scalding heat. The drum of hot water on her skin seemed to strengthen her legs and she was able to stand.

There was no soap, just a mist of fizzy disinfectant that came out of a nozzle attached to the showerhead in a simultaneous wash-rinse. The hot water alone was enough to sluice away what remained of the gel from her body. It was clear and brown, like glittering jellied shit. Perhaps the stuff was the by-product of some foul creature holed up in a bunker beneath the SDC headquarters. Some anomaly they kept as they kept her, feeding it drugs, using its dung to poison her mind. She pushed the image away. It was the drugs, but she could not shake the feeling of wanting the gel off her skin immediately.

She swiped at it angrily, first her arms and then her hips. She watched it fall from her in clear brown clots to the floor. The gel melted in the hot steam and dissolved down the drain with the water. She scrubbed the gel from behind her ears. She ran her fingers through her short hair that fell just past her ears. It was shorn at the temples to accommodate the headband-like device that she wore constantly. She had foolishly mourned the cutting of her hair when she first agreed to go with Fletcher, then she'd realized that she had never specifically chosen to wear it long.

She turned off the water and stood there dripping as she pulled the towel off the rack. Too weak to completely dry herself, she wrapped the towel around her body and leaned against the tiled wall. The agents would bring clothes and a hot cup of the worst tea, a luxury she had requested from Director Fletcher himself as it was not part of the protocol. She did not tell him that it was part of Thora's ritual to give her tea and cold lamb sandwiches when she awakened her from the pod, but she suspected that he knew.

She heard the mechanical whir and click of the heavy lab door opening. She looked through the tinted shower door, and her vision blurred in patches as Fletcher strolled through the doorway, his bald, brown head shining through the fog over her eyes like a beacon. He came to the shower stall and peered through the glass.

"Cassandra? You coming out of there anytime soon?" he asked.

"You'll forgive me if I'm a little disoriented," she said bitterly. She was not ready to face him and the memories of what happened on the island, that coupled with the fact that she felt especially vulnerable when coming out of the pod.

He slid the shower door back and stooped a bit, hand on his knees, his dark, red-rimmed eyes searching her face. The white hairs in his trim mustache glimmered.

"You'll walk it off," he stated and took her wrist to take her pulse. He gazed at the black windows that surrounded them. Ingman and his agents were gone. There were no clothes. No hot tea.

"How long has it been?"

"Two days," he said. "You know what I'm here for. I need to know what happened on Jove Island."

"I can hardly remember my own name right now," she said. "Weren't the others able to brief you?"

"You mean the ones who made it back?" he asked.

"I did what I could to protect them," she said. "Fabbro made it clear that if anything went South, I would be the scapegoat—"

He turned away from her. "Fabbro was a shit heel. He was one of mine though, and I wouldn't wish what happened to him on my worst enemy."

She felt panic rise within her. "You can't blame me for what happened. I warned you about Charybdis, I warned you about traps."

"I didn't expect four of my agents to be killed by one wraith, four people with families who are going to miss them…not that I expect you to understand such a concept."

She clenched her jaw. He often used that tactic, pointing out that she had no one else in the world besides Elle. He especially liked to question her importance to Elle.

"Are you that pissed that Thora wasn't there?" she asked, desperate now.

"I *need* answers," he said.

"Fuck you, Fletcher," she said. "Putting me in the pod isn't going to help the situation. It's not meant to be a prison cell."

He did not answer.

"Look, we landed on the island, Charybdis came out of nowhere—"

"You left out the part where you disappeared on the rest of the team," he said.

She faltered. Fletcher regarded her silently, his intent as lethal as staring down the barrel of a gun.

"If it weren't for me that island would have taken your whole crew."

"Tell me what you remember," he said. "This is your last chance."

She had a vision of Charybdis, the shift in her eyes as she pressed her forearm across Cass's neck and bore down. What had she seen in her attacker's eyes? Compassion? Whatever it was, it hadn't lasted long.

"Can I have some clothes first?" she asked.

He glanced down at her body as if just noticing she was nude save the towel. He shook his head.

"Talk."

CHAPTER TWO

The Subantarctic
Two Days Earlier

No amount of training could have prepared her for the icy waters off Jove Island, least of all the brief fifteen-minute lecture Fletcher had given her. A Chinook helicopter dropped Cass and the six-member crew, as well an assault boat. She churned through the freezing water along with the others and scrambled inside the boat. They landed on the rocky shore, a steep slope of more cold rocks ranging in sizes from pebble to boulder, in color from gray to black.

She was grateful to be on solid ground at least. They had landed on the eastern edge of a towering slope of rock, its summit jutting toward the sky. She was helping to unpack the equipment needed to negotiate the terrain from the assault boat when Fabbro signaled for her.

"Hunt, get over here."

He stood there, impatient of the seconds it took her to make her way to him. The man was as imposing as the landscape. He was six feet and about 260 pounds of self-importance. He raised his arm to show that he held the device used to remove the metal band that crossed her forehead from one temple to the other.

"Fletcher wants to make sure you have use of all your faculties," he said and passed the gray boxy instrument over the band. She caught a flash of a red laser and then the band fell from her head. Fabbro quickly caught it and stowed it away on his person.

She stood there for a moment, stunned that Fletcher had allowed the removal of the band. He rarely removed it. Since she'd allowed him to slip it on her, a mixture of shame and sadness plagued her.

Fabbro eyed her suspiciously and she noticed that a few others had paused their efforts to watch the exchange with a mixture of curiosity and she dared to guess (she would know for sure soon) fear. They knew what she was, and they'd heard the rumors that she could read minds.

It started as a shower of radio static, but not in the form of a sound in her ears. It came from the air around her, and her brain was equipped to tune in. She did not know the origin of the ability, only that it was one of Thora's crowning achievements, and that it made her a force to be reckoned with.

"Well?" Fabbro asked.

She rubbed at the sides of her head where the band had been attached, a safeguard that allowed Fletcher and the SDC to feel comfortable by suppressing her ability. The readjustment was overwhelming as she fought back the static, her brain separating the signals into six channels, one for each of the team Fletcher had sent to Jove Island.

Thora called it the pulse, a frequency emitted by the bioelectricity of the human brain, specifically how that energy changed when one experienced emotion such as fear, stress, the chemical changes in the brain.

In a matter of moments, she was in tune to the pulses of the trained agents, the high-pitched buzz of their anxiety, the steady hiss of their anticipation, not at all like Elle. Even when she was frightened or anxious, her pulse was to Cass like notes of flavor in a fine wine. She remembered Elle's pulse—a gorgeous warble that made her scalp prickle the first time she'd read it.

She nearly smiled savoring it all.

Fabbro scowled and moved close in a show of boldness. "Look, I give zero shits about whatever daytime soap drama you and Fletcher have going on. Just know this, he won't be there to save your ass if things go south."

She stopped smiling. "I understand."

"Good. We're going to be the best of friends you and me. You'll tell me if you pick up on anything."

She nodded in agreement and looked to the others.

"Don't worry about them," Fabbro said. "They just want to get out of here in one piece."

He turned and ordered them all back to work. This was her first time working with such a team, but she did not need to have the band removed from her head to know how they felt about her. In her brief encounters with agents like Ingman and his assistants, she found they all had chips on their shoulders. They were all the worst of the worst, war criminals, pillagers of the new age. All of them seemed to have a mutual hatred of her and saw her as the enemy living amongst them. Thora would have considered them beneath her. After all, they carried the baggage of a lifetime of memories, loves, and disappointments. They were burdened by free will.

Cass envied them those very experiences, and the freedom to pursue whatever life they chose no matter how unsavory. What crimes they had committed had been of their own volition, a choice to walk such a path. Cass had been forced for years to do things that she could not recall.

"Hey, zombie girl," said Kruger, a woman with a square jaw and arms that put them all to shame. Her eyes darted around Cass in a nervous type of energy. "We got a bet going. Did they build you in a lab or did you crash-land from Uranus?"

"That's enough," Fabbro said half-heartedly, grinning from Kruger's comment. He had handed her an automatic pistol tucked inside a thigh holster.

"I take it you know how to use one of these," he said.

She nodded and accepted it with shaking hands.

"We're giving the zombie with magic powers a gun?" Hister protested. He reminded Cass of a vulture. No matter what the distance he traveled or the condition of the terrain, Hister moved in swift strides, elbows tucked to his sides, fists clenched, his head always turning.

"Fletcher's orders," Fabbro told him.

She deduced that they did not know she carried a weapon more dangerous than the highest caliber automatic weapon. Just as she could read the pulses emitted by the human brain, she could weaponize the more powerful ones in the air around her.

The Aegis was an implant her handler Thora had planted into her brain at some point during their time together. The band Fletcher forced her to wear blocked her access to the Aegis, but she could feel it there always, a cold burn in the back of her brain.

Hister paced, his eyes on her as she strapped on the gun, his disapproval apparent. She didn't blame him. Zombie. Magic powers. Wraiths were a fresh territory for them. Though she was sure that they were all victims of some light programming.

She scanned them. There was Raglan. She'd been taking photographs with a small camera as the others geared up. Kruger stood with her arms folded, impatient to leave. Gray tilted his back to survey the cliff that slopped to the sky.

Jove island was situated north of the Antarctic Circle 3,000 miles away from civilization. The French government had once claimed the island and once ran a research outpost, but the unforgiving climate and terrain forced them to abandon the place. Eventually, it was sold to a bioresearch company called Oxylus, which happened to be another subsidiary of Olympicorp. There were few records of Oxylus that extended past the island and its ownership. According to public record, they were continuing the work of the former tenants. Cass knew that Jove Island was one of Thora's very private playgrounds.

Shortly after joining with the SDC, Fletcher brought in a doctor, a no-nonsense woman called Dr. Branch. She did not bother introducing herself and referred to Cass as "the subject." She had put a helmet-shaped device over Cass's head. The thing seemed innocuous, filled with a gray foam molded in the shape of a face. Fletcher's lot was big on sensory deprivation. Thora would have called it rudimentary.

To Cass's surprise, she could hear what she presumed to be Dr. Branch's voice in her ears.

"Tell me about your best memory," she'd said.

It was a strange thing to ask someone who had very few to claim for their own. Cass had decided that it would not hurt to play along. She told Dr. Branch that her best memories were of Elle and the time they spent together.

"Is there anything else you remember, a time before Kuwait?"

"You've read the file Fletcher keeps."

"There is always more," Dr. Branch had said, undeterred.

A flash of blue-white light lit up the interior of the device. She'd squeezed her eyes shut, the afterimage of the gray foam in the bright light burned into her vision. Another flash followed and it sent a blinding pain through her head. Yet another flash and more pain. She had blacked out after a dozen flashes and through the darkness of her mind came those memories of Jove Island and Charybdis. Though Fletcher was more interested in what she remembered about the freezing rock, there was another memory that Cass found most intriguing.

In those flashes of vision with Dr. Branch, she saw Charybdis, smiling and reaching down for her and picking her up. It was confusing until Cass realized in the vision/memory that she was only a small child. It became suddenly her earliest memory, something before Elle, and Kuwait and even Thora.

They began to scale the rocky slope as a light flurry of snow began to fall.

With the cold wind at her back and the icy rock beneath her, Cass set to the task of navigating the nearly vertical shore. She did not realize the gap she'd put between herself and the team until Fabbro called for her to slow down. He ordered her to wait for the rest of them. She did as he instructed. Did he think she would turn on them on high ground and take them all out? A part of her found the thought of watching them all fall satisfying.

She admonished herself for having such thoughts. It was in her best interest to cooperate with Fletcher. Besides, what loyalty did she owe Thora, Olympicorp, or even the mysterious Charybdis?

The rest of the group caught up with her, and one by one, they were taken by the view before them: a labyrinth of striated rock that jutted from the ground in angled columns, some were short enough to barely reach their knees, others were as tall as Fabbro. Beyond, towering over all, a plateau of black formation contrasting with the misty gray sky. Cass knew the view from her newly recovered memory. She knew that Thora had part of the east side of the rock hollowed out into a series of labs. She was to lead Fletcher's team there.

"Hey, what's that green shit?" Fabbro said, catching her attention. He gazed through a pair of binoculars toward the great rock plateau.

He handed her the binoculars and she looked at the plateau. She scanned the base and saw vines growing on the rocks. The vines were climbing upward and she panned in the direction of their growth to see that they reached the very top.

"It looks like some type of climbing vine," she said.

"I thought this place would be completely barren," he said. "It's so cold."

"I don't remember," she said, passing back the binoculars.

Raglan appeared. "Can I see?"

Cass handed her the binoculars and watched as she adjusted them so eager to explore Jove Island. There was no way she could be completely ignorant of the dangers hiding there.

They began to negotiate their way through the formations, quiet save for the whistling of the wind. After thirty minutes, they came to a shallow canyon and trailed down to cross it.

"I knew there would be some interesting formations here," Raglan said, stooping in the shadow of rock eroded flat like a tombstone. She pressed a flat palm against it, her fingertips tracing a vein of some glittering mineral. "This isn't like anything I've ever heard of."

"Are you a geologist?" Cass asked.

Raglan looked up at her and blinked as if she were truly shocked that she had spoken to her. "I'm sort of a jack-of-all-trades. Geology is a pet interest."

"Take a picture, we're moving," Fabbro said. He gestured with his chin toward the plateau towering into the sky.

They moved in a line—Cass, Fabbro, and Kruger, then Raglan, Gray, and Hister. An eerie fog crept among the rocks like clouds among mountains. She had kept in tune with their pulses and paused when she sensed the familiar static of a wraith.

"What is it?" Fabbro asked.

An explosion to their right, shards of rock, dust, and fog. She took cover behind one of the formations and felt the ground beneath her thrumming. She heard Fabbro yelling from somewhere behind her. She moved to peek around her cover. Another explosion sent her back to the rocky floor. A shower of dust and rocks pelted her back.

"Christ," Kruger shouted. "Gray's been hit."

"Anybody got eyes on what the hell is going on?" Fabbro yelled.

Another explosion came as an answer, this one farther away. And that strange pulse, she still heard it and knew it to be another wraith close by. A body landed next to her. It was Hister taking cover. He eyed her suspiciously, his gun drawn ready for action.

"There's someone out there," she told him.

"Where?" he asked dubiously.

"Not sure," she said, disoriented from the explosions.

"That's helpful."

She motioned to the east, and he turned to a group of rocks shaped like some prehistoric monument. The formation waited at the bottom of a slope and a light fog curled around the tops of the rocks in some facsimile re-creation of the volcanic activity that shaped them in the first place.

"Maybe," he said. "I can't see a fucking thing."

She gazed down into the valley. Something down there was the source of the strange pulse and was compelling to her. Another explosion. She startled and removed her gun from its holster.

"What are you doing?" Hister asked.

She stood slowly and turned to see Fabbro and Raglan cowering together, Kruger with Gray flat on his back. Hister grabbed her ankle and shouted at her just as another explosion rocked the chilly air. She shook him off and ran, sailing over the bank and down into the valley.

She hit the bottom and waited before slowly making her way to the fog-covered rock formations. The pulse grew stronger, indicating that the someone she sensed was closer than before.

"Charybdis," she whispered harshly.

No answer. Above, she could hear more explosions and the yelling from Fletcher's team.

Charybdis flew out of the fog, her attack completely silent, the long-bladed combat knife she wielded an arcing blur. Cass dodged the strike by the width of a hair. She felt the tip of the knife at her throat, slicing the dry suit there. She brought up her arm to dodge the counter blow, an expertly aimed fist. For a second, they grappled, their eyes met, and Cass saw a cold familiarity. Her attacker pushed her away, and the fierceness returned.

"Why are you here with those people?"

"I don't work for Mount Olympus anymore," Cass said.

"And you'd work with them?" she asked.

"It's complicated," she said.

"Thora wants me to kill you," Charybdis said. "That is my directive. Protect the island. Kill the Gorgon if she returns."

"It doesn't have to be like this. Hide from these people, get off this island. Thora would never be able to find you."

She was beyond listening. Cass could see it in her eyes. All that mattered now was her directive, the actions Thora programmed into her mind. The fact that she had stopped to explain it made no matter. Charybdis lifted the long blade, intent flashing in her eyes.

Cass focused on the cold spot always present in the back of her mind. The Aegis. Once activated, the chill claimed her from crown to core, more frozen than the waters of the subantarctic. She felt the pressure of air swirling all around her.

The world blurred and then blackened. She did see the afterimage of the look of alarm Charybdis wore as she was blown back several yards, her feet sliding across the rocks.

Charybdis managed to keep her footing. Undaunted, she sprang forward. Cass released the Aegis once again, and a stronger blast knocked Charybdis off her feet. She rolled into the fog and did not reappear.

Cass stood at the ready. She listened and felt for her pulse. After a moment, she discovered that Charybdis had not gone far. She was out there beyond the rocks, circling her and watching. Waiting. Cass's vision cleared a bit, and she focused her eyes in the direction of where she sensed her opponent.

Like a ghost, Charybdis lunged from the mist fist-first, swift and poised. Cass deflected the initial strike but succumbed to the follow-through. Charybdis grabbed her and they began to grapple. A swift knee to the abdomen came as proof that Charybdis was not only faster, she was stronger.

Cass jabbed her head forward, along with a blast from the Aegis. She felt the cartilage of Charybdis's nose give under her skull with a callous crunch.

Charybdis stumbled backward and brought her wrist to her nose as twin rivulets of blood trickled from her nostrils. She narrowed her eyes and curled her hands into fists as if to show that she was unfazed by the Aegis.

They stepped forward at the same time. Cass lashed out with a kick and Charybdis flew backward and landed on her side. Cass advanced as she scrambled to her feet. She dodged Charybdis's punches before connecting one of her own with Charybdis's collar bone.

A reply came with the thrust of her knee connecting with Cass's unguarded abdomen. She groaned and stumbled backward, and Charybdis pounced and kicked her in the middle of her chest. She felt her sternum creak and a few ribs give way.

Charybdis was on her again. Remarkably strong hands wrapped around her throat like thick cord. She felt the flow of her pulse slow, heard her heart pounding, a methodic whoosh-whoosh in her ears.

Cass tried to fight her off, and then she tried to summon the cold to no avail, squeezing her eyes shut with the effort. A blue-white flash. Was that what she would see as she died? The residuals of the SDC's little experiment? Then a memory. Strange. She saw Charybdis towering over her like a giant. Behind her was a blue sky with buildings, signs with Cyrillic letters. She was not looking at Cass but scanning a busy street as cars passed. She seemed as tall as a mountain. Then she looked down at her and smiled.

Then the vision fogged over; her limbs weakened as all of her energy was sucked up by Charybdis's vice-like grip. Cass opened her eyes and saw Charybdis staring down at her as she went about her handiwork, her lips curled into a snarl. She looked down into Cass's eyes and her fury swiftly faded. She spoke.

"I'm sorry, little one."

It was only a whisper, but Cass heard it over the ringing in her ears, felt it in her pulse as sadness. The wraith's sudden emotion startled her. The vision came again. She and Charybdis waiting at a crosswalk. They were hand in hand. She was looking up at her, a child, a stage in life she had never imagined herself to be. In the vision or was it a memory? Charybdis looked down at her and smiled.

"Let's get you something to eat, little one."

"Please," she replied, but not in the voice of a child, in the voice of her adult self as the blackness of unconscious threatened.

"Please."

She heard shouting in the distance. She was coming to, lying on the rocky ground. Fabbro's team surrounded her. She fought them at first, thinking they were her attacker. Hister grabbed her by the collar, and she could feel the press of his fist against her neck.

"Charybdis," she gasped.

"She took off," Fabbro said. "When you're done with your nap, we can go after her."

❖

Cass sat up slowly, her vision clearing as she looked at the anxious faces of the team. She stood on shaking legs and promptly threw up on the ground. The others jumped back like startled deer and scanned the mist intently looking for any sign of Charybdis's return.

"She looked like she was about to tear your face off," Krueger said. "Maybe we got the wrong one on our side."

"You sound like you're in love," she said, wiping her mouth with the back of her hand.

Fabbro came close, his gun in hand. "Why'd you take off on us?"

"She was out there—"

"I think we can all handle one weirdo," Krueger said.

"Shut up," Fabbro told her and turned to Cass. "You take off again, I'll shoot you in the back. Got it?"

She nodded.

"That freak makes an appearance again, I get first shot," he announced to the group. "We're doubling back to the plateau."

Once again, she led the way.

She wanted to tell Fabbro that the island was Charybdis's domain as much as it was Thora's, that all of them should be careful where they stepped. She clenched her jaw and locked the words back. There was no need to inflame Fabbro or Hister who prowled close behind her.

As they neared the base of the plateau, they began to encounter pale green vines growing from the ground. The vines were peppered with short, thick thorns that snagged their clothes and scraped against their boots. They tangled close in some places. Some grew higher than the tallest rocks curling in monolithic bunches like Van Gogh's cypresses.

Gray had taken some shards of rock to the side of his leg during the blasts earlier and his footing was unsure. He slipped trying to trample the vines.

Raglan told him to watch himself. She was curious about the mysterious plant life and snapped pictures. The vines had wrapped themselves around the rocks or ran along the ground in various lengths and girths. Cass followed one of the thick, curling vines with her eyes along the ground, around rocks weaving in between other vines.

"This vegetation cannot possibly be native to this climate," Raglan said. "It's an invader. It's amazing how it's thrived here. Cold. Little sun. Very little loose soil."

Raglan used a stylus to pry at some delicate tendrils growing from one of the main woody roots. The plant shuddered and stretched, wrapping around the stylus. She startled and gasped. She looked to Cass.

"This just reacted to touch," she said, showing the vine now curled around the stylus. "Like a Venus flytrap or mimosa. I mean, vines react to touch, but these recoil, move away from the touch. I'm going to take a sample."

"Help yourself," Fabbro said.

Cass watched with a growing sense of dread as Raglan attempted to saw away at the vines with a knife to no avail. She felt as if she were witnessing someone tapping live mines with a hammer.

"We should move on," she said.

"Right," Fabbro agreed. "This ain't a nature walk."

As they moved, Raglan fell in step next to her. "You know anything about these?"

"No," she said curtly. She did not remember anything of the plant. She noted that they gave off a strange pulse, not like one of the team or Charybdis, or even electronics like the rover. Somewhere between static and active, just a steady thrum. She looked around at the others as they made their way across the vines.

Gray stumbled and tripped. He went down hard and screamed. As they made their way to him, he reared up on his hands and knees howling. Kruger was the first to reach him. Cass followed and saw the palm of the hand he'd used to try to break his fall. A pointy wooden thorn covered in blood protruded right through his hand. The offending flora had pierced through glove, flesh, and bone.

"Shit, boy," Kruger said over the screams. "Today just isn't your day."

Fabbro cursed and knelt next to him, a large tactical knife in hand as he studied the wound. He attempted to lift Gray's hand from the spiky thorn, but Gray gave a tortured groan, his face contorted in pain.

"Goddamn this place," Gray screamed. He looked up at Cass pointedly. "Exploding rocks, killer plants, and now there's another one of those freaks out there stalking us. My hand. Look at my hand."

"Calm down," Kruger told him and glanced up at the rest of them with worried eyes. "He's losing his shit."

Fabbro stooped to study the wound and the ghastly thorn sticking nearly an inch from the top of his hand right through the glove.

"What are you going to do?" Gray asked. Blood ran in rivulets beneath his hand, creeping over the vines and rocks. Cass noticed another movement as she moved in for a closer look, the vine creeping around his wrist, the small tendrils clinging to his sleeve. Her eyes met Raglan's. She too had noticed.

Fabbro looked their way. "Take a moment from being in awe of this thing to help me assess this."

"Cut the vine," Cass said. "Cut it on either side as close to the hand as you can."

Fabbro and Raglan looked at each other for a moment.

"We should get away from these things," Hister spoke up. "Backtrack to where we found her." He tossed his head Cass's way. "We can treat Gray there."

"I'm for that." Krueger produced an axe with a black blade. She pushed past Raglan, stooped, and began to hack at the vine. Gray bit his lip, tears streaming down his face as he cursed the island. At first, Krueger's blows made no mark on the vine, and she began to huff, concentrating her efforts. A spray of water leapt up from a cut in the vine and startled them all. Krueger struck again bringing another mini torrent that splattered Gray directly across his face. Another strike brought more spray misting them all.

A new smell filled the air. Dull and rancid like raw sewage. Fabbro and Raglan grimaced and inspected their hands and arms where the water had fallen. Cass saw what looked to be watery green liquid staining the tears on Gray's face. He rubbed at it and sneezed.

"It stinks," he groaned. "God. Is it poison?"

Raglan brought up her arm and sniffed it. "Bad smells keep prey away. This plant does a lot to protect itself."

"It's to protect the island," Cass said before she could stop herself.

Everyone looked her way.

Fabbro took the axe from Kruger. "I'm done playing National Geographic. We're going to get Gray fixed up and then we're heading for the plateau. No backing off. No cute little detours."

He knelt next to Gray and threw a mighty chop in the spot where Krueger had left off. A chunk of the vine flew away. Beneath the thick skin was a pale pink flesh speckled with black dots like some bizarre watermelon. The awful smell intensified.

"This thing's tightening up around my arm," Gray cried, his eyes wide. "It'll swallow me whole if you guys leave me here."

"It's a plant," Fabbro deadpanned in between hacks. "Not an anaconda."

Gray laughed, a deep-throated chuckle that broke the tension among them. Even Fabbro smiled wryly. Cass felt her own smile pulling at her lips. Gray continued to laugh, his chuckle turning into a manic cackle. Fabbro stopped chopping to look at him, that same wry smile on his face. Gray began to rock back and forth overtaken by his laughter.

Kruger stepped forward. "I think he's in shock."

Gray, face stained green from the vine, his skin red from the hilarity, looked at her and laughed, the pain in his hand forgotten as it moved around the thorn. Blood wept from the wound.

"Shit." Hister braced Gray's shoulder to stop him from doing more damage. "Calm down, man, it's not that bad. We'll get you patched up."

He looked to Fabbro who still had that smile on his face. The green juice had spattered his front and his chin. He raised the axe again and brought it down on the manic Gray's wrist, completely severing it in one strike.

A collective flinch went through them followed by paralyzing disbelief. Gray brought the bleeding stump to his face, spraying blood across the bridge of his nose. His face registered what had happened and twisted in grief. He began to scream. Cass stepped back, her eyes on Fabbro. Something had changed in his pulse, his entire being seemed to hum with a strange vibration. Though sweat poured down his face, he showed no expression.

"Goddamnit, Fabbro," Hister yelled. "What did you just do?"

Raglan moved in and grabbed just below the stump. She began to tie it off with a tourniquet. She eyed Fabbro who stood and handed Krueger the axe.

"Fix that shit up, Doc," he said. "We got a date with the Shah."

"The Shah?" Hister asked, looking around at the others. "Is there something about this mission that we weren't briefed on?"

"He's lost it," Krueger said.

"I said fix that shit up," Fabbro roared, shoving Krueger. The others scrambled around Raglan and Gray who had gone completely catatonic after his unexpected surgery.

Meanwhile, the vines had covered his amputated hand.

"Leave it," Fabbro said coldly when Hister tried to retrieve it.

"Gorgon," he said.

She turned to him, shocked that he had called her by that name.

"We got a problem here?" he asked.

"No, sir," she said carefully. She looked to Gray and tuned in to his pulse. She found it intense as if he were covered by a swarm of buzzing bees. She was certain that it was the green liquid from the vine.

"Make sure Gray doesn't fall over again. I think the cold is getting to him," Fabbro said.

Raglan was busy binding Gray's wounded hand to his chest; her eyes were worried and fearful as they darted around the rest of the group. Her gaze landed on Cass's, and she quickly flicked her head to Fabbro.

Cass gave a slow nod.

Fabbro went quiet. He stared toward the plateau. Krueger and Hister stood close speaking in low, clipped voices. They were all frightened of him. For now, they were just observant of him, their pulses anxious like blips on a radar.

As Fabbro directed, they moved toward the plateau. She kept her eyes on Fabbro. Raglan and Krueger supported Gray. Hister lagged behind picking through the vines. For all of his posturing, he would not challenge Fabbro. He was a soldier following orders.

Gray began to hum, a tuneless song that grew louder as they neared the plateau. She decided to try to talk to Fabbro. His pulse had the energy of a crackling fire.

"Are we taking the Shah in dead or alive?" she asked.

"Wouldn't you like to know," he said.

"I'm on your side," she said.

"Are you?" he shouted. "You knew not to get any of that green shit on you. It makes me wonder what else you're not telling us."

"So you acknowledge that the green shit is bad. Hold on to that, turn around, call the extraction team, and tell Fletcher whatever you want. Tell him it was my fault."

He scoffed but did not speak. Perhaps he could be reasoned with.

Fabbro turned, un-holstered his gun, and aimed it at Gray who was still humming. Fabbro stepped close and touched his gun to the side of Gray's jaw. He used it to turn his face from one side to the other.

"You look okay to me, Gray. You crapping out on me?"

"His hand just got hacked off," Raglan said. "He needs medical attention. Drugs."

Fabbro smiled. "My old friend is going to be fine. Seems like I'm getting resistance from my team. Seems like you all want the Shah to get away."

"There is no Shah," Raglan said, her voice trembling as if she were about to cry. "I think that vine has some kind of hallucinogenic secretion. I don't feel right, and it only splashed on my hand, and it got on Gray's face, yours as well. Fabbro, I think you may be having a reaction."

"What do you mean you don't feel right?" Krueger asked.

"I dropped acid once," she said, and quickly added, "For scientific reasons." She gazed around at all of them. "I know this feeling. We should go."

Fabbro regarded her for a moment and lowered his gun. He turned away muttering something to himself. He was growing more agitated which told Cass that he was beyond reason at the moment.

He turned suddenly and fired at Raglan. Blood and brain exploded from the back of her head as the bullet made its way through. She staggered and fell to her knees before falling face first into the vines. Gray startled and nearly lost his balance. Krueger managed to hold him upright. Cass went down to Raglan and lifted her a bit. She was gone.

"Fletcher is not going to like this," Hister spoke up, his face red with anger and disgust. He marched up to Fabbro. "You killed one of your own."

"She wasn't one of us." He glanced at Cass. "The Gorgon here is more one of us than that mouthy know-it-all bitch."

Kruger attended to Gray who was sobbing like a child. "That didn't solve our problem, Fabbro. That didn't help us one freaking bit."

He raised his gun and fired into the air. Everyone cowered. Fabbro glowered at them. "That's enough of this shit. We're pressing on and I don't want to hear any more whining. We can't keep the Shah waiting."

When no one moved, he aimed the gun at Cass. She didn't flinch. She gently straightened Raglan's body and lowered her to the rocks. She stood and stared down Fabbro. She felt the coldness building in her head. One blast from the Aegis and Fabbro would find himself in worse condition than Gray.

He grinned. "Well, lead the way, Gorgon."

Hister helped Krueger keep Gray upright. They looked defeated and Cass felt sympathy for them but not much. She had warned Fletcher about this place. Now his team was, as Ingman and his cohorts would say, "tripping balls," one injured, another one dead by the hands of their so-called leader.

She was also angry at Thora and her ghastly vines. She could picture her cultivating the vine from a thorny seedling borne of genetic splicing to withstand the cold, to coil and slither, to bleed a hallucinogen when disturbed. Everything she did was methodical and well planned. The vines were just what Thora wanted them to be.

There would be more tricks on the island and Cass was sure that they were all headed toward one. Cass monitored Fabbro's pulse at her back as she picked over the rocks. She once again entertained using the Aegis to somehow disable him. She was not certain if the others would come to his defense, especially Hister.

When they were near the plateau, Fabbro began to move at a faster pace, sometimes barely making it over the rocks. When he put a good enough distance between them, Cass turned to the others.

"Turn back," she said. "While he's distracted."

Hister and Krueger looked to each other. Gray sagging between them was barely conscious.

"I'm not leaving Fabbro like this," Hister said. "Fletcher's going to want answers."

"He'll have his answers," Cass said.

"And if Fabbro comes after us while we're running?" he asked.

"He's not in his right mind," Krueger said. "Hister, you're the only one who didn't get that shit on you. I'll take shelter with Gray while you two look after Fabbro."

"Not a good idea," Cass said. "I'll go with Fabbro. You two can stay back."

"Hell no," Hister said. "I like Krueger's idea."

Fabbro shouted in the distance. Cass and Hister looked at each other and then immediately set to action getting Krueger and Gray into the center of a formation of stones that was almost ring-like. The vines had grown over the cluster.

When they caught up with Fabbro, he was caressing the black-and-gray-striped rock lovingly. Cass moved in closer to give it her once-over. The rock did not give off a pulse of course, but there was something else she could not read, an electric hum.

Hister called the two of them to a spot farther down the length of the wall of rock.

"Well, goddamn," Fabbro exclaimed when he reached Hister. "It won't be long now before the Shah is in our hot little hands."

If she had ever experienced a déjà vu moment, it was seeing the perfectly cut rectangular seam into the dark rock.

A door.

"You hear that, motherfucker," Fabbro screamed. "We're coming for you."

Cass looked to Hister. "You're not thinking of trying to blow this, are you?"

"We brought explosives," he answered. "But this place..."

He trailed off and Fabbro did not give him a chance to pick up his thought. He was unpacking the explosives and barking orders. She did not need to hear Hister's words or even the pulse to know that he was afraid. Thora's island was full of surprises so far. Who could predict what horror an explosion could trigger?

She watched helplessly as Fabbro and Hister set up the explosives. Fletcher's little excursion had already turned into what he would call a shit-show; he would be livid if she were the only one to survive Jove Island.

It was funny that she never questioned her own mortality on Thora's rocky maze. Even Charybdis had not been able to kill her. She began to doubt Thora's plans to end her life. Instead, her old handler would benefit from being able to wrangle her once again. Get inside her head to plant the seeds that would reprogram her, make her the Gorgon once again.

Hister and Fabbro were still setting up the explosives when a deep rumble came from within the rock. They startled and moved away. The three of them watched as the seam in the rock shifted upward emitting a series of hisses dressed in dust. Through the cloud, she could see an open doorway, and a darkened passage that was slowly lit by overhead lights coming to life.

She looked to Fabbro who stood there staring. Cass could not decide what was worse, the explosions or the open door.

"All right," Fabbro said, retrieving the gun strapped to his back while stepping forward. "Things are finally going our way."

Cass reached out her hand in front of him. "Disable the explosives."

"You're giving me orders?" Fabbro asked.

"She's speaking reasonably," Hister said. "I'm not going in there with this shit behind me, Fabbro. That's amateur hour and you know it."

"Fine," Fabbro said. "Get it together, quick while we keep an eye out for the Shah."

Hister went about his work while grumbling under his breath. Cass kept an eye on Fabbro and his vigil. She noticed that he was smiling.

"Do you hear that?" he asked and cocked his head.

Certain that he was hallucinating, she nearly discounted his claim, but then she heard it herself. Music. She could not exactly make it out, but this was Thora's island, so it was classical by default.

Fabbro quickly stepped around her into the hallway his gun drawn, ready for combat.

"Who's there?" he asked. "Make yourself known."

Cass peered into the dimness. She could better hear the music. It was coming from overhead speakers. Brahms maybe. She almost expected to see Thora standing there, but there was no one walking the checkered tile floor. Unless Fabbro had excellent vision, he was hallucinating.

Hister joined them. He looked down the hall, and seeing no one there, he looked at Cass with an exasperated expression. "Is that classical music?"

"Yeah, nice and cozy," Fabbro droned and shouted out into the empty hall, "Come out with your hands up, and I might not blow off your head."

Nothing.

"Guess we're going in for a closer look," Fabbro said.

He motioned for them to flank him, and they made their way forward.

They were not a few feet in when the rock behind them rumbled and the slab that covered the door sank, closing the way out.

"Shit," Hister exclaimed.

"This just keeps getting better," Fabbro said with a dry chuckle.

Cass remained silent. She fell back a few steps as they walked twenty yards, thirty yards, fifty…the hallway seemed to go on forever. The music never seemed to end. Cass felt her frustration mount as they walked further into Thora's domain. She was not the only one to sense that something was wrong.

"Wait," Hister said, stopping in his tracks. He displayed the face of his watch to Cass. "I checked the time just before we got here. Over two hours have passed."

Cass felt a chill down her spine, and it was not from the Aegis. A memory more chilling than the weapon in her head and the horrors of the island came over her. It was of her standing in front of a window staring out at a picturesque view of rolling green hills and a blue sky with clouds stretched thin by wind. She recalled being perfectly still but watching as the day progressed before her like time elapsed. The clouds were driven away with the light of the sun as the day darkened to evening. Thora came to her; Cass saw her in the glass of the window. It had all been one of her experiments.

"Lost time," she said aloud there in the hallway to nowhere.

"What?" Hister asked.

"Lost time," Cass said, but she could not bring herself to say more. "Time enough for someone to get inside your head if they know what they're doing."

They looked to Fabbro who had traveled on a few yards without them. Now he stood still, his gun raised like one of those green, plastic army men.

"Fabbro?" Hister asked, his voice cracking nervously. "Hey, Fabbro."

Cass startled when the lights dimmed to dark, followed by the flash of a bright light on the walls on either side of them as they came alive with images projected from some unknown point. Overhead, a lively classical piece began to play led by a piano. The image of a fountain appeared, an elaborate affair of Poseidon stabbing at the tendrils of a sea monster watched over by a court of sirens and horses springing from the surrounding pool. The picture changed to a statue of Hermes carrying the infant Dionysus. That image faded giving way to Perseus poised to slay Medusa, his foot on her hip, his hand clasping a handful of her serpent hair, sword raised high. The image struck a deep chord.

The walls changed again and there was the Winged Victory of Samothrace fading into Athena holding a spear in one hand, shield at her feet and Medusa on her breast. Then came the mask of Agamemnon. Then, Hercules wielding a club against the three-headed dog.

The hall went black save for the glow of a red light.

"What the hell was that all about?" Hister asked breathlessly.

"We shouldn't be here," Cass blurted.

He moved closer to her. "What are you talking about?"

"Let's find a way out, fuck Fabbro."

They both turned their attention to their team leader. He had not moved an inch during the little slideshow. His pulse no longer registered. He was gone. Cass shook her head at the dilemma. Fletcher was not going to be happy, but the longer she stayed in that place, the greater the chances Thora could get inside her head, if she already hadn't been successful. Cass feared she would not know the difference, that she could very well at that moment be standing like Fabbro, or like the statues from the images with Thora looming over her, a foot on her hip, paused to end her.

"Let's get out of here." She turned to see that Charybdis had appeared among them like a ghost. She clutched a large tactical knife in her hand.

Cass heard Hister behind her. "Put the knife down and step away."

Charybdis regarded him coolly.

"I'm giving you one more chance," Hister said.

"Get Fabbro away," Cass told him. "Just keep moving."

He started to argue.

"Just go, you're in charge now. You get to the others, and you get out of here."

"Shit," he said and moved away ushering Fabbro along while looking over his shoulder.

As Cass watched them, Charybdis made her move from the periphery, the blade of the knife shadow and flash. Cass avoided being sliced open. She grabbed the wrist of the knife-wielding hand and gave it a rough twist. The blade clattered to the floor.

Charybdis kept coming. She managed to get behind Cass and lock a forearm around her neck. Cass tried to shake her off, striking at her legs with kicks. Charybdis was strong and held fast in a vice-like grip.

Cass summoned that cold feeling to take over her brain. Charybdis's grip loosened but then tightened again. Cass tried again, another blast from the Aegis. The strain and lack of air made her weak in the knees, and as she fell, she tried to flip Charybdis from her back. They fell to the floor scrambling. She felt Charybdis's arm curl around her neck. Cass landed an elbow and felt the elastic cartilage and angled bone of her face absorb the blow.

Charybdis rolled away. Cass crawled a few feet choking on her own breath. She reached for the gun holster at her side. A boot-clad foot landed a kick just below her ear. She rolled to avoid the fall of another foot and found herself on her back, face-to-face with Charybdis who grabbed two fistfuls of her shirt and dragged her backward.

Cass flipped halfway over, twisting out of her grip. A blow to the center of her back sent her sprawling to the floor. A solid foot pressed between her shoulders, holding her to the floor.

"I won't be weak this time," Charybdis said above her.

"No, please," Cass managed, her mind flashing to the memory of Charybdis leading her by the hand across a busy street. The two of them smiling at each other, the only memory Cass had of her childhood.

She tried the Aegis again and felt a brief pocket of air form between her and the floor. The cold feeling got colder, so cold that for a second her vision went completely white. Charybdis noticed her falter and struck her in the back of the head with her fist so hard that her head banged against the floor. The taste of blood cleared Cass's head. She summoned the cold feeling once again and managed to use her arms as if she were doing push-ups. Her body pushed from the floor fast, rising several feet.

Charybdis tried to force her to the ground, but Cass managed to gain her footing. She let the cold feeling take over and saw the shocked look on Charybdis's face as she flew backward, stumbling to keep her balance. She dived right, escaping the Aegis's range. She landed next to Fabbro and scooped up his gun. She raised it, her face a determined sneer.

"Wait," Cass yelled. "Please don't shoot."

Charybdis glowered at her but miraculously did not pull the trigger.

"You said you wouldn't hesitate," Cass said. "Is it so hard to kill me because you know me?"

"It doesn't matter," Charybdis growled. "I have my directive."

"I was once like you. I had directives to harm people, and then I met someone who caused me to question why. I have a new directive. It's one that I made for myself. You can do the same. Leave the island and make your own life."

"Thora said that I am to kill you if you come here."

"Do you want to kill me?"

Charybdis nodded slowly. She raised the gun and fired.

This time Cass did not have to summon the cold feeling. It claimed her head and she felt a rush of air impacting her so hard she was knocked off her feet. As she fell, the wave shifted away. She hit the floor and scrambled to her knees to see Charybdis fly into the opposite wall. Her head whipped back violently once she made contact. Her eyes were closed when she fell.

Cass got to her feet, checking herself for wounds. She happened to look to the floor near her feet and saw one of Fabbro's armor-piercing bullets lying there whole. She looked back to Charybdis who wasn't moving.

Cass moved forward cautiously, her eyes never leaving the unconscious wraith. She moved in close and saw the gun still clutched in her fist. She stooped slowly to retrieve it. Charybdis's eyes snapped open, and she raised the gun. Cass grabbed her wrist, pinned her arm to the wall, and head-butted her. They scrambled over the gun, Charybdis trying to dislodge her with kicks and a blow to the neck. Cass wrestled her other arm down and struck with her head again. When she drew back, a fresh river of blood poured from Charybdis's nose.

"I don't want to kill you," she said. "Don't make me kill you."

Charybdis's jaw tensed as she struggled to free herself from Cass's grasp. Blood stained her lips and teeth. She faltered and spoke.

"Thora said that you would try to convince me to leave with you. She said that you would try to finesse me into going against my directives."

"I remember you; it is my only memory of being a child."

"I have no memories, only directives. Protect the island from intruders. Kill the Gorgon if she ever returns."

"But I'm not the Gorgon, not anymore. You could make the choice," Cass begged. "You could leave this place."

Charybdis closed her eyes. Her pulse was that of every wraith Cass encountered, a continuous, tenuous treble like the dying note from a violin.

"She'll be watching," she whispered. Her eyes opened and she looked past Cass and up toward the ceiling. Cass turned and saw the flat panel on the ceiling.

"You have to kill me," she said. "Only you can."

"No," Cass insisted. "Come with me."

"With people like the ones who came with you?" she asked. "You know what they would do to me."

She tensed, surging forward and pushing Cass to the floor. She loomed over her wielding a tactical knife, poised to strike. Their eyes met. Cass now clutched the gun; Charybdis had pressed it into her hands before knocking her off balance. Her first thought was to toss it aside and stand to once again appeal to her mercy, whatever connection they shared. Instead, she kept the grip of the gun clenched in her fist.

Charybdis would strike again, and Cass would fight her off. If she failed, she would never be reunited with Elle. Perhaps it was foolish to push Charybdis to slip Thora's yoke.

Charybdis moved forward in a blur.

CHAPTER THREE

Security Defense Collective Headquarters
Almaty, Kazakhstan

"I don't remember much after that," she told Fletcher. "I was able to make my way out of the rock, find Hister and Fabbro. Together they searched out the others who had already used the satellite phone to call in the cavalry. When they arrived, Cass was immediately fitted with the pulse blocking headband and sedated.

"How heroic," Fletcher said in an exaggeratedly bored tone. "I thought that the mythological names were a dramatic flair, but it seems you all live up to them. Charybdis the sea monster versus the Gorgon."

"I take it you didn't find her," Cass said.

"You don't sound disappointed," Fletcher commented. "Not sure how she escaped that place, but then, who knows what the hell went on. That place turned my crack team into unreliable narrators."

"She couldn't go against her directive. She didn't want to kill me either," Cass said. "She wasn't able to make the choice. She let me do it for her."

"And everything else you've told me?" he asked. "The rescue team came in contact with the vines. We had to take flame throwers to them, and they still have not been completely eradicated. They may even grow back for all we know."

She looked away from him and wished he would just allow her the dignity of being dressed in more than a towel while his cronies watched him interrogate her.

"We found Raglan's body, but no one seems to remember who shot her," he said. "Kruger vaguely remembers Fabbro chopping Gray's hand off."

"And Fabbro?" she asked.

"He'll never be the same. It seems the combination of the toxin in the vine and whatever was inside that rock took his mind to its breaking point. He's got a long road to recovery, but it's going to end in early retirement."

"And no one had anything to say about Fabbro losing his mind?"

"Maybe no one wants to touch this," he said, turning away from her and pacing away. "I can't blame them. This mission was a complete clusterfuck. We lost a few of our best agents."

"I warned them about Charybdis just as I warned you about going after Thora."

"This is a big game hunt. You don't turn back when the jungle gets thick."

She wanted to tell him that he could never catch up to Thora, she would always be ten steps ahead. He didn't have the intelligence, and he didn't have the resources. Thora would say that he didn't even have the pedigree.

"I don't think you fully appreciate me having taken you under my wing," Fletcher said. "Jove Island has made me rethink bringing you into the SDC. Maybe I've bitten off more than I can chew."

Fletcher had something up his sleeve, she was certain of it. She had fought succumbing to whatever methods he used to take control of her completely. She glanced toward the door.

"You'll be free to leave the lab. In a moment." He straightened, his head refracting sharp shards of light that burned her eyes. The drugs they'd fed her intravenously while in the pod were still in full effect.

"You can go to your room and have a proper shower and think about what I'm going to tell you now."

"What do you want, Fletcher?"

"I just want to remind you who brought you in, who kept you out of the hands of the Russians and who's been keeping Elle safe. It's not anyone in Washington."

"I am reminded every moment of why I'm here," she said.

"Then stop behaving as if you need reminders," Fletcher said. "There's someone from DC who wants to come talk to you. She wants to get a feel of your mental state."

"Shrink me?" she asked.

"Other than being a good judge of people, she's not trained to mentally evaluate you," he said. "But don't think it's at all informal."

"What does this woman want with me?"

"Word has gotten out and everyone wants to know if you're a zombie or a robot. In some circles, they may even be speculating as to whether you're a rubbery-skinned, bug-eyed alien."

"I get that a lot."

"On another note, we got another lead on Thora. You and I are going on the road tomorrow evening. Amir is in Egypt staying on the compound of a friend. The government there is putting together a team to raid the place. We've been invited to go along for the ride."

Amir was an old contact of Thora's, a human trafficker who knew her and Cass as British MI6 agents. She had given his name during one of her initial interrogations by Fletcher. He was one of the few contacts that she could remember, which meant Thora considered him important enough to keep in her memory banks.

"It was my impression that Amir had no idea of who he was really working for," she said. "Thora would have made sure of that."

Fletcher shook his head. "We need something to come of this Amir arrest. I was hoping that you can get him to talk. Scare him."

"Do I really have a choice?"

"No," Fletcher said. "And maybe you should be a little more excited about it, grateful for the opportunity to redeem yourself for allowing my agents to be killed and maimed."

Ire energized her and she was able to straighten. She still only wore a towel, which she clutched at with one hand.

"Fletcher, we both know that I traded one prison for another. Thora, for you, one handler for another. I made that choice to ensure Elle's safety."

She strolled toward the door which could only be opened by print recognition but could also be opened from the outside by whoever waited on the other side of the observation windows.

"Where are you going?"

"You said I could go to my quarters," she announced. "My clothes are there."

"You're not going anywhere until we're done here," he said, following her a few paces. "I've held up my end of the deal, or don't you remember our deal? I protect you and Elle from Olympicorp. She's still a part of the progressive media. Spending a lot of time with that mentor of hers, Anne Humphries. She's forgotten all about you."

The personal detail was meant to salt the proverbial wound. He also wanted to let her know that he was watching Elle, that he could put them in contact with each other whenever he pleased.

Cass turned to Fletcher slowly, that familiar cold feeling began to pulsate inside her head like an echo. She felt the air around her thicken and slow, like the gel in the pod, except it warmed her, nourished her. The Aegis. She touched her forehead to see that she still wore the metal band that was supposed to suppress the weapon in her head. In her mind, she saw that image of Medusa and Perseus, the anguish and pain on the Gorgon's face.

Fletcher took a step back. His eyes widened with shock for a second as he realized what was happening.

"That's not something you want to do now," he said. "For your own sake."

"You don't get to use her like that. It's best that you don't even mention her name."

"Don't forget your place, Gorgon." His shaking voice betrayed his threat. "Take my advice and stand down."

She stared him down, felt the chill in her brain run down her spine signaling that she had reached a threshold. If she did not reel in the power, she could make Fletcher regret the day he recruited her.

"Stand down, Cass," he said. Fletcher turned his head to the observation windows.

"Code gold. Code gold."

She heard the door behind her slide open and feet on the concrete floor. She turned to see a gang of lab coats and suits with helmets with plastic visors. All were armed with guns or high-powered stun guns on the end of batons. Ingman was among them, a smirk on his face.

She hated them all in that moment. It was a hatred so palpable that she could feel it as a pressure building inside her head, a pressure she just knew it would feel oh-so-satisfying to release. Like laughing with Elle in the sun. Before she could stop herself or the Aegis, she felt that cold shift within her.

A man in a lab coat flew off his feet toward the door. His body crashed into the frame. She watched as he fell limp to the floor in a crumpled heap. The others faltered a bit when their coworker went flying. They quickly regrouped and circled her like Spartans, their weapons drawn. Ingman was no longer smirking. He was saying something, but she could not hear him over the rushing of the Aegis in her ears.

She backed away from them, glancing at Fletcher. He had a syringe in his hand.

She took a deep breath and dropped to her knees. "Okay. I'm done. Just don't drug me."

"All right, everyone, show's over," Fletcher said to his cronies. "It's over, Ingman. Go take a smoke break."

The air was normal. The only currents of air wafted from the ducts. She turned back to the others, and the broken man on the floor stirred a bit and groaned.

"Somebody check on Heiberg," Fletcher said, closer this time. His forearm locked her swiftly in place. She did not fight him, only grit her teeth as the needle pierced her neck without prejudice.

"You want to know why I keep you in the tube?" Fletcher asked. "Everyone warned me. Zombie. Alien. Robot. You're not like the rest of us. Not like Elle."

"Fuck you," she said, trying to escape his grasp. The drugs had taken effect during his little speech and now he was lowering her to the floor.

"Just calm down," Fletcher said.

"We both know she's the only reason I'm here," she said, her voice hoarse.

He looked down at her dispassionately. "You should fear the day when she's no longer any use to us."

Cass woke in the sick bay, a large white room near the lab. There were usually a few occupied beds, but they had all been wheeled away. Someone sat close by, watching her. She tried to focus, but she had a splitting headache. Through the haze over her eyes, she saw a slight, brown-skinned woman with short, black hair.

"Elle," she said in a near whimper.

"You're a generation off," came a voice that sounded a lot like Elle's.

Cass's eyes cleared out of sheer will and she saw an older version of her love. The same mouth, but lined from years of smiling. Her eyes were what broke Cass's heart; they too were similar in shape and color as Elle's and still bright with a youth that belied the congresswoman's years.

"Mrs. Pharell?" she stuttered, not sure what else to call her.

She stood and moved closer. "Hello, Cassandra, please call me Regina. It's nice to meet you at last. How are you feeling?"

"Better, waking to see you." Cass faltered, realizing that despite the identical features, she was a stranger.

Sure enough, the smile faded and was replaced with a grave expression.

"I hope you feel like that after our conversation."

"Is Elle okay?"

"She's fine. She sends her regards. You could say that she sent me here."

Cass had to remember to breathe as her heart seemed to have soared into the stratosphere.

"When Elle returned from Indonesia, I knew something was wrong," Regina said, a forlorn look crossing her face like a shadow. "She has always told me and her father if she was leaving the States. I had to find out from Anne who told me about you and Kuwait. That makes two times my only child left the country without telling me. I didn't know what to think until Elle opened up to me at last."

"I'm sorry," Cass said. "We weren't ever going to see each other again, but I was just lost without her. In a way, she was all I knew."

Thora had been unable to reprogram Cass, erase her memories of Elle so she could go back to being the Gorgon.

"I understand," Regina said. "Elle is so determined to get you home."

Home. She had never had one, at least not like the Pharells'. It was something she often fantasized about; she and Elle living the life she saw in advertisements and television shows.

"I know you don't want to be here; I know you're trying to keep Elle safe, but what if you could help her and many other Americans stay safe? You don't have a country of origin, but we could make a place for you."

Cass stared at her for a moment. It was obvious that she had used her own connections to help find answers, all Elle's prompting, Cass assumed. Part of her wished that Elle would not have involved her mother, but part of her, mostly her soaring heart, was happy to know that her love refused to move on without her.

"Then you know the danger."

"We all do, even Elle. She was so broken, she felt guilty that she left you. She told me about the existence of the SDC, and I started digging around. Someone noticed and I was invited to join a congressional panel on terrorism. I was able to track you down and began to petition the Pentagon to take an interest in you."

"You're the woman from DC Fletcher told me about?"

"Yes," she said.

"And you're here on behalf of the Pentagon?"

Regina smiled. "Elle wants to make sure you're safe, and she wants you to finally have a decent life. You'd be monitored by the government, but they are willing to make you a citizen of the United States, give you a job with one of the bureaus, the military, whatever would be the best fit for you. I know someone who hopes you land in Texas."

"She's done all that for me? And you've helped her?"

"You saved my daughter's life. The two of you both lived through a harrowing experience. You need closure in order to move on."

"I care for her," Cass said decisively. "Fletcher says that I broke free from Olympicorp's control on my own, but I am convinced it was because of Elle. I would do anything for her including staying away from her to keep her safe."

Regina gave a slow nod, as if she were reluctant to agree. "She talks like you're some kind of hero, and of your abilities, which I must admit I didn't believe until Fletcher let me see video of what happened down there in the lab—"

That was not the first impression she wanted Elle's mother to have of her or their first meeting.

"I don't enjoy hurting people," she said.

"When they hurt you first, I think you do," she countered with a wry smile. "It's that power that you wield. You came out of that pod-thing a wounded dog, but you turned into a completely different animal when you activated that thing in your head."

The Aegis. They'd allowed her to watch and now she spoke of it with a mixture of awe and curiosity. She looked so much like Elle. The Pentagon knew exactly what they were doing by sending Mrs. Pharell to present their plans.

"You wield an extraordinary power that interests the United States government," Regina said. "No one would care about your story otherwise."

"Elle cares."

"That's Elle. I could never keep up with her crusades. Then, she gets mixed up with Loera, you, and Olympicorp."

"What do they want from me in return? Fletcher wants my loyalty, and he wants me to prove it by leading him to top Olympicorp members."

"The Pentagon is interested in the Aegis. They are also interested in access to more of your kind."

"Wraiths?"

"You understand them. You could help us help them. It would not be the first time the US embraced former enemies. As far as we know, you've been the only one to break from the programming. You were able to subdue Lyles. You were able to send a wraith cross-country to send a message to Elle," she said.

"That was a shot in the dark," she said. "I just wanted her to know that I was okay."

Regina nodded sympathetically. "What the Pentagon is offering you is a light security confinement in America. You can have visitors and phone calls, all monitored of course. What they want to do is study the Aegis for the purpose of extraction."

"And if they can't remove it?"

"Time will tell."

"I can see Elle in the meantime?"

"As often as possible," she said.

Still, it sounded too good to be true. "Fletcher made promises too."

"I understand your lack of trust after everything you've been through. It's why I came here personally. The Pentagon thinks that if you are in the right frame of mind, if you can be reasoned with instead of being treated like a prisoner, you might be a little more cooperative."

Cass weighed her words. "What if Fletcher is right about me? I didn't grow up with nice parents. I don't even remember my childhood. I'm not normal. I may very well be a monster."

Regina looked sympathetic. "You're losing the bit of humanity you were able to find, being cooped up here, I believe Fletcher wants that. It's easy to control a beast if you have the right firepower. It's harder to take down a whole, real person."

She had to look away as tears gathered in her eyes at her words. "And the Aegis? Does Elle know the Pentagon has plans for it?"

"Don't feel obligated to protect the weapon, for your own sake or Elle's."

Cass thought on the subject for a moment. She could be with Elle if the Pentagon deal went through; she could be free of the Aegis.

"I would give anything to be with her again."

Regina smiled and nodded. She had a quiet, confident grace. She was definitely Elle's mother.

"She will be glad to hear that. What about you, Cass? This is an opportunity for a new life. FBI, CIA, Homeland Security. Do you want to even go into intelligence or law enforcement? I mean you could do anything. You could be a chef, a firefighter."

They both chuckled at the idea.

Regina patted her hand. "I'll go back to Washington immediately. In the meantime, you stay strong. Play Fletcher's little game tomorrow."

"I will do my best."

"Take care of yourself," Regina said and leaned in and gave her a hug. She felt so much like Elle that Cass found herself in tears. Regina straightened while patting Cass's shoulder, giving her one final look before leaving.

Cass fell into a deep sleep and dreamed of America. There was sunshine, and people laughing and of course, Elle, smiling at her, leading her by the hand. It was heartbreaking because the whole while she knew that it was merely a dream. She woke and stared at the ceiling, let the tears fall from her face, and wished for the pod because it seemed her body could only rest when her mind was in stasis. A white coat came in a few minutes later and began to hastily remove the equipment monitoring her vitals.

"Fletcher says to escort you to your quarters," he said.

When he was finished removing the monitoring equipment, he presented her with a pile of clothes, the standard black skivvies, T-shirt, and khaki tactical pants. She dressed and left the bay to find the white coat waiting outside the door. She walked out of the infirmary with him trailing behind.

The building was once a facility for testing objects exposed to trace amounts of radiation. There were the dreary labs of the basement, and ordinary offices, once posh, now they were rundown. A slow elevator connected the two office floors, and a courtyard covered by a skylight too grimy to let much sunlight in but could not keep out the rain when it showered.

A few agents milled around. She reached her quarters, a small dorm with a closet shower. Once alone, she stripped her clothes from her clammy skin and hoped that the plumbing would be generous. Her prayers were answered when the stream stayed hot and steady after two minutes. She stayed under the stream and allowed the hot water to fall down her back. The water started to cool which meant that her hot shower was nearing its end. She turned off the water. She wrapped herself in a towel and walked half-wet to the main room, four gray walls, two chairs, a table, and a foldout couch.

She found the notebook charging on the table where she had last left it. She powered up the device and slid her fingers across the screen to access the one application, a limited internet browser with permissions to visit one site only.

The new Green Patriot logo brightened the screen, a white hand and a black hand partially overlapping in a green square. The morning's headline: *A third grueling night: Protests still underway in Omaha.*

And there was Elle Pharell, the Green Patriot's founder standing among protestors speaking out against the death of a black man by police. Elle had been there when the story broke, and never left, even after a riot squad fired tear gas on journalists and protestors. She seemed of course, nonplussed through it all.

Classic Elle.

It worried Cass that Elle jumped into any challenge feet-first, especially if she was championing a cause. The pictures of the young man murdered by the police flashed on the side of the screen beneath a fundraising link. She could not help but think of Rob Loera. His suicide right in front of Elle had started it all, her journey to Cass.

She sighed and watched the video. Elle interviewed people in the neighborhood where the killing had taken place. For the occasion, she wore little makeup and a baseball cap with the Green Patriot logo covering her usually perfectly coifed close-cropped hair. As always, she looked absolutely gorgeous.

Elle always remained poised and self-assured, even when she was spouting a few f-bombs. Elle spoke to a tearful young woman, a former classmate of the victim. The young woman was having a hard time speaking and, finally overcome by emotion, bowed her head. Elle embraced her as the woman shook with sobs. Cass felt tears in her own eyes at the sadness of the cause, at the grief of the whole movement. Still, the scene worried her. If she could talk to her, she would tell her that she didn't have to prove anything to anyone, that she had survived the worst.

Elle would have disagreed, because she believed in righting social injustices despite backlash and controversy, even at her own peril as she nearly escaped smoking metallic cannisters hurled by the police, but also made her a target for Mount Olympus as she was integral in them losing one of their most valued weapons.

Someone remembered to bring Cass food, breakfast, though it was time for lunch. She examined the tray from the mess covered with aluminum foil in an attempt to keep the food warm. She unwrapped it to find eggs, bacon, and porridge, all cold and no longer its proper consistency. Cass had long suspected that they medicated her food to slow her down, make her less of a danger. As usual, she ate it anyway and wished for more.

Her notebook chimed letting her know that she was receiving a communique from Fletcher. She answered and saw a text message that she was to head to the conference room.

She made her way suffering the stares of the agents as she went as they eyed the band around her forehead and the bruises on her face. Fletcher wanted to send them a message by allowing her to make her way without an escort. She spied him though, the escort from earlier lingering in the background. They were all vigilant of her journey as if they were put on alert and gave her a synchronized berth. She arrived at the location Fletcher requested and paused at the entrance of the appointed conference room. The space was dark save for the light of a projection of satellite photos on a bare wall. Fletcher noticed her and waved her in.

She glanced around and saw that there were a group of SDC agents gathered around the table in the far corner. They turned their heads when they noticed her, and she could see the shadows on their faces change in the light of the projector. There were a few whispers. They turned their backs to her, but she didn't need any special abilities to feel their awareness of her. Word had spread about what happened on Jove Island and they all had opinions.

"Have a seat," Fletcher said. "We were just reviewing the intel on Amir."

He slid her a stack of satellite photos that she picked up, conscious of the eyes on her. One of the agents stood and began to review the information the Egyptian government had given them including the myriad of crimes over several continents ranging from human trafficking to animal poaching. He'd opened a casino in the resort town of Sharm El Sheikh, a clean operation, but it allowed the SDC to track his movements to and from his friend's compound where he'd taken residence in order to oversee his new venture. Also, he enjoyed the nightlife, rubbing elbows with the region's elite.

She began to look through the pictures. A compound, six buildings, a lush garden and a pool, a wall around the perimeter.

"We're going in remotely," Fletcher announced. "The State Security Service is doing the takedown. They don't want any civilian casualties as there are an estimated twenty-five people on the estate at any given time, Amir's wife, children, his friend's family, servants, and of course, the bodyguards."

Fletcher looked around the room. "We're shadowing, so no cowboy shit. We've had enough of that his week."

There were a few chuckles and a few groans from those who thought it was too soon to be making quips about their attempt to crack Jove Island. Her eyes met Fletcher's as he stood.

Fletcher lifted a surveillance photo of the front gate setup, armed men in tactical gear in dark shades. "We'll have some agents on standby of course, you know, just in case."

"Once we get Amir secured, we'll follow the motorcade to a secure location yet to be named, but my guess is they'll hotfoot him to South Camp military base. "We'll ask Amir a few questions. After that, it's none of our business, though I am sure he will meet a nasty demise."

Cass glanced at the photos. She thought it was strange that Amir would surface right now, that he would put his name on something so public. Then again, if he indeed had moved into the right circle of elites, those who did not mind rubbing elbows with criminals, greed would have overridden any urge to stay underground.

The briefing ended and the agents began to stand and file out of the room. She waited until they were mostly gone to make her move.

"Just a minute," Fletcher said. "I want to talk for a moment."

As the room cleared, they regarded each other in silence.

"What bullshit did the Honorable Representative Pharell spill during her visit?" he asked.

"The Pentagon wants to make a deal," Cass said. "They want me to work with them."

"So, what, you're a free agent now?"

"I'm not naive, I know she told me what they wanted me to know."

"Yeah, just what you wanted to hear," he said. "Maybe I should have let you talk to her without that band on your head, the old telepathic lie detector."

His smugness annoyed her.

"Aren't I in your custody?" she asked. "You brought me in."

His smugness faded and she realized that he was simply a glorified warden, and the SDC her prison. He could do what he wanted within its walls, but her freedom belonged to someone else.

She felt her face flush in anger. "I haven't decided anything yet."

"You've made the decision. They're really pulling out all the stops. They even sent Pharell to dangle her lovely daughter," he said. "Why is it okay for them to use Elle against you, but not me?"

"Elle is advocating for me, her mother is using her office to actually give me a real life, not to keep me as a prisoner."

"That's exactly what they are using you for," he said. "You think the grass is going to be greener on the other side? You get your girl. What else did they promise you?"

"More than you have," she said and decided to test the waters, not that she ever expected Fletcher to give his honest opinion on the matter.

He raised his eyebrows and smiled like the cat that got the cream. "What did she ask in return? The Pentagon wouldn't have sent Mrs. Black Excellence, Regina Pharell, all the way to Kazakhstan to play games."

She paused again. She had no reason to tell Fletcher anything, especially after the way he'd treated her. Still, despite what she'd told Fletcher she had made up her mind about leaving to go to the States. How could she challenge the offer of such an opportunity?

"They want the Aegis."

"I figured that," he said. "I take it Regina has told you they can remove it without turning you into a vegetable."

"They haven't worked out the kinks," she said. "They want to study it first."

He nodded. "Makes sense, but I doubt the Aegis can ever be removed, not without killing you. Maybe if we had Thora, she could give us more insight."

"You'd never put me and Thora in the same room, especially with surgical access to my brain and the Aegis?"

"With or without you, Thora is going down. You want to be on our side when that happens, you want to be the one that apprehends her."

That was what it all boiled down to. He believed that she had a twisted obligation to continue to serve Thora and not ensure Elle's safety, as if Cass's concern was all a front.

"I have no loyalty to her. She altered my brain, she controlled me for years. She stole those memories so that I would each time be a killer with no conscience, a thief with an innate finesse, the ultimate mole, a plant, an assassin, she could program me to be whoever she needed me to be."

"Yet, you broke free," he argued. "Whoever or whatever the reason, you were able to slip the most advanced human programming anyone has ever seen."

That was their first mistake, they drew parallels between the brain and a computer when Thora would have compared it to a vast galaxy, a complex number of systems keyed in to a rhythm. The transfer of energy gives off energy, which is used to make more. An endless unchanged cycle just waiting for someone to tap in. She would have called them all fools and Cass the biggest of them all. But then Thora had her own tanks and put Cass in them countless times, erasing her memory after every mission and bringing her back, new and pliable. Because of Thora, Cass had no memories before she met Elle and her mind miraculously broke free.

"I just want to be treated like a human being," she said. "Sleep in a bed. Not wake up surrounded by a million eyes."

He sighed. "Being a human being is overrated. It's going to get you killed or worse."

Fletcher and his mind games. Earlier, he had likened her to something inhuman, now, he was contradicting himself.

"That may be, but I have to try," she said. "Is there anything else you need of me?"

"Not really, just some notes. Since this may be our last foray together, let's make the most of it."

She nodded in agreement and turned to leave him.

"I'll send someone to escort you down to the lab in a few hours."

She paused, cringing. He meant to return her to the pod. No soft bed to sleep a normal sleep. She left him and took a walk around the complex. She paused at one of the large windows in the courtyard and looked out at the day beyond. She could see cars rushing around the city, and a few cyclists the size of ants. As usual, her thoughts turned to Elle. The mere thought of being able to go to America to see her again and hear her voice in person filled her with a mix of anxiety and hope.

Someone moved close to her, and she looked to see Kruger at her side.

"Hey," the agent said.

Cass regarded her silently not sure what to say. Kruger seemed nonplussed that she did not return her clipped greeting. She simply stared out the window. Cass watched her profile for a moment before turning back to the view.

"You saved our asses back there," she said. "The last thing I remember after Fabbro shot Raglan was you arguing with him, facing him down. I told Fletcher that we would not have made it out of there without you. Thanks."

"You're welcome," she said.

They turned to face each other.

"Well, I've been reassigned, to where, I have no idea. Most likely Siberia," she said and chuckled. "After that island, an active volcano will seem like a picnic."

They turned to each other and smiled.

"Whatever you are, you did good by me, by all of us."

Cass felt a warm hand on her shoulder, the second kind gesture another person had shown her that day. Kruger did not linger and left her at the window.

She stood there for a moment before departing herself. She did not go back to the quarters designated to her, but down to the lab.

CHAPTER FOUR

Sharm El Sheikh, Egypt

Their cohort consisted of Cass, Fletcher, and a few SDC agents who did not look her way, let alone speak to her during the flight. Fletcher had her wear the band around her forehead to curb any unauthorized use of the Aegis or pulse reading. She used the opportunity to try to get some actual sleep, but sleep did not come. She stared out the window at the clouds beyond the window and allowed her thoughts to stray to Elle once again.

When the plane landed, she waited for Fletcher to say good-bye to his companions before exiting. They joined the agents who were already waiting in a black van parked on the tarmac. They drove through the desert past a slum of makeshift buildings. The terrain reminded her of Kuwait and her time there with Elle.

They were taken to an abandoned mill about ten miles from the compound where Amir was staying. Egypt's intelligence agency, the GID, had set up a skeleton surveillance base.

She saw a familiar form among them, Zahavi, the large Israeli man who had been part of the team Elle had hired to search for a village. Their eyes met and he furrowed his brow. He was a mercenary and offered his services to the highest bidder. She doubted if he had any qualms about their ideology. The last she saw of him, Zahavi had been bitter, with enough reason. One of his colleagues had been killed while taking Elle out into the desert to investigate Ziggurat.

She glanced over at Fletcher and noticed his eyes following Zahavi's movement.

"Is that who I think it is?"

"It's him."

"Small world," he said simply.

He reached over and removed the band from her head. The sensation of taking in the brainwaves of the people around her returned. She shivered as she soaked it all in.

"We're going on the move soon. We'll be in an armored vehicle so stick close to me," he said. "Just in case."

She agreed. They crammed inside the armored vehicle with four other people and surveillance equipment. She saw the points of view of other vehicles in the caravan on a bank of screens as well as from the outside, body cams mounted on the armed officials as they gathered for one last consultation before carrying out the mission.

She could see the lead vehicle closing in on the front gate, the panic of the compound's guards as they retreated, firing in vain. The iron gate crumpled under the assault. More men appeared, firing on the second vehicle. The mounted gun exploded in a staccato of bullets. She could hear them in the distance. On another screen a soldier took out an opponent who had taken cover behind a car. The body sparkled as bullets bounced off the car. They were armored as well. Zahavi passed into her view as inhabitants of the compound surrendered. Chaos. The women's faces contorted in agony as they were separated from their terrified children.

Outside, more men fell to the ground in surrender or death as the mercenaries moved deeper inside the compound. On another screen, she saw Amir, bleeding from the head, his hands zip-tied. She watched as he was escorted to the second vehicle and shoved in. On another screen, the vehicle backed away from the scene with a screech of its tires.

Once the dust settled, Fletcher exited the vehicle and motioned for Cass to follow him but told her to stay by the van until he returned.

Zahavi approached warily, glancing over his shoulder. He offered her a cigarette, and she took it and leaned into the flame of the lighter he produced. She mirrored his movements. They were just two people having a smoke amongst the ruin.

"Is this about the reporter, Pharell?" he asked. "My employers were tight-lipped."

"No," she said. "We are on the trail of Olympicorp."

He stubbed out his cigarette.

"How is Mo'Moh's family?"

"They'll make it," he said. "His son's studying to be a doctor."

A truck drove by and one of the men shouted for him. "Good luck, I hope you find the reporter."

That said, he trotted away and jumped on the back of a passing truck as it made its way toward the main gate.

Cass frowned at his last statement as she watched the truck disappear into the horizon. Fletcher appeared and directed her to another van. As she waited her turn to enter after a few officials, she saw the silhouette of Amir as guards loaded him into a different van.

Fletcher called her away from the scene. "We're rolling out soon. Stay close."

They joined a reformed contingent of the last caravan, smaller but joined by two rugged vehicles mounted with guns. They drove an hour south to what looked to be a prison complex.

They were taken to a room lined with large screens scrolling the rules of the proceeding in different languages. Three long tables were prepped with name cards and headphones to hear the interpreters. Fletcher placed a pair over his ears. She did as well as she was not certain she would be able to translate without an interpreter. Once, she could speak and understand a myriad of languages without thinking, one gift from Thora she regretted losing.

Men in brown military uniforms and black berets brought Amir into the room. He gazed around wildly. He was sweating profusely. His breathing so quick that his chest heaved.

"Is the prisoner well?" the translator asked for one of the dignitaries.

It was reported that Amir had been in a mild distress since his capture. There was some uproar over his treatment since. Meanwhile, the subject in question stared out at the room, his wild gaze falling on her. His breathing calmed to a hitch.

The lights flickered and she heard a crash of static in her ear followed by an ear-splitting buzzing feedback. She winced and removed her earphones. Besides, she found that she could understand the excited exclamations in Arabic, Russian, and French. Amir had collapsed and slumped over in the chair deathly still. A guard knelt next to him searching with his hands under Amir's shirt.

Someone shouted for a doctor. Cass looked to Fletcher questioningly and he just shook his head slowly.

"His pulse is steady," the guard announced.

The room calmed a bit as people hung back speaking in their varying languages into a collective murmur. She reached out and read Amir's other pulse, the one only she could feel. His brain sizzled like hot oil, nothing she could recognize as anything but dead static.

The officials tending to Amir stopped their efforts and glanced around at each other before moving away. Amir rose. Despite the bulk of his gut, he arced at the pelvis, his arms tucked at his sides. He was speaking, or at least trying to. Instead, his lips contorted, and a line of drool spilled forth. Amir's face dissolved into spasms.

The guards helped him back into his seat as a newly arrived medic slipped a blood pressure cuff around his arm. Amir changed again, his body shook and then he stopped. He was still and though he had that wild look in his eyes, his body seemed relaxed.

Then his pulse changed. It went from dead static to a pattern clearer to her. He smiled slyly as he glanced around the room as if for the first time. His expression morphed into a twisted grimace, his eyes rolled white, and he began to tremble again. The medic moved in and grabbed Amir's wrist. He quickly snatched it back to his violently trembling body. The medic backed away, a terrified look on his face.

Amir groaned as the shaking tapered off. He turned. The right half of his face sagged heavily and his voice slurred. Still, his words came clear enough to be understood.

"Certainly, I did not expect this kind of turnout for the simpleton Amir," he said and looked their way. "Cassandra, it is a relief to have found you at last."

She looked to Fletcher who stood motioning her to follow.

"Leaving so soon?" Amir slurred. "Cassandra, do you not have time to speak with me, your old handler?"

"Thora?" Cass asked.

"We're leaving," Fletcher said, urgency in his voice.

Amir smiled as if his lips were made of rubber. He stretched them thin, and they made a blubbering noise as air escaped them.

The others in the room glanced around confused.

"A new experiment of mine," Amir/Thora said. "Taking complete possession of a mind remotely."

"You're lying," Fletcher said. "Amir, Thora got to you first, didn't she? Drugged you. Told you to toy with us for whatever reason."

Amir gave another warped smile. "You're the one who took her from me. I suspect you made ridiculous promises that had to do with that reporter. Have you led her here under the pretense that Amir may know where she is? Or does she know that it's me you're after?"

"I'm after Olympicorp, and that path is taking me through you."

"And what makes you think I am the way through Olympicorp?"

Fletcher placed his hand on Cass's shoulder as he spoke to Thora. He wanted her to pay attention to his words and used the advantage of being in the room with her and not speaking through a hijacked brain.

"Where are you, Thora? I suppose you've got a bead on us; you know where we are. This place is swarming with military, guards, and officials," he said and muttered under his breath for her to get up and leave the room.

She stood in slow motion, as if in a dream.

"Cassandra," Thora/Amir shouted hoarsely. "Have they told you that your lovely reporter Elle was abducted six months ago?"

She turned to Fletcher remembering Zahavi's words. He'd said he hoped she found Elle. She began to step around the table, but Fletcher grabbed her arm at the wrist. She shrugged him off.

"It's been all over the news. Have they been keeping you in a cage, or perhaps it is your mind they have caged? I imagine they have all sorts of rudimentary tricks up their sleeves. Look at the screens in the room."

Cass turned her head to the nearest screen. Gone were the proceedings and in their place, the headline from a major news outlet.

Reporter still missing

The screen flashed to another video which featured a van in a parking garage, a woman who looked a lot like Elle being forced inside by masked men.

Elle Pharell taken from apartment garage, police investigate

Another headline read:

Where is Elle Pharell?

She stared hard at Fletcher who wore a guarded expression that turned into one of disbelief. His pulse was a jangly cluster of keys. He was beyond nervous. He was afraid.

"She's playing you, Cass," he said. "You can't believe anything she says. You said yourself, she's the bad guy."

"Is Elle safe?" she asked, her eyes locked on his. She thought of the tablet in her barrack, the one that could only access the Green Patriot. There were articles written by Elle, and videos of her in the field. If Thora could fake videos and articles, so could Fletcher.

"Damn you, tell me right now. I'll use the Aegis, I'll tear this place down."

He didn't answer, but when his gaze wavered, she knew.

"You sent me on a crusade to find Thora. You used Elle to manipulate me into allowing you to treat me like an animal?"

The cold feeling took her before she could consent. She was beyond caring who else stood in the room. Elle was somewhere, unsafe, even dead.

Fletcher gave up trying to reason with her. He stumbled around his chair in his haste to move away. He went for the gun he kept holstered under his jacket. She crossed the space between them and grabbed the front of Fletcher's suit. He tried to raise his arms in an attempt to break free, but she held him fast allowing the Aegis to buffer its will against his body.

Fletcher flailed, his face pained. She reined herself in and turned to see guns pointed in her direction. She dropped Fletcher and turned, arms raised. They were shouting for her to get on the floor. She turned her head quickly to glance at the table. Meanwhile, Amir/Thora was convulsing, a thick white foam issuing from his lips. Fletcher quickly collected himself as he arranged his suit and tried to look composed.

"Tell me where Elle is."

"I don't know," he insisted. "We think Olympicorp nabbed her to use to lure you back."

"And you didn't tell me? You were so sure Thora was on that island." Another blast of the Aegis. "Stupid man. You promised me a detail for her."

"I did what I had to do to bring her out of the woodwork," he choked out.

The floor beneath them began to shake. A few nervous shouts rang out in various languages. In a matter of seconds, the shaking escalated to a violent pitch, jarring the contents of the room. The lights flickered to darkness, leaving only the light of day creeping through the slats of the window panels. A prerecorded announcement overhead directed everyone to evacuate the building. Those not already making their way out began to crowd into the hallways. The military police remained certain she was the cause of the disturbance after her display with the Aegis. There were a few more guards, but they were assisting the medic attending to Amir by strapping him onto a rolling gurney.

She'd let go of Fletcher's suit during the strange earthquake. There was a plea in his eyes as he lifted the metal band for her to put back on.

"I swear, I don't know where Elle is," Fletcher said. "She was taken from the parking garage of her apartment back in August. By the time I got to Austin the trail was cold. It had to have been Olympicorp."

She was not shocked he would name them. "I am not putting that thing back on."

Fletcher made a show of laughing nervously. He spoke to her in Arabic. "Do us all a favor before this building comes crashing in on our heads, put on the yoke."

"And Elle's mother." She shook as the realization hit her. "She knew that Elle was missing."

"Which is why I warned you not to trust her. Now can we please get out of here?"

The room ceased its incessant trembling. The MPs decided to move in, shouting at her, their guns drawn. She raised her arms as they encircled her. Fletcher brought the headband from a pocket inside his jacket. He told the men in Arabic that she would be fine as soon as she put on the headband.

The men glanced around at each other but did not question Fletcher. The room shook again so hard that a chunk of the ceiling plummeted onto the table where Amir had sat only minutes before. On the gurney now, his still body was wheeled out of the room by the guards and the brave medic.

"You have your chance to get Thora. She must be close to be causing all of this," she told Fletcher.

He glanced at the door Amir had been taken through, then back at her. His nod told her that he was in agreement, and his pulse confirmed his resignation.

Thora was nearby. She would have the answers Cass needed. The building began to shake again, and she took the opportunity for escape.

She gave Fletcher a hard push with the Aegis ejecting him across the room and into one of the screens. She turned and ran the way Amir/Thora had gone. She could feel his pulse still lingering in the air strangely stronger than the other people around. She followed it; her feet pounded on the floor as she fled. Another rumble and the floor sloped forward and she crashed into a pile of debris. Something dull and angry poked at her ribs and she cried out. She pulled herself together and straightened. Through the chaos she could see a shaft of sunlight ahead. She scrambled forward and slipped through a newly made gap in the wall. She slipped out onto the street and a whirlwind of dust, debris, and piercing sirens.

Men and women in suits, some of them uniformed in black berets, jogged through the dust. They did not regard her as she passed. She ducked and sprinted across the compound toward the front entrance. She met with a large fissure, a newly formed canyon in the middle of the intersection. One of the vehicles they had arrived in was partially wedged inside the crack. She climbed over the car using it as a bridge. Men with uniforms surged out of the gloom. They demanded that she halt. Fletcher had raised the alarm. She gave them a taste of the Aegis and did not stick around to watch them tumble. She jogged down what looked to be a training trail as it was imprinted with the soles of dozens of boots. An emergency vehicle roared past. She began to run the path toward a series of outbuildings.

A sleek black car, tires spinning, zipped to a stop alongside her. The window glided down. Thora. Her gaze as piercing as ever, knowing, red-rimmed. But there were more lines on her face. Her crown of white hair framed her face, shorter than Cass remembered. It had always been white.

Cass broke eye contact and saw the smirk on Thora's lips as she forced her eyes away.

"Get in."

"Where is Elle?"

"I don't know her exact location, but I may know who does."

"I'm supposed to trust you? And end up like Amir?"

"I can no longer control you," she said. "If I could then I would have been able to get you on the island."

Cass paused. She could no longer read the strange pulse that had come from Amir. Another one of Thora's tricks to get her away from the melee.

"Don't you see what I've done? Just to be here? Just to pull back the wool they've put over your eyes."

"You've hurt a lot of people, Thora."

The authorities would be scouting the area soon, and two unaccompanied white women would stand out. She could not fight all that would come. She needed to get out of the area quickly and there was no alternative in sight. Thora had multiple plans, just like on the island. A fail-safe for every outcome. Cass was sure Thora had a contingency plan if she refused to go along with her.

"Since when do you care about collateral damage?" Thora asked. "Wouldn't you blow up the world to get your Elle back?"

"I can find her myself. I don't need you."

The car halted, and Thora opened the driver's side door. She climbed out of the car regarding her over the sleek roof as she hitched around leaning heavily on a cane of dark wood and silver, limping along the dusty road.

"In less than five minutes," she called to Cass, "no one will be able to get in or out of this place."

Their time apart had not been so kind to Thora. She had been injured. But then, it could have been an act. It was true that she could no longer control Cass, but that did not mean she was above manipulating her.

"We don't have time for this," Thora said, out of breath. She'd never had the problem before. She'd always had a graceful gait, thanks to long legs.

Cass thought of knocking her over, taking the car and leaving her stranded. A parting gift to Fletcher for all his hospitality. She could muscle her way out of the entrance. Try anyway.

Thora knew she could very well just do that. "I have the resources you need to travel away from this Hell-forsaken place," she said. "I can get you to the States. We could find Elle together."

Cass stopped and turned to look at her. Thora was out of breath and there was sweat on her upper lip.

"You aren't afraid of a crippled old woman, are you?"

Cass marched toward her, grabbed her arm, and pulled her along toward the car.

"I still have use of the Aegis."

"Of course you do," she huffed as she stumbled along. "Imagine my surprise to find that you'd supplicated yourself to the Americans."

Cass bit her lip as they reached the car. She pushed Thora against the passenger door of the still-running car. She turned, her face pained. A momentary look of fear. It was strange to see her weakened. Cass did not feel sympathy though her emotions swayed instinctively toward the sentiment.

"If you try anything I will use the Aegis," she said. "I am not in the mood to be merciful. I will toss you twenty feet in the air and be gone before you fall to the ground."

A slight smile tugged at Thora's lips. "I see that you learned how to talk tough among the Americans. I hope you have the nerve to back it up."

"I'll drive," Cass said.

She quickly walked around the car and slid behind the driver's seat. She smelled Thora's perfume all around her, light, flowery, and pleasant. She did not trust it. She decided that she would keep the window down. She would have to stay mindful of any of Thora's tricks to avoid becoming her thrall.

Cass watched her negotiate herself into a sitting position as she eased onto the seat. She reached over and slammed the door. The complete process left her out of breath.

"What happened to you?" Cass asked.

"Olympicorp. They ambushed me in Vienna. I barely escaped. My hip has not been the same since."

She put the car into drive and sped away from the scene.

"You're injured as well," Thora said. "Turn right here. When you clear these buildings make a left."

"I'll be fine," Cass said. "Where are we going?"

"The front gate," Thora answered. "I've paid good money for our safe passage through during this very small window of time."

The complex had deteriorated into chaos. A line of traffic halted their progress. Similar black sedans, military, and police vehicles. Cass glanced around nervously.

"Why have we stopped?" Thora asked.

"Traffic," Cass said.

Thora stared at her. "You haven't forgotten how to drive have you?"

"No, but have you not noticed where we are?"

"Since when have you ever had to worry about such a thing?" Thora asked. "Now please. Drive."

Cass gripped the wheel, felt her heart aflutter as she pressed down on the gas. There was a shallow dusty shoulder. A group of men in uniforms were watching the idle traffic. They noticed the car barely sliding through a narrow space between two cars, picking up speed as it headed their way. Cass did not falter, and they scattered as the undercarriage of the car encountered the rocky shoulder, metal shrieking. Cass watched them disappear in a cloud of dust. She skirted a barrier and maneuvered past a line of vehicles, one, an imposing jeep mounted with a gun. The stretch ahead was remarkably free of cars, and she could see the main entrance guarded by tall narrow towers flanking a metal fence.

"There," Thora said. "Slow down here."

Cass slowed the car. As they neared the gate, a half dozen uniformed men came from the dusty periphery, their heads darting as they talked among themselves trying to discern who was in the car.

"Shit," Cass said.

"Don't panic," Thora muttered.

The men were at the windows now, shouting and tapping at the glass. She looked to her old handler.

"It's fine," Thora insisted.

"It doesn't look fine."

"You sound like a child," she said and reached over to hit the automatic locks. "You could very well destroy them all, that is the beauty of what you are."

The men outside were more insistent. One of them tried the passenger door handle.

"You got any fire power?" she asked.

Thora looked as if she could not be bothered. She nodded toward the glove box.

Cass reached over Thora's knees, opened the glove box, and saw the silhouette of a gun.

CHAPTER FIVE

The Mist

A forest of towering evergreens. No sky in sight. Elle hovered somewhere in between the stillness, shrouded in a pale mist. She could hear her own breathing, and her heart beating in her ears. She could hear other sounds, distant but unrecognizable.

Then, there was the castle, hiding among the dark green trees like something she had been searching for but absent-mindedly overlooked. Shades of gray, weathered stone. Black, peaked turrets like the headdress of a sinister cult.

She tried to remember the significance of the place. Did her journey begin there? Was it her destination? It was just as familiar to her as it was a mystery. At the realization of her not knowing, she felt a panic within her as if she might suddenly plummet into a tangle of spiny branches. She felt desperate that she needed something to hold on to before she fell or floated off into the stratosphere.

Then, there was the net stretching out before her, nearly obscured by the mist. She suspected that it had always been there, just like the castle, unnoticed. She felt confused in a way that she was unsure of what she saw. She'd never had such a problem before. Focusing.

She needed to focus. That was all she needed here in the mist, complete focus on staying aloft. As for making a descent, she did not know if she should. The castle. The dark forest below.

Why was she so unsure?

The net was made of black line, the space between the links were of a curious jigsaw pattern making each link a different shape. Unlike the castle, she found she knew something of the net: it was not meant to ensure her safety. It would ensnare her if she made the wrong move. She knew this all purely by instinct. Her panic intensified as her senses steadily solidified.

The castle was not home.

The mist was not to be trusted.

The net was something to be dreaded.

She had been this close before, at the end of a journey of which she did not know the particulars. She got the sense that it was all tenuous, and that the alternative was darkness. She felt that it was imperative that she move.

She had to solidify herself somehow, distinguish herself from the mist. Her hand. She felt the urge to wave it in front of her face as one would do to someone who was daydreaming or in a trance. She lifted her hand. Nothing. Had she been paralyzed? Did her hand exist at all? She tried again and the errant limb appeared slowly into view. She took inventory. Four fingers and a thumb, five nails trimmed short, dark brown on one side, the palm lighter and lined. There was something else. An object clutched between her thumb and forefinger. It felt at once glossy and rough. On closer inspection she saw that it had print, a familiar dark green, gray, and black.

She turned her attention to the castle and noticed something had changed. One of those peaked turrets had been carved away by some force that had taken away the trees and mist leaving a brown piece of barren land in a bizarre shape of long and short curves. A symbol of something she knew, but like so many things, could not place. She looked to her hand and found the answer, that thing between her fingers was the piece of turret and the trees. The exact shape of the barren land. The jigsaw outline of the shape like the links on the net. Had her own hand caused such catastrophe? She had seen such mindless destruction before. She had lost loved ones to devastation. She inspected the object in her hand. Flat. Compact. She knew it then. The glossy picture side, the semi-rough cardboard backing. She lowered the object in her hand. The net retreated and fell creating a pattern across the scene below. The mist was gone. There was light, dim, and not natural. It gave her hand a weird shadow that covered the land as she laid the piece in place.

She looked away to the place where she sat physically. A room of glass-paneled walls and a black-tiled floor. Beyond, she could see people moving about. Some of them wore coral-colored scrubs. Two of them stood right outside her doorway. Talking.

Farther in the distance, another set of coral scrubs wheeled a slumped figure disappearing through a wall of light so bright that it stung her eyes. On the opposite end she was startled to see dark green treetops in the distance. In the place of the mist there was blue, cloudless sky and that brought her some comfort. She saw more people on a lawn of green grass.

"Well, look at you," a voice said, close by. "Hey. Yes. That's right. Come on out of it."

She tried to follow the voice with her eyes, but her vision blurred, and the world ran together in a mass of colors and shapes until she could no longer distinguish people from objects from empty space.

She blinked rapidly to clear her vision, but her lids felt so dry and heavy, ripping open and slamming shut. She tasted hot tears.

A clammy, feverish hand clamped over her wrist, making her scalp prickle. The contact made her realize how cold it was in the glass room. That voice spoke to her with a cheerful strain, a nervous urgency. A woman. Youngish. She could not tell. It was difficult to get hold of anything, let alone her basic senses.

"Come on, you can do it. Get out of your head. Try saying your name," the woman said brightly and then added urgently, "Do you even know your name? Are you that fried?"

She tried to speak to ask for help, because she desperately wanted to be able to answer the woman's question, as it was the very question she needed to answer. The only sound that she could muster was a wheezing breath that made her teeth rattle.

"That's not gonna work," she whispered harshly. "I need you to speak an actual word. Get your shit together and get out of the mist."

The mist. This woman knew about it. Had she been there before as well? Was that why they were here? The world further solidified around her. She saw the blurry outline of the owner of the voice. Slight. Pale. Black hair. Large, dark, searching eyes.

"I think I remember you. I think I remember that you were one of them."

She tried to reply to her again. She wanted to tell the owner of the voice to go and get help. The wheelchairs, the coral scrubs. Was this some sort of hospital?

"Do you know why you're here?"

She had stooped low and spoke in a harsh whisper.

"No. You don't. You're barely here. You could fade away, but I won't let you."

As if rebelling against the dark-haired woman's words, the world around her, including the woman, blurred into a white blaze across her vision. She could see an image beneath the white, a partially developed instant film photograph except the details never solidified. She could see hints of people and places before the white waxed into nothing. A man in her office holding a gun to his head. Then, a wide expanse of desert under clear, blue sky. Then, what could have been a night sky over the sea. This time, the image gave more details; there was a woman with blond hair on her bare shoulders. She loomed over her, a half-smile, like a secret on her lips. But before more could be revealed, the opacity burned away to a blinding white. Not that she physically saw any of this. The light came from inside her head flashing images, bloodied, broken, filthy people running in panic along a partially collapsed hallway. The white returned and gave way again. Then ceiling tiles, wires and insulation, shattered glass and daylight partially obscured by smoke.

A sharp pain up her arm and she felt her eyes widen from the shock. Her surroundings came into clean, clear focus. The dark-haired woman watched her as she pinched her arm and bit her own chapped bottom lip.

Her neck bowed, and her eyes fell back on the mist and castle. It had only been a jigsaw puzzle, and the last piece lay slightly askew. She had held that final piece. The puzzle looked to be one of those 500-piece affairs. She did not remember starting it. Had she put the entire thing together herself? She did not remember coming to that glass room or what lay beyond, let alone putting together a puzzle.

"Leslie." A different voice now. "Get away from her. Now."

The pain intensified, but her vision cleared presenting her with two women in scrubs with worried expressions. One of them shined a light into her eyes. The other spoke to the dark-haired woman, Leslie, in a scolding tone while trying to grab her arm. She snatched herself away, then dodged between the two in coral scrubs.

She tried to speak to them. She wanted to tell them about Leslie physically hurting her, harassing her, a mad woman on the loose. She wanted to ask about the place, why she hadn't remembered putting together the puzzle, why she was there with a woman who was obviously crazy.

Did that mean she was crazy as well?

"Has she come out of it? Is she out of beta consciousness?" Leslie asked. She was chewing her lip again and staring at her from the other side of the table.

"That's none of your concern," the nurse said.

"No, she's awake," Leslie insisted. She spoke directly to her. "Go on, tell them your name, idiot."

She felt anger welling up inside her. It was obvious that Leslie was not to be privy to her state of mind or why she was there. Also, she could not remember her name. Her annoyance with the interloper suddenly outweighed anything else.

"Fuck," she gasped from the effort and with as much triumph as she could mutter, "off."

The three of them froze and stared at her. Leslie's mouth hung open and she clutched at her collar at imaginary pearls, and she laughed.

"That's enough," one of the nurses said. "Your rec time just ended, Leslie."

"No way. Dr. Stevens promised an hour."

"You should have thought of that before you decided to bother another patient," another nurse said as another stepped behind Leslie and caught hold of her upper arm.

She tried to duck away, but they both grabbed her. She struggled with the other two. One of them shouted an alarm as they latched on to either side of her and tried to guide her away. She fought them, a rail-thin woman with wild eyes and unkempt hair. What was this place? The nurse had referred to them as patients. The realization brought fresh alarm, a din that rang louder in her head than the screaming and fighting in her ears.

"Welcome back," Leslie said as they dragged her away.

She watched the nurses escort her down a glass-paneled hall through a doorway. She glanced around; she could see that the walls of the room were not completely made of glass. They were divided horizontally, gray wall and glass panels. She looked out of the room she was in and could see into at least two others. Several figures in scrubs were watching her. She noticed another individual forgotten in a wheelchair stacking a tower of playing cards.

Beyond was a larger room and that was completely made of glass panels like a greenhouse. She could see sky and trees, a lawn with several people in wheelchairs, some in scrubs.

She felt tired and sore all over. Exhausted to the point where she could hardly keep her eyes open, and the whole scene began to flicker in front of her in blurry images like before when the world blurred together.

She felt sick, dizzy, and when blackness grayed the edges of her vision, she wanted to go to it just to escape the turmoil of her senses. A sudden curiosity claimed her as another form entered from the gloom trailing brilliance down the hallway, a beam of pure light. Once her perception of the world began to solidify again, she saw that it was a woman. She wore a white coat and a nimbus of curly auburn hair.

"Elle," the woman said. "How are you feeling?"

That name. Elle. It belonged to her. The relief caused her skin to prickle as if exposed to a chill. She tried to stifle the whimper that escaped her mouth, but it tumbled forth bringing sobs that made her chest ache.

The woman came closer, and Elle tried to shrink away, turned her head in the opposite direction. She gripped the side of the table determined to get up, to get away. She tried to tell the woman in the white coat to come no further, to leave her alone. The conviction rang in her head, but another pitiful whine escaped her lips. She squeezed the sides of the table so hard her arms began to tremble and throb with cramps.

"I'm Dr. Wyatt Stevens. You're at Gloaming Hill Recovery Center in West Virginia."

She watched the woman, Dr. Stevens, as she stepped even closer to the bed, reaching out her hand to further close the distance between them. Dr. Stevens seemed aware of her fear and slowly edged toward the bed as if she were some wild, wounded animal. The white coat seemed to hum as if it was wired to glow.

Elle moved her arm. It felt heavy and numb. Still, she lifted it clumsily and banged it on the center of the puzzle, shoving forward. It slid off the table and onto the floor. She heard the pieces fall and scatter.

"Elle?" Dr. Stevens asked. "Are you in any pain?"

"I don't know," she said in a trembling voice.

"Good," she said. "It's good to be able to finally hear you speak."

Then she was on her, her touch was light, but her presence and proximity felt oppressive. She spoke kind words in a velvety voice, but she wore a white coat in this gray room. She was one of them, but she did not know who they were.

"I'm going to take you to your room now, okay?"

Elle nodded and the world shifted as the doctor wheeled her out of the room. They passed through into a gray hallway with a black ceiling and a black floor. There were no more glass panels. To Elle, it felt like a strange world, far away from her own, as if there was nothing but darkness beyond those nondescript halls. The void at the edge of existence.

Though she was not actually walking, Elle felt out of breath. Tired. Her legs and back ached. Dr. Stevens touched her shoulder and said something in a jovial tone as they went along the gray halls, but the pain was too distracting to focus on her words.

They stopped at the only door Elle had noticed in their journey and thought that was strange. This door was open. Beyond, a room dimly lit by the warmth of a lamp.

"Here we are," Dr. Stevens said as she led her in.

Elle found herself grateful to see a bed even though there were a bank of monitors and equipment in the room as well.

"You must be tired," Dr. Stevens said, pulling back the covers. "It will be like that for a while." She saw Elle's hesitation and her face softened. "It's okay. I think you're out of the woods now. I always knew you would pull through."

Pull through. Elle recognized that phrase as one used for someone recovering from some grave illness. What had happened to her? She climbed into the bed, a captive to her fatigue. Why did she feel so tired? How had she put that entire puzzle together? When she was a child, her father would buy one for them to put together during the holiday break. They would always do the edges first.

Her father. Her mother. Did they know her whereabouts? Did they know what happened?

"My mom," she managed. "My dad."

"They are fine and will be glad to hear that you have asked for them," Dr. Stevens said, her voice a soothing balm that calmed the panic. She placed a hand on Elle's shoulder, her touch blanketed her whole body with drowsiness.

Elle closed her eyes. She felt Dr. Stevens watching her.

"Sleep well and come back to us soon."

The words and the soothing presence of the doctor brought her comfort and any other questions that she had were drowned out by the white noise of exhaustion. Sleep came in the form of a swirling darkness, but not the type of darkness that would not let her rise.

Elle slept and woke several times during the night. Each time, Dr. Stevens was there, standing next to the bed or sitting close by in a chair. Each time, she spoke to her softly, the way one speaks to a person who has just had a nightmare. Once, she held a cup with a straw so that she could sip water. She became a constant, like the smell of the sheets and the hum of the lights.

Once, when she woke there was another woman there. She had a cloud of gray hair. She did not wear a white coat, but stiff, dark clothes. A tie. A long brown face. She stood close to the bed and peered at her.

Dr. Stevens appeared once again like the dawn in the dark of night. She stood between her and the cloudy-haired woman. She spoke to the newcomer, her auburn curls moving as she spoke. The other woman's smoky voice echoed through the room.

She tried but could not make out any of their words. She had better luck when Dr. Stevens spoke, and she could better follow her portion of the conversation. Soon, the room darkened as her eyelids drooped and fell shut. Before she could think to combat the swirling black, she was asleep, and the blackness had merely invaded her dreams.

When she woke again, there was thunder. She could hear rain hitting the building. The overhead lights were on. Too bright. Her eyes flooded with tears at the sting. She shifted in the bed and heard herself groan as her body protested the movement. She thought of the gray room with the puzzle, and how the big windows looked during a storm.

The doctor was still there. Dr. Stevens. She was sitting in the chair next to the bed, studying the screen of a laptop. Dr. Stevens noticed that she was awake and smiled slightly. She was certainly beautiful—curls, creamy brown skin, and large dark eyes.

"Elle," she said. "You're awake."

Dr. Stevens stood and came close to the bed. She could feel the heat of the doctor's body. She flinched involuntarily as Dr. Stevens's hand landed lightly on her shoulder and the contact seemed to make the pain in her head inflame.

"Elle, can you tell me how you're feeling?"

The question echoed around her head for a moment, and then came a flood of memories. She was Elle Janine Pharell. Thirty-four years old. Five foot five. African American. Her driver's license number was 5329783. She liked Darjeeling tea in the mornings, and at night, cucumber martinis. She worked as a journalist for a popular internet news site, the Green Patriot. The affirmations paled in comparison to the other questions that weighed on her mind.

She glanced past the doctor to the room beyond, searching out the gray-haired woman.

"It's just the two of us, Elle," Dr. Stevens said. "I know things are hazy right now. Don't feel obliged to speak until you are ready."

Elle nodded, but Dr. Stevens's otherness distracted her to the point that she couldn't keep up with her words. Elle wanted to speak in return, ask the doctor questions, but once again, she did not know what to ask, or if she could string words together. The task seemed complex. She remembered the puzzle and the room with windows. The only memory she had of any of it was when she came of out that mist in her mind as if she had been trapped in there for some time.

"Where…?" Elle asked. She paused, furiously searching for the words. She knew them but they took a detour between her brain and her mouth.

"Go on," Dr. Stevens said. "You were doing fine."

Elle tried again. "Where am I?"

"The Gloaming Hill Recovery Center. In West Virginia."

"A hospital?"

"Yes, but much more. Privacy is valued. Our patients are high profile and so you can say we are off the beaten path."

Elle focused on her words, determined to comprehend.

"This place is hidden."

"Yes, you could say that," she said. "Are you in any pain right now, Elle?"

She nodded.

"Do you think you can describe it all to me?" Dr. Stevens asked.

Elle wanted to tell her about the pain in her eyes and in her head, how it made it hard to think, to corral and sort the words she wanted to say.

"I feel…confused," she said. Her voice fell soft like a dusting of snow.

"That's to be expected," she said. "How do you feel physically?"

"Tired," Elle answered.

"Yes?" Dr. Stevens prompted her.

"My head hurts. And my eyes."

Dr. Stevens apologized as she stood and turned off the lights and lit the lamp to a dim setting. She returned to her seat.

"How is that?"

"Better," Elle said.

She smiled in reply. "I know you have many questions. What's most important right now is for us to hear how you're feeling."

Us? Of course, she was not the only one there. Elle remembered the women dressed in scrubs, the gray-haired woman, and Leslie, another patient.

"I feel tired." She'd already said that. "I feel like I've been hit by a truck. Sore all over."

Dr. Stevens smiled that good-natured smile of hers. "Can you tell me where the soreness is located?"

"Legs. Back. My arms are hard to lift, and my head. There is a pain in my hand."

"Yes." Dr. Stevens scribbled something on a notepad she produced from her pocket.

"I don't remember how I got here," Elle said. "Something bad happened."

Dr. Stevens touched her hand. "You're safe now, that is what matters. I'm here to help you get through."

"What happened to me?"

"We have a process we must follow when a patient is in this particular phase of recovery."

"Does that mean you're not going to tell me?"

"I will in good time. Right now, and I know that this is difficult, but it is important to focus on your recovery."

There was that word again, she was in Gloaming Hill, a recovery center. She was in recovery. She had no memories, and she could barely string words together. Someone or something had hurt her badly, and any memories of the event were lost to her. She felt anger well inside her bringing a surge of energy to her body and mind. Whatever crime had been perpetrated against her, she was still strong.

The anger made her heady and then she felt herself spiral as if she might faint. Her eyelids felt heavy, and she saw Dr. Stevens's concerned face as she rushed closer. She placed her hands to either side of Elle's face now wet with tears and tilted her chin up. She urged her to breathe deeply and modeled the movements with her cheeks and lips.

Elle held on and did as she instructed. Together, they inhaled and exhaled several times. Her heart slowed its frantic beating in her chest, and the pain in her head subsided.

Dr. Stevens smiled. "There. You're fine. You're safe."

She removed her hands from Elle's face and wiped her cheeks and chin with something slightly damp that smelled sterile. The gesture caused her to cry again.

"Don't worry. Everything is fine."

She put an arm around Elle and watched over her as she trembled and wept. When Elle pulled away exhausted, Dr. Stevens pulled the covers around her and turned off the lamp. As Elle drifted back into the black, she felt her presence on her eyelids, warmer than the light of a lamp.

CHAPTER SIX

Gloaming Hill Facility, West Virginia

Elle woke to the smell of food. Her stomach rumbled. She wondered how much time had passed. Dr. Stevens appeared, smiling as Elle stirred.

"Wonderful. You're awake."

"Is it morning?" Elle asked as she glanced around for what smelled so appealing.

Dr. Stevens glanced at her watch. "It's a little closer to noon."

She sat on the edge of the bed.

"How do you feel?"

"Hungry," Elle said.

"That's to be expected," she said, smiling. "You had a rough night."

"I was dreaming, but I don't remember what my dreams were about," Elle said, preoccupied with food at the moment.

"Do you feel any pain? Anywhere?"

"Only in my stomach," Elle said.

Dr. Stevens chuckled. "I hope today's lunch is worth the anticipation."

She left the bed and retrieved a narrow tray balanced on tall spindly legs tipped with miniature wheels. On the tray was a mauve plastic dome on a brown plate, a gray plastic pitcher, and several cardboard juice cartons. To Elle's delight, there was a clear container with a green salad. It had red tomatoes, orange carrot sticks, and translucent slivers of purple onion. She relished the colors of the veggies. She reached for it first and popped open the lid. Whoever had prepared the salad had already added a light layer of a plain oil-and-vinegar dressing. There were half slices of cucumber as well. To Elle, it was the freshest food she had ever tasted. She was halfway through it when she looked up to see Dr. Stevens watching her.

"It feels like I haven't eaten in forever," Elle said apologetically.

"You're okay. It's just so good to see you up and about."

"How have I been eating?" Elle asked. "Is it like the puzzle?"

"The puzzle?"

"I was putting together a puzzle. I had the last piece in my hand, but I don't remember going to the room with the windows. I don't remember choosing that puzzle, let alone putting it together."

Dr. Stevens studied her a moment and sighed. "One of the nurses chose it for you. As for eating, you have been able to feed yourself, just as you are now."

"So why don't I remember putting that puzzle together? Or this place? Why does it feel like I'm waking up from this long sleep?"

"You haven't been asleep, Elle, but you have not been fully awake either. Honestly, we don't have a name for it. What else do you remember from yesterday?"

"The puzzle, the room with the windows, the nurses, and Leslie. She said she remembered me, but I don't remember her."

Dr. Stevens sighed. "Leslie. You could say her recovery is at an impasse. She will need more time."

"Did the same thing that happened to her happen to me?"

Dr. Stevens paused, seeming to weigh the question. "The circumstances were the same, but your recovery so far has been quite remarkable."

She removed the now empty salad container and lifted the dome that covered the plate. There was actual pasta, and chicken all covered in a white sauce with garlic bread on the side.

"Finish your lunch," Dr. Stevens said as she offered a plastic fork.

Elle stared at her for a moment before accepting. She took a bite from the dish and found it just as pleasing as the salad.

"Elle, my team is hard at work trying to figure out the physiological aspects of our patient's symptoms. It has been a long journey and we don't have many answers. Honestly, we've been waiting for a success story like yours."

Elle finished a bite of pasta. "What do you know?"

"We know that we are ready to do what needs to be done to get you better."

"I do this for a living you know," Elle said. "Asking questions."

Dr. Stevens nodded thoughtfully. "I've heard that you're tough."

Elle decided to take another approach. "So, I wasn't asleep, but I wasn't awake. I was feeding myself and putting together puzzles. I don't remember any of this because I wasn't conscious?"

"We call it beta consciousness. We find that our patients, with a little direction, can be led to complete simple tasks such as eating, bathing, and even higher-level thinking tasks such as putting a puzzle together."

Elle abandoned a bite of pasta on her fork. She thought of self-driving cars. "How could you do any of those things without being aware that you are doing them? Who's at the wheel?"

"You are, of course," she said. "Just not on a conscious level."

She glanced down at her meal, suddenly no longer hungry. It all sounded impossible. To think of herself truly mindlessly doing these so-called unthinking tasks with no emotions attached. The self, lost.

"What happened?" Elle asked. "What happened to make me like this?"

"We will discuss all of that soon. I don't want to overwhelm you right now."

"Why don't I remember?" Elle asked. "Did whatever happen affect my memory?"

Dr. Stevens slid the tray away without even asking if she was finished. Finally, a flaw in that bedside manner. "Elle, it's best that you don't get too excited or agitated at this point in your recovery. You've come so far in such a short period."

"So, knowing what got me here could threaten my recovery?"

"Yes," Dr. Stevens said. "It's a difficult thing to digest and you may not be ready for the memories those emotions could trigger." She paused, her voice wavering. "It can be extremely overwhelming. The more we can learn about this, the more we can help you."

Elle felt completely and fully recovered. "How long was I like that?"

"Six months," Dr. Stevens said simply.

"Six months," Elle repeated indignantly. "That's insane."

She gingerly shifted herself to the edge of the bed. Dr. Stevens made way for her slightly but stayed close restricting her movement.

"Six months, I've been in here. A zombie. And you won't tell me what happened to me."

"Elle, where are you going?"

"I'm leaving this place," she said. "So just get out of my way."

"Elle, this was just what I feared. You cannot allow yourself to get upset."

"You know what that sounds like? It sounds like a mind fuck. What about my life for six months? I just can't disappear off the scene. What about the Green Patriot? I want to talk to my mother, and I want to talk to Anne Humphries."

"That is not possible," Dr. Stevens said. "From what I understand, your mother has sought clearance to be able to speak with you."

"My mother needs clearance to speak with me?" Elle asked. "Do you hear the words that are coming out of your own mouth?"

She shoved herself over, gripping the railing. Her arms trembled from lifting her own body weight, and soon the rest of her followed. She doubted that she could even walk.

Dr. Stevens stayed close to keep her from getting off the bed. She looked concerned and opened her mouth to speak, but Elle interrupted her.

"How has Anne carried on with the Green Patriot? Can you tell me that?"

"I'm not sure," Dr. Stevens said. "I believe the official story is that you have an illness."

"Who's been taking my place?"

"I don't know," Dr. Stevens said, now breathless as if she were flustered. "My main concern is your recovery."

Elle glared at her. The Green Patriot started off as her dream, but Anne, her mentor, saw the potential for something more. They were approaching their tenth year online and they had started kicking around ideas for marking the occasion back in the fall. Elle tried to pinpoint more of that time but could not.

"I want to see my site. I want to see what is going on with the Green Patriot," she said, though she doubted the doctor would comply.

"Elle, perhaps you should rest."

"It would seem I've had plenty of time for rest here at Gloaming Hill. Putting together puzzles in a catatonic state. Sounds like the perfect vacay."

She tried again to get off the bed. "I have to pee, okay."

"Okay," Dr. Stevens said, moving away from the bed. "Allow me to help you."

"Fine," Elle said, throwing back the blanket that covered her lower half.

Dr. Stevens showed her how to lower the bed and then how she should swing her legs over. Elle allowed the doctor to help her stand on her shaky legs. They took a few steps together, shoulder to shoulder, then Elle walked on her own to the bathroom door. She turned and walked back to the bed, just to test her strength. Dr. Stevens hovered close as Elle turned and returned to the bathroom door. She noticed that the doctor was smiling.

"Very good," she said. "How do you feel?"

"Stronger," Elle replied. "Like I could walk right out of here."

"In due time," Dr. Stevens said.

"One moment please," Elle said before closing the door.

"Elle, please be careful in there," Dr. Stevens said.

"I've been potty-trained for some time now."

"That's not what I meant, Elle," Dr. Stevens said. "I must tell you we are not in any way physically prepared for how much you've progressed in such a short time."

Elle found herself face-to-face with her reflection in a small mirror. If she were to walk out of Gloaming Hill and return to Austin no one would have recognized her. Her skin was dull. Her hair was disheveled, sticking to her head in some places and tangled in others. She supposed that while in beta consciousness grooming had not been a top priority.

"While I was putting together puzzles you guys couldn't stick a brush in my hand?"

"What was that?" Dr. Stevens asked distractedly.

"Never mind," Elle said, noticing that next to the sink were her favorite skin and hair care products. At least the staff had done their research.

"Is everything all right in there?" Dr. Stevens asked. "Elle?"

"Fine," she said. "You could've warned me that I look like shit."

"You don't look like shit," Dr. Stevens said. "You're up and about and you're coherent."

"I suppose that counts for something," she replied under her breath.

"Elle?" Dr. Stevens asked.

"Okay, I'm going to use the toilet," she said, glancing around the bathroom. A narrow mat lay on the floor next to the shallow tub. There were a set of towels on a rack as well. The toilet was what one would expect in a place such as a hospital with a mounted bar next to it on the wall. She made use of it, flushed, and went to the sink to wash her hands. She paused to do something with her hair and cleanse and moisturize her face.

Dr. Stevens smiled when she came out.

"Well, don't you look refreshed."

"I feel refreshed," Elle said but yawned despite herself. "I'd like a shower though."

"Take a moment to rest," Dr. Stevens told her, moving back the covers on the bed.

Elle did not want to get back into the bed, but felt certain she would fall over if she did not.

"Let me know if there is anything I can do for you," Dr. Stevens said.

"Oh, there is plenty," she said as she arranged the linens around herself. "You can tell me where we go from here."

Dr. Stevens moved close to the bed. "We'll continue assessing you today and tomorrow, but soon we will start a regimen of physical therapy and tests. When you are ready you will start sessions with Dr. Branch."

"Who is Dr. Branch?"

"She is the head of Gloaming Hill, she's a neuropsychologist—"

"Wait, did she come here last night?" Elle asked.

"She did," Dr. Stevens said. "I didn't think you were awake."

"I remember. Barely," Elle said and yawned. "Like a dream."

"I should leave you to rest," Dr. Stevens said.

"I just woke up," Elle said.

"You shouldn't put too much strain on yourself," Dr. Stevens said as she began to gather her things from the chair where she had kept vigil most of the night. Elle did not think that she might be exhausted as well.

"Okay," she agreed, settling on the pillows. She did feel drained.

"Your nurses will come through to check on you soon," Dr. Stevens told her. "Rest."

When she was gone, Elle tried to relax against the pillows. She looked around the room at the gray walls, from the door to the banks of monitors with her vitals reported from the soft plastic band that glowed around her wrist. Besides the chair where Dr. Stevens had sat and the table where her food had been served, there was a counter and cabinet with a sink. No mundane art on the walls. No plants or books.

Though she felt tired, Elle found herself restless, her legs felt twitchy, and she could not keep her mind from racing through unanswered questions. She attempted to close her eyes, but the darkness behind her lids only made her dizzy to the point of nausea.

She sighed and tossed and turned.

Then she remembered the bathtub only feet away and the fact that a warm shower always put her right to sleep when she felt restless after a long day. She sat up in bed and stared at the door, just half cracked.

Surely, she was strong enough to give herself a shower. She would be careful. She would show Dr. Stevens just how well she was.

She lowered the bed and stood solidly. A good sign.

Elle made her way to the bathroom. She looked at her reflection as she entered creeping like a ghost.

She pulled back the curtain to see white tile and a showerhead and one knob. It all gleamed as if the thing had hardly been used or kept immaculately clean. It certainly looked more up to date than what Elle had seen of the facility.

She slowly stripped herself of the thermal gray pajama pants she wore and the matching top. She removed the underwear and gingerly stepped into the tub. The porcelain felt freezing cold beneath her feet. She turned the knob above the faucet. The metal gave a preemptive squeak before the water began to drip then spew forth in an even spray. She stepped forward and let the water fall on her, cool at first then gradually warming. Not as hot as she liked it, but warm enough. She stood under the water and relished the play of the slight pressure of dozens of tiny sprays of water.

She reached for the nondescript bottle of liquid body wash. She had not thought about a loofah or a washcloth, so she used her hands to lather herself, taking stock of her body as she did. She had gone a bit flabby at the waist. So much for sticking to that gym regimen.

Again, came the questions. What had happened to land her at Gloaming Hill? Why all the secrecy of what happened? Why could she not remember? How would she pick up the pieces of her life after six months in limbo?

Finished with her bath, she reached through the spray and turned the knob. This time instead of the clean squeak of polished metal turning she heard the torturous screech of rusty metal followed by a bang that was frighteningly familiar. The noise seemed to echo only inside her head so loud that her knees weakened, and she sank to the floor of the shower. She squeezed her eyes closed and saw light flashing behind her eyelids. She heard more noises. Screaming. Gunfire. Explosions. She feared opening her eyes for fear that she would find herself no longer in the pristine bathroom but somewhere else. Somewhere she should fear to be. She cradled her head in her arms, flinching as if the visions in her head were blows striking her body.

Hands seized her and she screamed. She opened her eyes and there was Dr. Stevens her face distorted with concern. She began to take Elle through a breathing exercise. After a time, she helped Elle to stand.

She wrapped Elle in a towel and helped her out of the hole in the rock, no, she was taking her from the shower to the bed and drying her as she spoke to her in kind tones.

Elle was able to gather herself enough to dress in new clothes, loose sweatpants and a UT T-shirt that was one of her own. She was glad to see it. She took refuge under the covers trembling uncontrollably.

Dr. Stevens sat on the edge of the bed and waited dutifully. Elle felt angry and betrayed by this woman she had come to trust in such a short time.

"You have to tell me," Elle said. "What happened?"

"You should rest now. There will be plenty of time to speak of why you're here."

"You'll be here when I wake?" she asked.

"Yes," she said. "I'll be here."

CHAPTER SEVEN

Gloaming Hill Facility, West Virginia

Elle began the transition from a troubled sleep to the darkness behind her lids. For a second, they seemed too heavy to lift and open her eyes. She'd been trapped in some dream with a snarling blond woman who snatched out at her from the darkness, tripping her up and tearing her clothes. She opened her eyes, and the darkness gave way to the dim room. As her eyes adjusted, she felt another presence in the room, someone watching her. Elle called out for the doctor. The lights brightened and she found herself face-to-face not with Dr. Stevens, but two women in blue-gray scrubs. One happened to be standing there watching her, balancing the backs of her hands on her hips. She had brown, shoulder-length hair parted down the middle, fanning her face.

The other was busying herself over by a counter, and she turned and walked over. Her hair was red and curly, tied up in a messy bun. Her smile was slight, her eyebrows arched quizzically as if she did not mean to be smiling at all.

"Miss Pharell," she said blandly. "I see you're awake."

Elle only stared at her too afraid to speak.

"I'm Nurse Grace," she said and pointed to the dark-haired woman. "This is Nurse Slick."

"We're glad you're up and about," Nurse Slick said. Her smile seemed more genuine. "We've been looking after you since you arrived here at Gloaming Hill."

"Right. So don't give us any trouble," Nurse Grace said. "This is not a democracy. We know what's best for you. So. No arguments."

She took a few steps back from the bed and looked to Nurse Slick who chuckled.

"How can I follow that speech?" She cocked her thumb to Nurse Grace. "She's been abstaining from caffeine; it's been a hard week for all of us."

"I just don't want any trouble," Nurse Grace grumbled.

Elle smiled nervously. She was sure that the nurses meant her no harm. Still, they were strangers to her, and it made her ill at ease.

"Nothing to say?" Nurse Grace asked. "I heard from Dr. Stevens that you talked her ear off yesterday."

"Give her a chance," Nurse Slick said and peered down at her. "You'll have to forgive us, Elle, our patients are usually non-vocal. Are you feeling well enough?"

"Yes," she said. "I'm good. Where is Dr. Stevens?"

"She'll be along soon enough," Nurse Grace said in a lackluster tone.

Elle eyed them warily as they wheeled a cart next to the bed. Their movements seemed more calculated than the doctor's, but nonetheless just as interesting. One of them produced another covered plate on a tray with plastic cutlery. She remembered throwing up her dinner in the shower the night before.

"I'm not hungry," Elle announced.

"Is that so?" Nurse Grace asked.

"You haven't even seen what we've got here," Nurse Slick said cheerfully. She had obviously gone to Dr. Stevens's school of bedside manner. She transferred the tray to the rolling bedside table. She removed the dome lid with a flourish revealing a dish of scrambled eggs mixed with vegetables and ham.

"I think that looks wonderful," Nurse Slick said. "You don't have to eat it straight away. We could even warm it up for you."

The other nurse let out a long, loud sigh at some running joke or understanding between them, the subtle nuances that arose between people who had worked together for a while. Elle and Anne had many.

"I was sick last night," Elle explained as Nurse Grace sidled up close and began to wipe her inner arm just above the bend of her elbow with a piece of gauze. Elle could smell alcohol. She tried to pull away, but Nurse Grace caught hold of her.

"Now, now," she said and produced a needle.

Dr. Stevens entered the room. "Good morning."

Elle turned in response to the sound of her voice and felt the sting of the needle. She winced as Dr. Stevens approached the bed looking sympathetic.

"She isn't very subtle, is she?"

"What was that?"

"An extra boost to get you through your transition," Dr. Stevens said as she watched Nurse Grace bandage the injection site.

"She hasn't said much to us yet," Nurse Slick said.

Dr. Stevens came close to the bed. "Now, Elle, you're going to hurt Nurse Grace's and Nurse Slick's feelings if you don't talk to them. They've been working with you all this time and doing a marvelous job of it."

Elle managed to agree, she couldn't have cared less about the nurses. If last night's episode was a clue of what she would face in recovery, they were the least of her problems.

"They'll be your only nurses," Dr. Stevens said. "So be nice."

They took her blood pressure, listened to her heart, and checked her reflexes. Nurse Slick shined a light in her eyes and looked up at Dr. Stevens.

"Her pupils are dilated."

Dr. Stevens walked around and flashed the light into her eyes.

"I want you to squeeze my hand as tight as you can," Dr. Stevens said. She offered one to Elle who slowly reached out to touch it.

"Don't be afraid of hurting me," she said and after a reassuring smile, "I have a high tolerance for pain."

Elle did as the doctor asked. She squeezed one slender hand, then the other, and finally both at the same time. She watched Dr. Stevens retrieve a pad from her coat pocket and scratch out some notes.

"We're going to do some tests in the next few days. We'll move at your pace, so if you feel tired at any time or uncomfortable just let me know."

Elle gave a slow nod.

"Good, we'll get started shortly. You can go to the bathroom and get ready. One of the nurses will bring you some fresh clothes."

Elle felt her anxiety rise as the doctor helped her out of bed and guided her to the restroom she had so boldly entered the night before. It was as white and pristine as before. There were some toiletries by the sink, and she brushed her teeth and combed her hair. She noticed that it all took quite a bit of effort physically. Her arms felt heavy and her neck stiff.

Cautiously, she pulled back the shower curtain. She reached for the faucet and paused. What if she heard that awful noise again and suffered from the same episode? Just thinking of it brought on the fear slightly, a ghost of a throb like the beginning of a migraine.

Her fingers brushed the cold metal, and she grasped the faucet and turned it, waiting for the squeak or the shriek she was certain would come. The knob made a clockwise turn in silence. The water came splashing down into the tub. Elle gasped. She watched it fall for a moment before peeling out of her clothes and easing under the spray. She washed herself quickly and without hesitation, then she turned off the water. Nothing. She stepped back out into the bathroom carefully. She stood on the mat and dried herself.

She redressed herself and left the bathroom. Back in bed, Elle tried to tune in the conversation between Dr. Stevens and Nurse Slick. They spoke in a hushed tone with their backs to her.

"I'm going to ask questions about your past," Dr. Stevens said when she returned to the bedside. "I want to know how much you remember."

"Sure," Elle said, looking forward to mentally retracing her steps for clues as to how she had come to Gloaming Hill.

Dr. Stevens started by asking her birth date, which she answered as if she were on a quiz show. The doctor smiled at her enthusiasm and asked the next question.

"What college did you graduate from?"

"University of Texas," she said. "Hook 'em, horns."

Dr. Stevens smiled. "What city did you grow up in?"

"Atlanta."

"In the same house?"

"No, we lived in Little Five Points until I was nine. Then we moved to Kirkwood. My parents still live there."

She could clearly see those places in her mind, sunlight through the leaves, sidewalks, and buildings, the people she knew who had populated them with her. In her mind, she charted and graphed them like a surveyor. They all seemed too big for her as she lay in her hospital bed answering the doctor's questions.

"Do you have any siblings?" Dr. Stevens asked.

"No. There's just me. When will I be able to see them? My family"

"Soon," Dr. Stevens said gently. "I believe Congresswoman Pharell is in the process of arranging something with the higher-ups. We email back and forth every day. Not that I am able to communicate so closely with the—"

Elle hardly heard the rest of Dr. Stevens's words after she mentioned her mother. She felt ill suddenly, dizzy and nauseous, like she had the night before in the shower. There was also the flash of light behind her eyes when she blinked as if someone were taking photos inside her brain. She saw her father at the top of cement steps smiling. Her mother with him. Behind them, the Georgia state capitol building. Her mother's swearing in. Elle had just graduated high school and felt all the hopefulness of the time. A fine memory. Yet, there was something off, a gray overcast, the squeal of tires. Gunshots. Her father grabbed hold of her and guided her through the pounding of feet, the blur of terrified faces, her mother's among them, and the sound of screaming.

"Elle?" Dr. Stevens asked. "Are you okay?"

"My mother," Elle said. "She was with me when, when what happened to me—"

"No, she wasn't," she said. That pen came out again and she shined it into Elle's eyes. "Why do you ask?"

Elle flinched at the sting of the beam. "I just remembered my mother's first swearing in at the Georgia state capitol building."

"Tell me," Dr. Stevens said.

"We were together on the steps. My mom, dad, and me. And then there was gunfire and people were afraid."

Dr. Stevens paused for a moment. "There was something in your files. That was some years ago. The culprits were members of a local militia..." She paused again as Elle stared, puzzled. "You don't remember any of this?"

She shook her head. "Not like that. There was no shooting. I remember it as being a lovely day. We ate Italian afterward."

Dr. Stevens retrieved a notepad from her lab coat pocket and quickly scribbled some notes. "We find that some of our patients experience extreme memory disruption, the alteration or combinations of one or more memories."

Elle wished she would cut the shit and talk to her like a human being without the vernacular-filled abridged version and deflection.

"I'm going to need to speak to someone I can trust immediately. I can't trust my own brain or body, and I can't trust you."

Dr. Stevens's sunny disposition darkened before her eyes like a suddenly overcast day. Her expression as grave as a storm. "Elle, I understand that this is a very difficult time for you, but the actions that we take right now are imperative to your recovery."

"Yeah, really?" Elle asked sarcastically. "Please share."

"I would first like to take some scans of your brain."

"What are you looking for?" Elle asked. "Or is that a secret as well?"

"It's not secret, I assure you. An MRI would be helpful to our study to observe certain centers of your brain and how they are processing at the moment."

"Your study?"

"There is still much that we don't know about your ailments. Honestly, it's been trial and error. We weren't prepared for you to be so advanced in your recovery."

Elle thought back to the glass-paneled rooms and the other patients. The only one of them who had been active was Leslie and she seemed majorly unhinged. Was that what happened to patients on their way to recovery at Gloaming Hill?

"I'm not cooperating with anything, not until I speak to my mother," Elle said. "You certainly can arrange that."

"That would take time that we don't have at the moment. I don't like to push patients into doing something they are not ready for, but right now we need to do this."

Elle stared at her for a moment. The earnest urgency in the doctor's voice gave her pause. Still, she did not want this woman to think she could be so easily railroaded. She felt her resolve weakening. She wanted answers and she wanted to fight for them, but she also wanted to trust Dr. Stevens.

"Okay. Fine. We'll do the brain scan. You have my full cooperation for now."

She smiled. "Good. I'm glad you're on board."

"For now," Elle reminded her. "What harm could a simple medical procedure do?"

"There is one caveat," Dr. Stevens said. "There is the chance that being inside the MRI could trigger a strong response memory."

"What's a strong response memory?"

"Like what happened last night in the shower. A memory invading reality. You might hallucinate the same sounds or experience changes in light, feel the same emotions, feel those fears or sadness."

"Is that what's wrong with me?" Elle asked. "My memories are all screwed up?"

A sad look crossed Dr. Stevens's face. "There is nothing wrong with you."

"There's definitely something wrong," Elle said. "What caused this?"

She sighed. "I want to explain everything to you."

"And I'm just supposed to just trust you people? Take your drugs and stay cut off from the outside world?"

"Wait," Dr. Stevens said. "Before we lose any more time, let's do the brain scan, and I will answer your questions."

"All of them?" Elle asked.

"As many as I am able," Dr. Stevens said.

Elle thought for a moment. She would agree to the terms, but only because she believed that the scan was needed. She could be rational.

"Okay, we'll do the scan."

"I'll get the nurses to prepare the imaging suite," Dr. Stevens said.

She disappeared for a moment and returned. "It looks like we're all set."

Elle stared at her for a moment. For all the fight she wanted to give, there was an anxiety that kept her from launching a full-scale tantrum. And as much as she wanted to tell the lovely doctor to piss off, she wanted the comfort she offered.

"I'm a little scared. No. A lot scared. After last night…"

"I understand. Just remember that you're safe here. I'd never let any harm come to you."

"I guess I kind of know that," Elle said. "But what am I giving up by accepting your safety?"

"You're ensuring yourself peace of mind knowing that Gloaming Hill is the best place for you to heal," Dr. Stevens said.

She sounded like she was quoting a pamphlet, but Elle doubted the place had an informative fold-out in glossy stock for patients and their loved ones.

"Are you ready?" Dr. Stevens. "The nurses are waiting."

Elle made her way out of bed and allowed herself to be ushered out into the hallway. It was her first time out of the room since she "woke" or became aware of herself in the glass room. The walls were a yellowing white with black trim, that same gray-and-black checkerboard floor. There were a few prints of paintings. Mostly vases of flowers. She did not recognize the styles as any artists she knew. They came to a dead corner and turned. They passed a doorway, the first since they left her room.

Elle felt tired suddenly and slowed.

Dr. Stevens turned to her with a concerned look. "We need to build up your strength with more walking. I'm afraid you haven't been doing much."

A shaft of light fell into the hallway from an open doorway. Leslie appeared and a crooked grin slowly claimed her face.

"Look who's up and about," she said.

"Leslie, please return to…wherever you're supposed to be right now."

"Physical therapy," she said. "But something urged me to go on one of my little jaunts and I am so glad I did, so I can see Gloaming Hill's latest champion. The famous reporter. The senator's daughter."

"Congresswoman's daughter," Elle corrected her.

"No. You two are not speaking," Dr. Stevens said as she looked from one of them to the other, her expression one a mother would give two feuding children.

Elle looked away from Leslie and felt those large gray eyes seeking her out. There were footsteps as several nurses approached. Leslie turned to them and offered her outstretched arms, hands dangling limply at the wrist as if she were about to be handcuffed. As they escorted her away, she looked back at Elle to say, "See you on the other side."

Dr. Stevens watched her go and looked at Elle. "Come. It's not much farther."

"She knows who I am," she said. "Have we met before?"

"She gets around, she listens to the other nurses," Dr. Stevens said, and her brow furrowed. "I must admit that it is a struggle to keep her contained."

They approached a darkened doorway, and as they neared Elle could see the glow of the equipment inside. They entered what looked to be a tiny control room dominated by four flat-panel screens. Nurse Grace sat in front of one of the monitors in a wheeled chair. She turned when they entered the room.

"Leslie is on the loose again."

"Yes, you could say we ran into her in the hallway," Dr. Stevens said. Her voice betrayed her annoyance with the situation. "That is something to discuss later. Right now, we have to focus on Elle."

She glanced her way and smiled. She flicked a switch and a dark panel next to Elle lit up revealing an observation window. On the other side, a dimly lit room waited dominated by an imposing machine. Part of it reached the ceiling where a knot of thick, black electrical cords dangled down into a boxy unit mounted with several screens. The scanner itself squatted on the floor, its tubular maw open and ready to receive its meal via a narrow cot sticking out like a searching tongue.

Dr. Stevens noticed her studying the monstrous-looking machine.

"Our scanner, it's the latest technology, but whoever designed it did not have the patient's comfort in mind."

She went on to explain more of the machine's components and functions, but Elle wasn't listening. There was something eerily familiar about it, and she thought of the mist and the castle. Of course, the castle was not a real place, it was a picture in a puzzle. The machine was real. Gloaming Hill was real. Still, she felt very much like she had in the mist. Disconnected. Barely there, as if her body and mind would dissolve into particles and float away.

She fought back a shiver and felt her anxiety heighten. She remembered Dr. Stevens's breathing exercises and began to do them furtively. It was in her best interest to be as cooperative as possible for now. She did not want to give the good doctor any reason to go back on her promise of giving her more information once this ordeal was over.

"Elle?" Dr. Stevens asked, gently touching her shoulder. "Are you having a hard time?"

"Was I here before?"

"Yes, we've put you in before. Several times. Tell me, do you have a specific memory of being here?"

"No, just looking at that machine, I felt something like déjà vu."

"What else did you feel?"

"I felt unnerved. Anxious."

Dr. Stevens looked over her shoulder to Nurse Grace. The two made eye contact and the nurse approached with a tray. She brought it to the counter near them.

"All prepped on my end," she said as she set it down.

"Good, then." Dr. Stevens looked to Elle. "I was hoping we could do this without drugs."

"What is that?" Elle asked.

"Something to relax you. After the scan you'll want a nap, but you'll be back up and about by lunch time," she said as she took and held Elle's arm a few inches above the wrist. She applied a bit of pressure. With her other hand, she retrieved an alcohol swab. She held it out to Elle, who went to take it, but Dr. Stevens held it fast so that the package tore open.

"Teamwork," she said and smiled. Elle, left with the empty wrapping, smiled too.

Dr. Stevens looked down at Elle's wrist. With her free hand she retrieved one of the syringes from the tray and removed the cap. Before Elle could protest, she expertly slid a needle into the IV port on her wrist.

Elle felt a tiny sting. She whimpered and felt her anxiety wane before it could swell. She looked to Dr. Stevens who gave that winning reassuring smile.

"We'll take a few minutes and then we'll go into the next room."

Elle nodded, though she did not feel ready.

"Just remember to breathe," she said. "I will be close by."

"Okay," Elle said. "I suppose I'm as ready as I'll ever be."

"You'll be fine," Dr. Stevens said. She helped Elle through the door that led to the machine. She showed her the table where she would lay and how it would slide inside the tunnel. Metal clanked and Elle nearly flinched at the sound. Dr. Stevens had her sit on the table.

"It should take about twenty minutes for us to get the scans we need," Dr. Stevens explained. "In the meantime, it's important that you keep as still as possible."

She showed Elle restraints, a brace for her shoulders and neck to keep her still. There were straps that she secured across Elle's legs. Dr. Stevens did not call them restraints. The word had invaded Elle's thoughts. She redoubled her attention on the doctor.

"—won't be able to stay once the machine is activated. I will be able to communicate through the intercom, but it is important that you don't speak unless you are experiencing extreme discomfort."

Dr. Stevens stopped speaking and regarded Elle for a moment as if she too could read her growing fear. "You'll be safe here. I promise."

Elle nodded as Nurse Grace entered from the control room.

"We're going to apply the brace now," Dr. Stevens said. She and Nurse Grace began to fit the straps over her shoulders and across her body. The brace consisted of a stiff plastic frame and Velcro straps. Elle winced at the tearing sound the straps made as the nurse adjusted them to restrict movement of her head and arms.

Elle scolded herself for the irrational thought. She needed healing. She would go inside the tunnel, and she would come out better. She told herself that Dr. Stevens did not restrain her to keep her subdued, but to ensure the best result. When the two were finished, her arms were bound to her body with the straps. Her hands close to her hips, her elbows tucked to her sides.

Dr. Stevens and Nurse Grace had worked silently, their attention on securing Elle rather than her well-being. The doctor's face turned on hers like the sun.

"How are you feeling, Elle?"

"I'm trying very hard to be okay," she responded.

Dr. Stevens straightened and spoke to Nurse Grace.

Less than a minute later, Dr. Stevens leaned over her and she felt the sting of an injection. She hadn't even bothered to discuss it with her at all.

"It's okay, Elle," she said. "Just breathe. We're going to go now."

She wanted to protest, but the world drifted away from her for a moment. And when she was able to gather her senses, she found herself in the dark. Something was over her eyes keeping her lids from opening. She nearly panicked but remembered that Dr. Stevens had placed a mask over her eyes.

Soft music played from above as Dr. Stevens promised. Flutes echoed over a steady drumbeat. Elle sighed. She did not recognize the tune, but she knew she had listened to this type of music somewhere before.

"Elle. Can you hear me?"

Dr. Stevens piped over the music. The intercom.

"I know this music," she said.

"Elle?"

"I went to Indonesia once. I ate fish for dinner and smoked shisha from a hookah pipe. This sounds like the music the locals played."

"We're going to activate the MRI now," Dr. Stevens said. Her voice sounded far away and tainted with static.

She waited and listened. She could hear a hum like a train from a distance. The noise deepened until she could feel its vibration in her shoulders. The stretcher began to glide slowly, sliding her forward feet-first. She grinned and thought that it must be what groceries on a conveyer belt felt like.

A dull clang above her head caused Elle to tense.

Dr. Stevens's voice once again interrupted the music.

"We're starting the scan now, Elle. Try to be as still as you can."

Somewhere inside the machine's shell, a whirring noise started along with a dull knocking. She forced her focus to the music. She tried to remember Indonesia and the players in the plaza, to recall the day around her. She was not able to remember much. Who had she gone with? She deduced that the trip had to be work-related as she had not taken personal time from her duties as head reporter for the Green Patriot since its establishment. Had Anne been with her? She could not remember.

A panel above her face began slowly descending. She vaguely remembered Dr. Stevens warning her that part of the machine would lower over her face once she was inside the tube. She focused on the music, determined to remain calm for the scan. She did not recall many details of her trip to Indonesia, but she knew she'd been happy that day. She tried to shirk the anxiety of not remembering, of being there in the tube, of being in the mist.

Slowly, the music began to fade. After a moment, static rose to a gritty buzz that pushed the music away. Elle fought the urge to raise her head or move her mouth to speak. She wanted the test to be over so Dr. Stevens could pull her out of the damned machine. A muffled metallic sound above her head seemed to punctuate her thoughts.

She tried to remind herself that she did not have to be afraid. She was safe in a medical facility with a kind doctor and decent nurses. Even if her mind was convinced that she was not in danger, her hammering heart would not allow her body to calm. Another metallic bong noise and then she could hear a woman's voice crooning. Elle made herself still and focused on just that voice. She knew it to be Lena Horne. She was singing "Stormy Weather." When she was a teen, Elle's parents introduced her to the movie of the same name, and she'd promptly fallen in love with the singer. There had been a moment of obsession that worried her mother. She always seemed wary when Elle would pick up a strange interest like Wicca or dirt biking, as if she knew Elle was doomed to become a lesbian and she had to make her conform as closely as she could to DC standards.

Another stray clang resounded above her head. Not the same muffled, mechanical sound as before; the noise had a rusty quality and was accompanied by a metal shriek. She felt the warmth of light on her eyelids. She realized that despite the mask placed over her eyes, she could see light: two parallel lines of dim blue light. She shuddered at the sudden cold that prickled her skin into gooseflesh. She began to shiver violently. Somewhere, Lena sang about walking in the sun once more.

Elle whimpered.

She was no longer at the Gloaming Hill Recovery Center in West Virginia. Though she could still hear the song playing, she could also hear the rumble of an engine and the drone. She was almost convinced, but she could still hear the song playing behind the rumble of an engine and the drone of an AC unit on full blast. Her eyes were unrestricted now and she was able to open them. She saw the long curls of freezing air falling from above. She saw bodies, some hanging from the ceiling, roughly swaying, their arms and legs dangling uselessly. They were dead and she was among them. She felt so cold and tried to move, but the room around them shook making the bodies dance to a cacophony of metal, the jangle of chains, the jolting of an axle on uneven terrain. She was in a narrow, frigid room.

She could not remember how she came to be there, but she was wearing the skirt of one of her favorite suits, along with the white short-sleeved blouse she paired with the ensemble. She still wore her heels. The cold had numbed her so that she could not feel them on her feet. A puff of white air, and a gray form moving in a lurching crawl through the cold mist, at first shapeless like a ghost, then clearer as it moved closer. She could hear breath exhale in labored puffs, and the saddest moan she would ever hear. It became clear to Elle the gravity of what complete misery she faced. The scrambling form was a young woman, her face a frosty white with rough red patches on her cheeks. She lifted her trembling head, her eyes half covered by stiff black tresses.

"Carrie?" she asked. "Carrie?"

Leslie. She was delirious from the cold. She was a stranger to Elle and at the same time the trouble-making patient at Gloaming Hill. Leslie crawled forward stiffly, groaning, certain that she had found Carrie.

The room lurched again, and Elle distinctly heard a car's horn, followed by another. She gasped as she realized that she and others had been tossed into a refrigerated truck and were being transported.

The woman she knew as Leslie reached out her hand. "Carrie. What happened?"

"I don't know," Elle said.

The truck lurched again, and she bounced against the frozen metal floor, her hand disconnecting from Leslie's. She heard a metal clang, the sound of the MRI machine, the static of the intercom, and Lena's sultry voice seeming to share her longing.

Elle began to call out for Dr. Stevens. The only reply was her cries fading into the freezing dimness.

"Carrie." Leslie's hand flopped against the floor like a wounded snake. The jolting of the truck had unclenched their hands. She was searching blindly for Elle's hand as she could no longer pick up her head. Elle stretched out her hand. There was not a degree of warmth between their fingers as they interlocked. She knew why Leslie had felt compelled to lead her out of the mist. This was no nightmare or vision; this was a memory. The two of them had survived a journey in a freezing truck.

Elle wanted out. Out of the memory/vision, out of the MRI, out of Gloaming Hill. She called out for Dr. Stevens. The light blinded her, but the music returned. She could hear her own panicked breathing. She felt Dr. Stevens's hands on her face.

Elle began to cry.

"You're okay now," Dr. Stevens said. "You're safe."

"I was gone," she sobbed. "There's something in the machine. It took me away. I was in a refrigerated truck with other bodies. I could not tell who was still alive and who was dead. Some of them were on hooks. Meat hooks."

"We'll just have to abandon the MRI today," Dr. Stevens announced to the nurses and leaned close to Elle. "You're okay now."

The two nurses appeared. They looked on, their expressionless looks of professional detachment betrayed by a glance between them. Elle noticed that Nurse Grace had a wheelchair, and she felt broken.

"I want to go home."

If Dr. Stevens or the nurses heard her, they gave no reply. They guided her from the MRI table to a wheelchair.

"I want to go home," Elle repeated as they settled her in. "I want to see my mother. I want to see my father. I want to talk to Anne."

Dr. Stevens came around in front of her, kneeling so they could see each other eye to eye.

"Elle, you're safe now. It's important that you keep calm," she said.

Together, they went through the breathing exercise. When they were done, the nurses were gone. It was just that machine and Dr. Stevens.

"Let's go," she said and wheeled Elle out of there.

The hallways seemed dimmer, and they met no one on their journey back to Elle's room. Dr. Stevens helped her back into that loathsome bed.

Elle wanted to pull away and storm out of there. Fight them if she had to. Still, she allowed the good doctor to tuck the covers around her.

"I'm not tired," Elle said.

Dr. Stevens nodded in agreement. "I know."

"So, was that a dream or a memory?" Elle asked. "The refrigerator truck, and Leslie was there. Poor Leslie. Is that what happened to us?"

"Elle, this isn't something we can afford to rush."

"Is that why I'm afraid all of the time?" Elle asked. "Why I see such horrible things when I close my eyes?"

A crestfallen look claimed Dr. Stevens's face. "As far as we've been able to piece together, the truck was one leg of your ordeal. There is not much more I should say at the moment. You'll meet with Dr. Branch soon."

"Ordeal? What happened to us?"

She stooped a bit, so they were at eye level. "It's important for you to remember, what you experienced back there is just a lost memory coming through."

"I can't disagree with that," Elle said.

"You were also under sedation, so it would be hard to distinguish what was memory and what your mind may have supplemented as details."

"Was Leslie there?" Elle asked. "Is that how you know?"

Dr. Stevens paused for a moment. "Yes, she was with you."

"Which explains why she is so interested in me," Elle said. "She's not unhinged, she's looking for answers. Like me."

"You and Leslie are not the same. Your cases are similar. That is all."

"She kept calling me Carrie. Did she remember that?"

"Elle, we need to slow down here." The usually calm doctor was getting agitated, even her perfect tresses seemed to frizz, and Elle felt her inner journalist rear at the smell of blood.

"I felt bad that I wasn't Carrie. I held her hand. I wanted to do something to convince myself that I wasn't going to perish in that place."

"Elle," Dr. Stevens said. "There is a great chance that you weren't conscious at all during that whole ordeal and any dramatics are the mind's way of coping with the lack of body heat."

"That's an awfully callous thing to say, especially if you weren't fucking there."

Dr. Stevens shrank visibly. "I'm sorry, Elle, but you must understand, I've seen how this thing works, what happens when my patients get bogged down in fear. They fail to see the big picture."

"This thing? What is it? Amnesia? Hysteria?"

"It's none of those, Elle. You shouldn't attempt to diagnose yourself."

"You're right, I should consult my local medical professional," she said and tilted her head mockingly. "Dr. Stevens, you've overseen my care. Could you tell me what the hell is wrong with me?"

Dr. Stevens was not amused by her sarcasm. She glanced at her watch. "You should rest now, Elle. I will come back to visit you later."

She felt anger, a wave of heat running up her spine. "You're just going to leave?"

"I have other patients to attend. I will send Nurse Grace or Nurse Slick to check on you."

"Don't bother," Elle said simply. "I'm not talking to anyone but my mother. I'm not eating either. You'll have to force-feed me."

Her words were spoken to Dr. Stevens's back as she briskly walked out of the room in two strides, white coat flying behind her.

Elle sighed angrily at the empty room.

Nurse Grace and Nurse Slick entered not long after. They wanted blood. For a test. She complied and when they asked if she wanted anything else, she told them that she wanted to talk to Dr. Stevens. They left after reassuring her that they would send the good doctor her way.

Dinner time came and the nurses returned with her meal on a tray. She was sure she smelled more of those bread rolls.

"I'm not eating," she said. "Not until I talk to Dr. Stevens."

"We'll just leave this here," Nurse Grace said and the two left once more.

Elle got out of the bed and rolled the tray to the door, lest she be tempted by those rolls. She felt exhausted and climbed back into the bed. They couldn't allow her to starve to death under their care. The world should know that places like Gloaming Hill existed, mysterious facilities with patients held against their will, not allowed to communicate with the outside.

She dreamed that she was starving to death, her systems failing one by one. Dr. Stevens watched over her silently. In her dream form, Elle was certain she could read sadness in her eyes and know what the doctor would say. She would say that she'd warned Elle, that she had tried to reason with her.

The nurses shook her awake, and as her eyes focused, she saw that it was Grace roughing her up while Slick stood passively in the background.

"Quickly now," she said urgently. "You're wanted in the sunroom."

"But it's nighttime," Elle said, not sure why she would be so fearful.

"Well, that's where she wants to see you," Slick said.

"Dr. Stevens?"

"Dr. Branch," Grace said. "Now let's get you there."

"Dr. Stevens mentioned her before," Elle said. "She's in charge of this place."

"Yes, so let's not delay any longer."

"Can I go comb my hair and brush my teeth?"

"This isn't a social visit."

Elle made a beeline for the bathroom. "Five minutes."

She did her thing and listened to them grumble outside.

Elle left the bathroom and announced that she would be ready to go as soon as she found her shoes. Nurse Slick produced the soft-soled sneakers and even helped her lace them. They escorted her out of her room and into the dark hall that lit up as they passed through. A power saving method for the nighttime. The sunroom was at the end of the long glass-paneled hall where Elle had come out of the mist. She could see the rooms, now empty of patients as she passed. The whole place had the air of a maze, the center a common room sparsely scattered with furniture. The only light came from a metal floor lamp with a lightbulb that flickered to look like a gas flame. It was hardly competition for the night above and beyond magnified by the walls and ceilings of paneled glass. A chip of moon and a scattering of thin gray clouds. And there, seeming to loom above it all, stood Dr. Branch, a woman with broad, round shoulders and a long, bovine face. Her hair was styled in a short gray-white afro cut closer on the sides and more of a hedge on top. She could have been a high school principal or a car salesman or a reverend if not for those eyes. They outshined the lights and certainly that bit of moon covered in clouds.

"Hello, Elle."

Elle spoke back. "Hello."

"I'm Dr. Branch," she said. "Dr. Stevens has mentioned that I would be talking to you."

"Yes," Elle said. "She said you would be my therapist and that we would talk about what happened to me."

A faint trace of a smile formed on her lips and vanished. "Yes, but I am afraid that she may have simplified my role in your care. Did she also tell you that I oversee things here? The staff, the patients, what outsiders are granted access, and let's face it, a place like Gloaming Hill could not exist without help from beyond these walls and windows."

"Yes," Elle said and was not sure what else to say.

"Also. I respect your mother and I am grateful that she was granted the proper clearance to allow her access to you. Still, I feel it's a conflict of interest. I can't afford to have parents of patients with influence over this and that."

"Is my mother coming here?" Elle asked, suddenly out of breath.

"If she were anyone else that answer would be absolutely not." Dr. Branch eyed her, sternly determined to continue her speech. Elle noticed that the doctor's head trembled slightly. A stroke perhaps?

"On the other hand," Dr. Branch said, "Congresswoman Pharell could bring us resources we surely need."

"Am I going to get to see my mother or not?" Elle asked.

"When and how will be decided at my discretion," Dr. Branch said with finality. "As I have explained to your mother and Dr. Stevens as well, no one is going to run roughshod over my protocol. Is that clear?"

Elle refused to allow herself to be intimidated. "Your protocol is keeping me a prisoner here. You won't even tell me what happened to me, how I got here. I've had to piece things together since I woke up here with no memories."

"That is for the benefit of your treatment. We are doing very innovative work here at Gloaming Hill. Those who don't follow their treatment plan fall along the wayside. I believe you have met Leslie. She was stubborn at first. She threatened to sue. She tried not eating. As you see, her methods did not work. Perhaps if her mother had clout in DC, she could have hurdled the red tape and talked some sense into her daughter."

"Is that what you expect my mother to do? Set me straight? I'm not some stupid kid. I'm being detained here against my will, and I haven't done anything wrong."

"Would you remember?" she asked. "Do you remember anyone you may have met? Perhaps for a story."

"Are you saying I brought all this on myself?"

"I could, but it would all be assumptions at this point," she said. "You're the only one who can tell the story, Elle. If we feed you information, your brain could very well supplement with details. We need more than details here."

"Don't you know what happened?"

Dr. Branch sighed. "Our sessions will start in the next few days."

"And what will happen then?"

"I specialize in a type of hypnotherapy. I will regress your mind back to that day in the truck since that is a memory that has come to you naturally. We will try to work our way backward from that moment."

"You're going to hypnotize me?" Elle asked incredulously. A hypnotist had come to her high school during senior year as part of the entertainment for fall carnival. He had put several of her classmates under, convincing them they were chickens or circus clowns, or at a frightening height. Hilarity ensued. "I like to keep an open mind, Dr. Branch, but that's afternoon talk-show fodder."

Dr. Branch smiled for the first time since their meeting. It was unsettling to Elle. To say she did not like the woman was an understatement.

"The technique I have perfected is so accurate it is the foundation of this facility, the treatment method of all of the patients here is centered around my studies of the mind and memory."

"That is what scares me," Elle said.

"Do you want to know what I think?" Dr. Branch asked. There was a calm in her voice, but it seemed insincere compared to Dr. Stevens's sweetness. "I think that you are letting fear get the better of you. I've seen this before. I believe you've had several run-ins with Leslie Thames. Dr. Stevens and I had many hopes for what her recovery could reveal. Her symptoms of fear and paranoia were too much for us to continue our course of treatment."

"Maybe if the medical professionals around here weren't so secretive about our symptoms of fear and paranoia, things would go smoother for everyone. Why the secrecy?"

Dr. Branch stood. "Dr. Stevens has conspired with your mother behind my back, which is something I find disheartening, but I also am at the end of my rope. If we don't start making some headway, there may no longer be a Gloaming Hill."

"Or they could just replace you," Elle added.

She returned to the desk and peered down at Elle. "Yes, they could certainly do that."

"I'm giving Dr. Stevens a chance and allowing her to take the helm here. Since this is her idea. She will reveal some things to you that I hope you will be able to accept. The nurses will return you to your room."

"When will I be able to talk to my mother?" Elle asked once again.

"Dr. Stevens will let you know," she said. "Good-bye for now, Elle."

She left her there for a moment with the darkness until the nurses came to guide her back to her room. As they walked through the silent hallways, their movement triggering the overhead lights, Elle listened for any sign of life. The sleepy murmurs of patients or the laughter of staff members. Instead, there was silence.

A new food tray waited for her along with a folded sheet of paper. It was chicken and creamed spinach, more dinner rolls, and a note from Dr. Stevens.

Please eat. The note read in a blocky print. *We will talk soon.*

She felt tears sting her eyes as she replayed her conversation with Dr. Branch. She'd said that Dr. Stevens had gone behind her back. Elle felt awful about giving the kind doctor a hard time and doubting her. She obviously wanted what was best, even if it meant breaking Dr. Branch's precious protocols. It made her feel hopeful.

Elle's stomach growled and she decided to eat while she turned over the conversation with Dr. Branch in her head. It seemed as if she blamed Elle for what happened to her. She tried to remember the time before she left for Johannesburg. What stories was she working on? Was she dating anyone? Even if she were flirting with a relationship, she didn't remember anything of it. She finished eating and busied herself with a puzzle on a separate tray. She fell asleep.

Elle woke the next day and performed what had become a routine at Gloaming Hill. Nurse Grace and Nurse Slick were like clockwork. They took her to the sunroom after breakfast. She did not want to wander too far in. It had been so long since she stood out in the sun, in green grass. The thought made her ill with dread. There were more coral scrubs in the sunroom, men who oversaw the place while the nurses chatted near the entrance.

When she returned to her room, Dr. Stevens was there smiling that smile of hers.

"The warden came in and woke me up in the middle of the night to talk," Elle said and made quoting fingers.

"I know. When I heard I thought you might be a little hungry afterward."

"Thanks," Elle said. "I guess my hunger strike failed."

Dr. Stevens approached the bed. "No problem."

"How do you tolerate her smugness?"

Dr. Stevens laughed and tried to stifle it with a stern expression. "She's strict but fair, and I am always giving her pushback."

"Good, she told me that you convinced her to get my mother access to this place. Maybe she can influence some changes around here. Me. I'm going home."

"Elle, you have it all wrong. Dr. Branch's treatment is renowned. Groundbreaking. If anyone can help, it's her."

"There is no way I am letting that woman stir around in my head."

"That's unfair of you, Elle. Dr. Branch has worked hard to get where she is today. I believe you know how hard that is for women, especially the ones who look like you and I and Dr. Branch."

"Wow, you're playing the Sista card?"

"It's not a play and you know it," Dr. Stevens said, amused. "Yesterday, Dr. Branch told me that she was glad she brought me on, that she needs someone she can trust to challenge her. We don't always see eye to eye, but we both want the same outcome."

Elle could not help but agree with the sentiment. Still, it did not ease her worry of what was going down at Gloaming Hill or Dr. Branch.

"We're here to help you remember what happened." Dr. Stevens continued to try to assure her.

Elle made a doubtful face.

Dr. Stevens removed a pack of UNO cards from her coat pocket, grinning her challenge.

"You any good?" Elle asked.

Dr. Stevens handed over the pack of cards and went to pull up a chair over Elle's bedside tray. "You'll have to see."

Elle sat up in her bed. Awake suddenly. She exhaled, out of breath, and reached out and switched on the bedside lamp. The dark no longer frightened her as much. Still, it comforted her to have light when unknown nightmares plagued her sleep. She no longer woke unsure of her surroundings. She knew her room at Gloaming Hill, as white as static. White walls and a stagnant Thomas Kinkade-type of landscape painting opposite her bed. She was anxious for her own apartment, to go visit her parents, to at least hear from them. She heard a shuffling sound near the door and turned her head.

In the glow of the lamp, she noticed that she was not alone. Someone stood near the door. Before her eyes could adjust, she called out to Dr. Stevens, before her sleep-fogged brain cleared to reveal that the figure in her door was definitely male.

"Dr. Stevens?" she asked. When she got no answer. "Nurse Grace?"

The intruder did not say a word, only stepped closer, into the light.

Elle gasped to see the young soldier, Sergeant Robert Loera, dressed in his service dress blue uniform jacket with brass buttons, tie fixed in a perfect knot, striped trousers, his cap on his head even though there was a hole in his face from his nasal cavity to his right eye.

The memory of his death came rushing over her mind, her office, the sadness in his eyes as he lifted the gun to his head apologizing, the explosion that followed.

"Rob," she whimpered.

"You've gotten yourself in a situation, Elle," he said. Strangely, his lack of a nose did not hinder his speech.

"This is a bad dream. A horrible dream."

The black cave of his face pulled up on one side into a grotesque smile. "You got caught sticking your little nose where it doesn't belong, dredging up your lies."

"You're dead, Rob," she shouted. "Just get out of here. You're dead."

He stepped closer, his wound wept fresh, wet blood that ran down the sides of his face and soaked the neck of his jacket with a black stain. "I'm here to interrogate you, to make sure you did not leak any information during your capture."

He punctuated certain words with a sickly wet noise, as damaged tissues rubbed together at the back of his throat.

She shivered. "You're dead. You're fucking dead."

"There is talk that they bombed that convention just to get to you, Elle," he said.

"That's not true."

He ignored her. "I'm going to need your statement to complete this investigation. If you won't cooperate, well, I'll be forced to use coercion."

She shook her head in disbelief. This investigation? She had to be dreaming, or hallucinating. Rob could not be back from the dead. Dr. Stevens had told her that her dreams could be lost memories surfacing or trippy nightmare fuel. Elle was certain that Rob's appearance was the latter.

"Unless you've defected, Elle, unless you're a terrorist now," he said. "It's better to tell me now than for them to find out. They'll do terrible things to you, Elle, and they'll make sure you remember every agonizing second of it."

She squeezed her eyes closed; it was only a dream. There was no way that this man who had died by his own hand was there with her in a covert government hospital. Elle opened her eyes. Rob stood close to the bed now, his brow bent over his broken face.

"You're being uncooperative," he said. "Makes me think you've got something to hide."

"I'm not hiding anything," she hissed in a panicked whisper. He grabbed her by the shoulders, and she screamed.

"You were planning it all along, weren't you? Then you staged your own abduction."

"Dr. Stevens," she half screamed, half whimpered. "Nurse Grace. Someone, help."

Rob lifted her out of bed, shook her as if she were a dusty rag.

"Tell me the truth. You've defected and you had them kill me."

"I don't know what you're talking about."

He stopped shaking her. His single eye gleamed at her suspiciously. Where another eye should have peered there was a dark cavity that seemed to go on forever.

She pushed forward with a grunt, an attempt to try to free herself, but he was too strong. He stifled her escape by pressing her close. She felt the coolness of his brass buttons, the prick of the bars affixed to his breast.

"They gave you a taste of your own medicine," he said. "They did not like the fact that you tried to profit off their handiwork. *Why* did they punish you, Elle?"

"I don't know what you're talking about."

He dragged her off the bed and she hit the floor with a thud. She felt a blow to her side. She rolled over, her body throbbing in pain. She looked up to plead for him to stop and saw that his face was changed. Instead of wounds from a callous bullet, the skin was fresh as if kissed by the sun.

The new face that loomed over her was no longer Loera's. In his place was a blond woman, at once beautiful and cruel. She snatched at her furiously as Elle tried to wriggle away.

"You're a self-indulged, degenerate little hack. There are millions out there, just like you. What makes you so special that they would come after you?"

"I don't know," Elle screamed. "I. Don't. Know."

"Throw stones and hide your hands," she said and kicked her in the side. "That's what you and your type do, isn't it?"

Her vision began to shade around the edges. By now she was familiar enough with the sensation of losing consciousness to know when she was close to a total blackout. Her mind and body exhausted, she curled into a ball on the cool floor and surrendered.

Chapter Eight

Sharm El Sheikh, Egypt
South Military Camp

Cass gripped the door handle, her gaze pinned on Thora. Outside the car, a half-dozen Egyptian MPs surrounded them shouting for them to open the doors. Her old handler was as calm as ever. It seemed like only seconds ago she was sitting with Fletcher and the Egyptian officials waiting to hear what he had to say about his crimes. Now, she was in a car face-to-face with Thora with over a dozen uniforms shouting for them to open the doors, aiming guns at the tinted windows. She was no closer to Elle and there was a gun in the glove box.

"One moment," Thora said and pointed her gaze past her out the window. Another group arrived; one of them wore a suit. There was a brief argument and the uniforms scattered. The man in the suit waved them ahead.

"Quickly now," Thora said.

Cass drove ahead and they were allowed through the gates. Cass sped up as they merged onto the main road.

"You made me think I was going to have to fight my way out of there," Cass said.

"We must be prepared for as many outcomes as we can imagine," Thora said. "I've survived this long using every tool I have at my disposal."

That was how she saw Cass, as a tool, only as good to her as the equipment in her head. That was the way it had always been. Thora had come back for her most valuable tool.

"How are we getting out of Egypt?" Cass asked her.

"First class of course," Thora said.

"And we're going to find Elle," Cass said.

"You've got the brawn. I've got the brains, money, and connections. I was thinking that we can pool our resources."

"Let me guess, resources that can shake the ground beneath a prison compound, the kind of tools that you used to turn Amir into a sock puppet?"

Thora made a face. "Tools such as the Aegis? I am happy to see the Americans have not pried it out of your head."

"Elle's mother visited me a few days ago. She asked about the Aegis. She wanted to know if I was willing to work for the Pentagon, that they would try to remove it," Cass said. "She didn't mention anything about Elle being missing."

Thora was silent. "I am not certain if her daughter's safety is her top concern. Elle's image has been tarnished and thus her mother's."

"Tarnished?"

"Her disappearance has raised some questions about why she went to Kuwait and what happened there. Her conspiracy theorist friend released pictures of you after the abduction, and the Green Patriot has offered a substantial reward for anyone with information about your identity."

Cass frowned. "It should be expected that they're doing what they can to find Elle."

"Everyone is making the wrong moves ensuring her safety. You. Her friends and cohorts. Her mother."

Cass stared out at the road ahead. Her heart felt low and heavy in her chest. Fletcher had been right, but then again, the bastard had known the truth the entire time. She gripped the wheel even tighter.

Next to her, Thora sighed. "Olympicorp plans to use Elle to get to you and you to get to me. It's been a race, but I have beaten them at every turn so far."

"And Elle? What if they've killed her?"

"They won't kill her. They're too desperate at this point."

Cass could not help but feel as if she were making the same mistake, once again trusting someone who promised her Elle. She resolved not to be played again. Thora would have money, passports, and transportation. When the opportunity was right, Cass would take what she needed and leave. She could no longer afford to gamble with Elle's safety.

"Where are we headed?" she asked.

"Nuweiba. I have a friend who will help us."

"And once we are out of Egypt?"

Thora looked annoyed, and Cass knew why. She was accustomed to her wraith, the Gorgon who never questioned her past.

"Germany."

"Not a big country, but you could be a bit more specific. Pretend you didn't program the world's geography into my brain."

"What an imagination you have," Thora drawled. "I really hope you won't be like this the entire journey?"

"Why? Because I can tell you what a monster you are."

"There are some who would call you a monster, as I am sure they have among that lot at the SDC. That is why they recruited you."

"You made me this way," Cass told her.

"I made you into something beautiful and lethal."

She laughed bitterly. "I'm a fucking mess."

Thora searched her face. "You are looking a little worse for wear. Have they been dragging you around the world searching for me?"

"Before we came here, I was in a pod for a few days," Cass told her.

"A pod?" Thora asked. "He was attempting to reprogram you? I doubt they have the knowledge."

"You know they had to try."

"Look at you. And that display back there at the gate. Hesitant. Fearful. I believe they've ruined you. The damage could be irreparable. I can't believe you allowed them to put you in a pod."

"I had no choice."

"You had a choice."

"What's the difference between what Fletcher has done to me and what you have done?"

"The difference is what I did made you great, and given the opportunity, I can make you even greater. That man only wants to use you for his own gain."

Cass paused, resigned that Thora had spoken the truth about Fletcher. He would have strung her along, tampering with her mind, not informing her that Elle was missing.

Thora watched her closely, obviously amused.

"You've done this your way, it didn't work. Now let me, the person who has watched over you all your life, help you.

When Cass did not answer she said, "I see why it was so easy for Fletcher to convince you to willingly be jailed and subject yourself to his crude experiments."

"And here I am, trusting in you. For all I know I could be in a pod right now."

"Stop it," Thora said. "Those fools, they practically returned you to me by bringing you to Jove Island. Ridiculous."

"I tried to warn them."

"Of course, you did." She gave a dark chuckle. "I'm glad they were too foolhardy to listen to your warning. My vine. How has it progressed?"

Nothing about Charybdis, a human being. She was more concerned about her deadly mutated plant. Cass felt her brow furrow. "We managed it fine."

Thora looked doubtful.

They reached Nuweiba in the middle of the night. They drove to a resort on the shore and were greeted like tourists. Despite the hour, the front staff welcomed them. At the front desk, Thora gave a phony name under which she had booked a room. She ordered food to be sent up right away. Cass carried the two suitcases she instructed her to bring from the car to the room.

"We won't stay here for more than thirty minutes," she said as they entered.

Cass sat in a chair and watched Thora move about the room opening the cases on the bed and tossing her some clothes while commenting on how skinny Cass was. She sent her to the bathroom to change and clean up. When she returned, there were dinner trays. Thora was already picking at the food arranged on her plate. Cass did the same, piling a bit of food on her plate and then sitting across from Thora. Not too close.

She stared at Cass as they ate in silence.

"What is this they've done with your hair?"

Cass absentmindedly touched her fingers to her temple. "Some device Fletcher used to keep the Aegis suppressed, and my ability to read pulses."

She raised her eyebrows. "Perhaps the pulse, but they could never suppress the Aegis. I believe you were hoodwinked."

Cass put down her fork. She did not doubt this as she had never tried to use the Aegis while wearing Fletcher's band around her forehead.

"The chicken is dry," she said in a bored tone and brought a cup of water to her lips.

"What happened to Charybdis? Did she leave the island?"

"She did and she will be joining us after the next leg of this journey."

"Is Charybdis my mother?" she asked.

Thora put down her cup and scoffed. "What gave you such an idea?"

"Fletcher brought in someone to dredge up any lost memories you didn't erase."

Thora rolled her eyes. "I take it they were successful, and you were able to recollect Charybdis. Do you remember who did this procedure?"

"She called herself Dr. Branch."

Thora nodded. "Yes, I have heard of her methods. Nothing to write home about."

Cass found the professional jealousy humorous; she did not recall ever seeing Thora exhibit any of what she called the baser emotions.

"If Charybdis isn't my mother, then why do I have a memory of her from when I was a young child?"

Thora made a grim face and sighed. "It was a mission, your first. She was an insert into a militia cult, you were her prop. A beloved baby daughter."

"The thing is, she remembered me too. She could have killed me, but she hesitated."

Another doubtful look. "Impossible."

"Then why did she not kill me?"

"There is no way she could end you. Even in your weakened state, Charybdis is no match for you."

"You didn't program her to kill me?"

Thora shook her head. "Absolutely not. I programmed her to do her best to subdue you short of death while I attempted to make a connection."

Cass remembered the darkened corridor, the slideshow, and the lost time. She pushed her plate away in disgust and Thora made a dour face.

"Trust that I have abandoned any prospects of reprogramming you. It's just impossible. Whatever happened in Kuwait has washed you clean of any influence I've ever had."

Cass frowned. "It was Elle. She saved me from you."

"Yes," Thora agreed to her surprise. "I am beginning to see that now."

There was a knock at the door, startling them both.

"Which reminds me, we need to get you armed."

Their visitor was only someone from the hotel there to retrieve them.

Cass and Thora left the room and the hotel. A small black car with a lighted taxi sign waited for them at the entrance. The driver was a man with small round eyeglasses. He did not speak, neither did Thora speak to him. He drove toward the sea and a dock with a line of cars waiting to board a ferry. A guard waved the cars into parking spaces as their occupants wandered onto the main deck. Cass climbed out of the car suddenly eager to stretch her legs. A rusted door led them to a mezzanine with a floor of metal grating. Below were a few storage containers, the logos worn away by sunlight and salt sea air. A man in a construction hat appeared. He regarded them both for a moment, his eyes darting between Cass and Thora as if he were not sure what to say to them.

"This way," he said and pointed the way to a set of metal stairs.

Cass felt nervous about the situation. She looked to Thora who took a step forward.

"You first," she told the man. "We'll follow."

He looked to Thora who nodded.

The ship began to move as they descended the stairs. Cass tried to feel out in the darkness for other pulses, but there was no one among the storage containers. She noticed that Thora began huffing halfway down but did not pause. Trembling, she took each step, her knuckles white from holding fast to the railing.

Thora stumbled once she hit the cement floor of the hold. Cass and their escort moved in to help her, but she waved them off. She grinned and made her way to the nearest container, a blue one with the faded logo of a black rabbit and white Japanese letters identifying the company and port. She limped to the narrow end where metal bars secured the opening. She reached up and wrapped her shaking hand around the bar and pulled. Cass heard two clicks and the hiss of compressed air. The opening lifted and a white light winked on inside. Cass stooped, not wanting to get close. She saw a bank of equipment on a pristine white floor.

Thora stepped in and turned to her.

"Well?"

"This how you've been traveling?"

"Not one of my favorites," Thora said. "I've tried to include all the amenities. Now really, we must hurry."

"I don't know if I want to go inside that thing."

"Please, it's larger than a pod, but I am sure you can manage."

"That's not funny. I don't want to be in a confined space with you. How are we supposed to get out of there if something goes wrong?"

"Your friend Fletcher will have every mode of transportation monitored from Egypt to the Med. This is a less public mode of transportation. Trust that I have thought out many scenarios."

"That's what I'm afraid of."

Thora lowered her voice. "Your incessant questioning. We are on the trail of your reporter. Is that a sufficient answer?"

Cass paused and glanced around them; the man was still there watching, not with the expectancy of a port worker with a busy shift to complete, but with a detachment she came to recognize as a wraith's. She read his pulse, a steady thrum like the machinery around them. He was programmed to serve Thora and no one else. Cass had no doubt that there were more like him planted where it suited Thora, blending in with the citizens of the world like ghosts.

"Excuse me if I'm a little wary of your benevolence," she told Thora.

"Don't call it that." She shook her head as she walked around the interior of the container. "I get you back, in some capacity, working with me, but I am beginning to doubt you'll be up for it when we have to face actual danger."

"I'm up for anything that will get Elle back."

Thora cast her a doubtful look. "I won't be able to do this alone much longer. There was not much time to allow myself to heal, and I am paying for it more each day."

"It sounds as if you need a nurse," Cass said.

Thora ignored the quip. She dismissed the wraith and bade her to come closer. Cass did so hesitantly, entering with caution.

"This container is engineered to react to my biometrics as well as yours," Thora informed her as she stood in front of a panel with a digital readout and a few buttons that she pressed in a sequence only she knew.

The door shut behind them and the space darkened for a split second before lighting from above. Thora took a seat on a chair mounted to the floor. She touched a control panel on the armrest and an image appeared on the far wall. It showed the outside of the container.

"A projection of our surroundings," Thora said. "We will be loaded into a large cargo boat at the next port and taken to Morocco."

"Won't we be jostled around a lot?"

"There is a stability system in place to prevent that," she said. She moved to a metallic box that held food and water. "The restroom is behind that partition."

Cass went to inspect and helped herself to water and some cubed cheese from the small fridge. Thora was in the process of hoisting herself onto a box bed mounted on the wall. "I do hope to catch up on some sleep. I suggest you do the same."

Cass said nothing. There was no way she was going to sleep. She went for the computer and skimmed the interface for a connection to the outside world not filtered and edited by Fletcher. The website had been fake, or she had been looking at a blank screen when she thought she was looking at Elle's latest reports at the Green Patriot. She felt a bite of anger at her naivety.

She searched Elle's name and saw the headlines. *Progressive reporter missing. Abducted: Did Elle Pharell know too much? Body found in Gulf, not Elle Pharell as speculated.* The last one frightened her the most. She clicked to load the article and read it. Some fishermen had stumbled across the body while crab fishing. A female fitting Elle's description, but no, it was a young prostitute from Amarillo. There was a statement from Congresswoman Pharell offering thoughts and prayers for the victim.

Another news source detailed Elle's last day in a timeline. She had left work after taping a show to run errands. The next day was Anne

Humphries's birthday party, and she went shopping for a gift. She visited a perfume shop and the pub where the party would take place. She then returned to her apartment. Cass scrolled down to see a grainy video of the parking garage where Elle lived.

Cass's heart began to hammer in her chest to see the shape of Elle carrying her shopping. She wore a scarf tied jauntily around her neck. She looked over her shoulder one way and then the other. She paused for a second before hurrying on. A deer sensing the nearness of the hunter, or Cass was reading too much into it.

Two figures entered the frame, one in a suit, the other in a hoodie and loose pants. Both of their faces were covered by the visors of black motorcycle helmets. Elle ran a few steps and another helmeted figure appeared and spread his arms. Even through the inferior quality of the video, Cass could see Elle scream as they all converged on her at once.

Cass felt her breath hitch in her chest as she watched. Suddenly, Elle used both hands to grab hold of either side of the nearest person. She drove her body forward lifting her knee swiftly. The assailant stumbled backward. Cass felt the corner of her mouth twist wryly, but it was only a moment of victory. The other two caught Elle's arms from behind just as a van pulled up blocking the camera's view. Seconds later, it sped away. The video ended in a freeze-frame of the garage.

Cass sighed out the breath she had been holding. She did not doubt that Olympicorp was behind Elle's abduction. She had seen too much in Kuwait. She was a reporter. She had inadvertently derailed the work of one of their best assets, Thora, by befriending Cass, which broke their wraith-handler bond.

Another headline caught her attention. The author was Tammy Crockett, Elle's friend who ran a conspiracy website. *Abducted: Did Elle Pharell know too much?* She clicked it and read through the article. Crockett pointed out Elle's trip to Dubai during the Bedouin revolt, and Rob Loera and his connection to Ziggurat. Cass saw her own picture, a still from the robbery she had committed in Prague, an event she did not remember since she was under Thora's thrall at the time. There was a caption beneath the image that described her as person of interest who could help in the investigation of Elle's abduction. There was a link with Crockett's email. Cass clicked and found that it was a generic website message box with the option to sign up for a mailing list. She hesitated, glancing over at the bunk where Thora slept. She turned back to the form on the screen.

In the subject line she typed: *The Gorgon.*

In the text she typed: *I will bring back Elle if it's the last thing I do.*

She settled back in her seat and closed her eyes. Her mind buzzed with questions about Elle's disappearance and what Olympicorp would do with her. The logical course of action would be to kill her on the spot. They had the resources to make it look like an accident. If they genuinely wanted her out of the way. No, Elle had to be more valuable to them alive than dead. Cass could think of no other reason than to use Elle as bait to get to her and Thora. Olympicorp knew about Cass rejecting Thora's programming. They knew, just like Fletcher, that the best way to get to Thora would be through her life's work, the Gorgon.

She wondered how the SDC came to be privy to the inner workings of Olympicorp's Patheon, the mysterious board of directors that led the entity. Thora had taken her to New York to show off the Aegis. Shortly after, they had been attacked. What had been the true meaning of that meeting?

She heard Thora stirring.

"Why did we go to New York?"

Thora snuffled. "What are you on about?"

"New York. We were attacked."

"You remember that," Thora said. "They wanted to take everything away from me, everything I had worked for, and that day I told them no."

"They wanted to take me away."

"Among other things," Thora said, hoisting herself into a sitting position. Her legs dangled off the bunk.

"So, Elle was taken because of you."

"No, she was taken because you two lovebirds just couldn't stay away from each other. Isn't that how Fletcher caught up to you?"

She was right, and the question she posed reminded Cass of her own.

"How did Fletcher find out about the inner workings of Olympicorp?"

Thora shrugged. "Olympicorp has infiltrated governments all over the world. The SDC sees itself as an enemy of corruption. Perhaps there is a double agent, perhaps someone high, someone like me that the Pantheon wronged."

Cass thought of all the people who would like to get even with Olympicorp, herself included, as they had given Thora a platform and resources.

She watched her move from the bunk to the computer. Cass moved over and watched her work for a minute hoping to get some clue as to where they were headed next. Music began to play overhead, and Cass felt her eyelids droop.

"You're welcome to the bed," Thora informed her.

Cass decided to take her up on her offer, and within moments she was drifting off to sleep. She startled awake once as she settled into the darkness behind her lids. She thought she heard footsteps and the bang of a gun. Thora must have heard her distress because she offered her drugs. Cass refused and out of stubbornness she fell asleep naturally.

She woke to Thora touching her shoulder.

"We'll be docking soon. I've been trying to wake you for the past twenty minutes. I thought I would have to give you an adrenaline shot."

Cass sat up and insisted that she was fine. She did not want Thora injecting her with anything. She moved to the observation screen. It was night now. She could see the bright lights of the port and the city beyond. Docking meant a crane lifting the container from the ship across the water to the loading zone.

"It won't be long now," Thora said and set to moving about the container gathering things into a metallic case. Cass watched her. She was energized by her rest.

"Who was my mother? My father?" She decided to ask.

"Do you ever let up?" she asked.

"Don't you know?" Cass asked.

"You have no mother or father. You were made in a lab."

"With the genetic materials of…?"

Thora sighed impatiently. "Other wraiths. I am not sure who."

"I find it hard to believe you would not find out that information."

"It doesn't matter now, and it didn't matter then," Thora said.

"Because I was simply a commodity, the raw material for you to mold. No memories. No life of my own," Cass countered.

Thora's lips stretched into a thin line, a sure sign that she was annoyed. "You understand and yet you pester me with your whining."

"How can you be so morally bankrupt?"

"The concept of morals is meant to control the unwashed masses," Thora said, the thin line curving into a snarky grin. "But I suppose that is what you want to be? I made you into something better."

"A killer?" Cass asked. "Someone who is programmed, who is not allowed to live their life freely, or even have their own memories?"

Thora scoffed, preoccupied with packing her metal case.

"Don't you feel any empathy? You left Charybdis to live alone in that harsh landscape," she said. "Were you going to leave her on Jove Island forever?"

"She is a wraith; she didn't have expectations."

"And that would have been my fate as well?"

Thora paused and looked up at her. "Of course not. You are different, unlike any wraith that has ever been created. When you were under my control, there was no doubt inside you, just the innate knowledge that you are special."

"I didn't ask for any of this," Cass said.

"This conversation is quite exhausting," Thora announced, her voice echoing through the container. "It's time to move."

Cass stood. She'd had enough of the small space. Thora opened the entrance, and they were greeted by a man in a hard hat and a black coat. Another wraith. Behind him stood Charybdis, her dark hair tied back in a ponytail, a pack slung over her shoulder. Cass felt a stab of apprehension since the last time they were face-to-face she was certain Charybdis wanted to kill her. She reined herself in but could not help but stare.

Thora instructed her to grab the metal case she'd been busy packing. Cass wanted to tell her to carry her own damned case, but it looked too heavy for her to manage with her bum leg. Cass picked up the case, her eyes straying to Charybdis and Thora, curious of their exchange.

As Thora stepped out of the container, she touched Charybdis's shoulder and the two made eye contact. Neither of them spoke a word of greeting as Charybdis fell behind Thora who followed the other wraith to the metal stairs that let out of the hold. Cass, lugging the case, caught up to them.

Outside, the night glowed from the lights of the port.

"Where are we?" she asked Thora.

"Morocco," she answered.

"I thought you said we were going to Germany."

"Eventually," Thora said.

The male wraith left them at some point, and Charybdis led them to a van. She opened the door and gave Thora her hand to help her into the passenger seat. She waited until Thora was settled. She glanced Cass's way but otherwise ignored her. She walked past to the driver's side and slid behind the wheel.

"Well, are you getting in?" Thora called.

Cass opened the sliding side door of the van and set the case on the floor inside before settling on one of the bench seats in the back

"What's in Germany?" Cass asked.

Thora sighed, her irritation apparent. She was not used to being asked questions, just her wraiths blindly following along.

"The answers that we both seek."

"Answers about Elle's location."

"Yes," Thora agreed hastily. "I am certain."

Cass turned over her words as Charybdis drove them to a small airfield. There they unloaded the van, and Thora handed her a passport.

Inside was the typical form naming her as Gabriele Ferreira, a Spanish national who had traveled to America and Germany in the past year.

As she followed Thora and Charybdis to the lounge outside of the boarding gate, she realized what the freedom of the documents in her hand could provide. She could go off on her own and find Elle, reduce the risk of Thora somehow drugging her and putting her in a pod. But where would she even begin her search? She had no choice but to trust that Thora would be true to her word.

Once they were seated in the lounge, Thora opened a laptop and stared intently at the screen while Charybdis sat next to her. She had not spoken a word since they met up in the hold of the ship.

Cass could not help but be interested in Charybdis. She watched her scanning the room at intervals. Her pulse was a steady strain that only wavered slightly when an attendant came by to offer them drinks. Thora ordered and the woman leaned forward attentively. If she was aware of Charybdis's steely gaze on her, she did not show it. If she had happened to be someone with ill intentions, she could end her with her bare hands.

Charybdis requested water when asked. Cass did the same. She leaned forward a bit to make eye contact.

"I'm glad to see you made it off the island. How have you been?"

Charybdis straightened, her gaze unwavering but expressionless.

"I'm fine," she said. "The journey was kind to me. I am glad to see that you are no longer with those people."

Cass glanced at Thora who wore a sly, amused grin.

"I was deceived," she said. "I should have known no one can be trusted in this game."

"Your place is here," Charybdis said. "With us. Just like before."

Thora frowned and she tsked as if she had used the wrong fork at the dinner table.

"Like before?" Cass asked.

"When we were all much younger," she said. "Grandmother, mother, and daughter."

"Your first mission," Thora filled in. "It's the only hiccup I've ever experienced with her. It's ridiculous how the human mind trips itself up with sentiments, chemical reactions that make us feel good, but ultimately robs humankind of its full potential."

Cass stared at her. "This is similar to what happened with me and Elle." She turned to Charybdis. "You developed an emotional attachment to a child you were programmed to believe was your own. When the job was over, you couldn't get rid of the attachment."

Thora was oddly silent.

"Your two best wraiths, their programming tainted by sentiments," Cass said. "Is that why you're on the outs with Olympicorp?"

"Are you quite finished?" Thora asked.

Next to them, Charybdis sighed as sadness briefly surfaced over the vacant mask she wore. "I realize now that you are not mine," she said. "But I would regret killing you."

Thora touched her knee and said in a begrudging tone. "I would never ask that of you." She looked to Cass. "Let's all settle down for the moment."

The attendant returned with their drinks.

"What's in Germany?" she asked Thora when the three of them were once again alone.

"The Great Mountain Hall, where Olympicorp keeps all of its secrets."

Cass eyed her suspiciously. There had to be something in it for her at their destination.

"What secrets do you hope to find there?"

"The ones that will end Olympicorp," she said with finality.

An announcement came from overhead. She and Thora boarded a small private plane along with a team of Swiss soccer players and their entourage, a bawdy bunch that gathered in the back and immediately began to pop open bottles of champagne.

It was then that Cass realized how posh their surroundings were. All leather and wood trim, the interior of the jet was ridiculously opulent. The seating was grouped in fours with a narrow table in the middle. She sat across from Thora and Charybdis.

The attendant prepared them for the flight and another came by to ask if they wanted food and drink. The three of them accepted the offer of an inflight meal. Thora requested another whiskey and soda to be brought right away. Used to the demands of the wealthy, the attendant brought the drink without delay. Cass watched Thora use the drink to wash down several pills.

The plane taxied to the runway and began its ascent. The football team cheered and continued their mirth.

At some point, Thora touched Charybdis's arm. Charybdis turned to her.

"Sleep now," Thora said.

Charybdis did not fall asleep immediately. She rolled her shoulders and settled into her seat, her body visibly relaxed. She looked out the window and her eyelids drooped and closed.

Thora caught Cass watching. "She is quite beautiful, isn't she?"

"Are all wraiths as aware as she is?"

"Not as aware, no, but all wraiths must have some kind of self-awareness. Remember, they have to blend into the world, they have to be able to make decisions on some level."

"That is why you recruit wraiths at a young age."

"Yes, that is one reason."

"And this is going on right now?" Cass asked. "There are children somewhere having their brains washed? Being put into pods?"

"Please, don't raise your voice," Thora said through clenched teeth as she forced a smile on a player passing to the restroom. "Once I take down Olympicorp, and you rescue your reporter, you and I could help all the wraiths."

Cass balked. "Help them or wrangle them? You could make your own army of wraiths to take over the world."

"That has never been something I desired," Thora said. "I was tasked with creating wraiths. It is the only thing I have ever cared about. For Olympicorp to turn against me is egregious."

"You were feeding people to their machine, that's egregious."

Another flight attendant approached; her cheeks were slightly flushed. She was giving away champagne, compliments of the footballers, and she had obviously partaken. Thora refused but ordered another whiskey and proffered her empty cup. Cass reached over and covered the glass with her hand.

"Please," she said. "My mother is on medications and is stubborn."

Thora laughed and began to protest.

"Please, Mom," Cass said sternly. "You must follow the doctor's orders."

The flight attendant shifted her gaze between them, her brow bent with uncertainty. Finally, she apologized, promised to bring seltzer water, and left promptly to see about the other passengers.

"Foul," Thora said.

"Your mind needs to be clear." She turned to watch the clouds through the window. "We have urgent business."

CHAPTER NINE

Württemberg, Germany

Cass had imagined that their destination in Germany—what Thora called the Great Mountain Hall, would be in a metropolitan area. They landed in Zurich and from there traveled to the German border, the only riders in a passenger van. Their driver was a wraith Thora called Milo. Cass noticed that they were headed toward the Black Forest.

They passed several picturesque villages of chalets with tall sloping roofs and cottages trimmed like cuckoo clocks. Tour buses piled with tourists and their gear appeared on the motorway around them on their way to fun places like Lake Constance to drink beer and enjoy the sights. She wondered what it would be like to be with Elle among them. She could see her in her mind smiling over her shoulder before skiing down a snowy slope.

Milo stopped the van in a dingy village, consisting of scattered buildings in a muddy rut long cleared of trees. The locals seemed to know Milo as a guide for wildlife enthusiasts and with his scruffy ginger beard he seemed less out of place than Cass, Charybdis, and Thora. The four of them huddled in a beat-up canvas tent where Milo and Thora studied a map.

Charybdis, who had been busy adding some attachment to the end of Thora's cane to make it more of a trekking pole, brought the finished product for her to test out.

Thora made the short lap around the inside of the tent, satisfied with the results.

"Are you sure you're going to be able to make this trip? With your leg?" Cass asked.

"I'm certain that I am up for the journey," Thora said. "Milo and I are going to procure a vehicle. You two stay here."

Cass and Charybdis agreed.

An hour passed.

It was cold, not Jove Island cold, but it would have been nice for Thora to leave them somewhere near a fire. She looked to Charybdis who stood at the opening watching the sluggish life of the village, which was not much.

Cass went to stand next to her.

"It's freezing," she commented.

Charybdis turned to look her way.

"It is."

"This sucks," Cass said. "Thora just left us out here like dogs and we wait obediently."

Charybdis regarded her for a pause. "Let's take a walk, then. It will warm us up."

"Really? You're going to leave after Thora told us to wait?"

"It's been a while," Charybdis said. "This is a small village. We can't go far."

Cass found herself grinning.

They set out on their walk, silent as they passed a particularly rustic structure.

"I think this used to be a village long ago," Charybdis said.

"Maybe," Cass said, glad to be moving.

There was a makeshift pub crafted in the same style as the rest of the village, with panels of wood covered in peeling, warped paint, and the roof patched with tin. A skinny chimney whispered welcoming smoke.

To Cass's surprise, Charybdis went right inside as if she were a regular. There were about three people at the short, sagging bar. There were buckets on the floor catching drips from the uneven ceiling.

"Look, darts," Charybdis said. "I'll play you a quick game."

"Okay," Cass said and followed her to the wall adjacent to the bar where the board hung inside a wooden cabinet with a missing door. The board was old with metal wire numbers instead of printed ones. The darts were piled in a discarded drinking glass. Charybdis separated them by color, red for herself, green for Cass.

"You throw first," she said.

Cass found the throwline drawn in chalk on the dusty floor. She straightened, aimed and threw. The dart landed on the thirteen just inside the triple ring. Her second throw hit the same spot and her third hit the bull's-eye.

"Not bad," Charybdis said. She waited for Cass to clear the board and stepped up for her turn. All three of her darts landed on the bull's–eye.

"You've played this before," Cass deadpanned.

"Maybe," she said and went to clear the board.

Cass took her turn. She was aiming for a bull's-eye. Her first attempt was successful, but her next two throws hit the three inside the triple ring.

When she turned back, Charybdis was sipping a beer from a pint glass. She handed her glass to Cass and hit another three consecutive bull's-eyes, the last knocking a previous dart to the floor.

Impressed, Cass asked. "Do you remember playing this before?"

"No, I just know. I think it's that way with kinetic things like games. Your brain doesn't remember, but your muscles do." She came and retrieved her beer. "When I saw those darts, my fingers tingled. They do that when I pick up a gun or steer a fast bike."

Cass watched in awe as she explained in her soft gruff voice.

"Is this true for all wraiths?"

"Thora says yes, but I've never asked another," she said and raised her eyebrows. "So?"

Cass shrugged. "I don't think I've ever noticed."

"Oh," Charybdis said. She seemed disappointed.

"Do you have a name?" Cass asked. "It feels weird calling you Charybdis."

"Why? What's wrong with my name?"

"I figured since you broke with your programming, that you would pick a normal name, not your wraith name."

"Perhaps it's best. Thora never told Olympicorp I broke with my programming. I continued with any assignments and then she sent me to Jove Island."

"She protected you," Cass said.

"She's trying to protect you now. You're special to her."

"The only thing Thora is interested in protecting is her work," Cass told her. "We just happen to be that work."

"Does it matter why?" Charybdis asked. "She has stayed one step ahead of Olympicorp since before they turned on her. Now she needs our help as she goes to face her judgment."

"Judgment?"

"Thora has chosen to face a member of the Pantheon who will decide her fate."

"Wait, Thora has done all of this running just to go to them willingly?"

"Approaching the Great Hall will not be easy," Charybdis explained. "But once we make it through, Thora will prove once and for all that she is worthy of facing the Pantheon as their equal."

Her tone had a prideful inflection and Cass pitied her. Charybdis's career should have ended after her mind refused to be washed of memories of her baby. Instead, Thora had continued to push her mind to its limits. The drugs. The pod. The mind fucks. Charybdis had been at it all a lot longer.

"Do you know what we'll be up against at the Great Hall?"

She tossed a dart. Another bull's–eye. "They'll try to stop us, but any wraiths they send will be turned against them."

"So, what? They blow us up? The end."

"Thora is more valuable to them alive than dead," she said with that same haughty tone.

Cass doubted a bloodthirsty group like Olympicorp, who made their own rules, would follow any code, even one of their own. "Getting myself killed in some power struggle between Thora and Olympicorp is not going to bring Elle back."

She smiled at bit. "Then don't get yourself killed, Gorgon."

"My name is Cass."

"Cass needs to stay here and practice her dart game. We're going to need the Gorgon at the Great Hall." She gestured behind her toward the entrance. Thora had found them. She stepped into the grimy bar her, cane in hand.

She turned to her. "You're giving yourself up to go on trial?"

"And Charybdis has taken it upon herself to fill you in on our journey," Thora said dryly.

"As if you did not put her up to it."

Thora scoffed. "Hanging with the Americans has made you paranoid."

Charybdis interjected, "She should know what we are facing, so she can prepare."

Thora moved close to her and removed a dart from the glass. "I told you that she is always ready. She's the Gorgon."

Charybdis looked doubtful.

Thora sighed and threw the dart. She hit the inner ring on the seven. She made a face, dissatisfied with her play.

"How is any of this going to get Elle back?" Cass asked.

"The Great Hall holds many secrets," she said. "All of them."

"What exactly are we up against?" Cass asked.

"Well, they won't send any wraiths after us," Thora said, raising her altered cane. "I have the Geist device."

"What is that?"

"Once activated, any wraith within a mile will become my thrall," she said, a smug smile on her lips, as close as Thora would ever come to beaming. "My falling out with Olympicorp started before Kuwait and it was all over this. I had you steal the plans, and in retaliation they sent you to what they thought would be your end."

Thora looked to Charybdis. "The Gorgon is my greatest weapon of all, and the Pantheon knows that."

"I'm no one's weapon," Cass said. "I'm a person."

"You are a weapon," Thora said. "The sooner you realize that the sooner you will see your Elle again."

She walked away with Charybdis following close. Cass did not move out of sheer stubbornness, then she stalked behind them stiff-legged. Outside, Milo waited beside a jeep petting a random dog. A midsize black-and-white speckled mutt. Charybdis went to inspect the animal as well and they all gathered around for a moment. Cass caught Thora glancing at each of their faces, her fellowship of wraiths. There was a pensive air about her.

"Well then," she announced when she met Cass's gaze. "Let's not dally any longer."

Charybdis helped Thora into the back seat and walked around the other side, leaving Cass to ride shotgun next to Milo.

They started the next leg of their journey on an overgrown road comprised of uneven ruts made by the tires of vehicles. As they drove in and out of copses of trees, the sun made an attempt to break through the clouds, but only a few rays were able to pierce through.

Cass asked Thora, "Why didn't you use the Geist device to wrangle me?"

She turned a bit in her seat. "You know the answer to that. It doesn't work on you, so I suppose you are actually asking if I tried."

"Did you?" Cass asked.

"No," she said simply.

Cass did not believe her.

Thora sensed her disbelief. "It would have been like trying to turn an apple into an orange. You are simply no longer programmable."

Cass glanced at Charybdis.

"Her experience shirking my programming was a lot different from yours. It was a small hiccup while yours was a complete break. Hers was intrinsic, yours extrinsic."

"What do you think happened?" Cass asked. "With me and Elle?"

Thora turned forward to look out the windshield. "I can't say."

"You have to have some theory—"

"I suppose you want me to say it was the power of love," Thora said sarcastically.

"Is that so difficult to believe?"

Thora laughed ruefully. "That is certainly not how any of this works."

The jeep stopped. They'd reached another outpost, two ramshackle buildings and a satellite mounted on a tall pole. Beyond, sparse forest dotted the rocky foothills that led to mountains looming among low clouds. The camp was kept by field research scientists who used wildlife cameras to capture the habits of a lineage of lynx. At least, that was Thora's explanation. As they exited the jeep, Cass saw a leaning caged run, the door secured with a short length of heavy chain. Inside, there was a lynx pacing back and forth on the bare ground. With its large paws, it covered the small area quickly as it regarded them with golden eyes.

One of the three-man team of scientists came to greet them. Bearded and tattooed, he did not look like a typical scientist. Cass nearly chalked his rough look up to the line of study in the middle of nowhere until Milo handed him a metal case.

He opened the case and smiled. Inside were several stacks of euros. His gaze met Cass's and his smile faded and he closed the case. He asked Milo in German about the women who had accompanied them, specifically Thora.

"I am more than able to make the journey," she announced in his tongue. "Now, where are the ATVs we've paid him so handsomely for?"

He stared at them for a moment and then tossed his head toward a netted camo tarp.

Thora gave him a dry *danke* and strolled toward the tarp. Milo trotted past her to remove the heavy tarp. Charybdis followed. Cass waited a moment to study the man's face and catch his pulse. While his face presented a calm, slightly annoyed demeanor, his pulse was like the rumble of distant thunder.

Cass caught up with Charybdis.

"What's going on?"

"It's illegal to go past this point," Charybdis whispered. "The land is a private preserve under the protection of the German government, but it's been the property of Olympicorp for five hundred years."

"Olympicorp has been around for so long?"

Charybdis stopped, a confused look on her face. "You don't know much about Olympicorp."

"I suppose not," Cass said.

"How can you possibly understand any of this if you don't know what you're up against?

She was watching Thora ease onto one of the ATVs. Despite her bravado with the so-called scientist, they all knew she'd been struggling with her injured hip.

"How much longer to our destination?" Cass asked.

"I'm not sure," Charybdis said.

"Will she be able to make the journey?"

"Of course," Charybdis answered without a beat.

"She's in pain," Cass said. "I don't need to read her pulse to know."

Thora took notice that they had not joined her and Milo.

"Don't linger, you two," she said. "We don't have a moment to spare."

Cass mounted one of the vehicles. She started the engine and looked over her shoulder at Thora and the rest. Beyond, the scientist watched, even over the engine, she could feel his pulse like the threat of a storm.

"What is it?" Thora asked.

"He's off," Cass said.

"He'll warn them of our arrival here," she said simply.

Cass was puzzled by the statement, but only for a moment. A sinking realization came over her, but before it could gel, Milo sped off on his ATV and Thora followed. Cass looked to Charybdis who was watching her.

"Go ahead," she said as she produced a gun from the pack she carried. "I'll catch up."

"What are you doing?" Cass asked.

"Eliminating the possibility of them following us," she said. "Or worse."

"You're going to kill them?"

Charybdis gave a smug smile at her innocence. "Go on. Thora will want you at her back."

"I'm not going to leave you alone," Cass said.

The smugness left her face, and a genuine smile remained. "You were always so stubborn."

She raced forward as if she were going after Thora and Milo but veered back around toward the researcher's camp. Cass scrambled to follow. Up ahead, the bearded scientist was joined by another man. They quickly split into opposite directions when they saw Charybdis double back; one disappeared into one of the shacks with the case of money, the other ducked behind the lynx's run.

Charybdis rode around the cage. As she did, the second scientist reappeared and aimed a gun at her back.

Cass unleashed the Aegis on him, and he lost his footing. He rolled on the ground and into the side of the shack from which he'd emerged. She dismounted the ATV and sprinted toward him as he aimed her way.

She blasted him backward and the entire little building rocked with the impact. He fell and did not move. She retrieved his gun and looked for Charybdis. She was close to the lynx, still astride the ATV. The scientist she'd chased lay on the ground, a bullet wound to his head. Cass hadn't heard the shot over the rush of the Aegis in her ears.

Charybdis looked up from her quarry and startled. She raised her gun and there was a loud pop. For Cass, the world went black for a few seconds. She fell to her knees. Through the blur, she did hear a gunshot and felt a body fall on top of her. She crawled away and Charybdis was there helping her to her feet.

Cass looked from her concerned face to the man at their feet and the wooden club he'd used to nearly knock her unconscious.

"You're okay," Charybdis said after using her hands to brush back the hair at the back of Cass's head to inspect the area. "It's going to be a nasty knot."

"Shit," she said as Charybdis walked her over to her ATV.

"Take a moment to collect yourself," she said and walked away. Cass watched her walk to the run where the wild cat was held, its furious pace now a panic from the sounds of gunshots and the smell of blood.

Charybdis picked up the chain as if it were something profane. She held the door of the cage with one hand and pulled away the chain with the other. It fell to the ground, useless.

The wild cat threw itself into the back of the enclosure bounding off the wire fencing and charged forward. Charybdis moved backward allowing the door to swing open. The lynx flew out of the run and stopped to turn a frantic 180 prepared to fight. Charybdis continued to back away, she too, ready to do battle.

The lynx gave Charybdis a warning growl before sprinting away from the camp. It disappeared down a rocky slope. She returned to Cass.

"How's your head?"

"I'm fine," she said. The ringing in her ears had stopped.

"Go find the trail and catch up with Thora and Milo," she said. "I'm right behind you."

Cass obeyed. She still felt woozy from the blow to the head, yet she managed to guide the bike to the trail Milo and Thora had taken. She and Charybdis found them a quarter of a mile away from the research camp.

Thora stood next to her ATV, her eyes searching as they approached. She saw the blood on Cass and her disheveled appearance.

"Were those second-rate animal wranglers too much for you?"

"She's fine," Charybdis said.

Thora would not be deterred. "Did you use the Aegis?" she asked Cass.

"I did," she said through gritted teeth. "The last one snuck up behind me."

"We can't afford that type of mistake," Thora said. "You must use the Aegis to its full abilities if we're to make it through this."

"What is this?" Cass shouted, exasperated, her pride hurt as much as her head. "What is possibly out here in the middle of nowhere?"

"Elle is here," Thora said.

Cass shot her a warning look.

Thora pointed to a patch of sky showing through the trees. "There," she said simply.

She looked and admonished herself for it, but then she spied it, nestled on the rocky shoulder of a mountain among the trees.

A castle.

The Great Hall.

CHAPTER TEN

Württemberg, Germany

As they traveled on, Cass could see the black turrets seeming to jut from the dark evergreens. It felt surreal to see the fabricated structures, achievements of their time, among the centuries-old trees seeming to compete to touch the sky. It felt like a dream that had once been familiar, but no concrete memories came to her.

They stopped in a clearing. Thora looked fatigued. She dismounted her ATV, her face red from the effort. Charybdis came to her aid.

"I just need to stretch my legs," she insisted, brushing her away. "Prepare a shot."

Charybdis went for her pack and removed a small case. She opened it and retrieved a clear orange cylinder. She removed the top to reveal a large, capped syringe. She moved close to Thora who was fumbling with the fly of her pants while leaning on her cane. She looked up at Cass.

"A little help?"

She moved in and offered her shoulder for Thora.

"Hold her pants," Charybdis said as she exposed her bare hip.

Cass saw that the area was heavily bruised.

She met Charybdis's gaze.

"It's fine," she said. "She's come this far."

"Can we please speed this up?" Thora asked. "And stop talking about me over my head."

Charybdis refocused on the task at hand. She uncapped the syringe and said gentle things under her breath as she jabbed the alarmingly blue-black skin at Thora's hip.

Cass watched the fluid inside the syringe empty.

"What is this stuff?"

Thora gave her a shrewd look. "Something to get me to the Great Hall."

She straightened and toddled a few steps forward fixing her pants. Behind them, Milo stood beside his ATV staring out at the trees.

She looked up at the castle. Up close she could see sections of missing stone in the tower. It almost seemed otherworldly under the backdrop of the gray sky and the mountain beyond. Like a fairy tale she had heard once but could not recall until now.

A sudden gust of wind rustled the trees.

Milo whistled to get their attention.

The air changed. The wind pushed their way, warm swirling with cool. Cass felt something, much like a pulse, but different, a brooding wail like a hurricane siren. She dared to think it was the pulse of a giant. Charybdis stepped forward, her dark hair whipping around her head.

The rustling in the trees grew wilder and the wind strengthened and warmed. Bits of wood and needles began to shower down on them.

"This is not good," Thora shouted and began to limp to her ATV. Cass, Charybdis, and Milo followed suit. As she started the ATV, Cass peered ahead at the trees whipping in the strange wind in such a frenzy that they were disintegrating. She could also see a black cloud, a stark contrast with the dull gray sky. It moved on the wind and seemed to be shining with bits of debris.

She turned to see the others jetting out of the clearing back the way they'd come. After a quick glance at the hastening black cloud, she sped behind them.

Their escape ended when Thora lost control of her ATV. The front wheels flipped into the air like an unruly horse rearing. She was dumped to the ground on her side.

Cass stopped and went to help her up. Her face twisted in pain, yet she glanced around and crawled away to snatch at her cane. Charybdis and Milo joined them. Thora attempted to get back on her feet, but she lost her balance.

They quickly propped her into an upright position. She groaned as she attempted to move to stand but stumbled even with her cane. Her grip tightened around Cass's arm as she peered up at the scene behind them, her face distorted in terror.

They were suddenly in near darkness as the swirling black cloud dipped low through the treetops. Bits of foliage flew, thickening the cloud. The glittering bits that formed it whipped and shredded at the trees shaving the branches to stubs. The massive old trees began to topple as the cloud settled closer to the forest floor. She could smell earth, and sap, and fresh wood as they were pelted with debris. She could see tiny shiny black metallic cones that had broken free of the cloud, one of which zipped past her face cutting her cheek.

"What is that?" Cass asked.

"Something I suspected would never exist," Thora said. "I am prepared."

She looked to Milo. She reached for his hand, their fingers grasped, and he was able to pull her up. She lifted her cane, and he took hold of the mud-caked end. Thora twisted the handle and the shaft of the cane began to glow in Milo's hands. He stepped back and the cane lengthened and fell away. He moved back away from them, carrying the glowing rod, his eyes shiningly blank.

Then, he ran. He jumped on Cass's ATV and turned it around, then gunned the engine toward the cloud, clutching the rod that had come from Thora's cane.

Cass stepped forward to stop him, realizing what was happening. Charybdis grabbed her arm and the two of them struggled in the dimness that had become the day as the forest was rendered to pieces.

A flash of light as bright as lightning illuminated the scene. Cass could see Charybdis and Thora suddenly, the angles of their anguished faces stark.

Still in Charybdis's grip, she turned to see the black cloud roll backward. The glittering pieces that comprised it seemed to recoil like an injured animal. The ones at the edges glowed with the same brightness as the rod Milo carried. They fell away, losing their glow and disappearing among the ankle-deep piles of broken vegetation. As they watched, more pieces began to glow and fall, thinning until the cloud was half its mass.

Thora stepped forward, entranced by the scene. She called for Milo. Just as she did, what remained of the cloud surged forward. The glowing pieces that hadn't fallen went black again. Milo was covered in an instant. His scream roared above the din of destruction, as the cloud ate him alive.

In a spray of blood, nits of his clothes, flesh, and hair mingled with the shredded body and tires of the ATV. A brief explosion from the engine punctuated the destruction. Now low to the ground, it surged their way.

Cass and Charybdis began to flee on foot dragging Thora with them.

"Use the Aegis," Thora wheezed, out of breath.

"Against that?" she asked.

"Yes, you have to try."

Charybdis stopped and Thora collapsed against her. "Try."

Cass turned away from them to face the cloud shredding through the trees. She took a quick breath and separated her terror from the cold feeling in her brain. She called on the Aegis and let the freeze claim her entire body. She felt the blast roll forth from her and made no attempt to hamper it. The world became a blur of green, brown, and shining black. She could hear a high-pitched buzzing like radio static as the cloud closed in.

She took a few steps back, the chill was too much to bear, but she knew she could not falter, even when the cloud slowed to a stop and began to swirl backward. Though her legs felt rooted to the ground, she took another step backward.

She felt Thora pressed against her then. "You have to give more."

"I can't," Cass managed.

"You can and you will or we're all dead." She gripped her arm hard enough to be felt through the cold. "And where will your reporter be then?"

She took stock of the chill in her body. She dropped her shoulders and threw back her head and let it completely take over. Just as when the conical bits of the cloud came in contact with Thora's rod, they glowed. Still frozen in place, they separated as the cloud lost its density. They lost speed, floated like confetti on a breeze, and fell useless to the ground.

Cass fell to her knees from the exhaustion, and Charybdis fell too, grabbing her jacket to keep her upright.

Thora was limping away from them. She went to inspect the cloud, now a smoldering heap of randomly sparking bits. She turned to them grinning manically.

"You did it."

"What the hell was that?" Cass asked.

"A weapon," she said and raised her hands in surrender when she saw the look of disapproval on Cass's face. "I didn't create it. It was no match for the Aegis. For you." She punched a fist into the air above her head and shouted toward the woods.

"No weapon formed against me shall prosper."

"Milo's dead," Cass told her. "You sent him to his death."

"His death was necessary," Thora insisted. "Don't you see? This is it. I need you to stop being afraid, hesitant, and might I add, slow. What if I told you that Elle could be in that castle? They've no doubt made every effort to impress."

"Is that true? About Elle?"

"I don't know," she said. "We have to think of all the possibilities. You and I are the only constants in any scenario. Do you understand?"

Cass looked to Charybdis. Thora had not mentioned her at all. She did not seem to be bothered about the omission.

"We're almost there," she said.

Cass looked back to Thora. "Let's go."

The woods felt colder once they fell under the shadow of the castle. They made their way through the landscape rocky from piles of rubble that were once part of the structure. A crumbled wall had been fortified with sections of chain-link fencing. Signs warned away any visitors, and outlined the penalties for disturbing a historic site.

It was not hard to slip through and make their way among a few outbuildings. A few of them were completely covered with large sheets of gray plastic material that billowed slightly. They entered a maze of broken walls until they found themselves in what was once a courtyard. Now the paving stones were broken and packed with dirt; stray plant life grew in patches of dim sunlight.

Cass felt uneasy as they moved along to a solid wall that had miraculously stood the test of time. Set in the wall was a large wooden door, bleached from age. Thora used her cane to push at the door. The wood groaned as the door slowly swung back. A red light winked on and off until it was steady. On the other side was a stone corridor lit by more red lights. The walls were the dark stone of the mountain and the floor beneath was paved with slabs of milky, glimmering marble.

"Welcome to the Great Hall," Thora said.

She walked into the red light and Cass followed. Her legs felt gangly, her movements awkward. The red lights above were suspended from the rock by cable in between the beams of buttresses. Bare red bulbs were caged in gilded domes. Charybdis gasped at the strange splendor.

As they made their way, the end of the corridor revealed itself, a gleaming white light, the transition between a wavering glow like a mirage. Cass realized that they were walking into the side of the tree-covered mountain to a hidden fortress within. She looked up at the rocky ceiling glittering in between the lights mounted on a system of metal beams.

"How old is this place?" Cass asked.

"Six hundred years, give or take a decade," Thora said, and shushed her when she opened her mouth to speak again.

Cass felt Charybdis's hand on her shoulder, reassuring and warm.

They came to the end of the corridor and two large wooden pillars carved into Grecian style statues. One was of a sneering bearded man, nude and wearing a sword and shield. The second was of a woman, her top half clothed, her bottom half the coiled tail of a snake. She held no weapons, and her expression was calm. The two held up a lintel above a great door carved with five tall ships sailing on choppy waves.

Thora paused to regard them for a moment.

"This is it," she muttered. "Be ready for anything."

She stepped forward and the door opened revealing a brightly lit room of glittering white marble floors, walls, and a gleaming ornate staircase.

Cass gasped at the drastic change. Blinking fiercely, she followed Charybdis and Thora inside. Her eyes followed the stairs up to the top where she spotted a small woman. Her hair was as white as the marble that surrounded her and like her surroundings, glittered with silvery streaks. Age had shrunken her face, and small, gnarled hands crept from the sleeves of a dark blue jacket.

Her eyes and voice, in contrast, showed no sign of frailty.

"Thora, what have you come here for?"

"Cavanaugh," she answered. "I've come for what is owed to me. Give it and save yourself some dignity."

The woman at the top of the stairs stared down at them for a moment, her expression haughty. There was something unsettling about her that Cass could not categorize. She did not seem to be worried that she was outnumbered. She reached out for a pulse but did not find one. She was not surprised.

Cass stared past her for any space that some formidable aid could come from to back up the old woman on the landing.

That's when she noticed that the stairs and the landing led to nowhere. At first, she thought that her eyes deceived her, but there was no structure beyond the stairs, just a solid looking fog or mist. She turned around in a circle and saw more of the white fog. The grand door they had come through had vanished.

"You've brought the Gorgon," Cavanaugh said.

"Cavanagh. Did you think I would come empty-handed?"

At the mention of her moniker, Cass reined in her shock and glanced at Thora, who had not flinched

"What secrets do you desire?" Cavanaugh asked.

"I want the place that I was promised," Thora said. "No one in this organization, besides you, has accomplished what I have."

Cavanaugh tossed her white head and walked a few steps, running her hand over the marble banister. "This place and its mysteries have changed hands before, but it has always belonged truly to Mount Olympus and the Pantheon."

"My work proves—"

"Your work belongs to us. You belong to us, Thora. Have you told the Gorgon? She's been observing our little exchange with most interest."

"She is baiting you," Charybdis said softly. "Don't give her anything to use against us."

Cass kept her gaze on Cavanaugh, and she stared back. Thora had yet to realize it, but she had seen through their ruse. Cass was certain that she was not the one being baited there in the great hall.

"Because of me, Olympicorp has the power to bring the world to its knees and right it on our terms."

"That is an era neither of us will live to see," Cavanaugh replied.

"Perhaps you won't," Thora told her. "With me as head of the Pantheon, the ideas of the old regime are out. Favored will be the ones who made themselves."

Cavanaugh smiled. "How ironic you should put it that way. You didn't make yourself; you were made just as your companions here. Someone like you could never head the Pantheon."

A figure shuffled out of the mist on wobbly legs. He was dressed in a Braves T-shirt and scrub pants. His feet were bare. His shaggy, dirty brown hair fell at his shoulders. She looked at the face and saw that the left side drooped heavily, the corner of his mouth permanently parted in a distorted grin. She recognized him.

"Lyles," Cass hissed. Though he currently looked like one of the mindless horde that had infested Kuwait, he had once controlled them thanks to a failed experiment by one of Olympicorp's subsidiaries.

They'd found a use for him after the disaster. Cass could read his pulse, no, she could feel it vibrating along the floor under her feet, up to her knees.

Thora scoffed loudly. "You've resurrected this ghost of your own negligence. A commemoration to the end of Mount Olympus?"

"What have they done to him?" Cass whispered.

She did not answer.

"Thora," Cass implored her.

Lyles tilted his head. "Cass? Cass?" He spoke in a too-loud voice that echoed over the marble. His tone was raspy and apologetic. "Don't mind this..." He used his right hand to gesture at his face. "I'm fine. I'm good. How you been? How's Elle?"

"A joke," Thora scoffed nervously. "Is this what you've brought against me?"

"He was much more useful to us than we could have imagined."

"Elle Pharell," Lyles broke in, slurring his words. "She told me...she told me."

"Do you know where Elle is, Lyles?" Cass blurted. "Have you seen her?"

"Don't speak to him," Thora growled under her breath.

"Elle," Lyles said. "I saw her in the mist."

Cavanaugh moved close and touched his shoulder. Lyles's knees sagged. He fell hard to the floor and began to seize, his entire body stiff and trembling. His pulse strengthened; Cass could feel it travel up her body to her stomach as if she had waded deep into water.

She moved toward the stairs but stopped when she saw that Cavanaugh stared down at her with a slight smile at her lips.

"Come up," she said in a soft, grandmotherly tone. "Isn't that what Thora promised you? That you would find your Elle here?"

Cass felt strong hands wrap around her arm. It was Charybdis. For a second, her face was a blur, and she would have snatched out of the grasp if she had not recognized her touch.

"Don't do it, little one," she said. She looked as terrified as she had in the woods when they were confronted with the strange black cloud, as if she were afraid that Cass would be shredded to pieces. Cass was sure that his pulse was a clue to the reason for her alarm. She was certain that she should flee the opposite way, into the mist.

"Don't be a fool," Thora shouted. "Charybdis, you are not to let her go."

"Haven't you figured it out yet?" Cavanaugh continued. "Thora's a wraith, just like you. We gave her freedom. We gave her autonomy to create. We could give the same to you."

"What is happening to Lyles?"

"Why do you care?" Thora insisted.

"She lies," Cavanaugh interjected. "You're the only one who can save him."

"She's in your head," Thora barked. "You must fight her."

"Lyles said he knows where Elle is," Cass said.

Charybdis held fast.

"Look at him," Thora said. "He's completely broken."

"Let her go," Cavanaugh commanded in a voice that carried over the thrum of Lyles's pulse. In response, Cass was able to break free. She started her ascent up the stairs, blocking out Thora's warnings, ignoring her own fear. She pushed past the old woman and knelt next to Lyles. He was shaking so violently that she hesitated.

She touched his shoulder, and the contact was like touching a live electrical wire. She felt her body stiffen and the white room around her blurred to gray and then black.

When she opened her eyes again, the interior of the castle had changed. The air was dim and dusty. The walls were stone and great chunks were missing revealing daylight through a dirty plastic tarp. The grand marble staircase had changed to rotting wood. She sat up and looked around for Thora, Lyles, or Cavanaugh. They'd vanished and she was there alone. She called out for Thora and got no answer. She stood and looked over the now dilapidated railing, a clutter of broken stone. She saw movement, a slight shadow. She reached for the gun at her waist and found nothing there.

She backed away, but not far enough where she could not lose sight of the figure picking through the debris and up the stairs. Cass hunkered down a bit and waited. The figure paused, waiting, and she could hear breathing. The head turned, scanning the second floor.

"Who's there?" a trembling voice asked.

Cass went numb because that voice belonged to Elle. She stood slowly and whispered her name. The figure spotted her and flattened against the wall.

"Elle, is that you?" Cass asked in a shaky voice. No answer came. She was shaking, not just her voice, her entire body. Hope flashed through her body in the form of a shiver.

"Elle, it's me. You don't have to be afraid."

The figure straightened in the near darkness.

"Who are you?"

That was her voice certainly. If only there was light, she could see her. She longed for nothing more than to see Elle standing in a shaft of sunlight.

"It's me. Cass," she said.

"Cass?" she asked in a gasp of disbelief.

She quickly made her way down the stairs. "I'm here."

Elle moved away from her but stopped. Cass could not quite make out her features through the dimness.

"Let's get out of here," Cass told her. "We can talk about it when we're far away from this place."

She ran to close the space between them. She reached out into the darkness and caught hold of her arms. She nearly drew the other body into her own, but there was something wrong with the touch. It didn't feel like Elle. Something was wrong.

Cass stepped away to see that it was Lyles. But she'd heard Elle's voice and she'd seen her form creeping through the darkness. She looked around, confused, and summoned the Aegis.

"Cass Hunt," Lyles said cheerfully as if they were old friends running into each other.

She gave him a shove, startled by his appearance. "Where is Elle? Where are we?"

He stumbled backward, nearly tripping over debris. "Elle. I don't know where she is. We're in the broken castle in the mountain."

Cass shook her head. "Where are Thora and Cavanaugh? They were here…"

"They're in the gloaming. In a white room."

She looked at him, puzzled.

"The gloaming," he said. "It's a place, but not a place."

Cass stalked toward him and grabbed the front of his shirt. "I'm losing my patience. Between you and Thora and Cavanaugh. All the mind fucks, the smoke and mirrors. You liked Elle, Lyles. She sympathized with you."

She heard a chuff and felt a sob come from him.

"I'm sorry," he cried as he sagged in her grasp. "I'm so sorry."

She took a breath and released him. Lyles was an innocent.

"I did see Elle," he said. "I saw her in a white room."

"A place that's not a place," she said. "Yes, you told me, but that doesn't make any sense to me."

"You were just in one." His voice quivered. "I was supposed to separate you from the other two, take you into the mist, but I was able to resist them."

"You did well," she told him. Whatever a white room was to Lyles, she was glad that he had been strong enough to help her.

"Where are the women I was with?" she asked.

"I can take you to them," he said.

He led her to the back of the staircase. The dimness faded to black, but she could make out the frame of a door. In the distance she could see a red glow like the ones in the passage that led to the great hall.

"This will lead us into the mountain?"

"Yes, but we may have trouble on the way."

She sighed. "There's always trouble. Lead the way, Lyles."

Cass did not know if she could trust Lyles, but what choice did she have? According to him Cavanaugh wanted her out of the way. That meant Thora could be in danger. Had she walked them into a trap?

Lyles led her down the narrow passage, dark but for the strange red lights. She could see him in front of her, his shaggy hair painted red by the scarlet glow. Occasionally, he would glance over his shoulder at her. He did not say a word. He'd mentioned that there would be trouble. She kept the gun Thora had outfitted her with behind her back. She eased the safety off.

"You've been this way before?" she asked.

"I think so," he said. "I learned to hold on to my memories, to know when I am in a white room and when I am not."

Again, with the white room. She could not imagine what horrors had been done to him since Kuwait.

He led her to a metal door with a hand wheel turn. He tried to turn it, but his arms were too weak. She took over and opened the door. It creaked loudly and she waited a moment before peeking around the frame.

On the other side of the door, there was an unremarkable hallway. She gave Lyles the go-ahead to show her the way. They moved down the dim hall. There were handle-less doors with glowing biometric scanners. Lyles moved passed them quickly but stopped at a large pane of observation glass. He stared into the darkened space, his face a blur in the reflection.

"I thought the war was hell," he said.

Cass felt her jaw tighten. Another life caught up in Olympicorp's machine. According to Thora, the castle in the mountain was six hundred years old. How many lives had been trampled in its wake? She felt dread to think that Elle was one of those lives.

"Let's keep moving," she said.

As they approached the corner, she could hear a jaunty whistle. Lyles stopped. She pulled at the back of Lyles's shirt. When he turned, she motioned for him to get behind her and showed him the gun. The whistling approached.

She rounded the corner quickly and saw a tall, thin, balding man, his back to them as he stared at a monitor. He gasped and stared behind her at Lyles.

"Osbourne," Lyles said. "Funny to run into you."

"What are you doing here, Lyles?"

"Paying you a little visit. Thought we could play with some of your toys," he growled.

Osbourne took a step backward.

"Where did Cavanaugh take Thora and Charybdis?" Cass asked him.

The man's brow furrowed. "It's over, Gorgon. Soon Thora will be where all defective wraiths end up, as will you."

"You're in no place to make threats, Osbourne," Lyles said.

A movement in the monitor Osbourne had studied caught Cass's attention. She saw a small space that she realized was pitch-black revealed in the grainy, faded green of a night vision camera. A figure lay on the floor, limbs constricted in a distress Cass knew well. Though the victim's eyes were covered by a strange piece of Olympicorp tech that resembled a falconry hood, she knew it was Charybdis.

She turned to Osbourne, her fury rising with the cold feeling in her brain. She had to temper both lest she kill the man who had the know-how to free Charybdis from the prison on the screen.

"You've fucked up, buddy," Lyles said. "You'd better start cooperating."

"Get her out of there now," Cass told him.

Without a word, Osbourne went to the almost seamless outline of a door. He pulled at a few latches and opened the door. Cass moved closer to see in person what was on the screen. Charybdis writhed on the small floor space. Her boots were gone but she still wore the clothes she'd had on when they walked into the Great Hall. She flailed her limbs, valiantly fighting whatever Osbourne was doing to her, though it must have caused her much pain. She'd lost control of her bladder.

"Get that thing off her," Cass told him.

He hesitated. "She'll kill me."

"You deserve it," she said.

Osbourne took a breath. "I should sedate her first—"

"No more drugs," Lyles interjected. He moved in a quick shuffle, the closest he could come to running in his state, and gave Osbourne a push.

Osbourne stumbled forward. He caught himself before he could fall. He tried to move around Charybdis without alerting her to his presence. She sensed him and managed to still herself. Osbourne looked back at them, his fear apparent. Charybdis lunged. He yelped.

Cass moved in to help. She touched Charybdis's shoulder as she was attempting to blindly strangle Osbourne.

Once she sensed her touch, Charybdis calmed. She turned trembling and leaned into Cass who embraced her.

"It's okay, now," she told her, though she doubted she could hear her through the device on her head.

Osbourne moved in and removed the thing and backed away as Charybdis lifted her head enough to give him a squinty glare as her eyes needed time to adjust to the light.

Cass helped her up and into a chair.

Osbourne tried to use the distraction to escape. Lyles may not have been fast enough to chase him down, but he did have the wherewithal to trip him. Osbourne fell to the floor.

He turned over quickly, looking at them with disdain.

"Not so fast," Lyles said, giving him a sloppy grin.

"Where is Thora?" Cass asked.

"I won't tell you anything," Osbourne said.

"You will," Lyles said, stepping forward. "Or maybe Cass here can help me give you a good old-fashioned lobotomy in one of those labs."

She left Charybdis to join him. Together, they lifted Osbourne to his feet and pinned him to the wall.

Cass tapped into that cold part of her brain and gave him a blast of the Aegis. He flattened against the wall banging his head and leaving a crack in the sheetrock. He cried out. At the same time, the force of the Aegis caused Lyles to lose his footing.

Osbourne was afraid, and she did not need to read his pulse to sense his fear.

Behind her, Lyles was on the floor hysterically laughing.

"Who needs a lobotomy? I wonder how much of that power of Cass's your bones and organs can take?"

He tried to bargain. "I can show you the way out. Leave this place. Whatever Thora told you, it's over now."

Cass gave him another blast of the Aegis and Osbourne's knees buckled.

Lyles rejoined her at a reasonable distance. "You want us to leave, Ozzy? We're just starting to have fun."

"Okay, okay," he said and took a shaky breath. "Go down this hall—"

"No way. You're going to show us how to get there, personally," Lyles told him.

"Good idea," Cass said and gave Osbourne a shove. He fell to the floor and gingerly picked himself up, then straightened his coat and tie before walking with a slight limp.

"No tricks," Lyles growled.

Charybdis was already on her socked feet. Cass was glad to see her back to normal. The three of them followed Osbourne as he led them to an elevator and pressed the sixth button on the control panel. There were no numbers. The elevator rose. There was a dull chime from above and the doors slid open.

She stepped out of the elevator into a warehouse-sized space, its ceiling high, the bare rock of the mountain. Below the rocky ceiling, a grid of steel girders had been mounted with lighting and other equipment. Then there were pods. Sleek and white, slim on one end and wide at the other. Not like the upright tubes Fletcher used. There were pods stacked on shelves encased in glass, and along rows stretching the width of the room. Each pod in the row was connected to a system of wires and cables that reminded Cass of Thora's vine.

Up ahead, she could see a group of people gathered under lights. Their heads were bent, intent on something. Cass crept forward, her gun drawn. As she neared, the group shifted and she saw the prone body of Thora on a metal gurney, her entire head encapsulated in a black helmet. She was attended to by four figures dressed in dark blue scrubs. Cavanaugh waited among them. She clutched Thora's cane in her gnarled hand.

She spoke sternly to the others as something on a monitor caught her attention. Cass thought for a second that she'd been noticed, but then Thora began to seize violently.

The scrubs sprang into action as Cass debated her next move. Charybdis appeared brandishing a gun and they raised their hands and backed away. She yelled at them as Thora continued to shake on the table.

The figure of a woman appeared in her periphery. Cass turned to fully see her, slight build, dressed in a gray trench coat and carrying an Uzi. A blast from the Aegis pushed her off her feet and a spray of bullets into the ceiling.

Cass turned to the others and saw that Thora had stopped seizing and the scrubs had scattered.

Cavanaugh stepped forward, a gun in her trembling hand. In the other, she held Thora's cane.

"I don't want to shoot you," Cass told her.

"Nor I you," Cavanaugh said.

"What are you doing to Thora?"

She smiled. "She's overdue for reprogramming. Just like you."

Cass recalled her words earlier. She'd discounted the revelation as more of their double-speak banter. Seeing Thora there on that table, her head covered in mind-control tech filled her with a daunting fear more powerful than the nanocloud.

"She was once the best," Cavanaugh said. "She excelled at everything we threw at her. Her handler was a brilliant man named Geist."

Cass looked to the cane she held in her hand.

Cavanaugh once again read her mind. "Yes, that very one. He trained her to program wraiths, and she excelled at that too. Join me. I can give you your reporter, but I doubt there will be much of her left when it is all said and done."

"Stop," Cass barked. "What do you know about Elle's disappearance?"

Cavanaugh continued to back away. The woman in gray who had attacked Cass had collected herself and joined her.

"Thora can answer your questions if you can rouse her. Ask about Project Songbird."

"Cass, we got a problem here," Lyles said.

On the gurney, Thora's prone body was beginning to convulse again. Charybdis hovered close, her hands on Thora's chest as if she could jolt her back to normal.

When Cass turned back to Cavanaugh, she was gone, as was the Geist device.

Shit.

Cass went to Thora and studied the helmet on her head before removing it. Her face twitched rapidly as her entire body shook with such violence the gurney rattled.

"Get that thing off her." Lyles brought Osbourne over. He stammered and hesitated for a moment.

"You have to promise me first, I want protection."

"Okay," Cass agreed.

"Help me lift her," he said.

Cass and Charybdis helped to raise Thora's seizing body into a sitting position. Osbourne ordered them to hold her head still. When they did, he pulled away the helmet-like device. Attached to the inner lining was a double-stranded cord. Cavanaugh's scrubs had plugged the other end into the base of her skull before the first vertebrae.

Osbourne pulled it away as if he were removing a Band-Aid. Cass winced at the meaty, sucking noise.

Cass settled her back onto the gurney. She was cold, but it was not the chill of death. She was still breathing.

"What's wrong with her?" she asked Osbourne.

"She needs adrenaline," he answered, glancing around. He went to a drawer and pulled out several small injection bottles.

Thora groaned. Her eyelids fluttered. Cass touched her shoulder and she responded with another groan. Cass leaned over and used her palm to pat the side of Thora's face.

Osbourne returned to the table with the bottles and began to prepare an injection.

Thora's entire body began to tremble, not as violently as before, but still as frightening to see. Cass felt her pulse. It was like a handful of coins tossed on the floor to bounce, roll, spin, and wobble. Without thinking, she grabbed her hand. To her surprise, Thora gripped it back.

"Good," Osbourne said. "She's still with us. Open her shirt."

Cass did so, revealing the pale, soft skin, wrinkled with age. A sports bra held her small breasts. Osbourne plunged the needle into her chest.

Thora tightened her grip on Cass's hand.

"The second one needs to go into the site of the prod," Osbourne said.

Cass turned Thora over onto her side. She watched as he slid the needle into one of the holes left by the prod. Once he declared that he was done, she eased Thora back against her arms. She removed the needle and tossed it aside. She felt Thora's body relax on her arm, then go limp. Cass looked at her face and saw that her eyes were wide open but not focused. Her mouth was slack.

Cass felt her heart stop. She looked to Charybdis who wore an expression of complete helplessness. Cass tried to reassure her, sure Thora would wake soon. She shook Thora and called her name.

Nothing.

She lowered her to the table and checked for a pulse in her neck. She could still make out her other pulse faintly. There was something there. She just had to wake up.

Nothing.

Cass felt her breath coming quick. She began to compress Thora's chest. She breathed into her mouth, then went back to compressions. She felt a groan in her throat, tears stung her eyes, and she had to steady herself. More breathing into Thora's mouth. More compressions. She could hear herself muttering but found she could not make out her own words. She paused to turn around, searching the room for some aid, a defibrillator, anything.

She heard a sharp gasp and turned back to Thora, who gripped the sides of the table and stared out wide-eyed. Cass leaned over her to let her know that she was there. Thora's eyes fell on her and she reached out to her. Their hands met and gripped each other as if they were both trying to save the other from drowning.

"You're okay," Cass told her.

Thora nodded and released a deep, ragged breath.

"My cane," she wheezed.

Thora sat up on her own, her chest rising and falling rapidly.

"Cavanaugh took it," Cass said.

"You should have shot her," she said. "I should be sitting here looking at her corpse."

"I think you just died," Charybdis said.

Thora ignored the comment, her focus solely on Cass. "You must go after them. Just leave me here."

"That's not part of our deal," Cass said. "I came here for information about Elle."

"If Cavanaugh gets away with that device this is all for nothing. Even if you save Elle, you won't be able to shield her or yourself from the fallout."

"Fallout?"

Thora roared at her. "This one time I need you to act without questioning me."

Cass backed away from the table.

"I've got things here," Charybdis said

Cass nodded. She checked her gun and sprinted back to the elevators where Lyles waited with Osbourne. She was certain that Lyles had whispered his plans of revenge while she was away.

"Cavanaugh and some others left with something that belongs to Thora," she said to Osbourne. "They're in a hurry to leave this place. Where would they have gone?"

He swallowed hard. "The helipad."

Of course, there was a helipad. "How do I get there?"

"Take this elevator," he said and pressed one of the buttons. "Once you get off, you'll go right. No left—"

Lyles thumped the back of his head. "No time for doubts, my friend."

Osbourne cowered. "Left, it's left, I'm certain. There is a cart to ride if you prefer. There is a long corridor. It will lead to another elevator. Press the button to the top floor."

She looked to Lyles for confirmation, but his eyes told her he had no idea.

"If you're lying to me, I'll let him do what he wants to you," she told Osbourne. "In the meantime, you'll help look after Thora"

They left the elevator and the doors closed leaving her alone.

During the ride she thought of Elle. All of this and she did not feel any closer to finding her. She'd found out more about her origins, and Thora's as well. It bothered her to think she would have that much in common with her old handler. If Elle were there, she would help Cass to navigate her tempest of emotion; her words and her touch would be a balm.

The elevator stopped and Cass stepped out. She found two long corridors on either side of her. As Osbourne had described, there were three carts. She jumped on one, turned the key, and went left as instructed.

She pushed the pedal to full speed trying to convince herself that she could not run faster. She needed to conserve her strength. The hall dead-ended at another elevator. There were three unmarked buttons. She pushed the top button. The elevator ascended and lurched to a stop. Even before the doors slid open, Cass could hear an engine and the blades of a helicopter.

She found herself on a concrete path carved into the side of a rocky wall, trimmed with railing. Above was the sky fully exposed, trimmed by the edges of the mountain. She peered down and saw a small black helicopter directly below hovering toward her.

Cass began to run down the path at full speed, her gun drawn. She was confident she could shoot the tail rotor and disable it. The result would be a crash, possibly harming the people inside. Not that they deserved her sympathy. Still, it would be easier to retrieve Thora's cane if there were minimal damages.

The helicopter continued to rise. She could see Cavanaugh watching her.

There was not much time to act. She raised the gun and aimed at the tail rotor. She fired. She saw the spark of the impact and heard the rotor give and sputter. She fired at the glass to unnerve the pilot and passengers. The bullets bounced off, but her ploy worked. As the helicopter began to lazily spin into a descent, she could see the panic on their faces.

The helicopter drifted as it spun, scraping the mountain wall. The rotors chopped at the rock sending a flurry of sparks. Cass took a deep breath and summoned the cold feeling in her brain and blasted the Aegis's power just beneath the skids. The helicopter bounced upward, dragging against the rocky wall of the mountain. The top rotor continued to spin, causing the now bent and broken blades to propel it along at a choppy gait.

Cass marveled she could use the Aegis to keep the copter aloft. She pondered how she could ease the thing down and avoid the crash as planned. She only had experience using the Aegis in short bursts, even with the strange black cloud that had pursued them in the woods. She pulled back, and the helicopter tilted forward in a nosedive.

Cass turned her attention and the Aegis to the cockpit sending a blast to try to upright the copter. The effort caused the copter not to right itself, but instead to succumb to the force of the damaged rotors and spin, nose down. Still, it remained upright. She tried again to pull back the power of the Aegis. The helicopter dropped a few feet, but easier this time. Cass leaned over the railing as it sank, ignoring the pain, the stinging fire of the cold the Aegis brought.

The helicopter fell the last ten feet onto its side. Cass went after them via metal stairs at the end of the scaffold. When she reached the wreckage, she saw that the scrubs were trapped inside. She climbed onto the landing gear and peered down into the cockpit to see their frightened faces.

The engine was on fire.

Cass pried open the door. The pilot had not survived the fall.

She regarded the disorder of bodies inside the passenger area. She could feel the jangle of their pulses, their fear. Among them, she could see Cavanaugh, limp, still clutching the Geist device. The pilot had not been the only casualty. Cass thought of Thora, barely out of whatever the scrubs had done to her, insisting that she fetch the mysterious weapon.

Cass locked eyes with one of the surviving passengers. "Give me the Geist device."

Without a word, the woman slid the cane out of Cavanaugh's grasp. She handed it to Cass who realized that this was the woman in the trench coat who had brandished an uzi at her earlier.

"Please," she said. "Allow me to talk to Thora."

"Who are you?" Cass asked.

"Dr. Greta Liang," she said.

Cass studied her for a moment and offered her hand. She seemed to know Thora. If she wanted to turn, she should have the chance. She was certain that Thora would not turn down the aid of a new minion.

She reached out her hand and helped her climb out of the overturned helicopter. The others reached out their hands for her begging for help.

It looked as if Thora had a few more underlings.

She freed the rest of them from the wreckage. She stayed long enough to supervise them with extinguishing the smoldering craft. None of them seemed too concerned with Cavanaugh. What had she died for? A weapon? How had she lived? None of her colleagues had stopped to mourn her and were quick to slither to Thora.

Cass turned away from the wreckage in disgust.

CHAPTER ELEVEN

The Great Hall

Thora was on her feet when they arrived. She was inspecting some equipment and speaking with Osbourne. Lyles was stretched out on the gurney, not as an experiment, his arms were folded behind his head. He was taking a nap. The scrubs and Dr. Liang waited on the fringes, standing in a row like privates in the army waiting to be addressed.

She saw Cass and smiled, reaching out for the Geist device. "I knew you wouldn't fail me." She raised her eyebrow when Cass did not immediately relinquish it.

"I don't know if I should give this to you."

Thora gave a grim smile. "You don't have to. You can keep it for yourself."

Cass gave her a hard stare and handed her the cane. Thora returned it to her side and looked to Dr. Liang and the others watching their exchange.

"I didn't instruct you to take prisoners."

"She said she wanted to talk to you. I suppose the others do as well."

"I know of a few of them," Thora said.

Dr. Liang took a breath. "My loyalty is to Olympicorp not Cavanaugh. We had a good working relationship and once we were even fond of each other, but for me time weathers such feelings."

Thora scoffed. "Cassandra, Dr. Liang is a true cultist. She sees Olympicorp as a religion, man's true salvation. She will gladly let others stand on her shoulders, blind to the fact that the so-called enlightened are mad only for power and wealth."

Dr. Liang looked to Cass. "Perhaps I have been blind in the past. You spared our lives twice today. You used your ability to save us. Cavanaugh would have wrangled the both of you."

Thora scoffed again and looked to Cass, then Dr. Liang. "Despite your sentimental words, I have use for your intellect and knowledge. I extend the offer to you as well, Dr. Osbourne. It will not be an easy road, but I will never stand on your shoulders."

Charybdis appeared. She moved slowly and glanced about with red-rimmed eyes. She saw Cass and smiled.

"It seems I am not the only one in your debt," Thora said.

"What about Lyles?" she said. He was still napping on the gurney oblivious to the scene around him.

"I'm not a babysitter," Thora said.

"You have to at least get him to civilization and set him up with a passport and money to go wherever he wants."

Lyles sat up. "That," he shouted. "That is exactly what I want."

"I suppose we have the resources here on the premises," Thora said and looked to her new underlings. "Correct?"

Osbourne nodded.

"Don't forget your promise to me, Thora," Cass said. "Where's Elle? What is Project Songbird?"

Thora seemed surprised at her last question.

"Well?" Cass asked.

"Osbourne, you seem to know your way around here. Can you show her to the archives, help her find any information she asks for," Thora said.

Osbourne nodded. "Right this way."

As they were leaving, Thora announced that she was hungry.

The archive was another large room, except instead of pods there were rows of tall glowing shelves. She and Osbourne arrived there after an elevator ride and a long walk down a silent corridor. Dark and quiet save for an electric hum, the space had a library feel. Just in case anyone could ever forget they were inside a mountain beneath an ancient castle, the walls that encased the dark paneled shelves were naked rock.

Osbourne showed her to a black podium with a flatscreen on top.

"What exactly are you looking for?" he asked.

"What do you have about Project Songbird?"

He typed out the words, then stood back a bit and looked expectantly toward the shelves. Cass looked too. A few seconds into their vigil, a strange figure zipped between the aisles up ahead and disappeared around the bend. Cass took a few steps to follow, but the figure returned gliding toward them. The head was arrow-shaped, the body was segmented into two parts. It had no legs, only whirring wheels somewhere underneath. It stopped in front of Cass, a readout glowing a blinking blue as it registered her, the obstacle in its path. After a moment, it extended one arm which held a tablet.

"File number 6735-29A," the robot announced in a female voice. "Have a lovely day, Dr. Osbourne."

Cass took the tablet. There was a padded cover with a flap to protect the screen from the robot's grippers. She exposed the glowing screen. It felt like Kazakhstan and her time with Fletcher. Like then, she hoped to find information about Elle only to find that it was all a ruse.

On the tablet's main screen there was only one icon, a blue circle with white trim. She tapped it with her finger and two more icons were revealed, a video icon in the shape of a triangle turned on its side, and another a file icon.

Cass tapped the file icon and found an empty white space. She scrolled to look for text but found none. She walked over to Osbourne who waited patiently.

"What does this mean?"

"The information was wiped," he said.

"You guys go through all of this," Cass said as she gestured at the endless rows of shelves. "Just to erase information?"

"Olympicorp erases what is no longer useful," he said. "I am not that familiar with the record keeping practices, but I know this organization. Secrets keep us in business."

Cass turned her attention back to the tablet. She tapped the video icon. The screen flashed to show a video of an office space. Sitting in front of the video to the left was a desk with what looked to be vision testing equipment. Sitting to the right was Elle, but not the Elle Cass knew.

She had to be about fourteen or fifteen years old, on the cusp of womanhood. Her youth brought to Cass a sense of nostalgia and a sense of dread. In the video, young Elle wore her hair in a banged bob, a teen's idea of a mature look. The punk rock band T-shirt, multiple bracelets, and seashell necklace betrayed her real age. A woman spoke to Elle off-camera, and she answered.

Through their conversation, Cass was able to gather that Elle was under the impression that she was being interviewed for a junior camp counselor position.

"Very good then," the interviewer said. "Now, I hope you don't mind me recording this for the rest of the selection team."

"No, I don't mind at all," she said, and in typical Elle fashion, asked about the bulky piece of equipment that occupied the desk.

The woman asked Elle about school and extracurricular activities in which she participated, as well as her family life.

Young Elle spoke with a practiced confidence that would later come completely naturally as she grew older. She even cracked a joke and chuckled a bit.

"At Camp Blue Creek we like to get to know about our counselors personally. The positions carry a lot of responsibility as you know."

"Sure. Anything for Camp Blue Creek."

"Tell me about your best memory," she said.

On the other side of space and time, Cass felt as if the floor would crumble beneath her. She'd heard that voice before saying those exact same words. One of Fletcher's cronies who had flashed her brain and questioned her at the SDC headquarters.

Elle paused thoughtfully before answering. "It would have to be the day my mom was sworn into office of the Georgia legislature. I was so proud of her that day, well, I still am. She worked hard to get where she is. Imagine all the little girls like me who will visit the capitol in Atlanta who will see her picture hanging in the main hall."

"That is so wonderful," the woman said. "I am sure she is quite proud of you as well."

Elle smiled shyly. She had no idea of the peril she was in sitting with that woman.

"Now for the grunt part of the interview," the woman said. "We're testing the vision of all the candidates. It's a liability thing."

The two shared a few more pleasantries before the interviewer instructed Elle to look into the viewfinder and describe what she saw. Cass gasped as Elle did so and quickly snatched her face away.

"What?" she asked, clearly upset to the point that she was breathless. "What is this supposed to be?"

The woman behind the desk asked her what was wrong, her tone flat with a fraudulent concern. Cass knew the tone well, the lull before something awful came from a man in a white coat, or Thora or Fletcher.

"What did you see?"

"Something bad," Elle sniffed. "Why?"

"What did you see?" the woman asked again.

"A baby. It was injured. The jaw…it was gone. Why did you show me this?"

"It's just a test. To check the nerves of our candidates. What if a camper falls and breaks their leg?"

"I am certain that I would know to keep calm in an emergency situation," Elle said in true Elle fashion.

"One can never tell. Look again. You'll notice it changed."

She hesitated. "Are you sure?"

Slowly, she ducked her head to peer through the viewfinder once again. She looked up toward the camera. Her eyes seemed to have lost all expression.

"What did you see this time?" the woman asked.

Elle did not answer, instead her shoulders dropped. She seemed to have gone completely limp. Cass knew exactly what had happened. The woman was washing Elle. But why?

"Elle?" the woman asked.

Nothing.

The overhead lights lowered to near darkness and the camera self-adjusted. A minute passed and the woman stepped into the frame. Cass recognized her as the owner of the voice, the woman Fletcher sent to drag what memories she could from her brain. Dr. Branch, at least a younger version. Instead of a lab coat, she wore a bright yellow sweatshirt emblazoned with the so-called camp's logo. Her hair was styled into a short black afro. She wore a pair of gold-rimmed glasses.

Cass did not keep a tally of people who had wronged her. She found, especially in Thora's case, that the lines between enemy and ally were thin. She only wanted Elle back. Seeing Dr. Branch handle Elle pled the case for vengeance, as Cass never on her own volition wanted so much to end someone's life

In the video, she straightened Elle back into the chair, arranging her hands in her lap. She used a light to check her eyes and rolled back her sleeve and injected something into her veins. A man entered the room and hovered over Elle, touching her with pale thin hands.

He left a few moments later. Dr. Branch returned to her original place. All was quiet for a moment and then the lights began to dim. Strangely, music began to play, the rhythmic tinkle of a piano accompanied by a somber horn led into a brash bluesy chorus of horns. A woman began to sing in a sultry voice about stormy weather. A red glow rose like the sun of an alien planet and then it began to pulse bathing Elle and the room in seconds-long flashes. Cass figured it to be an earlier version of the techniques Branch used on her in Kazakhstan.

The song continued, reaching its climax, the singer crooning about feeling heavy hearted and sad. All the while Elle lay there in the flashing red light. When the song ended, the overhead lights brightened, and Dr. Branch announced that they were ready to continue. Elle opened her eyes and blinked rapidly.

"Just look this way and explain why you think you would be the best fit for our junior counselor program," Dr. Branch said sweetly.

Cass waited.

Elle straightened and her eyes opened as alert as she was when she first entered the office. She did not react to the flashing red light or the interviewer's voice. She sat there non-blinking and still.

"I love Lena Horne."

"Yes, she is a wonderful singer," the interviewer said. "Did you know that she was the first black performer to sign a contract with a major motion picture studio?"

Elle smiled a sleepy grin that Cass knew well from their few morning encounters. She felt a dull ache from her heart to her stomach, a sickness that felt terminal and outweighed all the hope she had for her and Elle.

On the screen, the interviewer continued as before, asking the same questions about Elle's school life. Elle answered normally, her body relaxed. Her eyes told of something else. They watered over and dripped tears, the left eye began to spasm, a rapid tic that pulled at that entire side of her face.

The video ended there.

Without a word, Cass left the room, clutching the screen under her arm. She made her way back toward the pod warehouse to find it deserted. Osbourne reminded her that Thora had requested food. He directed her to a mess hall where Lyles was serving up steaming bowls of soup while Liang and Thora sat in deep discussion. Her old handler had found herself a pleasing acolyte.

Cass tossed the tablet in between them.

"What did you monsters do to Elle?"

"I did nothing to her," Thora said. "Project Songbird was a collaboration with the Americans. We introduced them to a new technique for washing sleeper agents."

"You knew about this the entire time. Were you ever going to tell me?"

"Would you have believed me?" she asked.

"You're saying that Elle is a sleeper agent. How?"

Thora straightened in her chair. She was weary and in definite need of some rest.

"I was not involved in the project and did not know of it until your paths crossed. It is my theory that Olympicorp intentionally exposed you to her to discredit me and my work."

Dr. Liang interjected. "I can confirm that," she said in a shaky voice.

Cass pointed to the tablet. "What are they doing to her here?"

Thora raised her eyebrows. She took a moment to skim through the video, Liang peering over her shoulder. When she was finished, she sighed.

"Tell me, Thora."

"This mind-control technique freezes part of the mind, the task, to implant information, intelligence, directions that could be thawed over time or by a series of triggers, such as that song."

"She's a civilian. She was a child," Cass said, but doubted that mattered to anyone present. Thora looked nonplussed.

"Why did they do this to her? How did they get access to her?"

"It does not take much to be a candidate," Dr. Liang spoke up. "She was young, bright, and ambitious. The American government had been known to recruit students through schools or even summer camps. The kids then live normal lives until they are activated."

"They were in the background the whole time," Thora added. "They molded her. I would deduce that they influenced her choice of career. It gave her a platform to cast the net to snare people like the solider and you."

She noticed that Charybdis watched the exchange silently. Had she known what was happening with Elle?

Cass asked Thora, "What do you mean snare?"

"As you and other wraiths have the ability to read brainwaves, the Americans have created a specific pattern for agents like Elle to emit which disrupts programming," Thora said. "I suspect she may have influenced Lyles, triggering the fall of the Olympicorp facility in Kuwait."

Thora looked to Liang who nodded in agreement.

Lyles spoke up. "I saw her in the white room. I can find her again."

Cass ignored him. She stared at Thora. The more she learned, the deeper a feeling of dread welled in the pit of her stomach.

"Do you know who took her?"

"I am certain it was the Americans," Thora said, turning her gaze to Cass. "With all the press around her disappearance, her trip to Kuwait during the so-called Bedouin revolt, her involvement with you, who they are calling a terrorist."

"Why would they set her up like this?"

"Because the Americans are opportunists with deep ties to Olympicorp and the Pantheon. Elle will be the mouse the housecat brings to the owner's hearth."

"I have to find her," Cass said, frantic now. "I helped you, Thora, now it's time you fulfilled your end of our bargain."

"Do you not see or are you being willfully blind?" Thora asked, standing with some effort. "Those warm and toasty feelings that you have for Elle are all false."

Cass backed away from her shaking her head. "You're wrong."

"It's time that you shed this ridiculous romance narrative. Now you know the truth about me as well. You've seen it." She motioned to Lyles and Liang. "You have witnesses on both sides here to attest—"

Cass summoned the Aegis before she could rein herself back. The air left the room for a split second before returning in a short burst that rattled the walls. Thora stumbled backward onto Liang. Charybdis stepped in between them.

"How ridiculous. How foolish," she declared, straightening with the aid of Liang. "You've been tight-roping without a net. It's a wonder you haven't been killed. Elle's your handler now, and she's not a very good one."

"Elle freed me," Cass said, furiously blinking back tears as she spoke. "She's the way for me. She's my future."

"You're not free, you're a fool."

"Then our partnership has ended. You don't know where Elle is, and I doubt you'd take time from your tour of vengeance to help me find her."

They stared at each other for a moment.

"Are you a wraith?"

"Yes, I was Echidna," Thora said. "I was given autonomy in order to create wraiths."

Cass turned to Charybdis. "And you knew this the whole time?"

"Yes, I knew," she said.

"It was not her place to tell you," Thora said. "It was mine."

"You know what life is like for wraiths," Cass said. "You continue to enslave and torture people?"

"I gave myself purpose. Unlike you, I realized my potential."

"I'm giving myself purpose," Cass said. "And my potential will not be spent oppressing others, contributing to a monstrous cycle."

"I brought you to the truth. None of it is a mystery anymore. You know what you are now, what you were meant to be, and what I did to make you great."

"I'm not as blind as you think. I'm going to save Elle. No one deserves this fate, not even you, Thora."

"I know where to find Elle," Lyles announced.

Thora smirked. "Ridiculous."

"I've seen her with my own eyes," he insisted. "You saw her too, Cass."

She thought for a moment of Elle, lost and crying in the dark. It had seemed so real.

"What happened to us earlier, Thora?" Cass asked. "One second we were together and the next, I woke up in ruins chasing after Elle."

"I found myself with a yoke around my neck," Charybdis said.

"You were in the white room," Lyles said.

"What? Where is that?"

"Somewhere in the gloaming," he said.

Thora scoffed. "No offense, sir, but look at the state of you. Whatever Cavanaugh thought she could learn from you was a shot in the dark. A last-ditch effort to try to hold on to her power."

Cass made a show of ignoring her. It was clear that Thora did not want to hear what Lyles had to say. There had to be a reason.

"Tell us more about this gloaming," she prodded him.

"When they brought me back from Kuwait, I was in worse shape than I am," he said. "I was having these experiences. When they would put me in those pods, I would leave my body and fly."

His last statement elicited a bitter chortle from Thora. "Which was a bad reaction from the drugs in your system combined with the toxin from Kuwait."

Osbourne cleared his throat. "Actually, we were able to learn a great deal from Mr. Lyles about shared unconsciousness. This discovery led to some revelations about mind programming."

Thora began to protest, but Cass spoke over her.

"So what is shared unconsciousness?" she asked Osbourne.

"Just what it sounds like," he answered. "Imagine an asset, taken prisoner, or in a remote location, or a wraith lost to their handler. They could communicate, coordinate. The handler could reprogram a wraith from afar."

"Theoretically." Thora interjected.

"Until we took a closer look at Lyles," Dr. Liang spoke up. "Cepilon, that toxin he was exposed to in Kuwait, was the catalyst for the anomaly."

"When Cavanaugh would put me under, I could hear Elle. Calling out. Afraid."

Cass felt her skin prickle at the thought.

"Were you able to find out anything about her location?"

He shook his head. "She's confused, afraid."

"Do you think there could be a way to communicate with her?" Cass asked.

Dr. Liang looked to Osbourne who shrugged.

"Perhaps," Dr. Liang said. She began to furiously type notes into a tablet.

"Elle was also exposed to Cepilon," Cass told them.

Thora was beyond agitated. "If there is any merit to what he's saying it could take years of experimentation to nail down a method."

"Perhaps," Dr. Liang repeated. "We could use the Geist device."

Everyone stared at her waiting for an explanation. Thora raised her hands in exasperation and walked away.

"The Geist device synchronizes the brainwaves of anyone who has been programmed, thanks to Cepilon, Lyles was able to connect a large group of people in a hive mind. Now, he can pull anyone dosed with Cepilon into a white room," Dr. Liang said. "Elle was exposed in Kuwait, but that has been some time."

"I see now," Osbourne said. "The Geist device could work as a satellite."

"Or a beacon," Dr. Liang added.

"Have you two forgotten that you work for me?" Thora asked. "We do not have time for any of this. It could take days. Weeks. Years."

"You promised to help me find Elle."

She sighed. "And how much time should I devote to this endeavor of yours? How long before you see reason?"

"You wouldn't be here if I hadn't destroyed the nano cloud," Cass reminded her. "You would be on that table."

Thora relented. "Three days. I will give you three days to sort this out."

Cass gave her a doubtful look and her reply was a smile. "You will have to go into a pod."

"I've done it before. For Elle, I can do it again."

Thora stared at her for a moment and turned to Dr. Liang.

"Prepare her."

CHAPTER TWELVE

Gloaming Hill Facility, West Virginia

Elle woke in her room at Gloaming Hill, not in the bed, but on the floor. She heard a groan and startled. There was no one in the room. The tortured noise had come from her own throat. She tried to move. Her body felt heavy. The bed towered above her; it may as well have been as tall as a skyscraper. The room was dim save for the white light that glowed in the space between the door and the floor.

She was curled into a fetal position, shivering on the cold tile. She slowly stretched her legs to straighten her body. As she did, pain struck like a lightning bolt, and she shrieked, clamping her eyes closed until she saw stars in the darkness there. She writhed on the floor trembling, trying to discern the origin of her injury.

Something else came to her in the dark beneath her eyelids squeezed shut from the ache: a vision of her old friend Rob Loera. He had come to her the night before, but that was impossible because Rob was dead. It had all been some horrible nightmare. She remembered his face, crumpled from the self-inflicted gunshot wound. She remembered the day he came to her office, distraught. She'd tried to calm him, but as she would later consider after the incident, he had come to her so that she could witness his end. Had he come to her because he did not want to be alone? Was it revenge because their work together did not provide the healing they'd both hoped for? Only Rob knew that, and he was dead.

She felt hot tears on her face. His family had chased her out of the church on the day of his funeral. They blamed her. A multi-generation military family, they could not handle that one of their own had come back from battle unable to cope. They claimed that she had made Rob into a sideshow to promote the Green Patriot and her own career.

The door opened and a pair of sensible brown leather loafers walked into the room. She craned her head up and saw Dr. Stevens.

"Oh my God. Elle."

The doctor crossed the space between them and knelt to examine her as she called for the nurses.

"What happened?"

"I fell off the bed," she groaned the words through gritted teeth.

"I noticed," Dr. Stevens said. "Can you sit up?"

"Something hurts really bad," Elle told her.

Nurse Grace entered and gasped. She joined Dr. Stevens and the two of them helped her into a sitting position. In the process, they determined the source of Elle's pain when the nurse touched her right arm. Elle cried out and felt tears on her face.

"I think she may have landed on it," Dr. Stevens said as she gently attempted to straighten Elle's arm, bringing a fresh agony. "We're going to get you something for the pain as soon as possible."

After examining the offending appendage, she looked to Nurse Grace.

"We may have a fracture on our hands. We'll need to X-Ray."

"Do you think you can stand with our help?" she asked Elle.

"I think so," she said, and they helped her to her feet. They guided her back onto the bed. They lifted her clothes and checked her for bruising and found her hip badly bruised, as well as the elbow and upper arm on which she had landed.

"What happened last night?" Dr. Stevens asked.

Elle paused for a moment, not sure how to answer.

"Do you remember?"

She nodded. "I had a bad dream about Rob Loera. I must have thrashed around and fallen out of the bed."

The nurse and Dr. Stevens exchanged frowns, and then looked down at the rails on the side of the bed that would have prevented her from falling off.

"We should make sure that the side railing is secured each night," Dr. Stevens said.

Nurse Grace lowered her eyes. "Yes, that was careless of me."

"Let's just all be a little more mindful in the future," Dr. Stevens said.

She looked to Elle and gave a weak smile. "You too. We have enough work to do without a broken bone or a concussion to slow us down."

Elle nodded. She was watching Nurse Grace leave the room, at the same time, her eyes happened to wander toward the door, and the floor at the corner of the frame.

She knew what the object was as soon as she saw it, and despite the distance and its size, she knew it in exact detail, could feel it in her hands.

Still, she did not believe it was there, just some remnant from her dream that lingered to mock her and glint in the full light of day. Had it been there when she woke on the floor, next to Nurse Grace's white shoes? She tried to remember.

"Elle?" Dr. Stevens asked. "Are you all right?"

Suddenly, she felt as dumb as she did the day she woke from the coma. The doctor's words took a few seconds to register.

"I'm fine."

Dr. Stevens straightened, concern on her face. "I was asking you if you remember any details of the dream about Loera."

"Oh," she answered slowly, her eyes on the button. "I don't."

"Perhaps we should do a scan as well," Dr. Stevens said as she helped her back into a sitting position. "There really is no way to know if you hit your head last night."

Elle gave her a wan smile. "You're the doctor."

Nurse Grace returned and prepped her arm before producing a needle as Dr. Stevens looked on as if she were training a resident. Elle shrank away. Suddenly, she did not want the pain to end, at least, she did not want her senses dulled. She wanted to keep her focus on what she was certain was a brass button, the type that would come from a military dress jacket.

"It's just some morphine, for the pain," Nurse Grace said.

"Sorry, I guess I'm a little jumpy."

Nurse Grace finished injecting the meds and left promptly. Elle felt a heaviness settle over her, spreading, edging out the anxiety. It brought on a queasy feeling like car sickness. Her eyes kept bouncing back toward the button.

"Are you really, okay?" Dr. Stevens asked. "You can tell me, you know."

"Yes, I just feel sore and exhausted."

"Of course." Dr. Stevens patted her leg. "I heard you talked to Dr. Branch."

Elle nodded remembering the clandestine visit in the sunroom, their conversation, and the hope of seeing her mother.

"She can be quite brisk, but I suppose she has to," Dr. Stevens said.

"She said that I would be able to talk to my mom."

"Yes, we're still in the process of making arrangements for that."

"Okay," Elle said. It was hard to divide her attention between Dr. Stevens and the button. She was almost certain that it would not be there when she looked back. That would prove it was only a hallucination. She would tell Dr. Stevens about it and the doctor would gravely insist on taking a look inside Elle's skull for a concussion. The button would be gone because it had never been there in the first place.

She could just tell Dr. Stevens what she saw. She would help Elle figure things out.

While she trusted the doctor, she feared that tiny, shiny object more. She was afraid that Dr. Stevens would see the button and that meant Rob Loera had really been there the night before, that he was back from the dead.

"Tell me what you remember about that dream," Dr. Stevens said.

"Rob was here in my room, and he was very violent, angry with me," Elle said. "I'm not sure why. He was treating me as if I had committed treason." She stopped and remembered that Loera had not been her only visitor the night before. There had been the blond woman as well, cruelly shouting at her as she lay on the floor.

"Elle?" Dr. Stevens asked as she touched her shoulder. "Is something wrong?"

"I'm fine," Elle assured her, though her skin prickled with goose bumps at the thought of the blond woman from the night before. If she searched the room would there be some physical evidence of her as well? The thought frightened her more than zombie Loera or someone posing as Loera to fuck with her head.

"There was someone else from last night," Elle said. "There was a woman."

"Someone you know?"

"No. She was a stranger, about my age. White. Blond. I don't know who was more frightening. Her or Rob."

Dr. Stevens studied her for a moment before reaching out and patting her hand.

"You really gave me a fright, Elle. I didn't know what to think."

"I'm fine," she said. "My arm doesn't hurt so much now."

Dr. Stevens stood. "That would be the drugs taking effect. I'm going to get things ready for a scan. Sit tight."

She exited the room, leaving Elle alone. Well, not exactly alone. There was the button, waiting at the base of the doorway's frame. The doctor would not be away too long. If she was going to get a closer inspection of the button, Elle would have to move quickly.

She lowered the bar on the bed. Even with the morphine, she could still feel a deep dull ache in her arm. She sucked in a breath and slid over the side until her feet touched the floor. Using the bed to lean on, she limped around to the edge. She felt as if she had been hit by a bus. She teetered toward the door, until the button lay between her feet. She stooped over it, expecting it to vanish before her eyes.

The button waited, reflecting the light overhead and casting a shadow on the floor. For a second, she was afraid to disturb the button. She did not have time to hesitate.

She crouched, cradling her hurting arm close to her side. She slowly let out the breath she had been holding as she inspected the button. It did not roll away like a fragile dust bunny, but stood solid, the army insignia etched into brass. Her fingers brushed the button. It moved the width of a hair. The contact startled her. She gasped and scooped it into her palm. The brass felt cool in her hand, the weight familiar.

The button was real.

Rob had been there.

"His face," she said aloud. "How? Why?"

She relaxed her shoulders and took a deep breath. She straightened, made her way back to the bed, and climbed in, out of breath. She made sure to secure the railing back into an upright position.

Once settled, she opened her hand and there it was, as real as the bed beneath her or the room around her. Its existence questioned everything. Dr. Stevens would of course, have a logical explanation of how the button got into her room. Would the doctor's reasoning be a valid rationalization or outright lies?

She heard Dr. Stevens's voice and leaned over to pull out the drawer of her bedside table. She tossed the button in and closed the drawer just as the doctor entered with Nurse Grace who pushed a wheelchair.

"It's just a precaution," Dr. Stevens said. "Besides, you should reserve your energy."

"Okay," Elle said numbly. Nothing made sense anymore, and she should have been angry. She could confront them and demand to see her mother so that she could know what exactly was going on at Gloaming Hill.

Instead, Elle allowed Dr. Stevens and Nurse Grace to help her into the wheelchair. She went along with their tests. She waited quietly as a splint and sling were applied to her arm. They returned her to her bed, and she ate the food from the tray placed in front of her. Dr. Stevens waited around. She seemed worried because Elle had gone mute, giving short answers to their questions. She gave up after Elle finished the late breakfast and left.

It was not until she was alone that Elle allowed herself to replay the events of the night before inside her head. There was the meeting with Dr. Branch in the sunroom. Why had she sent the nurses to come for her at night versus the daytime? Then, there was the appearance of Rob and the blond woman. The whole experience was just a dream/hallucination, a mix of her memories of the Gorgon, the pit, and her guilt over Rob's death. Maybe someone at Gloaming Hill wanted her on edge.

She recalled the exchange with Rob in her head. The scene remained, faded at the edges like any bad dream as the day wore on. He had called her a traitor in so many words and suggested that she knew something about what happened to him.

There was still much about what happened that she did not remember. Just as she dreamed the memories recalled during her therapy in the padded room, her unconscious could have conjured Rob and the blond stranger to bring a vital fact to the surface.

She was no expert on the mind, sadly, not even her own.

Her thoughts turned to the button.

She retrieved it from the drawer, not at all surprised that it was not just a shiny, brass, engraved hallucination in the palm of her hand. The button was cool to the touch and very much real. She put it between her lips and touched the engravings with her tongue as if she were a blind prospector. She resisted the urge to return the button to the drawer and sat there for some time cradling it in her fingers.

She heard the door open and slid the button into the pocket of her sweatshirt as Dr. Stevens slid into the room.

"How are you, Elle?"

"I'm fine, I guess. Tired."

"I fear last night was more traumatic than a sprained wrist," she said. "Perhaps a change of scenery would help?"

"Are we leaving this place?" Elle asked.

She laughed a bit, bowing her head. When she looked up her expression seemed to Elle to be bashful.

"We're only going to my office," she said. "I thought we could have lunch there."

Elle regarded her silently. How could she trust the smiling charming doctor after the night before? She imagined the doctor disputing all the details of Rob's appearance. She would say that he was dead and dead people did not come back to life. She would say that Gloaming Hill was a high security facility. She would say it all with her brow bent in concern and would comfort her. All the while Elle would seethe in her doubts.

Because she knew what she'd seen.

"Something's wrong," Dr. Stevens said. "I can tell."

"Yes, something is wrong," Elle said, her frustration at its peak. "I'm here. I had a whole life before this. I didn't materialize here to be your patient."

"Of course, you didn't." She sighed. "Come with me and we can talk it out. I have comfy chairs."

"Do you have cocktails?"

She laughed, briefly her cheerful self. "I have ginger ale."

"Fine," Elle drawled.

Dr. Stevens went for the wheelchair and Elle tried to refuse, but before she knew it, she was being wheeled out of her room and into the dimly lit white halls of the Gloaming Hill facility. As they started their journey, Elle imagined zombie Rob Loera in his dress uniform roaming those same halls.

"Why does this place always seem so empty?" she asked.

"We keep the patients scattered throughout. Some are still in comas. Others are in various stages of treatment."

"Are there many?"

Dr. Stevens did not answer, and Elle turned a bit in the chair to see a smile on her face.

"What?"

"There's that reporter we all know and love. Asking all the questions."

"Well? How many patients?"

"About thirty."

She wanted to ask if any of them had been in the refrigerated truck with her and Leslie, but she noticed a set of double doors up ahead of them. She knew them to lead to the sunroom. They passed and Elle saw that it was empty. They came to yet another set of doors. Dr. Stevens swiped a card through a reader mounted to the wall. The doors popped open revealing a short hall with three doors, one looked like an elevator.

They stopped in front of a door of gleaming, light colored wood, with a brass plate etched with Dr. Stevens's name. She reached over Elle to use a key to open the door.

"Welcome to my home away from home," she said as she pushed Elle into the spacious office, day compared to the sparse, dim night of Elle's room. Art hung on the walls, and a rug covered the floor.

A large brown leather sofa dominated the middle of the space. Elle left her chair to claim it without being invited. It looked antique and comfy, as Dr. Stevens had described. Next to it a shelf crowded with books captured Elle's attention. She tried to study the titles, but found that the letters trembled, as if they were threatening to blow right off the spines.

Dr. Steven sat on the opposite side and watched Elle examine her new surroundings.

"How do you feel?"

She laughed. "I made myself kind of dizzy trying to read the titles of your books."

"They are mostly medical volumes." Dr. Stevens walked to the shelf and scanned the titles. She turned with a small paperback. "Here's something light." She stretched her arm out proffering the book. "Promise me you won't tire yourself."

"I promise," Elle said, accepting the slim volume.

"I wish I had something fun, like one of those awful celebrity magazines."

"I doubt you would have one of those," Elle said.

Dr. Stevens put her hands on her hips and pretended indignation. "I happen to be fond of reading trash. When I'm in the mood."

Elle glanced down at the book in her hand. To her surprise, the cover, a picture of a tapestry depicting the tree of life, was familiar.

"*Dobhale's Myths and Fables*," she read aloud. "I read this in high school."

Elle opened the cover and studied the list of chapters. She read each one aloud but stumbled a bit over the words. She could decode and comprehend the combinations of letters and words fine. She just found it hard to tame her eyes enough to move across the page. The print trembled as if the words would crawl off the page. She traced them with her fingers like a grade-schooler not yet completely familiar with the concept of reading.

She flipped through the pages to a dog-eared page. Bold letters named the section of the chapter, *Medusa and the Gorgons*.

"As explained in chapter five," she read aloud. "As punishment for her rape by the sea god Poseidon in the temple of Athena, the goddess cursed the Gorgon Medusa with a crown of serpents and a gaze which turned men into stone."

On the opposite page was an illustration, an etching of Perseus triumphantly holding the head of Medusa, her body at his feet. Elle remembered how she'd felt angry as a kid reading about how wise Athena punished a maiden for her own sexual assault. Even then she made the connection to modern day victim blaming.

She looked up to see Dr. Stevens watching her with something more behind her eyes than her usual charming cheer. To Elle, the look was haunted.

"Everything okay?" she asked.

Elle nodded. "This whole story is fucked. It just confirmed how sick the world is."

The doctor leaned across the table and retrieved the book. "You're safe here, you know."

"It's safe here," she repeated, though not completely convinced. "I know."

They were silent for a moment. "You dreamed of Loera last night. I read about him in your file, as well as some research of my own."

"A man killed himself. Because of me," Elle blurted.

"You blamed yourself?"

Elle turned away from her. "Everyone told me that I shouldn't. I don't think I ever really dealt with it."

"You understand that couldn't be your fault."

"You weren't there."

Dr. Stevens sighed and removed her white coat. Underneath she wore gray trousers and a blue blouse with a collar tied into a clever bow. The type of outfit Elle would have worn to the Green Patriot. As Dr. Stevens had so far kept herself covered in the lab coat, Elle hadn't noticed her elegant shape. She scolded herself for noticing. This wasn't a coffee shop date.

"I'm sorry that on top of everything you have to relive what happened with Loera."

"You should have seen the looks I got after that happened."

"People can be cruel."

It all started when while traveling Elle found that she crossed paths with many veterans and enlisted soldiers. Some of them were angry at her for her views on the war in Iraq and were determined to defend their country in any arena. She spent a lot of time debating, but even more time listening. She learned a lot just listening.

"I remember those pieces you used to do," Dr. Stevens said. "The interviews with soldiers. I enjoyed them."

"I wanted to help. I wanted to bring attention to the matter. I wanted to help vets, but then there was my career. Those stories got the Green Patriot some sponsors with deep pockets."

Dr. Stevens shook her head. "Just because there was some benefit to you does not spoil your intentions."

"Yeah, my intentions were good, but you know what they say about those," Elle said.

"You gave a voice to those who didn't have one."

"I was driven and ambitious, and it cost a man his life," she said.

Dr. Stevens took one of Elle's hands and held it in both of hers. They felt so warm, and despite it all, they brought comfort.

"We all get caught up in our passions and ambitions. I want to be this brilliant doctor and save my patients, but I cannot shoulder the blame for the cause of what ails them. You are as brilliant a reporter as I want to be as a doctor. It's not your fault that the military complex is fucked up."

She covered her mouth and widened her eyes, shocked at her language, and laughed.

Elle could not help but grin. "My bad habits are rubbing off on you."

Dr. Stevens smiled. "I could use some of those."

"I've never told anyone how I felt," Elle said. "About Rob."

"It's hard, I know," Dr. Stevens said. "All of these memories rising to the surface and bringing back all of those emotions, it's overwhelming."

"It's not just the memories, it's how palpable everything felt last night. It felt like he was there. I could feel the buttons on his coat. You say it's all part of whatever happened to me, but I don't even have a grasp of what that is."

Dr. Stevens did not seem to have a reply. She walked around the couch, away from her. "We should get lunch."

"Why can't you just tell me?"

A grave look passed over the doctor's face. "There will be a time for answers, Elle. It would be unethical for me to go against protocol."

"Isn't it equally unethical to leave me in the dark?"

"Not in this case," she said and went to her desk to bring lunch over. "I brought outside food. Subs from Zoey's. It's a popular spot."

She presented two brown paper bags and two cans of soda. Elle tried to remember the last time she had soda.

"I brought turkey and ham," Dr. Stevens said. "Both are great. I didn't know if you had a preference."

"I'll have turkey," Elle said. "But don't think you're off the hook."

She handed over the bag marked with a letter T written in a thick black marker. Elle recalled going to places like that, mom-and-pop restaurants and shops without all the bells and whistles of chains with their logos on everything. It was one of the reasons she liked living in Austin. She imagined Cosmo's Subs crowded with families and college kids. She imagined Dr. Stevens among them smiling at little kids and chatting with the owner.

"This was very thoughtful of you," Elle said as they unwrapped their sandwiches.

"It's nothing," Dr. Stevens said, taking a bite.

Elle did too. At first there seemed nothing out of the ordinary about the sandwich. The bread was fragrant and soft. There was turkey, cheese, veggies, and a light sauce like mayo but with a spicy tang. It was indeed tasty.

"Wow," Elle said.

Dr. Stevens raised her eyebrows and smiled around her chews. "Right?"

They both laughed at their one-word communication. After silently savoring the first bite of her sandwich, Dr. Stevens asked Elle about her arm.

"It feels okay," she said. "Not really painful at all."

"Good. Make sure to let the nurses know if you feel anything at all," Dr. Stevens said. "I don't want this to be a setback."

They fell into a silence once again. Elle realized that she was hungrier than she had thought. She took a sip from her soda. As she returned the can to the table, she felt the contents slosh and fizz beneath her fingers. She also felt something akin to the nostalgia of Austin's mom-and-pop eateries, yet with a sense of dread.

She recalled sitting in what looked to be an old hangar, the metal rafters covered in bird droppings. There was a stony-faced woman. She was talking to Elle, asking her things about the Gorgon, whoever or whatever that was. She did not like what Elle was telling her. A bald man in a suit waited nearby.

The memory was vivid but fleeting leaving Elle stunned, a bite of masticated sandwich in her mouth. She realized that Dr. Stevens was asking her if she was okay, and she swallowed hard. She'd suddenly lost her appetite.

She felt Dr. Steven's hand on her shoulder, and then cool, dry fingers on her face.

"Elle? Are you okay?"

"I think I just remembered something."

Dr. Stevens had abandoned her lunch and Elle wondered how long she had been absorbed in the memory of the hangar. It seemed to run through her mind in a few seconds.

"Are you certain it was a memory?" Dr. Stevens asked.

"Is it possible to have a nightmare when you are fully awake?"

She leaned forward. "Tell me."

Elle took a breath. "I remembered a woman. She had a Russian accent. She was asking me questions. Interrogating me. She brought me food in a paper bag."

"You say she was interrogating you. What did she want to know?"

"She wanted to know about the Gorgon," Elle said, and she looked to the mythology book on the table. She remembered the dog-eared page about Medusa. "Who or what is that?"

Dr. Stevens sighed and touched her fingers to her temples.

"You want to tell me," Elle said. "A good reporter always knows."

"Elle," she said, her tone a warning.

"Why was I with the Russians? Are they behind what happened to me?"

"I'm not allowed to feed you information."

"To tell me the truth about what happened to me?"

"Our plan for your complete healing—"

"Has it ever worked for anyone?" Elle asked. "It doesn't seem to be working for Leslie."

Dr. Stevens's brow furrowed. "That's not fair."

"Who is the Gorgon?"

"I can't. I just can't," Dr. Stevens said.

"You can," Elle said. "Or is this place just a cover-up? Am I being silenced here until someone can figure out how to clean up their mess?"

"You know that's not true."

"Then who is the Gorgon?"

Dr. Stevens's hands were now curled into loose fists on the table, not in aggression; she was trying to mask her body language. She more than likely wanted to wring those hands. She was wrestling with breaking Gloaming Hill's precious protocol.

Elle felt a little guilty. She liked Dr. Stevens and did not want to cause her any distress. She reached over with her good hand and touched one of those loosely curled fists.

"No one knows who the Gorgon is," she said. "The name could belong to a terror cell, or a scientist, or a spy. We are hoping that you will fill in that information so it is important that as your memories return, they not be tainted by details you have been fed."

Elle backed away from the table a bit, her mind reeling. Dr. Stevens watched her closely.

"Am I considered a witness?"

"In some part, but our first priority here is to make you better."

"I wonder," she said in reply. "Dr. Branch, Rob, the Russian lady. It feels like I did something wrong to make me a prisoner here."

"You're not," Dr. Stevens said, uncurling her hand to hold Elle's. "You're a patient. My patient."

"Is the Gorgon why you have a copy of Dobhale's myths?" Elle asked. "Did you want me to see that?"

Dr. Stevens's mouth pulled down at the corners. "I didn't expect you to make the connection. It was careless of me."

"That is not a word I would ever use to describe you," Elle said slyly. "You took the risk that I would be triggered."

"After yesterday, I just wanted to see what would happen if we made an attempt to stimulate your memory. Dr. Branch of course was against it."

"But you did it anyway," Elle said.

Dr. Stevens gave her a pained look as she let go of her hand.

"I won't tell her," Elle said.

She gave a wan smile. "No, I will have to do that."

"Why?"

"Because I was right," she said adamantly.

Elle could not help but chuckle. She decided she would give Dr. Stevens a pass for the time being.

Dr. Stevens sighed. "Your mother will be here in a few days. Dr. Branch and I plan to have a frank conversation with the both of you about your recovery."

"I'm a grown woman. I don't need my mother to be able to digest what is happening."

"I know," she said. "I gave Dr. Branch my word that I would honor this compromise, and I broke my word by bringing you here, giving you that book. It was reckless."

She stood and returned the book to its place on the shelf.

"Don't talk like that," Elle told her. "You're trying to help me."

"So is Dr. Branch."

Elle suddenly felt tired both mentally and physically. "I just want my life back."

"That will happen. I promise you."

Elle did not answer. She felt alone, adrift in her own mind, and then there was that button tucked away in the muff of her sweatshirt. She wanted to remove it and shove it under Dr. Stevens's nose. Something was not right about Gloaming Hill; Elle had known it the moment she awoke. She could steel herself against a pretty doctor and her sweet attempts to smooth things over.

Dr. Stevens returned to the sofa and sat close to Elle. "Dr. Branch wants to do one of her sessions with you before your mother's visit."

The hypnotherapy sessions. Of course. More smoke and mirrors.

"I don't think you're ready, to be honest," Dr. Stevens whispered.

Elle turned to face her.

"I couldn't convince her otherwise," Dr. Stevens continued in the same tone.

"I'm ready to move forward if it means getting out of here."

Dr. Stevens surprised her by looking stung. "You don't understand. Dr. Branch's technique, it can be very hard on the mind and psyche. You will more than likely find yourself reliving some traumatic events."

"I'm not afraid of the truth," Elle said.

"I know," Dr. Stevens agreed. "And I don't want to scare you. I suppose I just want to prepare you. Dr. Branch is not the type to give you a pep talk beforehand."

Elle nodded. She expected as much from their initial meeting. Still, Dr. Branch had consented to allowing her mother to visit.

"Maybe I will be able to remember more about who or what the Gorgon is."

That pained expression returned to Dr. Stevens's face. "Come, let's finish lunch and I will take you back to your room."

Elle returned to the table, and they finished lunch in relative silence. She insisted on walking back to her room, pushing the empty wheelchair through the nondescript white corridors of the facility, Dr. Stevens at her side. They said their good-byes at the door with the heaviness of a conclusion to an awkward date.

When she was alone, she removed the brass button from the pocket of her sweatshirt. She held on to it while she reviewed the conversation, she'd had with Dr. Stevens. She admonished herself for not pushing for more answers. She felt tired, her brain foggy. She could not control her thoughts about Loera, the button, the Gorgon, and her upcoming session with Dr. Branch. She was most anxious about the coming night and closing her eyes to sleep.

Nurses Grace and Slick came to check on her in the late afternoon and then returned to bring her dinner and an injection for the pain in her arm.

"My arm doesn't hurt," she told them.

They exchanged glances. "Of course, it does, Elle."

Too tired to start a dispute, she dutifully extended her arm.

Nurse Slick administered the shot while Nurse Grace presented her with a coloring book and a set of waxy colors.

"I'm not coloring," Elle said drolly.

"Why not?" Grace asked. "It's soothing and passes the time."

"Because I'm not in second grade."

They exchanged looks again.

After the nurses left, she took a long hot shower and returned to find the coloring book on her bedside table. She picked it up and thumbed through the pages to find it filled with scenic places in black outline, the details numbered for each color. She stopped at a two-page spread of a castle tucked in a forest. Its towers peaked into black cones much like the castle from the puzzle, but it was not the same castle. Or was it? Elle turned away from the spread and settled on a picture of a flowery meadow. She enjoyed coloring in the flowers but grew tired while filling in the grass. When her eyelids began to droop, she put the book and colors aside and closed her eyes for the night.

CHAPTER THIRTEEN

Gloaming Hill Facility, West Virginia

The next day, Dr. Branch entered her room shortly after noon. Elle had just finished communing with the mysterious button. Of course, it was still there, cold at first, then warmed by the heat of her hands. Just as she returned the button wadded in tissue to her bedside table, she looked up and noticed Dr. Branch standing in the doorway.

"Hello," Elle said.

"Good afternoon. How are we today?"

She gave a brief smile and entered the room pulling at the lapels of the jacket of her skirt-suit combo. She rolled her broad, round shoulders as she surveyed the room and Elle. She carried a clipboard outfitted in black leather. It held a tablet of gray, lined paper. Her hedge-fro in the full light was white at the top and transitioned from light gray to a darker gray at her temples, ears, and nape.

"Great," Elle said hopefully. "My arm feels okay." She was sitting on the edge of the bed waiting for Dr. Stevens to take her to see Dr. Branch. She'd come by that morning, her usual sunny self. Elle expressed her apprehension about her session. She was looking forward to being escorted by Dr. Stevens as if she could leech some of her endless energy and optimism.

Instead, she got old stone-face.

Dr. Branch approached the bed. "Dr. Stevens tells me you had an episode the night after our conversation."

"If seeing your dead friend and ending up passed out on the cold floor is what you would call an episode."

Dr. Branch glanced down at her clipboard. She removed some clear framed readers from her pocket and put them just below the bridge of her nose. Better to stare at Elle over them, which she did for a moment as if she were looking for her to say more.

"I slept well last night," Elle stammered.

"That's good," she said and glanced down at her. "Dr. Stevens described it as quite an ordeal."

"It was at the time," Elle said. "Now it all seems like old hat."

Dr. Branch pursed her lips, unmoved. She regarded her with dark eyes. "The biggest mistake you can make right now is downplaying your anxiety or your fears," she said in an admonishing tone. "How are you feeling about your stay here?"

"I'd like to get back to my job and my life."

"Last time we spoke you compared Gloaming Hill to a prison."

"I don't know what else to call a place that will not allow me to leave or make contact with the outside world."

She agreed, unmoved by the sarcasm in Elle's tone. "I'm hoping that today we can get some answers to assuage your fears."

"My fears?" Elle asked. "I'm trapped in a creepy hospital where I barely see other patients, no one will tell me why I'm here, and let's not leave out the hallucinations/night terrors of my dead friend."

Dr. Branch had the nerve to add to the tally. "You're also afraid that the world has gone on without you. Which is valid, as it has."

"It's a reasonable fear. A consequence of being here. If your life was stripped away from you, wouldn't you worry about things here at Gloaming Hill?"

She paused as if considering the possibility. "There are other competent folks who could take my place. That would bring me some solace. Your news site is doing quite well."

"Yes, it is. And just as you said, Gloaming Hill would be okay, but it would irk you that you couldn't be here to run things the way you would run them," Elle said.

"True," Dr. Branch said. "But sometimes we have to wait on the sidelines of life until it is our time to get back in the game."

Elle hated sports metaphors. "It's daunting though to think of what my life will be like when I am able to return home."

"I want to show you something," Dr. Branch said. She lowered her clipboard to show Elle. There were some notes scribbled in the margins, a symbol-riddled shorthand she could not decipher. Otherwise, the gray page was empty. She placed her writing pad in the middle of the tray table where Elle had done her coloring.

"My method of hypnosis is a journey into the mind to access your lost memories," she said. "It requires you and me to be in sync. I want you to picture the place in your brain where all your memories are stored as a maze of hallways. Imagine it as a physical place that you know."

She touched the tip of the pen to the paper. She drew one line, and then another, crisscrossing them until she had drawn a five-pointed star that ended at the same point it had started, the type a primary school teacher would use to mark a good grade.

"Think of these hallways as being lined with doors. Some only have one or two and some have many."

Dr. Branch traced over the star following the same pattern as she spoke.

Elle assumed that she was scratching out what looked to be a diagram or allusion to her mind-maze analogy, so she paid close attention.

"Some of these doors and hallways have been forgotten but can easily be accessed," she continued. "Some doors are barricaded with crime scene tape, warnings that the rooms behind them hold awful memories. Things to keep you away."

Elle noticed that each time she traced the symbol, she extended the points.

"Some of these doors are bricked shut, and some you just have to talk yourself into tearing off that tape and just going in."

Now the points of the star were solid black, while the center of the star remained a perfect white pentagon. She could see the stress of the paper as Dr. Branch retraced over drying ink. It would bleed through soon, and the pressure of the pen tip would make a crude embossing of the star image on the pages that followed.

"Our search will be a random one," Dr. Branch said. "I can't navigate your unconscious. I can only link it to your conscious."

She found Dr. Branch's voice lulled her, despite the doodle. Her anxiety, though, remained coiled and ready to strike, but tamed for the time being. She wanted to ask Dr. Branch some questions she had prepared about the session, but her tongue felt heavy as if she'd had one too many martinis. She found that she was too relaxed to be afraid.

"Well," Dr. Branch said with finality. "It looks like we are ready to begin."

Then, they were moving, out of the room and through the maze of nondescript white corridors of Gloaming Hill. Elle couldn't feel her body, her feet, and legs as she walked. Her eyes blinked rapidly of their own volition, and she saw that damned red star in the nanoseconds of darkness behind her lids.

They stopped at a stainless-steel door with no handle.

Dr. Branch simply pushed it with her flat palm, and it opened. Inside, two chairs waited in the middle of the room. One chair sat in a squatty recline, the back ergonomically curved and padded with gray upholstery. A small screen hung above it suspended from the ceiling. The other chair stood on bending legs, an insect-like thing with a spindly aluminum frame and a gray plastic backrest.

Elle thought of Dr. Stevens's cozy office with art and books. It was the opposite of the room. This was Dr. Branch's place for sure, cold, colorless, and sterile.

Glancing around the room, she noticed that gray cushioned pads paneled the walls. It occurred to Elle that the décor of the room told its story. She imagined other patients unruly under Dr. Branch's hypnosis. They fought unseen attackers or mistook Dr. Branch for the villains in their dreams. She wondered what her own chances were of going berserk in the padded room.

"I don't like this room." The sound of her voice echoed only in her head.

"Focus on me for now," Dr. Branch said.

She helped Elle onto the squatty chair below the screen. She leaned over and strapped her in with Velcro straps. Up close, she smelled faintly of magnolias, Elle's favorite flower. She closed her eyes and settled into the chair. It was wide enough that she could rest her arms at her side. Her eyes still closed, she listened as Dr. Branch sat in the chair next to her and moved closer.

"Elle?"

She did not answer.

"Elle, open your eyes," she said.

She did. She looked at Dr. Branch. She had been to a therapist before. At the moment, Elle could not remember why she started seeing the woman.

Her eyes strayed to the screen above her head.

"What's that?"

"It's a tool," Dr. Branch said. She reached up and touched the frame around the screen and it glowed a deep red. Elle tensed and Dr. Branch touched her shoulder.

"Don't look at the screen just yet, look at me."

She did so reluctantly.

Dr. Branch peered down at her with dark eyes. "In just a moment, I'm going to show you something on the screen. Then, I am going to have you close your eyes."

Elle nodded, afraid to open her mouth.

"Okay. Now, look at the screen."

She did, though loath to investigate the monitor, afraid of what she would see, of who might be looking back at her. The screen no longer glowed completely red, but white with a red star in the center, constructed just as Dr. Branch had drawn.

"What do you see?" she asked.

Elle explained exactly what she saw.

"Good," Dr. Branch said. "I want you to keep your eyes on that red star, in fact, the more you look at it, the more you will find you cannot take your eyes from it."

Skeptical, she looked away from the screen and directly at the doctor. At this display of stubbornness, Dr. Branch's lips pulled into a half-smile. Elle turned her attention back to the screen, back to the star. It started to flicker.

"It's blinking," she said.

"No need to speak right now," Dr. Branch said.

Elle tried to look away from the screen again but found that she could not. In her periphery she could see Dr. Branch and the padded walls behind her. The star continued to blink in the center of her vision. She could not move her eyes or shift her vision. It felt as if her eyes themselves had become monitors.

She whimpered. "I'm having a seizure."

"You are not having a seizure," Dr. Branch said, some amusement in her voice. "Just focus on the star."

Elle moved her leg to prove to herself she was not paralyzed, that only her eyes remained fixed, frozen in one place.

"Tell me of your greatest fear," Dr. Branch said.

This was how it all began didn't it? With talk of fear? She did not answer; she did not want to answer. She wished the doctor did not want to talk of her fears, but then she supposed there was not much else to talk about at Gloaming Hill.

The star disappeared into a white background. Even with it gone, she could see its ghostly green after-image on the white screen.

"Elle," Dr. Branch said sternly. "I asked you a question."

Behind the doctor, the gray padding on the walls had taken on a silvery sparkle. She squinted trying to see without looking. The padded walls were alive, suddenly crawling with dancing sparkles. A hallucination. The star. The walls. They were all part of Dr. Branch's little sideshow. She heard the first notes "Stormy Weather."

"Elle?"

"My worst fear is…" She decided to go along with the game. "Not ever leaving Gloaming Hill, staying here forever."

"And why would you end up here forever?"

Behind Dr. Branch, the walls darkened and turned red. She watched out of the corner of her eye. She didn't have to turn her head to see.

"I need you to focus," Dr. Branch, said noticing her distraction.

"Did you know that the walls are changing color behind you?" Elle asked.

"Focus," she said. "Please just answer my previous question. Why would you end up at Gloaming Hill forever?"

She sighed and decided to let Dr. Branch have her little funhouse.

"If I were to lose my mind."

"What would cause you to lose your mind?"

"I feel it…slipping."

Dr. Branch waited, silent, for what, Elle did not know.

"I don't like this room," she said.

The padded walls were now a bright red, and shiny, with a slight iridescence she found familiar. She wanted to inspect it, but she was pinned like an insect in a specimen frame. She realized she had once been close to the sparkling red, admired its color, and caressed it with her hands. She could not remember when. She found it hard to concentrate, especially with Dr. Branch and her questions.

"Why do you fear you will lose your mind, Elle?"

"Because I'm frightened all the time, because my dreams feel so real, and the world when I'm awake feels like a dream."

She paused, out of breath, too tired to cry.

"Tell me what color the walls are," Dr. Branch said.

She gave a short, giddy burst of laughter. She wanted to ask her what the hell color she thought the walls were.

"Red. Sparkly."

"Is that so?"

"I know this isn't real. You bring people here to drive them nuts."

"That's not true," she countered. "The walls are a projection of a place that made you feel comfortable and brought you immense joy."

"Yes," she agreed. The memory loomed close; she anticipated it as she would a breeze rolling in her direction on a sizzling summer day.

"Tell me the place."

"The Luling Bowling Alley." She giggled, almost embarrassed. The great troublemaking, educated reporter's happy place was a small-town bowling alley. She saw the place clearly in her mind, the lanes, and the Formica counter for renting shoes, the neon trim on the walls.

"When did you first go there?"

"It was back when I first started out as a reporter. There was a labor strike at a nearby factory. I was covering the story there. There were three of us in the crew. I turned out to be incredibly good and I had never bowled."

"Describe the place for me."

She felt giddy visualizing the place. "There were about ten lanes, and murals of longhorns and wild horses stampeding through space on the walls. The murals glowed under black lights. There was a bar where they served junk food—malts and shakes and burgers and fries. Beer. The seats in the booths were covered in the original red sparkly vinyl from the fifties."

"Sounds like fun," Dr. Branch said.

"I go back every now and then to bowl. I've tried it at other lanes, but I don't really enjoy it anywhere else."

"Picture it in your mind. Can you see every last detail? Smell those burgers cooking?"

As Dr. Branch spoke, Elle found that she could see the Luling Bowling Alley coming to life around her. She could smell the burgers and popcorn. It felt as if she were dreaming, though she did not remember closing her eyes in sleep.

"Elle?" Dr. Branch asked. "Can you see it?"

In disbelief, she took a deep breath and laughed a bit. "Yes. Yes, I can."

Elle found that her eyes were no longer fixed in one position. She no longer lay on the chair in the padded room beneath the screen. She was standing on her own two feet in the middle of the bowling alley, near the shoe rental counter. She could hear country music. She smelled popcorn and beer, cleaning chemicals, and the leather of bowling shoes. The main lights were low; the disco balls were spinning, staining the wooden floors with blue squares of light.

She tried her voice. "Is this a dream? A memory?"

Dr. Branch spoke. Her voice still sounded close as if she were sitting next to her in the padded room. The music faded into the background.

"It is not a dream or a memory. This is your safe place, Elle."

"It seems so real, but I know it can't be."

"You are envisioning with the expert eyes of your unconscious, a construct pieced together from memories of the bowling alley. This is the place we will use as a main entrance to the hidden parts of your mind."

Intrigued, Elle continued to explore the bowling alley. She admired the detail of the place, right down to the red vinyl. All of it seemed more vibrant than she remembered.

Dr. Branch's voice piped in overhead. "Elle, I want you to move to the nearest exit."

"You want me to leave?" Elle asked, reluctant to do so. She wanted to pick up a ball and bowl a set.

"For now," Dr. Branch said. "Walk out the door and tell me what you see."

In the distance, a red and white exit sign began to glow brighter than it would in reality. She approached it, uncertain. She turned down a hall, past a carved wooden sign that marked the restrooms, and a payphone. Double doors stood at the end of the hall; each had bar handles that crossed horizontally.

The red letters of the exit sign began to flash on and off in the same pattern as the star.

Dr. Branch somehow knew of her hesitation. "Go on."

She reached for the handle of the door, anticipated the cool metal under her hand. She had yet to touch anything in this strange consciousness. She pushed one of the bar handles, heard the metallic click as the door unlatched.

From memory, she anticipated that outside waited a typical Texas evening, the lights of the small town over a parking lot of pickup trucks and compact cars. The stacks of the factory glowing in the distance.

Instead, when she opened the door, she did not see the back parking lot of the Luling Bowling Alley, but a ruined building, clouded with the smoky dust of debris. Broken ceiling tiles and insulation littered the sodden blue carpet beneath her feet. Shafts of sunlight slanted here and there, while broken red backup lights winked on and off staining the scene.

She heard different music then, a familiar song, one she had heard so many times that she could recognize it by the first notes of music. "Stormy Weather."

Dr. Branch's voice piped overhead though not as clear as before.

"Where are you, Elle?"

"I'm in a new building. It looks like someone drove a tank through it."

"What do you see?"

She described the gaping hole in the ceiling, how she could see the sun through the haze, a ghostly glowing ball, a speck in the sky compared to the destruction below. She could still hear Lena Horne singing about being weary all the time.

Like Luling, she saw the place in clear detail, the trickle of water from broken pipes, furniture bent into unrecognizable shapes, personal effects rolled in a filthy breeze stirred by an unknown force.

Elle peered through the haze and saw figures in the distance. They lurched forward through the dust and smoky red light on unsteady legs. The walking wounded shuffled through the wreckage of the blown-out building. There had been an explosion, this was the aftermath.

"What is this place?" Elle asked.

She heard Dr. Branch call her name, her voice a drawled whisper, but Elle could not make out what she was saying.

She wanted to go back to Luling. She would even take the padded room with Dr. Branch. She turned her attention back to the others. They did not seem to be any closer than before. As if in a dream, they continued their broken shuffle in the distance.

Elle did not want to stick around to find out. She would get back without Dr. Branch's guidance. This was her mind, and she could navigate herself back to the place in her mind designated as Luling.

She turned to go back the way she came. Instead of a door, she found the walking wounded, their procession just yards away.

"Dr. Branch," she called out nearly in a panic. "Dr. Branch."

Even the music was gone.

They were upon her, their faces blurred by a cloud of smoky dust from the debris that seemed to move with them. She could see their bodies clearly. She expected to see wounds through torn clothes and mangled limbs, but besides their limping zombie march, they were intact. They shuffled right at her. She winced, expecting them to tear her to shreds. They lurched closer. Instead of attacking her, they parted around her like a flock of birds coming upon an obstacle. She tried to recognize their faces. One of them bumped into her but seemed unaware as he stumbled to a stop.

At his cheeks, red patches showed from beneath his translucent skin. He opened his mouth slowly, as if to speak to her. Instead of words, a thin cloud of condensed breath swirled from his lips. He continued in the wake of the others.

She watched them lurch on until they disappeared around a broken wall. She stood alone once again in the ruined building, cut off from Dr. Branch. A chill claimed her, causing a shiver through her body. The sensation took her breath away, and she marveled at the frigid blast, a steady cold that crept around her.

"Dr. Branch, I'm freezing in here. Is this right?"

She thought of the padded walls and knew that other patients experienced worse than cold. She shivered again and could not stop.

"Elle." Dr. Branch's voice returned.

"I'm here," she said, relieved to hear her again. A wave of warmth rolled through her.

"Elle, go back to Luling."

The red emergency lights faded and left blackness in their absence. She welcomed the dark, and even more, the new, dim light that followed. She expected the neon lights of the Luling Bowling Alley, instead she found herself on her stomach on an icy concrete floor, a red puddle directly in her line of sight.

The cold soaked through her skin and caused her bones to ache. She noticed the clothes she wore, a short-sleeved blouse and skirt, were useless to ward off the cold. They stuck to her body as if she had been doused in water before she was tossed into the truck. Not a bit of warmth remained inside her, or strength. She could not move. Her body was frozen in place. She would die soon, she figured, drift off into sleep as her bodily functions failed.

The center of the puddle moved. She flicked her eyes up and saw large slabs of meat hanging on hooks. They swayed slightly in the frigid breeze. She lay in some sort of refrigerated room.

A drop of blood fell from one of the slabs and landed in front of her. She realized that the entire room rocked gently, that the room moved. Another drop fell. She wanted to move away from the foul puddle, did not want any of the blood to land on her, though that would be the least of her troubles.

She heard a moan so close she thought it her own. The cold had numbed her so she could not feel the breath entering and exiting her lungs, let alone a moan. She wondered if she would notice when her breath would stop altogether.

The moan came again, a tortured sound from above among the slabs. She looked up and found the cold had not numbed her stomach. It clenched at the part of her ribs in its threat to revolt. A young woman with red hair hung above her suspended from a hook, like a butchered animal carcass. Still, she lived, her breath escaping parted lips in thin, short puffs barely visible. Her skin was blue, her lips purple, the only color left besides her clothes was her red hair.

"Carrie."

A voice came from the sluggish bodies, and she could see Leslie, calling her that strange name and reaching for her hand.

Above, the woman on the hook's eyes fluttered and followed the movement below. Elle guessed that this was the Carrie that Leslie was calling for. She opened her mouth as if to speak to call out to her friend, and her jaw trembled. A half-dead woman's cry for help to a half-frozen woman.

Oblivious to her, half-frozen out of her mind, Leslie continued to call Elle Carrie and reach for her hand.

She gave a cry of her own, and the anguish appeared before her in the form of a swirling cloud of vapor that died as soon as it was born. She tried to get up, to raise her upper body with her arms, like a push-up, and found she could not.

Dr. Branch's voice piped in her ear like a loudspeaker on the fritz.

"Elle, come back to me."

She felt relief to hear the doctor's voice. She tried to respond, but could only lay there shivering. It occurred to her that she was not physically in the back of a refrigeration truck. She'd somehow survived the actual ordeal, but the memory would certainly kill her.

"Come on, Elle," Dr. Branch said. She sounded worried.

Once again, her vision began to darken, and she knew she was leaving. The woman on the hook did not have such a luxury. Soon, everything went black, and she was nowhere. At least, she felt warm again.

CHAPTER FOURTEEN

Gloaming Hill Facility, West Virginia

When Elle opened her eyes and saw her drab room, she smiled. She felt a hand on her own. Dr. Stephens was there with a gentle smile. Elle reached for her. She could not help herself. She felt as if she had been lost for a long time. She felt worn out.

"Welcome back," Dr. Stevens said.

"Hi," Elle managed.

"You've been out for a few days," she said.

A few days? She tried to sit up but found that she did not have the strength. Her arm was still in the sling and had been fastened close to her body. What had happened?

"You're okay," Dr. Stevens said, sensing her panic. "After your session with Dr. Branch, we had to take drastic measures."

"What?" was all Elle could ask.

"A medically induced coma," she said. "We needed to stabilize you, or all our work would be lost. Dr. Branch will be pleased to know that you are awake."

Of course, she would. What had she done to Elle? She tried to remember and found that she did not have to put in much effort. The bowling alley in Luling came to mind, which puzzled her at first until she recalled that it was her landing place, the doorway to horrible memories of being in a blown-out building with shuffling injured people.

"What…what happened? What did I remember?"

Dr. Stevens sighed. "You recalled some of the events that brought you here."

"The building? Where was I?"

"You were in Johannesburg, South Africa, covering an event, the World AIDS Summit. Terrorists targeted the event. They set off bombs."

Elle knew then. Her session with Dr. Branch had brought the lost memories to the surface and they'd taken their place in her mind with the others. She could remember the flight out and talking over the details with Anne as she relaxed in the tub at the hotel room. She remembered riding the shuttle bus to the convention center with some other reporters and chatting amicably. They had planned to get drinks and dinner after.

None of them suspected that in a few hours they would be trapped in the rubble of the building, that some of them would be dead.

Elle bowed her head and began to cry. She felt Dr. Stevens's hand on her shoulder. It was warm and comforting.

"I am so sorry you had to go through any of this."

"Why would someone do such a thing?" Elle asked but quickly retracted her question. "I know these things happen, I put it on full display for the world to see. There are maniacs out there who plan these attacks hoping to fulfill some grudge they have with society."

"It's okay. You're safe now. We're on the right track here to help identify them, but that's not what's most important here."

Elle wanted her to stop telling her that she was okay. She was not okay.

"What do you know of them so far?"

"Elle, I can't discuss that with you. Not right now."

She would not be so easily put off. "I saw Leslie. Was she able to give any information about who bombed the convention center and kidnapped people?"

"She has not been as successful as you in her treatment," Dr. Stevens said and then lowered her voice to a conspiratorial tone. "Not that I should be discussing other patients with you, Elle. You're so close—"

"Close to what?" Elle asked. "Getting out of this place? Remembering who kidnapped me? I'm not sure I want to remember."

A brief look of panic crossed her face. "You must not say that, Elle."

Seeing that she had struck a nerve, she asked, "Why would I? It's been nothing but a horror show so far."

"Let's take a moment to calm down," Dr. Stevens said. "Remember to breathe."

Elle took a moment to go through the breathing exercises. When they were done, they were silent watching each other. Elle broke contact. She stared toward the opposite side of the room and the bathroom door. They'd brought in more equipment to monitor her.

"Your mother postponed her visit until you awoke again," Dr. Stevens said cheerfully. "She can be here by the morning."

Elle did not answer. She was tired of the same runaround and Gloaming Hill's secrets. Her mother had the clout to get her away from there. She turned to see Dr. Stevens; her palms were pressed to her eyes and gently massaging in slow circles. She removed her hands and Elle saw the tiredness in her brow. How long had she kept vigil over her?

"You're upset," she said.

"I'm perpetually upset," Elle said.

"How about some food?" she asked.

"I guess I could try."

"I'll get the nurses in here to clean you up, remove the catheter and IV. Then, we can get you a nice soup for dinner."

"No Zoe's?" Elle deadpanned.

Dr. Stevens smiled. "Maybe in a few days. Okay?"

"I'm going to look forward to that," Elle said. "I'm glad you were here when I woke up."

Her words were rewarded with a smile.

When the doctor left, she sat there for a moment regarding the silent room, waiting for the nurses. When they did not come, she leaned over the side of the bed and was able to reach the stand and pull open the drawer. She eased it to the end of the track and gave it a shake until a balled-up tissue bounced into view.

She pushed the drawer back and retrieved the scrap of tissue. She unfolded it almost expecting the button not to be there, as if her session with Dr. Branch had knocked something loose in her brain besides memories.

But there it was nestled in the tissue in all its brass, eagle glory. She ran her fingers over the talons, one set clutching arrows, the other an olive branch, as was the duality of all things. She thought of Dr. Stevens and Dr. Branch. They too were dualities of the same institution. They both had good intentions. Still, there was something wrong about Gloaming Hill.

Elle returned the button to the drawer. The nurses still had not arrived. She lay back and closed her eyes. She felt tired but not sleepy. She lay there waiting haunted by the memories stirred up during Dr. Branch's session. When the nurses came, she was glad for the noise of their presence, glad to drown out the horrors that played in her head.

Before finding herself at Gloaming Hill, Elle never had trouble getting to sleep, nor did she ever sleep so much. Even as a kid, she'd subsisted on five to six hours a night and would wake refreshed. She usually just went on until she could no longer keep her eyes open, a habit she carried into adulthood.

For the next few nights, a peaceful rest eluded her. When she did sleep, her dreams were a mix of nightmares and memories from her session with Dr. Branch. She woke often, breaking from the darkness to the dimness and silence of her room, out of breath and damp from sweat.

Her mother was scheduled to visit the following afternoon, and Elle found herself fretting about how that would play out. She fantasized about her mother taking her from Gloaming Hill, and she would be cured of her fear. She'd dreamed of the broken, confused people from the convention center in Johannesburg. What woke her was the smell, something acrid in the air, overpowering even in her dreams.

She sat up in bed and opened her eyes to see someone standing next to her bed. She blinked to fully clear her eyes from sleep and saw the silhouette of Rob Loera's ruined head. He was speaking—not to Elle—in a bitter, anxious monotone.

"Rob?" she asked.

His head was bowed as he droned on. "We dropped at thirty-three degrees north, sixty-five degrees east at oh-six hundred, found the enemy, fired on the enemy, we got return fire—"

"Rob," she said a bit louder.

His head shot up and he waited in the darkness, stone still. Elle wanted to see if she could inspect him for clues. She reached for the light switch.

"Don't you fucking touch that light," he growled.

She snatched her hand away. "Who are you really?"

"I'll ask the questions here, Miss Chief Correspondent."

He straightened and marched around to the other side of the bed. Though the room was dark, Elle could feel his gaze upon her. She could feel a fresh violence along with his presence, like a black cloud.

He scoffed. "Answer me this, Elle, you've been in contact with the one they call the Gorgon? She told you about Project Songbird, didn't she?"

"I don't know what you're talking about."

"I've got the intel. I've been sent to verify it."

"You're not real."

Rob shifted and leaned forward. "Then why are you here, Elle?"

"I'm here because—" she stammered. "Someone bombed the convention center in Johannesburg, and they brought me here."

"That's the story you tell everyone, to account for the time you spent with the Gorgon, betraying your country."

"I don't know the Gorgon. What I do know is you're not here, Rob. You're dead."

He reached for her. "I'll get you to talk."

She quickly slid over to avoid him. She went for the lamp again. Just as her fingers turned the switch, Rob swiped it off the table and it crashed to the floor. A crescent-shaped beam of light fell across the room. It exposed him, skin paled with the pallor of death, the wound in his face black and green with rot. He still wore his uniform. One of the middle buttons was gone.

"My eyes were opened," he said. "They were closed my whole life. I am resurrected to see these atrocities."

"You can't be dead and standing here," she told him. "It's insane. It's impossible."

He reached into his jacket and removed a large Army-issue black-handled knife.

"You're going to tell me what you know," he said. "The Gorgon. Project Songbird, all of it."

He took two steps closer to the bed.

She began to scream. If this was all a dream or a hallucination, or even some twisted reality, someone would come to her aid.

Rob grabbed her arm, twisted it, and pressed the blade of the knife to her throat. She felt her skin give and a trickle of blood run down her neck. She screamed and tried to remove his hand and the weapon.

His other arm snaked across her neck and her screams dissolved into a wretched choking, muffled by the lack of air. She struggled wildly as he pulled her halfway off the bed. She tried to break the contact between them to no avail. Her body tired fast; her lungs felt as if they would cave in on themselves. The world became a black-gray blur. He was able to hold her. She squeezed her eyes shut not wanting to see what would come next.

"It's time for you to finally be punished for your treason," he said into her ear.

He lifted the knife high.

She groaned. Panic roared in her ears like a passing freight train; her vision blurred and ran together, sparkled black when she blinked.

She saw the knife plunge down. The blade disappeared from her sight. She felt it slam into her chest with a resounding thud, followed by a blinding blackness like a black bag over her head.

❖

Elle found herself once again in the mist. She could feel the soft static of it around her, the sensation strange yet comforting. Nothing to see, nothing to hear. She was tempted to float there as she was sure that it was a place where undead soldiers could not reach. She would be safe there, somewhere between consciousness and unconsciousness. Gloaming Hill could have her body.

Somewhere in the distance, if the mist could be measured in terms of space, she could hear music. It was moving closer to her or she to it. She rejoiced to recognize "Stormy Weather." She felt as if she were hearing the voice of an old friend.

"What song is this again?"

A question from a voice she did not know. A woman, close to her ear, sleepy, sultry.

The mist solidified into shadows and through it, a faint glow alternating between pink and blue. Her mind struggled to process the shapes and colors that formed before her. Slowly, things came into focus. She found that she was lying on her side facing a window as rain dripped down the glass. The wall around the window was white and reflected the soft glow of pink and blue while absorbing the cool gray of a rainy morning. There were buildings beyond the window mounted with neon trimmed digital advertisements changing and flashing. She did not recognize any, but she did notice that the bold lettering was Korean.

She could hear the rain and music. "Stormy Weather." She felt warm sheets against her naked skin. She startled when she felt the heat of another body behind her. An arm constricted around her waist, pulling her closer.

"What song is this again?"

That voice from the mist, not so disembodied this time, its owner a mystery that she could solve by turning over. She tried, but that arm held her with a tender swiftness she could not resist.

"Please, don't go yet."

Before she could protest, she felt hands gliding appreciatively over her hips, over her stomach to her breasts. The woman behind her let out a sigh and Elle found herself matching it with one of her own. Kisses landed on her neck and shoulders.

"Elle," the woman whispered in between kisses. "Is this a dream?"

She did not have an answer for the woman. Even if she did, she doubted that she could put together an intelligible sentence. If it was a memory, Elle was not familiar with it. She had never been one for one-night stands, and she had never gone to South Korea with any of her past girlfriends.

Lena Horne sang about how she just could not get her poor self together, and how weary she felt. As she lay there being kissed and caressed by a stranger, Elle could not help but relate. She too was weary of Gloaming Hill and the terrors that haunted her mind, nightmarish memories that she could not imagine living through.

Dream or memory, being in that place, in that stranger's arms, made all those fears suddenly seem so small.

No longer able to hold her curiosity at bay, Elle turned over and saw her.

In the dim light of the rainy morning that softened her features, she smiled at Elle, a crooked half smile, bashful, with a promise of mischief. She knew this woman, though now with her tousled hair she seemed a harmless lover, and she was in that moment.

Elle stiffened and tried to pull away, but the woman held her fast.

"Don't go," she said, and that smile turned into a crooked pout. "Please."

"I can't be here," Elle said, not sure what else to say as she made her escape, winding the sheet around her as she stumbled around the room. She spied the door.

"Wait, Elle, please."

"No. This isn't real," she told her as she picked clothes from a chair and dropped the sheet to dress. The place was small. A kitchenette that fit on one short counter. A table folded from a wall, and Elle saw a bottle of wine and stained glasses.

"What is this place?" she asked.

"The mist." Elle spied the door and made her way toward it.

As she went, she looked over her shoulder to see the woman rise from the bed slowly shedding the covers. Shirtless, she wore a pair of underwear. Her limbs were long and well-muscled. Elle found herself familiar with the woman's form and her mind flashed to memories of that same body beneath her as the two of them quivered together.

"I've been looking for you," she said.

"No," Elle protested the memory and the stranger. "You were with Rob. He came to my room and hurt me."

"What? I would never hurt you," she said, moving closer.

"Get away from me. You're a liar."

Elle went for the door, opened it, and stopped in her tracks. She'd expected to find a narrow hallway lined with doors to similar tiny apartments. Instead, there was the void that was the mist.

She looked to the stranger who seemed just as bewildered.

"Come away from there. Close the door," she said, a panic in her voice.

She was afraid of the mist, which surprised Elle. Did she not know that the mist was benign? Simply a placeholder for the consciousness. The thought frightened and thrilled her. How had she become so acquainted with the mist?

"Elle," the stranger warned her. "Whatever you think is on the other side of that door, it's not something you can trust."

"You're wrong," Elle told her and walked into the mist.

CHAPTER FIFTEEN

Gloaming Hill Facility, West Virginia

Dr. Stevens woke her midmorning with a gentle shake, then began to buzz around the room chattering about her mother's visit that afternoon. Elle felt a rush of excitement at the anticipation of seeing her mother. That feeling soon gave way to a rising dread. Rob had been there in the night, and Elle had escaped him in a fever dream. She began to touch her hand exploring under her T-shirt, certain that she would find a wound, sure she had been stabbed by her dead friend during the night.

Dr. Stevens's smile quickly waned as she registered Elle's growing panic.

"Elle, is everything okay?"

"I saw, Rob," she said, out of breath from the sudden panic. "I saw him again. Here."

She moved to sit up, and Dr. Stevens placed a palm on her shoulder.

"Calm down, Elle, tell me what happened."

"It was just like last time," she said. "He was angry with me. He wanted me to tell him about the Gorgon and something called Project Songbird."

"And then?" Dr. Stevens asked.

Elle put a hand to her throat as she remembered. "He put a knife here. I felt the blood. Then, he stabbed me in the chest. I was so scared, I ended up in the mist."

"The mist?"

"I was there before I woke up here."

"Elle, I've never heard of—"

"Never mind that. Rob came back last night. He was here."

"I'm sorry that you keep being plagued with these hallucinations. They sound terrible."

She sounded genuine, but Elle had her doubts, in fact, she had the button. She sat up, leaned over, and reached into the drawer of the bedside table. She glanced at Dr. Stevens who watched with a curious expression as Elle pulled the drawer to the end of its slide and retrieved the wadded tissue.

"He wasn't a hallucination. He never was."

Hands trembling, she unwrapped the tissue to reveal a single, plain, flat plastic button. She glanced up at Dr. Stevens who had been peering into her hand. Their eyes met.

"What's this then?" she asked, reaching for Elle's hand.

She snatched it away into her closed fist. "This is wrong."

"What's wrong?"

"This button, someone must've switched it while I was out."

"Elle, who switched what?"

As if she did not know.

"The buttons," she said and realized how crazy it sounded. "It was Rob—the person pretending to be him. They switched the buttons."

"Elle, there was no one pretending to be Rob. It was a hallucination."

"Hallucinations don't lose buttons from their coats. I found it on the floor the first time he was here. I've kept it here in my drawer. I've looked at it again and again."

Dr. Steven looked concerned. "Elle, why didn't you tell me about this?"

"Because it was proof," she said. "This place is not what it seems."

"You should have reported this to me right away, instead of hiding it." Dr. Stevens walked away from the bed and went to the door. She closed it and turned back to her. "You should have told me what you were feeling."

"So you and Dr. Branch could sweep it under the rug? What I want to know is why you'd terrorize me like that? Was it a part of your so-called treatment?"

Dr. Stevens was visibly shaken. "Elle, you must stop this. I would never be a part of something like that. We've kept you safe here, and will continue to, even if we have to protect you from yourself."

"I saw that button, day after day, I touched it."

"That doesn't mean anything in this case, Elle, you should have told me. I would have helped you sort things out." She shook her head. "You should have told me."

"That can't be true. You're fucking with my head," she shouted.

The door opened and Nurse Grace entered.

"Is everything okay, Dr. Stevens?"

"Fine, everything's fine," she answered without turning away from Elle. Her voice was cheerful, but her face was dour and tinged with panic. "Just let me finish talking with Elle here. Today is a big day for her."

Nurse Grace muttered something and left. Dr. Stevens closed her eyes at the sound of the door closing. She did not open them for a moment.

"Okay, we're going to talk more about the button situation, you and me. Until then, I don't want you mentioning this to anyone, especially during your mother's visit."

Elle balked at her demand. "I'm going to do more than mention it."

For the first time since Elle had come to her senses to find herself at Gloaming Hill, an exasperated expression crossed Dr. Stevens's face. She ran her hand through her hair. She'd officially lost her cool. No longer the cheerful doctor, she was furtive, nervous.

"You'll have your answers today, Elle. Your mother has been insistent. I thought it would be a good thing, but now I am beginning to have my doubts."

"You're trying to frighten me."

"I'm trying to warn you. A long-lasting hallucination like this, it's a setback to your treatment. Seeing Rob, feeling like you have physical evidence of his presence, believing that we would set you up."

"I'm not delusional."

Dr. Stevens sighed. "I can't tell you what to say to your mother today. You should lay it all bare, as you say. I believe the two of us can sort this out together. I'm confident that we can."

"Why should I trust you, when I can't trust my own mind?" Elle asked.

"Because I'm the only one on your side," Dr. Stevens said and promptly left the room.

The nurses came to help Elle prepare for her mother's visit since she was hindered by her injured arm. It all felt loaded, their banter, their movements, as if they knew something she didn't. The wadded tissue remained on the bedside tray, not even acknowledged as trash to be tossed away. She did not want to touch it, let alone look at it. Everything, from the button to the nurses, to her mother's visit filled her with an intense dread.

Dr. Stevens returned for her shortly after breakfast. As usual, she was smiling, but the smile lacked its usual luster, as if it were a mask pasted on. Elle realized that she was nervous as well. They walked to her office and stopped in front of the door. Dr. Stevens took her good hand and gave it a quick squeeze. It seemed she wanted to say something but thought the better of it. She opened the door.

Elle saw her mother standing in the middle of the room. Dr. Branch was sitting on the sofa behind her balancing a clipboard on her sturdy knees. As she and Dr. Stevens entered, Elle's mother opened her arms wide, beaming, her eyes shining with emotion.

Elle took a tentative step forward, then quickened her step until she was in her mother's embrace. She closed her eyes and smelled Fracas, complemented by the cocoa butter pomade she used to keep her hair in place. Elle could have been five years old, sixteen or thirty, and her mother would have smelled the same. She thought of speaking, but her brain would not form the words.

She took Elle's hand and guided her to the sofa to sit next to Dr. Branch. Still holding Elle's hand, she sat in an opposite chair. Dr. Stevens brought a box of tissues as she pulled up a rolling chair.

The four of them sat for a moment dabbing their eyes, even Dr. Branch. Elle found that though her face was wet with tears, she felt numb. It was like she was not there clutching her mother's hand. She almost expected to hear Dr. Branch's voice overhead guiding her through to the Luling Bowling Alley.

"It's good to see you up and about, baby," her mother said.

The term of endearment embarrassed her, as it had always been used in private. "I've been doing a lot better."

"Dr. Branch has kept me in the loop with your treatment, and I met with Dr. Stevens this morning and she is very optimistic."

"No one is giving me any answers, Mom. I can't have access to anything. I can't call Anne or even look at the Green Patriot."

Her mother paused and glanced briefly at the doctors on either side. "Dr. Branch and Dr. Stevens have told me you've had a hard time being cut off from the world. I warned them from the beginning that you would fight that."

"Just tell me," Elle said. "What happened to me? What is this place?"

Her mother sighed and glanced around at the doctors who watched expectantly, looking to her to lead the discussion. She could not help but think of Dr. Stevens's warning earlier that she was the only one on Elle's side.

"There has been a surge of attacks, foreign and domestic," her mother explained. "The reasons behind the conflicts are evolving. It's no longer country against country. It's zealots and mercenaries teaming up to make their dissatisfaction known to the world."

Elle snorted. "Yeah, it's been like that for a while."

Her mother gave her a look. She disliked snark and sarcasm. "An old friend brought me in on this Chemical Terrorism Commission, an inquiry into terrorist attacks around the world using chemicals and other agents to cause mass destruction."

"Wait. Chemical terrorism?" Elle asked. "Is that what happened in Johannesburg?"

She looked to Dr. Branch, then Dr. Stevens. The looks on their faces told her what they refused to say outright. Her mother shifted in her seat.

"So, they didn't just blow up the convention center, they blasted everyone with poison?" Elle asked.

"Yes," Dr. Stevens said. "We don't know much about the chemical nerve agent they used, only that it affects the areas of the brain in a similar way to PTSD. Anyone exposed experiences a chronic state of high alert."

"If only it were so simple," Dr. Branch cut in. "There is a progression of the symptoms which we have been able to slow with medically induced comas, something we think those responsible are also aware of."

"Progression?" Elle asked.

"Hallucinations, paranoia, and delusions," Dr. Branch said bluntly.

"They've figured out a way to make people psychotic," Elle said.

"I would not describe it as psychosis," Dr. Stevens said. "There is still much to find out about this agent and its effects."

"There is also the matter of missing time," Dr. Branch said.

"Missing time?" Elle asked turning to her mother.

"After the initial attack on the convention center, the perpetrators raided the scene and abducted several people."

"And I was among those people," she said numbly as everything began to fall into place. It explained the refrigerator truck and her inexplicable fear of certain sounds.

"You were missing for seven weeks," her mother added. "We did everything possible to try to locate you."

Dr. Branch leaned forward revealing a tablet.

Elle leaned forward to peer at the screen and she saw herself.

"During that time this surfaced," Dr. Branch said and touched the screen. The image came to life. Elle stared into the camera. Her face was gaunt, her eyes shining with fever, her untamed hair trembled in a billowing wind. The sky behind her was a clear blue, the sun at its highest point in the sky. The wind roared across a mic as the camera panned out to show a rusting barge, an unknown sea rocked below the horizon.

"The Western world must embrace a new way of thinking," she said, her voice raspy and shaky. "The citizens of the US must cleanse their psyches of capitalism, imperialism, and religion, a trial by fire where only the strong of mind will emerge as their own personal messiahs. Those like me have been called upon to make the sacrifice."

"What the actual fuck?" Elle retorted to the image on the screen. "That's not me."

"We've looked into that," her mother said. "The video has not been edited or altered."

She continued, spewing nonsensical New World Order conspiracy theory drivel that even her friend Tammy Crockett, the staunchest of conspiracy theorists, would have ridiculed.

"Okay, just make it stop," Elle said.

Dr. Branch did so.

"They had to force me to say those things," Elle said. "I would never—"

"Of course," her mother said. "This footage has been kept under wraps. I will make sure that it never sees the light of day."

Elle shivered thinking of the consequences of anyone ever seeing the video. It could ruin not only her career, but Anne's as well as her mother's. It was the first time she felt violated. Someone had forced or coerced her into discrediting herself.

"Who are these people?" Elle asked. "Why don't I remember any of it?"

"We've theorized that you purged those traumatic memories. It would explain why you don't remember the shooting at your mother's swearing in years ago."

"You don't remember the swearing in?" her mother asked.

Elle shrugged. "It seems like a bad dream I had once."

Her mother looked concerned. "You did take that hard. You were so young. I guess this isn't our first run-in with extremists."

"Elle, your experience has given us some leads, but there is still little that we know," Dr. Branch added. "There have been some questions raised about the months before Johannesburg and someone you crossed paths with."

"Who?" she asked.

"A person of interest in the bombing and presumably the abduction and torture of you and others, as well as similar attacks," Dr. Branch said.

"So, what is this, some kind of interrogation?" Elle asked them.

"I would never allow anything like that to happen," Dr. Stevens said.

"I know that," Elle said begrudgingly. "I don't mean to lash out. If only this was explained to me when I came out of the—" Mist. She'd almost said mist. "When I woke up here."

"Just breathe, Elle." Dr. Stevens knelt in front of her and led her through the breathing exercises.

"I can't do this," Elle whispered.

"You have to be strong right now," Dr. Stevens said. "You can only tell them what you know. What you remember. We'll stay the course for the treatment, and eventually you'll remember more. They'll just have to wait for the rest."

Elle nodded dumbly. She realized that she clutched Dr. Stevens's hand tightly. Her mother looked on; her mouth was pulled straight at the corners. Dr. Branch wore a perturbed expression.

"I think we should take a break," Dr. Stevens announced. "I can bring us tea and coffee."

"Wow, refreshments?" Elle asked in disbelief.

"Decaf for me," Dr. Branch spoke up. "You know how I like it."

Dr. Stevens was up and on the move. She crossed the room to the door swiftly as if she could outrun Elle's protests. Dr. Branch needed her coffee, after all, and Dr. Stevens knew exactly how she liked it, which peeved Elle even more than being ignored.

"Congresswoman, what can I get for you?"

"Regina," her mother said, equally nonplussed. "Black tea—"

"Two bags, two sugars," Elle finished for her. As a kid, she would bring her mother tea when she was at home working in her office. She would prepare a mug for herself and curl up in an old leather chair with a book. "I suppose I'll have the same."

"I'll be right back," Dr. Stevens said.

Dr. Branch left as well giving the excuse that she had a quick phone call to make.

"How have you been?" her mother asked when the room was clear. "Really?"

"Considering everything, good."

"Are you eating well? Sleeping?"

"Eating yes, sleeping no. There's just not enough to do during the day to tire me out, I suppose."

"You always go-go-go until you drop."

"Right? All I do here is puzzles and coloring books," Elle said. "Coloring books, can you believe that? It's like time evaporates here."

Her mother looked concerned. "Part of me wants to take you away from here."

"Don't talk like that. Your new doctor friends may not like it."

She ignored the barb. "They know of my conflict. I shouldn't be here. We have to be objective here. Give and take."

"So, what do I need to give them in order to leave Gloaming Hill?" Elle asked.

Her mother nodded solemnly. She reached over and took her hand. She spoke in a faint voice that was almost a whisper. "I don't want you to ever blame yourself for any of this. You're not here as some sort of punishment. You're here to get well, and this is a place where you are guaranteed to be safe."

"Mom," she said, suddenly feeling apprehensive. "What is going on? Am I in trouble?"

"You're not," she said. "I just told you that."

"Then, am I in danger?"

"You're safe here," her mother reiterated. "Safer than you would be out in the world."

Elle sighed in frustration. "You know what, Mom, I expect them to jerk me around with these half-answers, but not you. Why can't anyone just come out and tell me what the hell is going on?"

"It's a matter of national security first of all," she answered. "That makes it crucial that you remember what happened on your own, without being fed information."

"I've been told," Elle said. "But I can't accept that. I just always feel like something is creeping up on me like a dark shadow that will swallow me whole. It feels like I have zero lifelines here."

"I'm sorry you were hurt and taken away from your life," her mother said. "Your father and I want you home. Your friends and colleagues want you back at the Green Patriot."

"I know," Elle said, hearing the emotion in her voice. "And I want to get back to my life too, but if it's time for me to know, I need to know. I'm losing my mind in here."

Her mother changed the topic to Elle's dad and his endeavors as reverend over a small congregation outside of Atlanta, their family home, and the social events of the past year.

Elle asked about Anne Humphries and her apartment in Austin.

"It's all waiting for your return," her mother said. "Your father and I were wondering if you'd like to come home to Atlanta once you're released. You know we would take loving care of you."

"That sounds good, Mom," Elle said, looking forward to cooking with Dad in the kitchen and having wine around the fire pit out back on a chilly fall evening.

"We'll be together soon," her mother said.

"How is the Green Patriot handling my absence?" she asked.

"As far as anyone knows you are recovering from injuries that occurred during the Johannesburg incident."

"And that's it? No one is asking any questions?"

"Of course, they are. Anne and I have both made statements that you want privacy while you heal. Everyone has respected that wish, even your conspiracy theorist friend."

"Tammy Crockett," Elle said and could not help but smile. "This all would be right up her alley."

"I don't want you to worry about such things right now."

Dr. Stevens and Dr. Branch returned together. Dr. Stevens carried a tray with four paper cups with plastic lids. She was smiling until she saw Elle's face.

"Is everything okay?" she asked.

"No, it's not," Elle blurted. "Let's get on with this. I want to know who that person was."

The three of them exchanged glances. Her mother gave a nod.

"Dr. Branch has a picture to show you," Dr. Stevens said. "You're to tell us if you recognize the person. If you don't, that's fine. If you do recognize the person in this photo, we need you to tell us everything you remember."

Elle read the gravity of her words. She thought of the button. Was her mind so unstable that it could play such a trick on her? She thought of Rob. Did she carry so much guilt about his death that her mind could conjure him so vividly?

"Elle?" her mother asked.

"Show me," she said. "Show me the picture."

She looked to Dr. Branch; she was watching Elle intently.

"If I recognize this person, if I remember anything about them, I won't hold back."

"Good," her mother said. "When you're ready, Dr. Branch will show you the picture."

"Mom," Elle said. "I'm ready."

Dr. Branch looked to Dr. Stevens who nodded. She leaned forward and lifted a page from her clipboard revealing the picture. She recognized herself squinting in the setting sun, and a woman with shoulder-length blond hair and a narrow face. Elle knew her as the woman from her journey through the mist.

"Do you remember her?" Dr. Stevens asked.

"I know her," Elle admitted. "But I am not sure how or where."

She couldn't tell them about the dream in the middle of the mist.

"It's okay," her mother said. She seemed relieved and Elle felt a pang of guilt.

"Who is she?"

"She's exactly like those men who attacked us during my swearing in," her mother said. "Someone with a grudge against society, someone who would do atrocious things to get people to pay attention to their twisted rhetoric."

Elle thought of the dream from the mist, and that woman holding her, and kissing the back of her neck while her hands explored under the sheets. She'd seen her before, the first night Rob had come to her. She felt Dr. Stevens's eyes on her but did not look her way, as she was not sure she could hide the truth.

She had to say something. "Maybe I connected with her for a story." Because that was a benign possibility. That was how she'd met Rob.

"We've considered that. We were not able to confirm with Anne or anything in your phone or laptop," her mother said. "We searched everything, and we could not find a trace of this woman in your personal or professional life."

"Who is she? What is she?"

"A terrorist," Dr. Branch said, and Elle was afraid that she'd seen right through her. "She was a part of the attack in Johannesburg. She had a hand in your abduction and whatever happened from between then and when you were found with a half dozen others on a rusty barge in a catatonic state."

She looked to her mother and Dr. Stevens for confirmation. They were both agitated. Dr. Stevens's brow was furrowed, and her mother had wiped all trace of emotion from her face because she did not like to show her hand.

"We all agreed that this isn't an interrogation," Dr. Stevens said.

"I thought so as well," her mother added.

"This was a gamble we didn't need to take," Dr. Branch said.

"We don't know that yet," her mother argued.

"With all due respect," Dr. Branch said. "This is not your area of expertise. You should not be here."

"You needed someone to jolt the life into this program of yours, Doctor, if not for my daughter, then for your long-suffering patients."

"Do not bring my patients into this. None of them have had their pictures taken with a known terrorist."

Dr. Stevens stood. "The two of you just stop right now. I will be the first to admit when I'm wrong, but we don't have to allow this meeting to deteriorate just because there was not some aha breakthrough."

She glanced at Elle. "Let's just take a moment to breathe and rethink this."

"What's done is done," Dr. Branch said.

Elle's mother huffed and turned to face her.

"Can you tell me more about what is going on with this mysterious woman?" Elle asked.

Instead of answering, her mother looked to Dr. Branch in an exaggeratedly expectant manner. She'd taken her mask off.

"A few months before," Dr. Branch said. "She was being watched by UK intelligence concerning another incident involving chemical weapons."

"Wait," Elle said, pointing to the picture in Dr. Branch's lap. "Is she the Gorgon?"

She looked to Dr. Stevens again. Her glance was unwavering; still, she did not say a word.

Elle turned her attention to her mother.

"Yes, that is what she's called."

"Did you remember something?" Dr. Branch asked.

"No," Elle said. "I'm connecting the dots here, just like you. A few days ago, Dr. Stevens gave me a clue."

"A clue?" her mother asked.

"We were here in her office, and she showed me a book about mythology," Elle explained as she motioned to the bookshelf.

"A little experiment I wanted to try," Dr. Stevens said. "Something to trigger a memory."

"It worked," Elle said. "I remembered a Russian woman interrogating me about the Gorgon."

"We were hoping Dr. Stevens's experiment would work again," her mother said.

Elle looked to her mother. "You knew about the Gorgon?"

"She is a key player in all of this," her mother said. "Finding out who she is and what she knows about the toxin used in the attack is integral."

"Is the woman in the picture the same as the woman you saw in your room?"

Elle hesitated. She looked to Dr. Stevens who gave a quick nod of assurance.

She nodded. "I saw Rob Loera too."

"A hallucinatory experience," Dr. Branch chimed in. "The toxin is still working its way out of your system."

"When Elle told me about her experience, I figured it had to be the Gorgon she was describing," Dr. Stevens explained. "It seemed like Elle's memories of her were beginning to surface."

"And my stance remains the same," Dr. Branch said. "We need to stay the course and follow the treatment regime as it is, no theatrics."

"I would have to agree," Dr. Stevens said.

Elle straightened. "It feels like I have to clear my name now."

Dr. Branch opened her mouth to speak, but her mother was quicker.

"That isn't how anyone here wanted this to go down."

"Which is why we need to be on the same page," Dr. Branch said. "With this level of transparency, we're putting a lot of trust in you, Elle. We'll need your complete honesty."

She did not have to tell them about the cozy apartment on a rainy day, that place beyond the mist. Perhaps it was like the button from Rob Loera's dress jacket. Something she imagined. A nightmare residual of a wild hallucination. Dead people did not come back from the grave, and she most definitely would never find herself in the arms of a known terrorist.

"I'll be completely honest," Elle repeated Dr. Branch's words.

"And if it's something you don't want to see," she said. "Something that would be difficult to accept."

She had a dreadful feeling that they knew about the dream beyond the mist. She recalled Dr. Stevens's words that morning: *I'm the only one on your side.* Elle dismissed the thought. They would have busted her by now.

Elle looked to her mother. "I'll be truthful. I won't let you down, Mom."

The atmosphere seemed to soften after that, and they all were watching her, gauging her reaction. The meeting was over, and it was time for her mother to leave. Elle's nervousness about lying gave way to sadness.

"Where are you going? Home or DC?" she asked.

"Home first, but in a few days, I'll be in session."

"Would you be able to call me?"

"We will see," she said, glancing at the doctors, and Elle was satisfied that her mother would get her way.

"You'll give my love to Dad. And Anne."

Her mother stood.

Elle stood too and they awkwardly embraced around the sling. Her mother kissed the side of her face, something she had not done since high school graduation.

"Your car is waiting, Congresswoman," Dr. Stevens said.

Her mother moved away. "Dr. Stevens, I see that you have been taking extra care with my daughter. I greatly appreciate it."

"It's my pleasure," she said, and the smile was back though dampened by the somberness of the occasion. "We're doing everything we can to get Elle back to you."

"Thank you," her mother said as they shook hands. She turned to Elle.

"You stay strong. You're a Pharell, never forget that."

They embraced again and she was gone, followed by Dr. Branch. Dr. Stevens watched them go, a worried expression on her face. She glanced at Elle, then realized she was observing her and quickly smiled.

"I brought you some truffles."

Elle felt her spirit lighten at the prospect. "Chocolate truffles?"

"Well, it's not the fungi," she said. She went to her desk and returned with a gold-colored box. "I was going to pass them around during our meeting, but I went with tea and coffee instead."

"Great. More for us."

Dr. Stevens chuckled while opening the box with a flourish to reveal a row of round bonbons, some dark, some creamy brown. Each was topped with little bits of flower petals or tiny curls of fruit or nonpareils.

Elle selected one with a swirl of caramel on top and took a bite. She closed her eyes, relishing the flavors.

"Good?" Dr. Stevens asked.

Elle nodded and finished the sweet.

Dr. Stevens sat next to her in the seat where only moments before her mother had sat. She chose a truffle from the box and devoured it whole. The two of them were silent for a few moments as they ate chocolates.

"How are you feeling, Elle?"

"Overwhelmed, exhausted."

"I'll take you to your room to rest," Dr. Stevens said. "We can talk later."

"Not just yet," Elle said. "How am I supposed to trust my own mind after the button?"

"You can," Dr. Stevens said. "And if you aren't sure, let us know. That's why we're here."

"Mom trusts you," Elle said. "I think she believes I screwed up, that I invited this Gorgon person into my life. I think Dr. Branch does as well, but not you. Why?"

"One meeting with a terrorist doesn't implicate you. Elle, you may not have even known what she was truly about."

"So why would she target me? Because I'm a journalist?"

"That could very well be," Dr. Stevens said. "Her type is not exactly trustful of the media."

"Still, she had me read that statement. She may not like the media, but she knows that it can bring attention to her cause."

"I was against them showing you that video," Dr. Stevens said. "It was too much for you right now."

"I've seen worse reliving all of this," Elle said. "To think, I may have somehow brought this all down on myself."

"You're safe, you have your mother looking out for you and Dr. Branch as well, believe it or not," she said. "And I am always here."

CHAPTER SIXTEEN

Gloaming Hill Facility, West Virginia

A few days after her mother's visit, Elle was back in Dr. Branch's chair, in that room with the padded walls. It all blurred around her as she transitioned from consciousness to trance to the bowling alley in Luling. For a moment, it felt as if she were flying in a dream. Then, she was back in Johannesburg exploring her mind for lost memories.

Elle had traveled to South Africa to cover the World AIDS Summit. She arrived the night before and stayed at the Radisson. She'd worn a cream-colored blouse and the skirt of her favorite suit but had left the jacket behind because of the heat that day. She carried a medium-sized bag with a camera and a tripod to do her own videography. It was strange that Anne hadn't sent someone with her.

She would have walked the short distance to the convention center, but the air-conditioned shuttle bus seemed like an oasis on wheels. She felt adventurous as she always did when traveling abroad.

After flashing her laminated pass on its red lanyard, security allowed her to file into the glass-paneled lobby. She attended a round table of reporters. Their discussion, avoiding bias against people living with HIV and AIDS. Elle spotted a familiar face in the crowd briefly. The Gorgon. There, then, gone again.

Elle did not remember the sound of the blast, shortly after, only the force of the hot wind that knocked her to the floor. The room shook and everything went dark for a moment. Dazed, she heard the rise of a chorus of panicked screams throughout the building. Sparks showered through a mist of smoke and dust. She had fallen and been partially covered by broken ceiling tiles and a light fixture. She freed herself and stood on shaky legs.

Around her, the others collected themselves. She stumbled with them toward a red exit sign that was somehow still intact. They did look like zombies as they rose and began to move, stunned, covered in dust, and smeared with blood. Water from the broken water cooler ran over her favorite, most practical pair of pumps. Her feet slipped out of the wet shoes as she made her way through the ruined building.

She thought of hazardous building materials released into the air, asbestos, dioxin, lead. She learned from the 9/11 tragedy that the clouds of toxins dispersed from destroyed buildings were just as dangerous as the causes of their destruction.

A wall of debris fell with a thunderous crash. More screams rang out in response, then cries of relief as shafts of light lit up the dimness. Everyone surged forward to be rescued. Elle hung back. She was not injured as far as she could tell. Blinded by the high-powered flashlight the newcomers wielded, she shielded her eyes with her hand. Dressed in black camouflage and helmets with black visors that covered their eyes, they entered the hall single file through the breach of broken rubble. They carried rifles with silencers on the end, flashlights mounted on top.

"Elle Pharell," one of them shouted. "Where is Elle Pharell?"

The muzzles of the guns flashed as the figures in black fired on the remaining attendees of the World AIDS Summit. Elle scattered with the others. She tripped over some debris, and someone stepped on her hand. She managed to get to her feet without being trampled. She moved again with the others. Like a panicked herd of animals, they ran, blinded by fear.

They came to another wall of debris where other black-clad gunmen waited. Beams from their guns played over terror-filled faces. There was no place to run. One of the gunmen stepped forward and pointed his weapon at her. Before she could beg them not to shoot, she felt a stinging pain in her leg. She gasped and looked down at her thigh and saw the fletching of a dart.

Everything went dark and she heard Dr. Branch's voice. It brought her comfort, a reminder that she was not really in Johannesburg and everything she saw was just a memory.

"Can you recall any of their faces?" she asked.

"I don't know," Elle said. "It happened so fast."

"Let's continue," Dr. Branch said.

The refrigerated truck. Leslie, who, like Elle, would later become a patient at the Gloaming Hill Recovery Center in West Virginia, mistook her for Carrie, who hung above them on a meat hook swinging in the frigid breeze. The cold did not affect Elle like before and she was able to see the end of the journey.

The truck stopped, then there was the sound of creaking metal as the doors of the trailer swung open. A light swept across the space revealing the true horror of the scene. Elle saw several frozen, unmoving people as well as poor Carrie hanging.

She heard voices and heavy footfalls. She was too stiff and weak from the cold to move to see who entered the trailer. A pair of booted feet stepped into her vision. The beam of a flashlight crawled over her.

"Get them out," a woman's voice said. "I'll get Pharell."

In Dr. Branch's chair, Elle felt her body tremble as her mind connected the memory of the voice with the face, and a flood of images like when she sank from the mist and found herself at Gloaming Hill. She saw that face, the eyes, the mouth pulled into a half smile, felt the touch of hands all over her at once.

She turned Elle over and onto a sort of stretcher. She was stooping over Elle with a flashlight under her chin as if she were going to tell a scary story.

"You made it," she said, her words appearing as shadowy condensation. "You've run the gauntlet."

Her voice was low, but her tone was hopeful. She rose, and soon Elle began to glide across the floor of the trailer. She was dragging Elle along on the stretcher. Above, the dark ceiling of the trailer gave way to a red glow that brightened and dimmed as she was moved along a cavern-like hall tunnel. They were underground, Elle deduced from the rocky walls and ceiling. Dull red lights glowed overhead dangling from crooked wires.

The memory faded to black, and she was back at the bowling alley in Luling under the multicolored glow of the black light murals of cows in outer space. She called out for Dr. Branch but got no answer. She wandered away from the mural and toward the lanes. She found it strange that the place was completely dark. During her last session, and when she passed through as she transitioned, there had been light overhead, just like in real life.

She called out for Dr. Branch once again. No answer.

A familiar figure in the dark stood there watching her. She began to move away. If this was supposed to be her safe space, why was the Gorgon there? She tried to move around the bar area, move to the back exit, get back to remembering. The Gorgon copied her movement, blocking the path.

"What do you want from me?" Elle asked.

She did not answer.

"You're a terrorist," Elle said. "You hurt me and countless other people."

"One man's terrorist is another man's savior."

"That's a horrible thing to say," Elle told her.

"They made you forget," she said. "Even now, even this." She raised her arms to gesture around them. "It's all here to make you forget."

"You're wrong," Elle said. "This is where I will remember the truth."

"You'll remember what they want you to remember," the Gorgon said.

PA static crackled above them, and Dr. Branch called out for Elle.

"I'm here."

There was relief in Dr. Branch's voice when she spoke again. "I'm going to guide you out. You've gone far enough this session."

"No," Elle blurted. "I saw her. I saw where the Gorgon took me after the attack. She's here with me."

Static. Then Dr. Branch's voice. "It's time to get you out."

"No," Elle said. "We're so close. I just know it."

The Gorgon was gone. Vanished. Elle moved past the bar and toward the restrooms. She heard Dr. Branch calling for her as she made her way to the back exit. She burst through the door and felt her own rush of relief to find a swirling black.

Red lights above, dimming and brightening as Elle's body lurched along. She recognized it all vaguely like a recurring dream. She was back on the stretcher; the Gorgon dragged her along a rocky passage.

The light changed, a dim buzz like dusty fluorescents. She heard a metallic shriek followed by a bang. She smelled water. Before she could register anything else, she was unceremoniously dumped onto a cold, wet dirt floor.

Elle began to writhe weakly; she was able to turn over on her side, her fingers scrambling in the loose dirt and rocks for purchase. The Gorgon stood above her.

"Get up," she said. Her voice was deep and smoky, and it was hard for Elle not to think of the memory, or was it a dream of the tiny apartment in Korea, the woman who now spoke so sternly, kissing her ear between sleepy whispers.

Elle did not move. Her eyes rolled up to look at her captive. She tried to speak a plea, but only a slurred babble came out of her mouth.

"Get. Up."

"I can't," Elle groaned.

"You have to," she growled in return. "You've been deemed an asset to the cause."

Perhaps it was the gravity of the Gorgon's voice, but Elle struggled to her hands and knees, tried to stand, but fell back into the dirt where she began to sob.

"Enough," her captor said. "You'll have to be stronger if you want to survive."

"Just do it now," Elle whispered. "Just kill me."

"You don't know what you're saying," her voice had softened.

Her captor hauled Elle to her feet and waited until she stood steadily.

Elle whimpered as she lurched along leaning on the woman in black.

The tunnel ended. They entered a large room with a paved floor and cement columns. Several pieces of furniture were scattered throughout, tables and chairs. A rack of guns hung on a wall. A bank of boxy monitors had been piled on a long desk. They displayed what Elle figured were exterior angles of the hideout.

She shoved her. "Keep your eyes down. You'll make these guys nervous."

"What is this place?" Elle asked.

The Gorgon gave no answer as she marched her through the room to another dimly lit tunnel. Elle could hear voices, people as they cried out in agony. She tilted her head, not able to figure out their location, but the tranquilizer had left her disoriented and unsure of what she heard or saw.

They'd stopped in front of a narrow hole next to a rusty grate of metal.

"Prime real estate."

Like déjà vu, Elle understood immediately. In the distance, someone screamed for their mother.

"No," she said. "Please no, please no."

The Gorgon flinched but did not seem moved. Her face became a blur as she shoved Elle forward.

Her already unstable footing completely failed. She tripped over her own feet and fell into the hole. She landed on her side, stunned. She rolled over grimacing from the impact. Through half-closed lids she could see the woman in black above covering the hole with the grate. She peered down to watch her.

"Elle?"

Dr. Branch was calling her back and Elle was ready to leave this memory behind. As in a dream, the scenery dissolved, and she stood in the Luling Bowling Alley. The dim lights brightened until they were blinding. Everything went white.

She opened her eyes to see Dr. Branch standing over her.

"What was that all about?"

Elle looked around, disoriented from the transition.

"You're never to do that again," she said. "I guide the session, not you."

"I wanted to see more," Elle said.

"I understand, but we do not know the repercussions of a patient-led session," Dr. Branch told her. She glanced at her watch. "Dr. Stevens wants us to meet her in the sunroom."

Elle climbed out of the chair. Her legs felt a bit unsteady as she followed Dr. Branch out of the room and into the hall. Unlike Dr. Stevens, Dr. Branch walked at a quick pace, her heels clacking on the tiled floor. Elle found herself lagging a few paces behind.

They reached the sunroom, but Dr. Stevens was not there. Dr. Branch glanced around impatiently. Elle did so as well, curious of other patients. She saw two, one in a smaller observation room just off the sunroom completing a puzzle, a nurse in coral scrubs nearby. The other patient was parked in a wheelchair staring blankly out the glass at the woods beyond. Elle tried to recognize any of them from her remembrances of the explosion in Johannesburg but found that she did not.

Dr. Branch waved a nurse over. Elle had seen him around but never really spoken to him. "Dr. Stevens should be here shortly, if you could keep an eye on Ms. Pharell here."

He nodded. "Hello, Elle."

"Hi," she said.

"This is Nurse Rollins," she said. "Don't give him a hard time."

Elle gave her a thumbs-up transfixed by the day beyond the wall of glass panes. The sky was packed with looming white stacks of clouds. Below, the mowed spread of green lawn sprouted tiny purple blooms.

"Am I allowed to go out?"

"I don't see why not," Dr. Branch said distractedly.

Elle went for one of the folding chairs and then the door. Rollins came to help by holding the door. She smiled at him as she made her way out. On the grass, she slipped off her shoes. The lawn was always trimmed not too long and not too short, the perfect length for bare feet. She set up her chair among a patch of the purple blooms. She sat and folded her legs under her like summer camp. She turned her face to the sky and closed her eyes. She felt the light of the sun shining on her closed lids.

One of her first memories of her father's sermons was him saying something about the light of God's face shining on the faces of people. The sermon was about overcoming discouraging circumstances like David's followers as they fled into the wilderness from Absalom. She was five at the time, and based on her knowledge of the world up until then, the sun was God's face looking down on the world. She walked out of church that day in her little patent leather shoes with her face tilted up to the sky feeling what she thought to be pure glory.

Elle laughed to herself to have remembered such a thing when she was in such a struggle to retrieve her lost memories of her abduction. This recollection brought her joy, the same she felt as a child innocent enough to believe that the light of God shone down on her face. Unlike the memories that haunted her at Gloaming Hill, even the lost ones such as her mother's swearing in.

Perhaps that was the key. Happiness. She would have to share that with Dr. Stevens.

A pair of hands suddenly covered her eyes. She smiled thinking it was the doctor playing a game.

"We don't have to go inside yet, do we?" Elle asked.

"I won't stop you," came the reply.

The voice did not belong to Dr. Stevens.

Leslie stepped around the chair to face her. Dark circles shaded her eyes, otherwise her skin was as pale as the moon. Elle remembered the refrigerator truck and how she had wept for Carrie.

"Hello," Elle said.

She crinkled her nose, her brow bent. Her stare was hard and unreadable.

"I've been looking for you."

Elle felt a chill down her spine as if she were back in that truck. She thought of the Gorgon's words to her in that vision at the end of the mist.

"There are some things I want to talk to you about as well."

Leslie raised her eyebrow. "We don't have much time. The nurses are looking for me."

"Who is Carrie?"

She covered her mouth and Elle, thinking that she was overcome by the memory of a lost loved one, felt a pang of sympathy. Leslie moved her hand away to reveal that she had been hiding a giggle. Elle straightened in her chair, startled at the response. She realized that trying to compare her experiences of Johannesburg with Leslie's would not be so simple.

"I saw her in a session with Dr. Branch," she said gently. "Do you visit with Dr. Branch?"

"No," she said.

Perplexed, Elle wanted to ask why, but she doubted that Leslie would know. She was not stable enough to have sessions with Dr. Branch. They were mentally grueling.

"Carrie was a friend of mine," Leslie said. "We traveled together to third world countries providing health care to people who needed it. Basic stuff. We went to Johannesburg to find more resources for helping people with HIV and AIDs."

"You're a doctor?"

"I was trained as a nurse," Leslie said. "But when you're the only person with medical knowledge in a five-hundred-mile radius…"

She trailed off and just stared for a moment.

"You were fighting the good fight," Elle said to be encouraging, but Leslie just shook her head and tears welled up in her large gray eyes and shimmered in the sunlight.

"Is that why you were in Johannesburg?"

Leslie inhaled sharply. "We're meant to die here. This place is not what it seems."

Elle felt a sinking feeling in the pit of her stomach at those words. She looked behind her at the sunroom for Rollins or any of the nurses. She could see no one. Was everyone on the alert looking for Leslie?

"You don't believe me," she said. "You've got blinders on."

Elle decided to play along. One of the staff would come along soon. "Tell me, what am I being blinded to?"

"You're the reason we're all here, and our time is coming to an end."

"I don't understand," Elle said. "I know that terrible things were done to us, and the people that did those things are still out there, waiting to strike again."

Leslie laughed. "Yes, terrible things were done to us, and terrible things still are happening, even as we stand here talking. The perpetrators are here at Gloaming Hill."

"That's just not true."

Leslie stepped back. She regarded Elle with dark-ringed eyes now filling with tears. She produced a scalpel. Elle recoiled in her chair. Fear gripped her colder than her memory of the ride in the refrigerated truck.

"What is that for?" she asked.

She blinked several times before once again fixing her with that stare. "Ask me about Carrie."

"Okay, how long did you know her?"

Leslie's face crumpled into a sob. She trembled. "I don't know."

Elle reminded herself to breathe. She wanted to genuinely express her sympathy, she had after all, been through the same terrible things, but she did not want to further upset the woman standing there with a scalpel.

"We all lost memories—"

She shook her head. "I don't know anything about Carrie other than what they put into my head. They've done it before. That is my role, the grieving visitor. My tears corroborate their narratives."

Another breath. Elle forced herself not to turn around to see if anyone was coming. She did not want to seem disingenuous to Leslie's emotional state.

"I don't understand, you must explain it to me."

"False memories," she said. "You see, I'm a perpetual victim, one of the many players needed for an operation like this. They've done it before. They're doing it to you right now."

"What exactly are *they* doing, Leslie?"

"Everything here is a lie. The doctors, the nurses, they are all like me."

Leslie came close and Elle saw that fresh scratches crisscrossed her left forearm, the skin that surrounded them irritated halos. She crouched before the chair, the pupils of her gray eyes wide as if she were in the dark. She was staring past her, back toward the building. Elle turned to see Nurse Slick, Nurse Grace, and Nurse Rollins approaching. They all looked different in the full light of day.

"But I have a secret, a message in a bottle, a message for you."

She grabbed Elle's hand quickly and raised the glinting blade of the scalpel above it.

"Thora says to look at the full moon," she said.

By then, Rollins had reached them. He grabbed Leslie by the arm and snatched her away from Elle. She tore away and ran a few paces and stopped. She stretched out her arm, brandishing the scalpel. She shook her head slowly, like a naughty child refusing to give up their game.

"I wasn't finished talking to Elle," Leslie said. "I have to tell her."

"Put the scalpel down," he said. "This area is restricted to you right now, Leslie, you're going to have to leave."

Nurse Grace and Nurse Slick moved in closer, positioning themselves between her and Elle. Leslie stumbled away from them, glanced over her shoulder to the woods, and turned back to them all with a triumphant grin.

"I'll run into the woods," she said.

"You'll do no such thing," Nurse Slick said with finality. "You'll go back to your room."

"My room," Leslie said with a mocking drawl. "Ever notice, Elle, how time passes when you're in your *room*?"

"Shut up," Nurse Grace said. "You're only going to make more trouble for yourself."

"What do they have you doing in there?" Leslie asked. "Coloring? Puzzles? Crafts? You ever lose track of time?"

"Get her out of here," Nurse Grace said, and Nurse Slick went to Elle and touched her shoulder. At that moment, Rollins made an awkward lunge for Leslie who once again avoided capture. She sliced at him clumsily, and he managed to grab her wrist.

"They keep us in the mist mostly," she shouted to Elle as she struggled. "They feed us nightmares and tell us what to fear."

"Get her out of here," Nurse Grace bellowed to Nurse Slick. "Leslie, I'm going to take you back to your room myself." She quickly crossed the distance between them, and either her quarry was slow to react or stunned into submission by the nurse's will, but she was able to catch Leslie's forearm in a death grip.

The scalpel fell into the grass.

Nurse Slick had also gotten more aggressive as she pulled at the arm of her charge. She found Elle frozen, fixated on the scene playing out in front of her, the words of the other patient replaying in her head.

Leslie tried to thrash her way out of Nurse Grace's grip. Rollins had joined the fray and both of his big arms wrapped around her. She screamed, kicking her legs, but his muscles strained through his shirt as he tightened his grip.

"See?" Leslie shouted in anguish. "This is how they really treat us."

Elle did not want to see this. She tried to convince herself that Leslie deserved the rough treatment because she broke the rules, whatever they were. She wanted to turn away, to leave the room and return to the safety of her own bed. She stood and allowed Nurse Slick to guide her away. Upon turning, she saw that Dr. Stevens had arrived.

Elle looked to her pleadingly, but the doctor strode past her without so much as one of her reassuring glances.

Leslie screamed upon noticing. "Get away from me, you bitch."

Dr. Stevens did not say a word. She removed a syringe from her pocket and quickly prepared it. Upon seeing the needle, Leslie let out another piercing scream, a wordless cry, the type of anguish only an insane person could feel as their mind conspires against reality. She fought wildly, like some snared animal. She would cease her struggle to curse, then start up again.

Dr. Stevens moved closer, and Leslie lashed out with a kick catching her in the thigh. Unperturbed, the doctor restrained her legs in one swift movement.

"You should just kill me," Leslie screamed.

"Hold her," Dr. Stevens barked at Nurse Grace as she moved in with the syringe. She squeezed Leslie's upper arm and drove the needle home.

"I've been compromised," she shrieked.

"It's okay now," she said. "It's not your fault."

Leslie's eyelids drooped; her body went limp. She sleepily murmured a few more curses before she succumbed to the drug mixing with the blood in her veins.

Rollins sagged with her and struggled to catch his breath. "She came out of nowhere, started talking to Elle."

"Get her to her room," Dr. Stevens said and walked away from them toward the building. She took hold of Elle's arm as she went.

"Are you all right?"

"I think," Elle said as tears filled her eyes. "What is wrong with her?"

Nurse Grace spoke up. "She's unstable. You can't believe a thing she tells you, she—"

She quieted when Dr. Stevens raised her hand. "I'm going to take Elle back to her room," she said curtly. "You can assist Slick and Rollins."

She guided Elle back into the sunroom and through the corridor that led back to her room. Elle felt a flash of dread as they went. She thought of Leslie's words. Had she said that her room was the mist? She suddenly did not want to go back there. She looked to Dr. Stevens and saw the worried expression on her face. She wished that the doctor could bring her some comfort, bring the reassurance she often brought Elle, but she felt too unnerved by the encounter with Leslie.

"I don't want to go back to my room. It's lonely."

"Would you like to go back to my office?" she asked.

Elle nodded. She thought of Leslie and wondered where the nurses would carry her off to, what would happen to her in that other place.

In a few moments, they were in front of Dr. Stevens's office door though they had not changed directions. Had Dr. Stevens's office always been so close to her room? It was so difficult to map the nondescript corridors of the facility.

Inside, Elle settled on the comfy couch. Dr. Stevens brought her a bottled water and bade her to drink. She sat next to her and sighed.

"I never wanted you to see anything like that here."

"I'm sorry," Elle said.

"It's not your fault, or anyone else's," she said. "Leslie can be... difficult."

"What happened to her?"

"She's very ill."

Elle sipped her water.

"I need you to tell me exactly what she said to you out there."

"She said that everything here is a lie, that nightmares are planted inside our heads," Elle explained. "If I was in a different place mentally..."

Dr. Stevens bowed her head and straightened. "I'm glad you're in a good place. What else did she say?"

"She said that she had a message in a bottle, that it was from someone named Thora."

Dr. Stevens took a breath, and she reached out to clutch Elle's hand as if she would fall over if she didn't. A coldness claimed her eyes, and her usually cheerful demeanor, already dimmed, seemed to fade entirely.

"Thora?" she asked. "Are you certain of that name?"

"Yes," Elle answered, her own dread rising. "Who is that?"

"Don't mind that," Dr. Stevens said gently. "I need you to think carefully, is there anything else she told you?"

Elle thought for a moment. "No."

Dr. Stevens stood. "I want you to stay here for a moment, Elle. I'm going to lock the door. Only I have the key. I do not want you to open the door for anyone."

"What?" Elle asked. "What's going on?"

"Just give me a few minutes, please," she said and left.

Elle sat for a moment listening to her own breathing. Who was Thora and why had the mention of her name caused Dr. Stevens to go into a near panic?

She heard the unmistakable rattle of a door handle. She startled and looked toward the only entrance to the office. The latch handle moved in an agitated jiggle then stopped. A stern knock followed and then silence.

Elle stood hoping that it was Dr. Stevens. She had misplaced her key. She walked a few paces and paused. The knock came again.

"Wyatt? Elle, are you in there?"

It was Dr. Branch.

Elle debated answering her. Surely, Dr. Stevens did not mean to include Dr. Branch among those she should not allow admittance. Then again, she had been in a near panic when she'd left. Another knock. The handle rattled vigorously and stopped. Silence followed. She stood staring at the door, her heart hammering in her chest. She tried to comprehend what was happening.

Elle kept her eyes on the door, glancing only at the clock on the wall.

The door opened, and Dr. Stevens appeared. She did not enter, only motioned for Elle to come to her. Before she could move, Dr. Branch stepped into the doorframe behind Dr. Stevens who turned and backed into the office.

"What is going on here. Wyatt?"

"It's time," she said. "I've already rang the alarm."

"Wyatt, do you know something I don't?" Dr. Branch entered behind her, a strange smirk on her face. She spotted Elle.

"None of that matters," Dr. Stevens told her, stepping backward as Dr. Branch advanced. "Gloaming Hill is compromised, but I suspect you know that already."

Something was wrong, the way Dr. Branch kept calling Dr. Stevens by her first name in a sly, mocking tone. Dr. Stevens became increasingly nervous each time. Elle could feel tension waft through the room like a freezing cold draft.

Dr. Branch frowned. "You're the only one who's acting squirrelly here, Wyatt."

Dr. Stevens stepped backward and glanced over her shoulder at Elle. She reminded her of a spooked horse, ready to rear and bolt.

Elle decided to speak up. "I'm tired, I'm very tired."

Dr. Branch looked to her. "You'll get the chance to rest, very soon."

"Back off," Dr. Stevens growled suddenly. "I won't hesitate."

"You spook so easily," Dr. Branch said. "Your kind usually does; the mind begins to deteriorate early when it's been tampered with as much as yours."

"Trust that I'm fit to defend this operation," Dr. Stevens said.

In a sudden flash of violence, Dr. Branch lunged and shoved Dr. Stevens to the floor.

Elle screamed and went to help her. Dr. Branch moved in to stop her. She grabbed Elle's shoulders in a remarkably strong grip.

She whimpered and tried to pull away. Behind them, Dr. Stevens was back on her feet shedding her white coat, which she tossed to the floor. Elle noticed that she wore one black brace that stretched from her elbow to her wrist. Her feet were spread apart, her arms up and bent at the elbows. A fighter's stance.

"Oh, Wyatt," Dr. Branch said without turning. "You don't want to do this."

"There's no point in us trying to reason with each other," Dr. Stevens said. "Let's just get this over with."

Dr. Branch shoved Elle backward.

She fell hard on her ass, her vision blurred from the pain. When her eyes cleared, she saw Dr. Branch removing her suit jacket. She wore a black silk blouse with a jaunty bow at the collar. She went for her watch as if to remove it. Instead, she pulled the crown and removed a length of shiny garrote wire.

The two doctors circled each other carefully, their usual clinical, professional demeanors changed into something with a lethal edge. Elle watched in disbelief, frozen in the spot where Dr. Branch had dumped her.

Dr. Stevens struck at Dr. Branch with a viper's quickness. Dr. Branch was quicker. She dodged, got behind her, raised her arms, and attempted to get the wire around Dr. Stevens's neck. The two of them parted quickly with an agile grace that left Elle in further disbelief.

Dr. Stevens bit her bottom lip and struck again, her gloved blow landing on Dr. Branch's silk-clad shoulder producing a blue spark and the crackle of electricity. Dr. Branch cried out and stumbled backward. Dr. Stevens advanced and attacked with her gloved hand. Dr. Branch side-stepped to avoid it, and as she did, she drove her elbow into Dr. Stevens's midsection. She doubled over and Dr. Branch grabbed a fistful of auburn hair and shoved her to her knees.

Dr. Stevens tried to strike out with her gloved hand. Dr. Branch slapped it away and pulled her close trying to secure the other end of the garrote wire up and under her neck. She began to strangle her earnestly. Dr. Stevens's arms flailed out. She made a gagging noise and Elle knew Dr. Branch would kill her, right there in front of her eyes.

Elle moved forward, her legs numbed by fear. Not sure what to do, she grabbed Dr. Stevens's gloved hand just below the wrist and brought it back to connect with Dr. Branch's side. She roared but held on to the garrote. She turned her body to block any further interference from Elle, dragging Dr. Stevens with her.

Elle noticed the tall bookshelf behind them. She ran to it and slid her fingers between the wood and the wall and pushed. It didn't budge. The doctors continued to struggle. She pushed harder, gritting her teeth as she used her entire weight to lean against the shelf. She felt it tilt forward and slowly lean over. Several books slid off and pelted Dr. Branch's back. A particularly heavy volume fell from the top shelf and slapped the back of her neck, calling her attention to the falling shelf. She released Dr. Stevens and shouldered the shelf as an avalanche of books fell to the floor.

Elle went to Dr. Stevens who was sprawled on her back clutching at her throat as she struggled to choke in air.

"I'm fine," she wheezed, though the angry red mark left by the garrote dripped with blood.

There was a crash behind them, and Elle looked over her shoulder to see that Dr. Branch had tossed the empty shelf aside. She reached into the pocket of her skirt and removed a scalpel sheathed in a plastic case. She tossed the case as she stepped forward, the blade clenched in her fist.

Dr. Stevens pushed Elle away and stood. She was still visibly out of breath from the tussle with the garrote. She and Dr. Branch met again with force, the scalpel slicing through the air wildly. Dr. Stevens hissed and moved away clutching her arm above her brace-clad hand. Blood spilled on the nice rug at her feet.

Dr. Branch gave a smug smile and attacked again. Dr. Stevens stepped sideways, deflecting the blade and delivering a quick blow just below her ear. As she stumbled back, stunned, Dr. Stevens grabbed hold of her scalpel-wielding arm and brought it down over her raised knee. The fingers extended in pain, dropping the blade to the floor.

Dr. Branch snatched away and spun around, her injured arm tucked close to her body. She turned, her eyes flashing with deadly intent. Dr. Stevens snatched up the scalpel.

"Please stop," Elle sobbed at them. "Stop this."

"It's okay," Dr. Stevens said, her voice trembling. "Breathe." She took a deep breath as she always did to model the technique for Elle.

She tried but could only get out a sob.

Dr. Stevens breathed out. Her body visibly relaxed. she brought the scalpel low.

"Give this up," Dr. Branch said. "You can go for reprogramming. All can be forgiven."

Her reply was a shake of her head. She was still breathing in deeply and out slowly.

Dr. Branch scowled. She shifted her weight, and with her injured arm braced against her, she stalked forward, her good arm extended. Dr. Stevens's arm sailed forward to meet her. She raised the blade and with one fierce swipe, sliced Dr. Branch's neck.

Elle gasped when a red jet of blood arched forward and splashed Dr. Stevens's slacks. Branch staggered forward and fell to her knees clutching her neck, trying to choke in air, her eyes wide with terror and shock. Blood showered through her fingers and down her torso. She fell onto her side, still trying to use her weakening hands to stop the bleeding.

Dr. Stevens stumbled backward and dropped the scalpel. She reached out for Elle.

She ran to the doctor and embraced her. "Are you okay?"

Dr. Stevens nodded. She covered her mouth with her knuckles as she looked down at Dr. Branch who had stopped moving, a spreading pool of blood around her head.

"Why did she attack us?" Elle asked.

"We need to get out of here," Dr. Stevens said absent-mindedly but made no move to leave. She seemed transfixed on the body of Dr. Branch.

"Dr. Stevens?"

She looked away and smiled serenely. "I'm going to take you to your mother. She'll know what to do."

"Anywhere but here," Elle said breathlessly.

"Hey," Dr. Stevens said. "It's going to be okay."

She stopped at her desk and removed a first-aid kit. She quickly patched her bleeding arm with gauze and wrapped it with a bandage. She then removed a syringe which she prepped with a solution from a small metallic vial. She slid open another drawer and removed a black gun.

Elle concluded that there was more to her genteel doctor than she could have ever imagined.

Dr. Stevens approached her, syringe in one hand, the gun in the other. She took Elle's bare arm and squeezed to expose a vein and held on when Elle tried to pull away.

"I don't understand," Elle said.

Dr. Stevens gave no words of reassurance. She slid the needle under Elle's skin.

The shot made her woozy and brought a haze across her eyes that nearly blinded her.

"Everything is going to appear much different from now on," Dr. Stevens explained. "Stay close to me no matter what you see. Remember to breathe."

Dr. Stevens caught her hand and pulled her toward the door and opened it. She peaked out into the hall before guiding her out. Someone had turned out all of the lights. Elle's vision cleared and her eyes adjusted to the dimness. At least she thought so.

What made her question herself was the fact that she did not see the sterile halls of Gloaming Hill, but old cracked brick, lit with dull red bulbs every few yards. She thought at first that she had somehow slipped through the mist and her mind was introducing her to some new terror she'd repressed.

She looked back to Dr. Stevens's office door. Instead of the welcoming warm-colored wood there was rusty metal with a latch-bolt like a prison door. The sight caused her to stop in her tracks.

"Elle," Dr. Stevens said. "We must go, now."

She turned to her. "What is this place?"

Without a word, Dr. Stevens pulled her along. After a few twists and turns, they came to another solid metal door with a card reader on the wall next to it and a camera mounted on top. She opened the door to reveal a darkened room with a desk and a bank of monitors. A small lamp lit the startled face of a man in camos. Before he could speak, Dr. Stevens lifted the gun and shot him.

The explosion echoed throughout the small room. Elle did not have time to cover her ears. Dr. Stevens ushered her through another door.

Sunlight flooded the space. She saw the man who'd been shot still on his feet clutching his chest desperately reaching for his radio.

Once again, her eyes took a few moments to adjust. She blinked furiously, registering cars, pavement, a chain link fence, and buildings. She turned around looking for the woods, for Gloaming Hill. Instead, she saw an old industrial building looming above.

Then, Dr. Stevens was shoving her into the back of a car. She slid in after her and scrambled over the driver's seat and behind the wheel.

Elle heard an engine start and then they were moving. She went from one window to the other, trying to figure out where exactly they were. She saw a strip mall, comprised of the typical stores found in any across the world, certainly not a hidden government facility in the middle of the woods.

The car stopped at a red light. She felt a stinging in her hand. She turned away from the sight of a line of cars waiting on the next lane to see Dr. Stevens wearing a guilty look as she pierced Elle's hand with a needle.

"What did you do?" she asked her.

If Dr. Stevens answered, she did not know. Blackness washed over her vision, leaving her in the darkness of her unconsciousness.

CHAPTER SEVENTEEN

The Great Hall

Cass sat in a chair with a warm towel around her shoulders. Globs of glittering gel littered the floor beneath her feet. Just a few feet away, the pod waited, still partially full of the gel that had cushioned her body. She could hear classical music playing somewhere in the lab. Through her blurry vision, she could see a figure approach. Though her senses were dulled, she knew without seeing that Thora, Dr. Liang, and Lyles were in the room. Their pulses came to her clearly.

It was Dr. Liang who'd come close. She'd brought a cup of tea.

"How long has it been?" Cass asked.

"Eight hours," she answered, and after a moment, "Did you see anything?"

"No. At least I don't think so," Cass said.

They had agreed on twelve-hour stretches in the tank. Thora had calculated the time, along with what drugs and how much. Liang and Osbourne had watched closely as she took them through their paces.

"Lyles was fading," Liang explained. "Thora pulled the plug, for now."

She tried to focus her vision and glance across the room. She could vaguely make out Thora attending to the other pod where Lyles lay. Her vision cleared, but at a price. The overhead lights were blinding. Pain stabbed at the back of her eyes and crashed against her jangly nerves.

"Drink your tea," Liang said.

Cass brought the steaming cup to her lips. She recognized the déjà vu of the situation; her times in Thora's lab, sitting in front of a fire, her body tingling from the residue of pod gel evaporating from her body, a cold lamb sandwich in her hand, a cup of tea in the other. Back when she was a wraith, she'd seen Thora as a kindly doctor figure, attending to her with a stern care.

Cass stood on shaky legs and limped her way.

She was leaning over Lyles. He was propped up in the pod his eyes still covered with the protective goggles.

"You should not be walking so soon," Thora said.

"I'm fine," she said.

She glanced up from her work. "If only your friend here was in better shape."

"What happened?"

"Olympicorp has not been easy on him," she said.

Cass peered down at Lyles. His pulse lumbered. She sighed.

"Is he going to be okay?"

"Like you he needs rest," Thora said. "I take that to mean you didn't see anything while you were under. I told you that this was the wildest guess one could conjure."

"This is the only lead we have to find Elle," Cass said. "As long as Lyles is willing to help, we'll keep trying."

Thora turned her attention back to Lyles. The gel weighed down his shaggy hair. His face was relaxed; the side affected by the tortures he'd been through lay completely slack.

"Easier said than done," she said. "He's not waking."

Cass moved closer. She reached out and touched his cold arm as if the contact would wake him from his stupor.

"And what of our bargain?" Thora asked. "Remember, three days."

"Yes," Cass said begrudgingly. "Three days."

Charybdis entered the room, back to her old self. She saw Cass on her feet and smiled.

"Did you get any results?" she asked.

"I don't think so," Cass told her. "I remember white fog and just floating. I think that is what Lyles referred to as the gloaming."

"Let's walk," she said. "I've been doing some exploring."

"Don't be long, you two," Thora said. "There is much work to be done here."

She followed Charybdis out of the lab. After a few twists and turns plus an elevator ride, they were outside of the mountain under trees. It was nighttime, and Charybdis pointed up at the sky glittering with stars.

"You'll find Elle," she said. "I know you will."

"We got nothing, and Lyles might be done," Cass said. "I need a plan B."

Charybdis shrugged. "I've searched those archives. I wasn't able to find anything else about Elle or Project Songbird."

"It was the Americans' operation," Cass said. "We're looking in the wrong place."

Out of frustration, she let the cold feeling take over her brain and blasted the air with the Aegis. The vegetation around them fluttered in the wind wildly for a few seconds, a momentary storm in the dark German woods.

"Wow," Charybdis remarked dryly. "That's a pretty amazing trick."

Cass smiled at her, but her smile soon faded.

"If all else fails, I'm going to America. I'm going to speak to Elle's mother, anyone who can help me."

Charybdis looked concerned. "I should go with you."

"Would Thora allow that?"

"It doesn't matter," she said.

The revelation shocked her, but at the same time she was proud of Charybdis for finally being able to start to break free.

"You're Thora's right hand."

"She'll find another," Charybdis said. "She has her choice of wraiths."

"Did you know she was a wraith?" Cass asked.

"I did. She told me many years ago when I was struggling with losing you. She opened my mind to what is possible for those like us."

"She is impressive," Cass said.

"You're even more impressive," she said to her surprise.

"Because of Thora."

She reached out and touched Cass's shoulder. "I'm not talking about the Aegis or the pulse, or how very adept you are at kicking ass."

She smiled. "What else is there?"

Charybdis laughed. "No, because you made the decision to love someone and you're risking your life to save her."

"She freed me," Cass said. "Maybe whatever they did to her gave her the ability to break my programming—"

"Maybe she tapped into your humanity, something Thora couldn't take from you."

"Maybe," Cass said. "What if I am too late?" She posed the question to Charybdis who happened to be there with her, but also to the night sky as a sort of lament.

"If she is as strong as you say, she'll make it."

Cass thought of Lyles lying in waste in the pod back in the lab. Her heart sank to think of Elle in the same way.

"We should get back to the lab," Charybdis said.

❖

They returned to the lab where Thora sat with Liang looking at the readouts on several monitors. Cass spotted the images from brain scans she guessed to be Lyles's. He was out of the pod and lying on a gurney, a pillow propped under his head.

"I'm still here," he slurred.

She went to the gurney and they clasped hands.

"I lost you," he said. "In the gloaming. I'm sorry."

"It's okay, Lyles," she said. "It's taking me some time to catch on."

"That's something we don't have much of," Thora said. "Another round too soon could prove to be deadly."

"When can we get a do-over, Doc?" he asked.

"When you are fully healed," Liang broke in.

"There's been irreparable damage to the brain," Thora said. "To continue at any course could result in death."

They were silent for a moment. Cass could not ask Lyles to risk his life any further.

"Well," he spoke up. "We'll try again, first thing in the morning."

"You do understand what Thora is saying?" Cass asked. "You've been through so much already, Lyles. You deserve to rest and live out the rest of your life."

He nodded briskly. "I also heard irreparable brain damage. Look, Cass, you don't see what I see when I close my eyes. At any given time, I'm tripping through the gloaming, not here, nor there, not even in my own mind. Perhaps it would be best to cut the tether and just float."

"You don't mean that," Cass said.

"I do," he said. "I can try to help you find Elle on my way out. That would make it all just right. Don't you think?"

Charybdis moved in and touched his shoulder.

"Thank you, Lyles," Cass said. There was no more she could bring herself to say. Trying to talk him out of offering his life would have been harder. She noticed Thora watching her slyly and felt a wave of guilt.

"We should all get a good night's rest then," she said. "We'll take turns looking after Mr. Lyles here and start bright and early."

Cass volunteered for the first shift. She watched Lyles nap, and at some point she closed her eyes as well.

She dreamed of Elle.

They were in bed, in a small apartment. Soft music played as a gentle rain fell outside the window. She knew that it was a dream, one of those sweet, fuzzy around the edges types. She'd experienced them before, Elle in flowing white, hovering above where she slept, or Elle in a wild garden of flowers completely nude.

In this dream, Cass pulled her close, kissed her. Similar interludes they'd shared during their brief moments together had been harried by the danger of being discovered by a pack under the hive mind control of Lyles, or by Thora and Olympicorp, or the SDC.

Then, in the dream, Elle had run away from her and out a door where there was nothing but the strange fog that Lyles called the gloaming.

She woke startled, her entire body wired as if she had been wrapped in a blanket charged with static electricity. She found Lyles staring at her.

"You were there," he said. "In the white room."

She gathered her senses. "It was only a dream."

"Think of it as more than a dream," Lyles told her. "When day crosses over to night, the conscious and the unconscious. The gloaming."

"What does that mean?" she asked.

"It's the time between dusk and night, a very brief time, a magical time," he explained as if his words made perfect sense. "In this case it's the place between conscious and unconscious, that's where you find the white room."

"Lyles," she said, rubbing her temples. "Thora would say that was complete nonsense."

"She doesn't believe that," he said. "Do you?"

"I wanted to believe Elle and I had a special connection, that it could save me, save us both."

"And now?"

"I don't know." She lowered her head. "None of that changes the fact that I want Elle to be safe and happy even if it's without me."

"You let go of your faith," he said. "But just because you have a different perception of something doesn't mean you have to stop believing. You came in contact with Elle just now. It wasn't a dream."

"Thora says it would take years to develop whatever we're doing here into an exact science," she countered.

"It sounds as if you're ready to give up," he said.

"I can't," she said. "I won't."

He smiled. "You have the gumption. You just need the spirit."

She smiled back at him. "What about you, Lyles?"

"What about me?"

She hesitated. "I'm just sorry. You deserved better than this."

"Now don't go feeling sorry for me," he said, reaching out his hand. "Just keep in mind what I've told you."

She took it.

Osbourne entered the room to cover the next shift of watching over Lyles. She stayed around long enough to see that he was once again resting comfortably before leaving. There was a dormitory section, a maze of cubicles with tidy cots topped with thick mattresses. She checked in on Thora and Charybdis to find them deep in slumber recouping from their adventures in the Black Forest.

Cass claimed one of the empty cubicles and fell asleep as soon as her head hit the pillow.

She did not dream.

Cass hurtled through the gloaming, filled with a panicky feeling as if she were in the middle of a crash-landing. Her body was tucked inside of a gel filled pod somewhere in Germany but her consciousness was in a void of swirling white and constantly changing gray shadows traveling at the speed of light. She had become familiar with traversing the gloaming over the last two days. Like the Aegis, the gloaming had become something that was always there waiting for her to tune in. Even in her sleep, she searched for Elle.

She came to a hard stop and the gloaming scattered revealing black at first, the absence of light which solidified into forms. She would have squinted to make them out but realized that she did not perceive this place with her senses.

The space developed around her—a counter, narrow lanes flanked by ruts, a rack that held dark globes.

A bowling alley.

Once her mind recognized the type of space, it brightened with color. A mural under black light, a disco ball shooting out a pattern of reflected squares on a rainbow-colored carpet printed with a confetti of geometric shapes. Country music played faintly overhead. Much like the apartment Cass had found through the gloaming, this place had remarkable detail.

She noticed Elle then standing there watching her from the middle of one of the lanes. Cass stepped forward calling her name.

Elle turned and ran, crossing over the lanes.

Cass gave chase, past a snack bar and a sitting area for bowlers to enjoy beer and refreshments in between games. She followed the Elle-shaped shadow down a narrow hall and a floating sign that read: restrooms.

Their chase ended through the swinging doors of the restroom. Cass heard the creak and bang of a stall door. Inside, she saw that the walls had been scrawled with what looked to be salacious newspaper headlines about

Elle and what happened in Kuwait. She heard soft crying come from the stalls.

"Elle?"

"Please, just leave me alone."

Cass' heart broke to hear the hopelessness in her voice. She crouched low.

"Elle, I don't know exactly why you're so afraid of me," she said. "I think I may have a good idea, this place isn't real, I think you may be stuck here."

"You're the one who's not real. You're a nightmare, a demon."

"That's not true," Cass said. "I've been looking for you Elle, I fear that wherever you are, you're in danger."

"Why should I trust you?" Elle asked. "You hurt me. You killed all those people in Johannesburg."

Cass flinched. The words stung, though she would never purposely hurt Elle, she had indirectly, just by knowing her. As for killing people, she had done that as well, perhaps not in Johannesburg. She let the guilt wash over her and stood firm. She could make all of it right.

"Where are you Elle? Do you know?"

Silence.

"Please, you have to tell me, I can help. I can get you home."

"You'll come and take me away, put me in a freezing truck. Lock me in a cage."

"Elle, I would never do that," Cass said.

"You're the Gorgon."

Hearing Elle say her wraith name made her blood run cold. "I was, but then I met you. I'm Cassandra Hunt. Cass for short. You were the first person to call me that," she said.

"I don't remember that," she said. "There's a lot I don't remember."

"I know, you could say that I've been through the same ordeal," Cass said. "I had no memories either. Someone kept erasing them from my mind."

The creak of a stall door. She looked up to see Elle peering at her through a sliver of an opening. Cass straightened.

"I don't know what to believe anymore," Elle said her voice trembling. "I thought the doctors would cure me, but everything has gone wrong."

Cass took a tentative step forward.

"Do you know where you are?"

"No. Not anymore. I was at Gloaming Hill."

"Gloaming Hill?" Cass asked and immediately thought about Lyles.

"It's in West Virginia, it's a facility where I was supposed to get my memories back," Elle said and choked back a sob. "I don't know what's real anymore."

"It's okay," Cass said. "I'm going to figure it out."

The door swung open and the mist filled the room in billows. The next thing she was aware of was cold air. Strong arms lifted her from the gel and she sat up sputtering the stuff from her lungs. She could not hear or see anything, but the pulses of everyone in the room came through.

Something was wrong.

She tried to speak and found that she could not.

"It's okay," Charybdis said close to her ear.

Cass did her best to express her doubt.

"It's Lyles," she said. "He's flat-lining. They've been working on him for twenty minutes."

She looked in the direction of the pulse, and through her bleary vision she could see the shape of the other pod. Beyond, she could see a table and a body, and the figures of Thora, Liang, and Osbourne.

Cass took a moment to gather herself. She hoisted herself out of the pod, her hands and feet slipping in the gel. Charybdis knew better than to attempt to stop her, and helped her to her feet and guided her toward Lyles on the gurney.

As she neared, she could make out better exactly what was happening. They were trying to keep him alive. They didn't know what she did. Thora saw her watching and shook her head dispassionately.

"He's gone," she announced.

"You have to keep trying," Cass insisted.

"He's brain dead," Thora said. "You can feel it can't you?"

She turned away from the scene. She could not stand to see him dead, knowing that he made the sacrifice to save Elle. The last few days had taken a lot out of the small team, but Lyles had paid with his life.

Charybdis came to drape a towel around her shoulders and comfort her.

"Did you find the white room?"

"I did," Cass said. "I saw Elle."

"Can you be certain that it was her?"

She looked down at her trembling hands still covered in the gel from the pod. She could not be sure. It could have all just been a fever dream brought on by the drugs, or one of Thora's tricks.

"She's in danger," Cass said. "She told me that she was in West Virginia, at some facility. She called it Gloaming Hill. That has to mean something." She looked around at Thora, Osbourne, and Liang. The latter two looked wrung out from their efforts to save Lyles's life. None of them had an answer.

She went to him and touched his forehead slick with the gel.

"I'm sorry," she whispered. "I'm so sorry."

"What exactly did you see?" Thora asked behind her.

"I saw a bowling alley this time," Cass said. "Elle was there and she didn't seem to know me. She called me the Gorgon."

Thora studied her for a moment. "I think I am beginning to see the purpose of this white room and the gloaming."

Cass turned and eyed her with suspicion. "Or have you always known?"

She scoffed in reply. "Has my participation in this experiment not proven that I had nothing to do with your reporter's disappearance?"

"Elle," Cass said. "Her name is Elle. She's somewhere scared out of mind because some scientists want to play God."

"You're no better," Thora accused pointing at Lyles. "You didn't mind sacrificing him."

Cass felt white-hot anger roiling inside of her. "I'm going to the states."

"Wait," Charybdis said. "How will you know where to look?"

"She told me that she was in West Virginia, I'll start there."

"Foolish," Thora said.

"Go back into the pod," Charybdis suggested.

"And waste more time?" Cass asked.

"You'd rather go on a snipe hunt?" Thora asked.

"I have to try," Cass said. "I don't expect you to understand."

"I understand," she said. "You judge me and yet you so easily used Lyles. He put his life on the line in some ridiculous sense of honor."

"What would you know? You send wraiths to do your dirty work."

Thora stared at her for a moment, then reached inside her jacket and removed a small envelope. She tossed it across the distance between them. Cass caught it.

"It's a passport, money, you can get to the States," Thora said.

Cass turned the envelope over in her hand to test the heft. She looked to Thora. There was nothing left to say. She looked to Charybdis.

"Come with me. You said you would."

She shook her head. "I can't. I must stay here with Thora."

"I'll do this on my own," she said and left the room.

Charybdis followed her. "Where are you going exactly?"

"The States."

"Yes, I get that," she said and grabbed her shoulder. "Can you stop for a moment?"

She shrugged her off. "I don't have time for this."

"You'll get killed."

"You don't understand," Cass said.

"Stop saying that," Charybdis told her. "You're not the only one who will sacrifice everything for someone they love."

Cass stopped, stunned by her words.

"Then come with me."

"I have to stay. That is my sacrifice."

Cass nodded. She understood.

They embraced.

"You will always be my little one. Now go and don't forget about me."

"I won't," Cass said. "Mother."

CHAPTER EIGHTEEN

Jefferson County, West Virginia

Elle opened her eyes to find herself stretched out in the back seat of a moving car. It was night and she could see the sky and ghostly clouds. A full moon seemed to sink into the murky black of the sky like a bright pebble thrown into a puddle.

They were no longer at Gloaming Hill.

She sat up, groggy. She saw Dr. Stevens at the wheel. She noticed Elle and looked over her shoulder to give her a quick once-over before turning her attention back to the road.

"You're awake," she said.

"Where are we?" Elle asked.

"We're on our way to DC," she said. "I'm taking you to your mother."

She remembered the bloody fight between her doctors that had ended with Dr. Branch's death.

"What is going on?"

"Gloaming Hill was compromised, by a terrorist cell. I had to get you out of there."

"Do you have a phone?" Elle asked. "I want to call my mom."

"Phones can be traced," Dr. Stevens said. "We're going to meet her."

Elle was still under the effects of the syringe Dr. Stevens had given her and felt wobbly and foggy-headed. She rolled down the window for the air. She breathed in the smells of the highway—exhaust, and the crisp fall she'd missed. She was away from Gloaming Hill. She was free.

In the rearview, Dr. Stevens watched her. Elle did not feel free.

They stopped at a motel. It occurred to her that she had no idea where they were. She asked Dr. Stevens as she guided her to the front desk. She parked Elle on a sofa while she booked a room for the two of them. The woman at the front desk identified herself as the owner. She explained that there was a pool on the premises as well as a communal area that was open twenty-four hours and stocked with a foosball game, a vending machine, a computer, and printer/fax. She kept eyeing Elle suspiciously.

The room was clean and cool. Dr. Stevens ushered her in and dropped the two bags she'd brought from the car and shuffled to the bed to sit. She sighed and massaged her temples. She looked up when Elle moved to sit on the opposite bed.

"This must all seem incredibly insane," Dr. Stevens said and crossed the space between them to sit with her.

"Can you please explain to me what happened back at Gloaming Hill?"

"Dr. Branch turned," she said. "Leslie, I understand. But Branch?"

"What do you mean she turned?" Elle asked.

Dr. Stevens stared at her for a moment and rose from the bed to pace the small space.

"We need to get rest. We need food and a shower."

"Why can't you just tell me?"

"I will, I swear, I just need a moment to think."

"Why do you need to think? If it's the truth."

Dr. Stevens gave her a wounded expression. "You must trust me, Elle."

"You killed Dr. Branch."

"That is unfair. You were there. She attacked me first, and had she succeeded, I can't fathom what she would have done to you."

She came close and touched Elle's face. "I can't possibly let any harm come to you, Elle. You do believe that don't you?"

"Yes," she said. "I believe that, but—"

"Then put that trust as well into my promise to you. I will explain everything."

Elle sighed.

Dr. Stevens smiled brightly and went for the phone on the nightstand between the beds.

"We'll order pizza. And soda."

She was putting on a brave face, Elle supposed, but it did nothing to soothe her worries. Dr. Stevens ushered her into the bathroom with instructions to shower. She left the door open when she left. When she was gone, Elle inspected the tiny bathroom for a window and found none. She resolved to take her shower.

She moved back the curtain revealing dull blue tile that at least appeared clean. The water was nice and warm once the tap ran for a few minutes. Elle showered and stepped out to dry herself. Dr. Stevens was there waiting with a towel.

"You'll have to wear the same clothes," she said apologetically.

Elle accepted the towel and quickly wrapped it around herself. Her hair was damp from the shower and, with no hair products in sight, was threatening mutiny. She lamented not having any of her usual travel luxuries, or the fragrant-less bottles at Gloaming Hill.

Gloaming Hill.

The place was now a lifetime away. Someone would have discovered Dr. Branch's body by now. Nurses Grace and Slick would notice Elle's disappearance. Someone would check the cameras. Would they contact the local authorities? The Feds?

"Hey, you, okay?" Dr. Stevens asked softly from the doorway.

"I'm fine, I guess," Elle said. She had not realized that she stood in the same spot, her body partially dry under the towel.

"It's all yours," she said of the shower.

"After we eat," Dr. Stevens said. "Go ahead and dress yourself."

She left the bathroom.

Elle stared at herself in the mirror. In the garish light of the hotel bathroom, her appearance was as gaunt as Dr. Stevens. She supposed what they had been through during the last twenty-four hours had an effect. Still, that did not explain her sunken cheeks.

Gloaming Hill haunted her mind—her doctors fighting each other until one of them was killed, and the strangely ominous words from Leslie. She'd mentioned the mist and memories implanted in her head.

Outside the bathroom, the phone rang. She stepped close to the door to eavesdrop. It was just the front desk.

"Send him over then, please," Dr. Stevens said, obviously annoyed.

Elle's stomach growled and she began to dress. When she stepped out, Dr. Stevens was closing the door and holding a pizza box and a small plastic bag heavy with bottles of soda and water. She passed them to Elle and turned to lock the door before peering out the window. A sliver of light from the delivery car's headlights slashed across her face. She squinted as it passed, her brow bent, a knot at her jaw.

They ate on the bed in silence. Dr. Stevens would not allow her to turn on the television which worried her even more. Elle managed a few slices, a few sips of soda, and an entire bottle of water. After her meal she found that she could barely keep her eyes open.

She helped clear away their dinner. When Dr. Stevens pulled back the covers, Elle slid underneath them fully clothed. As she tucked herself in, Dr. Stevens knelt next to the bed.

"You should rest too," Elle told her.

"I will, when this is over."

"What exactly is this?" she asked.

She sighed. "It's me keeping you safe. I told you. Trust me."

Elle wanted to, but there were too many questions and her mind seemed clearer since leaving Gloaming Hill. She reached out and touched the knot under the bruised skin and Dr. Stevens's jaw.

Dr. Stevens closed her eyes, seeming to relish the contact.

"You need to ice this," Elle said. "These places always have ice machines."

She opened her eyes. "I will. Now it's important that you get some sleep."

Elle settled back on the pillow and closed her eyes.

Elle dreamed of the silent white halls of Gloaming Hill. As usual, the place was empty of the steps or voices of its staff and patients. There were plenty of doors, like the one to her room, and Dr. Stevens's office, and the padded room where Dr. Branch held her sessions. She found herself before the last, and in the way that dreams work, she was inside the room.

That is where the dream ended.

She was in the mist then, flying fast. The mist faded to near darkness and dancing neon streaks. When everything went still, she was in the Luling Bowling Alley in all of its dayglow, red vinyl, vintage glory.

It was strange to be there without Dr. Branch's voice guiding her. She realized that she never needed anyone's guidance in the places beyond the mist. Luling. She wondered if Gloaming Hill was one of those spaces.

The Gorgon stepped from the shadows.

Elle ran across the colorful carpet to the restroom.

She slammed the door to the stall and perched on the toilet.

The lights snapped on.

Elle could see the walls were all tagged up with what appeared to be typical bathroom graffiti. Bold, black, hand drawn letters. She saw her name and though the Gorgon was in pursuit, she slowed to read them.

Reporter Turned Terrorist.

Blood, Bodies, and Screams: Reporters Describe Aftermath of Johannesburg Attack.

Congresswoman Denies Daughter's Involvement.

They all read like accusatory headlines, each one worse than the next. She heard the Gorgon enter the restroom. She was the one who was the terrorist and she wanted to drag Elle into her criminal world.

She'd hidden in one of the bathroom stalls and waited. She heard the Gorgon enter, but there was something different about her. She wasn't rough and cold as she'd been in the lost memories revealed to her during Dr. Branch's sessions. She was soft and sweet as Elle had encountered in the bed of the little apartment in South Korea.

She seemed to understand Elle's plight and promised to save her.

Elle woke alone in the darkness. She sat up in the bed and looked over at Dr. Stevens. She was propped up on the pillows in a sitting position, but her eyes were closed and gentle snores drifted from her with the rise and fall of her chest.

She did not bother calling her name. Instead, she tested the soundness of the doctor's sleep by slipping out of bed and creeping through the darkness to the toilet. She peed, washed her hands, and looked out at Dr. Stevens. She was still in the same position and snoring lightly.

Even if she could move fast and silent, Dr. Stevens could wake and spot her.

She made her decision. Her mind felt clearer despite having just crawled her way out of the mist. She made her way to the door faintly illuminated by light that had slipped through the tightly shut curtains. She slowly opened the lock and bolt on the door, then eased it open.

Elle slipped out into the night. The motel complex consisted of one row of rooms in one building and an office in the other. She could smell chlorine nearby and knew there was a pool close by. She went to the common room. It was a cluttered affair with all the amenities the owner had described, outdated, but there. The computer was an old Dell with a boxy white monitor. There was no internet.

There was a phone, a black cordless unit mounted to the wall. She picked up the receiver and pressed the call button.

There was a dial tone.

She wracked her brain trying to remember any of her parents' numbers. She paced nervously certain Dr. Stevens would wake and come looking for her. She focused on recalling any of Anne's numbers and could not. One phone number did come to mind, the main number to the Green Patriot studio. In the automated system there was an option to get in touch with specific departments and staff via extension.

She dialed the Green Patriot with shaking hands.

It worked.

"You have called the Green Patriot Studio located in Austin, Texas."

Elle had never in her life been so happy to hear the robotic voice. She listened to the automated voice list options. When prompted, she entered her extension without hesitation: 622.

She found herself listening to her own voice directing her to leave a message. She could try, but would anyone be regularly checking her voice mail? It just wouldn't do. She heard the tone signaling her to speak. She remained silent for a few seconds. Dr. Stevens would be coming for her.

Nine-one-one? Could she trust the local authorities? They would take her back to Gloaming Hill and have questions about the corpse of Dr. Branch. Flashes of the dead doctor, a pool of blood spreading beneath her, spreading to cover Elle's inner vision. She feared she would be next.

"Help," she whispered into the phone. "Please I'm at a motel in Virginia. Something terrible has happened. Dr. Branch is dead."

The time allotted for leaving a message ended and the voice asked if she would like to record her message again. Elle pressed the button to end the call.

She remembered that Anne's extension number was either one digit higher or one digit lower than her own. They'd always joked about it.

She had to try.

She hit the redial button and entered 623 when the automated voice told her she could.

There was a click and then the familiar Mississippi drawl.

"You have reached the voice mail of Anne Humphries here at the Green Patriot."

Elle took a deep breath exhaled and at the beep began to speak.

"Anne, it's me, Elle, please pick up."

She hung up and tried again, waited through the whole automated spiel. She would leave a message and calmly explain where she was and pray Anne got the message soon.

The ringing stopped and she heard a ragged breath. "Elle?"

"Yes. Anne. It's me."

"Elle, is it really you?"

"It is, please, I need help. I'm in West Virginia, somewhere in Jefferson County. I'm not sure where. There's a motel. It's called the Breezeway."

"Are you safe?"

"I don't know," she said. "Nothing makes sense. I just want to come home."

The receiver was suddenly snatched away from her. She turned to see Dr. Stevens, her brow shadowing her eyes. She looked even more worse for wear than when they had arrived at the motel. She looked ill.

"That was very foolish, Elle," she said, returning the phone to its place on the wall.

"That was very, very foolish."

She grabbed her arm just above the wrist in a death grip. Elle tried to pull away, frightened by the violence she displayed and the wildness of her appearance. This was not the same woman who had brought her sandwiches and let her nap on the couch in her office. The gentle doctor had fled.

The phone began to ring.

Dr. Stevens ripped the entire unit from the wall with one tug and viciously slammed it on the floor. A few plastic pieces flew across the floor in different directions.

She pulled Elle along, out of the common room and back into the night. Elle tried to struggle, but she was too weak. They returned to the room. As she closed the door behind them, Dr. Stevens gave her a hard shove. Elle fell to the bed on her stomach. She rolled over quickly to see Dr. Stephens grabbing things. The black leather case. The duffel bag. After placing them by the door, she turned to Elle in a fury.

"Who did you call?"

Elle turned away from her, refusing to answer.

Dr. Stevens approached the bed. She grabbed Elle's face, her nails digging into the skin as she forced eye contact.

"Who did you call?"

"Anne," she answered. "Her office number at the Green Patriot was the only one I could remember."

Dr. Stevens released her and stood. "We have to go."

"I'm not going," Elle said. "You're scaring me."

Her face softened but not by much. "I know you're scared; you should be, Elle. This is a very frightening situation."

"Why can't I call Anne?" she asked. "Why can't we call my mother?"

"That is why you have to trust me," she said. "We have to go about this the right way. It's a matter of life and death."

She stood and reached out her hand.

Elle did not take it.

"You'll feel differently when you're face-to-face with your mother," she said, her hand still extended.

Elle took it and stood. At the same moment, Dr. Stevens produced a syringe. Elle barely felt the prick.

Dr. Stevens guided her out of the room to the car. For Elle, the world went black, she could still feel the crisp night around her. She heard the car door open. Dr. Stevens forced her inside with a rough shove. Within moments, they were moving.

"We're changing locations," Dr. Stevens said. She was not talking to Elle.

"I'll deliver her to DC, just be sure you're ready to receive her."

The rest of the conversation faded with the darkness as the mist settled in and carried Elle away with it.

She stepped from the mist and into the apartment in South Korea. The place was brighter than usual, the source of the light, the blue and pink glow of the neon sign beyond the window shining like an exploding star. Elle knew who would be there when she opened the door.

Her handsome brow bent with concern. "Are you in trouble?"

"I don't know," she said moving further into the space, but keeping her distance. She felt frantic. "I was able to get away. I was able to call Anne. She said she's taking me to DC. I remember earlier she said she was taking me to my mother."

"Just a moment," Cass said. "Slow down. Something's not right. This place, it feels different than before."

"We don't have much time," Elle said.

Cass studied her for a moment. She tried to close the distance between them, but Elle wasn't having it.

"Sorry," Cass said, shaking her head furiously. "How do you know we don't have much time?"

"I don't fucking know," Elle growled as she motioned toward the window. "Does any of this make sense to you? Are you even real?"

"Okay," Cass said. "You were able to get to a phone. You called Anne Humphries."

Elle felt alarm at hearing her speak her friend's name. She continued her account cautiously unsure of what to share.

"I gave her the address to the hotel, but Dr. Stevens found me. She drugged me again."

Cass frowned. "Who is Dr. Stevens?"

"She was my doctor at Gloaming Hill," Elle said. "I'm beginning to think that she's not a doctor, and that Gloaming Hill isn't a real place."

"I think you're right," Cass said.

"Everything seemed so real," Elle said. "I saw Loera there. I saw you."

"Loera is dead and I haven't been on that side of the world."

"I know," Elle snapped. "I'm not delusional."

"No, you're not," Cass said. "I know they can make you feel that way, the people behind Gloaming Hill, I know the horrible things they can do."

"What did they do to you?" Elle asked. She was not exactly sure who they were. She remembered then her friend Tammy, a conspiracy theorist. She would always tease her about the mysterious "they" that sprayed the skies with chemicals and wiped LSD on public door handles.

Cass sighed. "They made me a killer. They erased my memories and I knew nothing but what they wanted me to know. I was supposed to kill you."

Elle shrank and waited for the tide to turn. For Cass to suddenly become the Gorgon and throw her into a hold in the ground. Instead, they both stood facing each other.

"I just couldn't bring myself to harm you," Cass said. "I couldn't forget you, no matter how much they tried to erase you from my mind."

"I don't remember," Elle said, though she desperately wanted to.

Cass moved closer. "It's okay, we'll get your memories back, but first I have to find you."

The door popped open and the mist rolled in fast. Cass and Elle looked to each other and knew their time together in that moment had ended.

"Find my mother," Elle said. "She'll be able to help you."

Cass reached out her hand, and Elle reached back, but it was too late. The mist carried them away.

CHAPTER NINETEEN

Austin, Texas

The Green Patriot studio was in a maze-like office park on the outskirts of town tucked away among clusters of tall pines. Cass lurked among them. Anne Humphries parked her hybrid under the carport marked with her name, unaware that she was being watched. She looked small and frumpy bundled up in a coat and scarf to ward off the mild winter chill. She gathered a handbag and a laptop bag and slung it over her shoulder. Humphries punched the lock button on the remote attached to her keys, then turned to the building. She gasped when she saw Cass standing before her in the dim early morning light.

Anne slipped her glasses on her face and narrowed her eyes.

"Goddamn you. Where's Elle?"

"I don't know," Cass told her.

Anne reached into her bag. "I'm calling the police."

Cass stepped forward from the shade of the trees.

"Don't come near me." Anne puffed up with a fierceness that caused Cass to hesitate. She did not want to do anything to hurt Anne Humphries or bring any attention to their meeting.

"Please," Cass whispered frantically. "She made contact with you a few days ago."

"I have no idea what you're talking about," Anne said.

"The hotel in West Virginia," Cass said to jog her memory.

Her eyes widened. "So you do know where she is."

"I know as much as you know, Anne," Cass said. "That's why I'm here."

She paused phone in hand, her thumb hovering over the screen as if to reiterate her threat to call the police.

"Elle told you everything that happened in Kuwait," Cass said. "You know about Olympicorp and what they did to me. I think the same thing has happened to Elle, but it's not Olympicorp, it's her own country."

Anne pocketed her phone. "Once, I trusted Elle's judgment. Hell, I depended on it, but she changed after Kuwait. Then, after she came home from Indonesia, she started training for the apocalypse."

"What do you mean?"

"She bought guns and went to the range to learn how to shoot them. She took this insane stunt driving course, not to mention the self-defense classes," Anne said. "It was as if she were getting ready for something."

Elle had learned a lot from their time in Kuwait, and after the scene on the boat, she felt defenseless. Now standing there before Anne, she felt guilty.

Anne eyed her with suspicion. Her pulse was a deep bass throb that reverberated from her. Tenuous when Cass first approached, now it mellowed. "I always wondered what she was leaving out of the story."

Cass faltered and glanced around them nervously. She thought of Project Songbird, the video of young Elle, the white room and the gloaming. "She may not have known what she was leaving out."

Anne studied Cass for a moment as if she were not sure what to do next. She motioned to her car and pointed her key fob to unlock the door.

"I'll call Tammy," she said. "In the meantime, I'm not letting you out of my sight."

Cass had been traveling nonstop for the last day and a half. During her journey, when she was able to close her eyes, she was scouring the gloaming for Elle. It was good to finally sit and rest. She listened to Anne make phone calls explaining that she would not be in the office that day.

"No. No, I'm fine," she explained and sighed. "Yes, I will try to take it easy. Well, I'm trying to keep positive. Yes. Fine. I'll see you tomorrow."

Anne looked over at Cass apologetically. "Everyone seems to think I'm going to shatter any day now. God, I feel like I've aged ten years in the past few days."

As they drove through the streets toward downtown Austin, Cass stared out through the windshield, unsure what to say to this woman who loved Elle as much as she did. She listened to her call Tammy Crockett and leave a message on her voice mail.

"When Elle called me the other day, I didn't know what to think," Anne said. "It was the middle of the night, I wasn't sure if I was asleep and dreaming."

Cass took an anxious breath. Anne was not the type of woman to let things lie, let alone chalk things up to a dream.

"I called back and found out that it was the Breezeway Motel. The woman at the front desk described Elle. She told me she was with another woman who checked in using the identification of a woman who's been dead for the past eight years."

She and Cass exchanged knowing glances. "You did your own investigation."

"Of course, I also did my due diligence and called Regina right away," Anne said. "She said she would pass the information along to the authorities, but I haven't heard from her."

Cass had an inkling that Elle's mother had reported the information but not to the proper channels. The last time they had made contact in the white room, she had implored Cass to find her mother. The mist had not allowed her time to lay out her suspicions about Regina. Besides, Elle had just come to trust her somewhat.

"Tammy is working on getting some surveillance footage."

"Has she found anything?"

"She'll get back to me as soon as she does," she said. "I've come to trust her and even started to buy into her conspiracy theory rhetoric. Now I'm far from naïve. Of course the government doesn't disclose all its dealings, and there are some far-out things that have been revealed to be true…"

Anne trailed off and turned to Cass. "I'm rambling. Where have you been all this time?"

"Kazakhstan," she answered. "After Indonesia, I was picked up by the SDC, the Securities Defense Collective, a collaboration between intelligence services around the world. I was promised Elle would be kept safe if I cooperated with them. All lies. They messed with my brain. I was never told that Elle was missing."

"I've never heard of the SDC," Anne said as she absentmindedly negotiated through traffic.

"It's underground," Cass said. "Regina Pharell has connections. She came to visit me there."

Anne straightened in her seat.

"She didn't tell me that Elle had been abducted. She acted as if she had a deal with the Pentagon."

"A deal?"

"A chance at a normal life, and in exchange the Pentagon would study the weapon implanted in my head."

Anne chortled bitterly. "Regina always seemed so loving and supportive of Elle. I can't believe she'd turn on her. There have been some horrible things said in the media, but they're all speculation."

Cass had the feeling that Regina's betrayal of Elle had happened years ago.

"Where are we going?" she asked Anne as they entered a residential area.

"I'm taking you to my place," she answered.

Cass felt a bit of apprehension but did not protest. She reminded herself to be on guard. After what happened in Atlanta at the Pharell house, she was not sure who to trust.

Anne's house was a little bungalow in a neighborhood of hilly, sloping streets. She invited Cass in past a small porch trimmed in vines and hanging with potted plants. The inside was warm and tastefully decorated with a menagerie of antiques. She could not help but think that Elle had been there. If she had been in Anne Humphries's place with a cozy house and a normal life, she would never have let Elle go away with some mysterious stranger.

"Have a seat," Anne said as she led her to the living room. "Do you drink coffee?"

"I'll have water," Cass said. "Lots of it."

Anne grinned. "I'm going to bring you some food, so don't argue with me about it."

Cass smiled wanly. "I won't."

Anne disappeared down a hall. Cass glanced around. She spotted a framed picture of Elle smiling in front of a backdrop of blue sky, framed by trees, her short ebony hair tousled by the wind. Cass was touched to see her captured so beautifully in one single moment in time. A memory that could never be tainted, unlike all the ones she had of Elle, danger hanging like a black cloud. She felt weak suddenly, like her legs were made of sponges and would not hold her weight. She realized that she had stood and walked close to the picture. She heard Anne's return and quickly wiped away the tears that had pooled in her eyes.

"That was a nice day," Anne said behind her. "She teased me about hanging that picture."

She turned to see Anne depositing a tray loaded with ice water, a carafe of coffee, a beer, sandwiches, fruit, and other goodies. It made her eyes water even more. She took the water offered her and promised to eat soon. Anne was kind to her, but she had a shrewd eye.

"Tammy called back. She's on the way."

"Okay," Cass said. She removed an SD card from her pocket and handed it to Anne. "There is something here you need to see. It's not pretty."

Anne took the card and placed it on the coffee table before going to the door where she'd hung her bags on a hat stand. She returned with a laptop. She took the card and slid it into the slot on the side. After a moment, she gasped. She watched young Elle on the screen as Dr. Branch hypnotized her. She closed the computer and stood gripping it in her hand. Her lip trembled as she paced the living room.

"What is this?"

"A collaboration between Olympicorp and the US government. They called it Project Songbird."

"What were they doing to her?"

"A mind programming technique to prepare Elle to take down people like me."

Upon speaking those words, a sadness took over and she could only stare at that picture of Elle. Anne sat back down next to her on the sofa. She reached over and gently touched her knee.

"Tell me."

She told Anne about the pulse and how she could sense and read the shift in people's moods through the patterns of their brainwaves.

"Elle was altered in the same way I was, except she emitted a pulse that could disrupt the programming of others, like Loera, and me."

"Why would Olympicorp assist in creating something that could harm them?"

Cass shrugged. "Somewhere along the way they programmed wraiths to create others. I suspect it caused a division. Project Songbird was a way to even the playing field."

Cass remembered Thora's words, explaining it aloud, hearing it from her own lips solidified the truth in her mind. What she and Elle thought they felt for each other was simply an anomaly.

"You don't know for sure Regina knows about this," Anne said. "Perhaps she's only using her position to find her daughter, including lying to the woman she holds responsible for her disappearance."

Cass reluctantly agreed.

"On the other hand, I expected her to make a lot of noise about this phone call," Anne said. "I offered to get the story out. She won't even return my phone calls."

She sighed in frustration. She checked her phone.

"Tammy's here."

The doorbell rang. She went to answer it

Tammy entered the room, her eyes landing on Cass. She was a tall, broad woman with a cap of short dreads. She carried a backpack and a leather bag with a computer cord spilling out. She regarded Cass with a mix of awe and curiosity.

"She's actually here," she said to Anne in disbelief.

Cass stood and offered her hand. "Cassandra Hunt. Nice to meet you."

"Tammy Crockett," she said, and they shook hands.

Anne directed them to sit. "I know this isn't a social call, but I have refreshments."

Tammy kept her eyes on Cass. She got right to business.

"Where have you been all this time?"

Cass told her about the SDC.

"A secret international intelligence group?" Tammy asked. "You're shitting me."

"Regina visited her there," Anne blurted.

"You mean Congresswoman Reginia Pharell?" Tammy asked in disbelief.

Cass nodded.

"She didn't mention anything about Elle's disappearance," Anne added.

"She said that she was there representing the Pentagon. They want to attempt to remove the Aegis, the implant inside my head."

"Implant?" Tammy asked as she and Anne exchanged looks.

Cass straightened and allowed the cold feeling between her eyes to spread. A draft of air swirled around the room, stirring a short stack of magazines from a table.

Anne and Tammy startled and instinctively reached for each other, their eyes on Cass.

"That just didn't happen," Anne huffed, out of breath.

Cass stared down at her, searching her face. "I'm sorry. I didn't mean to scare you."

Tammy gave a dry, nervous laugh.

"You can do that because of an implant in your head?" she asked. "I mean, how powerful is that thing?"

Cass thought of the nano cloud and shivered inwardly.

"I've taken down a helicopter."

Anne gasped. She picked up her laptop and presented it to Tammy so she could watch the video of young Elle.

"You need to look at this."

Tammy watched the video at once charmed by the younger version of her friend and apprehensive of what would happen. When it was over, she rubbed her eyes. "Do you think Regina knew about this? Shit."

Anne looked at them both shrewdly. "We need to tread lightly here. Were you able to get footage from the motel?"

"I'll show you," Tammy said and unpacked her own laptop from one of the bags, She set it up on the coffee table and the three of them leaned in to watch.

In the video, Elle walked a bit unsteadily past a row of doors. A car passed, momentarily blocking the camera's view. Elle paused like a frightened rabbit and then toddled inside the front office.

"She's alive," Cass said.

Tammy advanced the video seven minutes further. A woman appeared. She went into the office and exited a few minutes later with Elle in tow. The scene changed to a different view; it was of the room where they were taken. Tammy sped up the video and the woman exited with Elle leaning heavily on her. She placed her in the back seat of a white sedan before returning to the room and exiting with a few bags and a black boxy case.

"Who is that?" Tammy asked.

"Dr. Stevens," Cass said without thinking, remembering what Elle had said in the dream.

"You've come across her before?" Anne asked.

"No," she said. "I've never seen her until now."

"Well?" Tammy asked.

Cass took a deep breath. "I have been in contact with Elle."

"How?" Anne asked. "When?"

"I'm not sure how to explain it," Cass told her.

"Try," Tammy said bluntly.

"Lyles was there."

"The man from Kuwait?" Anne asked. "I thought he'd been killed."

"He was alive," Cass said. She thought of him lying in the pod, covered in gel. "Olympicorp found another use for him. It seems he picked up a new ability."

She paused not sure where to start. Unlike with the Aegis she couldn't perform a demonstration of the gloaming or the white room for Anne and Tammy.

"Lyles claimed he could make contact with Elle with his mind," Cass said.

"Like telepathy?" Tammy asked.

Cass thought for a moment. "That's close, but not quite what I'm trying to describe. It's like a dream but there is a transition state like floating through a white fog and then you're in another place."

Anne and Tammy squinted at her shrewdly. She stammered.

"Lyles called it a white room."

Tammy startled a bit. "Did you say white room?"

"You've heard something?"

"Uh, yeah," she said. "It's associated with remote viewing, tapping into someone's waking mind and seeing what they see. The CIA experimented with using remote viewing to gather intelligence."

"So what is a white room?" Anne asked impatiently.

"A place that exists in the mind of another person," Tammy said.

"Where did you hear this information?" Cass asked.

"A few years ago, a woman called in to several radio shows that share conspiracy theories, the extremist right ones, the extremist left ones, and all the ones in between."

Anne chuckled dryly. "How many conspiracy theory radio shows are there?"

Tammy gave her a snarky smirk in reply. "Well, she made the rounds. She would call in and go on about mind control experiments, and of course what she called the white room."

"So how was she different from the other weirdos that call in to those shows?" Anne asked smugly.

Tammy shot her a look. "I can find the audio if you need it."

Cass told her that she would like to hear it. She absentmindedly accepted a sandwich placed into her hands by Anne. She took a bite and chewed distractedly.

"Is this the famous database?" Anne asked as she peered over Tammy's shoulder.

She scoffed in reply. "Like you've never searched it before. Here is one, the Dark Horizons podcast." Tammy turned her laptop around.

A male host with a British accent announced a number where fans of the show could call in to give their opinion on the featured topics or tell their own story.

"Our first caller is Leslie, and she will not say where she's calling from," the host said in an amused tone. "I've been told that she is being quite theatrical. Let's hear what she has to say."

There were a few seconds of dead air and then the grainy sound of a telephone.

"Hello?" asked a raspy voice.

"Yes, Leslie, we're on the air live. My producer tells me that you have something important to tell us about something called a white room?"

"Yes," she said. "These people have figured out a way to get inside your head, and I'm not talking in a general sense, I'm saying they can now literally feed you a false reality. You're thinking you're living your life, going to work, making love to your wife, on a nice vacation. No. You're hooked up to a machine in the basement of the CIA."

The host interrupted. "Why would the CIA want to hold someone in the basement believing they're going about their normal lives?"

"Because that's total control of someone, ensuring that they will be compliant, and completely captive. Then, they slip things into your unconscious, your very psyche. They could have you do anything, and you wouldn't even know. You wouldn't be able to stop yourself."

Tammy stopped the recording. "She rants on like that for another two minutes, but there was another call to a radio station in Portland. They've been doing this midnight conspiracy theory show for several decades. That show is where the story took off in the community."

"Explain to us, what is the white room?" a female host asked. "Where is it located?"

"I'm so tired," Leslie replied. Her voice reflected her claim, a weak, harsh whisper. A promise of the mystery she revealed.

"What's wrong? Are you ill?"

"Yes, they can make you sick if they want. They always have that connection. We need to rise up and break free before they make everyone like us."

The host was sympathetic. "I know you're ill, Leslie, but you wouldn't have called in to the show if it wasn't important."

"It is important."

"Tell us, who is 'they' and why have they made you ill?"

"If they succeed, they'll be able to make us all sick. That's why the white room is important," she said.

"Okay then, tell us about the white room."

"It's not a physical place. It's a collective place, an anomaly of all their experiments. The white room is a safe space. If they've tampered with your mind, like they have with mine, it's the only place where they can't control you."

Another host chimed in. "And they control your thoughts, how?"

"No one can control our thoughts, but they can manipulate them. The white room is the only escape."

"But how?"

The caller, now even more agitated, threatened to hang up. "You aren't listening. Through suggestion, hypnosis of the entire consciousness. That's how they implant memories."

Tammy stopped the recording.

"The voice doesn't sound familiar," Cass said.

"This makes MK Ultra look like a cakewalk," Tammy said. "The CIA did their mind control experiments on unsuspecting Americans and Canadian citizens; their own agents, women, and children."

The three of them were silent for a moment. Cass saw young Elle sitting in that office with that horrible woman. Anne must have been thinking the same thing because she stood throwing up her hands.

"We need to get in touch with Regina," she said. "If she knows anything we're just going to have to get it out of her somehow."

Tammy balked at the idea. "I'm not sure we should put ourselves on her radar. I don't want to end up in a white room or worse."

Anne was pacing but paused. "Cass, you were able to make contact with Elle in the white room, why don't you do it again?"

She shook her head. She explained Thora's Geist device and how it had been the catalyst for the connection through Lyles. She told them about the few times she had encountered Elle in the white room after falling asleep. "I'm able to search for her, but I can't seem to get a bead on her. They've been drugging her so that could be affecting things."

Anne slumped, feeling devastated for her friend. "We've got to do something. They've been doing these awful things to her, perhaps for years."

Tammy frowned and tilted her head. "What was it like?"

Cass told them about the gloaming and the apartment that looked to be in South Korea, she then described the bowling alley where she saw seen Elle.

Anne grinned wryly. "That sounds like Luling."

"Luling, Texas?" Tammy asked.

"We did a story out there," Anne said. "On our downtime we went to some bowling alley and Elle just went on and on about it."

She rushed away leaving them in her living room. She returned a few moments later with a photograph. She passed it to Cass.

In the picture, Anne and Elle were toasting with two pint glasses, in the background Cass recognized the mural from the bowling alley. It was beyond surreal.

"That's it," she said in amazement. "Do you know anything about an apartment in South Korea?"

"I don't think Elle has ever been," Anne said and shrugged.

"When you were in this white room, the two of you were talking like we are now?" Tammy asked.

"Yes," Cass said and remembered Elle in her arms in the white room, the first time she'd stumbled through the Gloaming. "Everything was so real."

"Maybe we could re-create Thora's lab," Anne said. "We don't have all the pieces and parts, but we could at least try."

"You're starting to think like a conspiracy theorist," Tammy said. "I do know someone who does sensory deprivation therapy."

"We don't have Lyles, or the Geist device," Cass said.

Anne let out a restless sigh. "You said that Elle told you she was being drugged by the Stevenson woman. Is there anything else she mentioned that could help us?"

"She told me about the facility where they held her. She was afraid of me at first, as if she did not know me anymore," Cass said. "She told me to find her mother."

"Damn," Tammy said. "We can't risk that."

Cass straightened. "Elle said Dr. Stevenson told her that she is taking her to her mother, but she didn't exactly trust her."

"I don't know about ya'll," Tammy said, "but all roads seem to point us back to Regina; either she's in on the whole thing or she's using her connections to find Elle on her own."

She looked to Cass. "Either way, I think it's time you two sit down and have a real talk. No bullshit."

Anne fetched her laptop. "I'll check her social media," she said. "That I can do."

"What has she been up to?" Tammy asked.

Anne squinted at the screen. "Business as usual according to her social media," she said. "She attended an alumni thing last night. Tomorrow she'll be at the Howard homecoming game."

"Then I have to go there," Cass said.

Anne touched her shoulder. "We're going with you."

"I should go alone," Cass said. "Just in case there's danger."

Anne and Tammy looked at each other as if their first thought was to argue, but they seemed to simultaneously change their minds.

"We'll make ourselves useful here," Tammy said. "I'm going to send you off with a copy of both those videos."

"I'll arrange your passage," Anne said. "A helicopter service that we use for the Green Patriot. They can get you to DC by tonight."

"If anything happens," Cass told her, "make sure that video gets out."

Tammy produced a small notepad and jotted something down. She ripped off the page and handed it to her. "That's the credentials for a public message board and VPN to access it from. Almost un-trackable."

Cass thanked her. "Elle is lucky to have friends like you two."

"Also, I have something to show you," Anne said, taking her by the arm toward the door. "Remember when I told you Elle was preparing for the apocalypse?"

They drove downtown. Cass allowed herself to close her eyes, to get some semblance of a nap. She startled awake when Anne stopped the car in front of a brownstone with a red awning. Anne pulled her lips into a grim smile and, without a word, slipped out of the car.

Cass climbed out onto the sidewalk and followed Anne to the entrance. She punched in a code and opened the tinted glass door. A small lobby ended with a bank of three elevators. Cass felt her heart accelerate. She knew this place, though she had never set foot in the building. There was a familiarity. The brick walls and wooden floors and wrought iron trim.

As the elevator doors slid shut, she looked to Anne.

"This is Elle's place," Cass said when she realized where they were.

"Correct," Anne said. "You've never been here, have you?"

"No, I haven't," Cass said. "I just knew."

"You two are connected," Anne said. "I noticed when she came back from Indonesia. She was changed."

The elevator stopped and she followed Anne a short distance to a door, then watched her unlock it. Elle's apartment. Cass shivered when she crossed the threshold. She could have sworn that the place still smelled of her soap, her perfume.

"She has a safe here that she told me to check if there ever was an emergency," Anne said. "I guess this counts."

They were standing in the living room. Blinds and curtains shut out the sunny day, darkening the space. Still, some stray bands of light seeped into the room. The place was free of dust and Cass realized that Anne had been coming there and keeping up with Elle's apartment.

She followed Anne to Elle's bedroom. One of the walls was exposed brick and on it was mounted a neon sign shaped to spell out the words *Stormy Weather*. Anne caught her staring.

"Her favorite song," Anne said. "It pisses me off that something as innocent as a song was actually a part of the horrible things they did to her."

Out of curiosity, Cass plugged in the sign. It buzzed alive, a glowing pink reminding her of the billboard outside the window of the apartment in Korea, or was it the white room? She looked at Anne who watched solemnly.

She hauled out a black duffel bag and handed it to Cass. Inside was clothing sized for her, several pairs of jeans, a gray T-shirt with the words *The Kewpies* in a jagged silver-colored font. There was a light, black hoodie, a pair of black moccasins, and motorcycle boots. Cass's eyes watered to think of Elle gathering those things and storing them away. There was also a small lockbox and Anne handed her the key.

Cass opened it and found two compact Glock handguns, ammo, and a retractable baton. She picked up the baton and flicked her wrist to extend it to its full length. She'd had one on her in Kuwait, with Elle.

If Anne was surprised to see the guns, she did not show it.

"I suspect you can do more damage without those things."

"The Aegis is not always dependable," Cass said. "Guns are practical."

"She told me that if anything ever happened, that this stuff was here. I told you that after she returned from Indonesia, she wasn't the same. It was frustrating and I must admit I was not a good friend to her."

"I have my guilt about Elle too," Cass said.

"We have to do everything we can to get her back," Anne said. "Let's get you to DC. We have some time to kill if you want to clean up."

Cass felt herself blush. She had not showered in a few days. She realized that she must have looked terrible, not that she felt much better. She went to the bathroom and upon looking in the mirror, confirmed her realization. It was strange to be in Elle's shower, using her products, her bath towel.

Once dry, she dressed in jeans, T-shirt, hoodie, and boots. She returned to the bedroom. Beyond, she could hear Anne on the phone arranging her trip to Washington. She went to the metal lockbox. She tucked one of the guns into her boot and the other in the waistband of her jeans. She slipped the baton into the muff of the hoodie. She noticed something strange about the underside of the lid of the lockbox.

Cass tapped at the lid. Something was off. She took the box to the bathroom and pried at it with a nail file. A metal plate fell away revealing a small wad of money and an envelope. Inside the envelope were two Texas driver's licenses and two passports. Elle's picture was on one set of identification with a different name and a Houston address. The other set had pictures of a woman with features similar to Cass. She was blond and a bit heavier but the same height. If Cass presented the ID as her own any differences could be explained away by weight loss. The name below the picture was Jessie Harden and she lived in Fort Worth, Texas.

It occurred to Cass that if she had ever gone to the States that Elle had prepared to run, never to return. She left the bathroom and showed the IDs to Anne who was just finishing up her phone call.

"Well, that will come in handy," Anne said. She paused when she saw the passport with Elle's picture and a different name. She sighed and plopped onto the couch, having come to the same realization Cass had.

"I've made peace with the fact that I may never see her again," Anne said, her tone haunted. "If, when, you do find her, you two run."

Cass agreed.

CHAPTER TWENTY

Washington, DC

Elle slept in the mist. Through it all, she was aware of time passing. A day passed. Two days passed. She knew because she felt that faraway feeling except she still felt tethered to the world, aware, just floating, buoyant on the in-between of being awake, of being conscious, and the void and uncertainty of what lay beyond. She knew she was in a moving car, and she knew that Dr. Stevens piloted that car. When she was able to open her eyes she saw the sky beyond the windows, a crisp fall day. She sat up slowly and met Dr. Stevens's glance via the rearview mirror.

"You're awake," she said.

"Where are we?" Elle asked and, peering out the windows, saw that they were traveling on Interstate 270 South and were currently passing through Rockville, Maryland.

Dr. Stevens reached over to the passenger seat and lifted a white bag which she offered over her shoulder. Elle took it.

"There's tea in the center console here," she said.

"No coffee?" Elle complained as she gazed out the window looking for a clue about where they were headed. Dr. Stevens was being tight-lipped about their destination but had to know that she realized they were close to DC.

She did not seem worried.

"We're headed to Pleasant Plains."

Her mother's old stomping ground. She often went down for the football games.

"Howard?"

Dr. Stevens did not answer.

"Maybe then someone will be able to tell me what's going on," Elle said dubiously.

"Eat your breakfast," Dr. Stevens told her. "You'll need your strength."

She sat back in the seat and opened the bag. There was a croissant with bacon, eggs, and cheese in a foil wrapper. Her stomach growled. She unwrapped the sandwich and took a bite. Before she knew it, half the sandwich was gone. She reached for the tea and took a sip. Dr. Stevens had fixed it just the way she liked.

They were passing through Bethesda, and she felt even closer to her mother, and answers about Gloaming Hill, the death of Dr. Branch at the hands of Dr. Stevens, and all the weird behavior since then.

She finished the sandwich and the tea. She tried to blink the cobwebs from her head, even her senses (except taste) were dull. It was the drugs Dr. Stevens had forced on her; she just knew it. She felt angry at the once calm, sweet doctor.

They were taking the College Park exit now. Elle watched the scenery change to the familiar landscape of Pleasant Plains. Her mother had taken her many times to her alma mater, had even tried to convince her to attend. Elle had bigger plans. She wanted to be a journalist, and the University of Texas had a course taught by the illustrious Anne Humphries.

Dr. Stevens pulled the car around to the back of Burr Gymnasium. She parked but left the car running. She turned to look at Elle. Her face was haggard, and Elle doubted that she had gotten any sleep at all. Her eyes were sunken, the skin around them ringed dark. They stared at each other for a moment.

"You have no idea how important you are," she said.

"I just want to see my mother," Elle said. "I just want to go home."

"I know," Dr. Stevens said. "I just want you to know that it has been my greatest purpose to be able to accompany you on this part of your journey."

"Can you finally tell me what's going on?" Elle asked, sensing there was more the doctor would tell her.

She closed her eyes in a moment of serenity. "Today, you will fulfill your purpose and once you have, it is going to change everything."

"I don't understand," Elle said.

"You're going to open the door to change the world," Dr. Stevens said, and her usual charm had returned, but Elle knew better. There was something manic in her eyes. She reminded her of one of those religious zealots.

"I'm not sure how. I feel so weak. So tired."

Dr. Stevens smiled that serene smile that was unlike any she had ever worn at Gloaming Hill. It had a tinge of coldness and paired with that look in her eyes.

"You're ready. It's time," she said, turning around and settling in her seat. "Just sit back for a moment." She closed her eyes and breathed deeply, like they used to do at Gloaming Hill.

Elle followed suit.

"Stormy Weather" began to play, which startled Elle into opening her eyes. Dr. Stevens had also opened her eyes.

"It's only the radio," she said and closed her eyes once again and breathed in deeply.

Elle nodded.

She'd heard the song thousands of times, knew every note and nuance. There was something more sinister under the music. It wasn't like the buoyant mist; it felt heavier. No, not heavy, but hindering as if she were tethered to a millstone while slogging through gelatin. She didn't like it, but she continued to breathe in and out.

Beyond the music, she could hear the deep rumble of a truck. She pried open her heavy lids to peek. In the side mirror, she saw that Dr. Stevens had slipped out of the front seat. She was standing with a dark-haired, brown-skinned woman. Just beyond, a gray food truck idled.

Then, Dr. Stevens was helping her out of the car. Elle stumbled forward, her feet nearly numb to the ground beneath them. Dr. Stevens guided her around the side of the truck. The woman Dr. Stevens had been speaking to watched expressionless as they passed. A troupe of colorful, dancing anthropomorphized snacks loomed over them, a logo pasted on the side of the food truck. Their eyes were black dots, their limbs skinny black lines. It made Elle think of the Luling Bowling Alley.

A door slid open revealing a group of people gathered in the dimly lit interior. They wore aprons or T-shirts with the same dancing snacks. Half a dozen eyes stared out. Sure, they were normal human eyes, but they were just as dead as black dots.

"Don't just stare at her," Dr. Stevens told them. "Get her in the truck."

A set of strong, pale hands appeared and helped load Elle aboard, leading her up the steps and through the cab. Dr. Stevens followed and the door was shut firmly behind them. The woman outside had not joined them.

Those same pale hands plopped Elle onto a short stool among hundreds of bags of cotton candy packaged in transparent plastic bags. Dr. Stevens leaned against a counter and tilted her head back as she took a long pull from a water bottle. She finished it halfway and passed it to Elle who drank the rest. The others watched intently, their shuffling feet the only whisper in the tiny space.

"Where are we going?" Elle asked.

"To the football game," she said. "I told you that already."

Elle did not remember. She did know they were there to see her mother. She had something especially important to tell her and it had to be loud enough for the whole stadium to hear.

Dr. Stevens picked up one of the bags of cotton candy. She pried open the plastic and swapped with her for the empty water bottle.

"Why are we in a food truck?"

"Because we have lots of snacks to sell," Dr. Stevens said around a bright smile.

"I don't understand." Elle reached into the bag and took a bit of the fluff and placed it on her tongue. She felt the mass grow warm and melty in her mouth as it dissolved into sugary syrup. Just like when she was a kid.

Dr. Stevens took her pulse and then turned to the others.

"We all know what our roles are here today," she said as they stared with dead eyes. "The truck is our cover. Those of you left behind are to keep up appearances until the final event."

A cart was rolled forward. They all leaned forward, and Elle could see a black box because they shone a light while Dr. Stevens inspected it. Seemingly satisfied with what she saw, the doctor helped one of the others carefully load the black box into a backpack.

"Also, the Gorgon will be in attendance. It doesn't matter. Once we get her into the press box, I'll initiate the final event."

Elle watched them, aware of the eerie scene but also feeling the pull of the mist. Part of her wanted to drift away while part of her was certain that she should be concerned about Dr. Stevens and her new friends.

The truck began to move. Dr. Stevens sat next to her on the bench. She studied Elle for a moment, then took her hand at the wrist and checked her pulse.

"How do you feel?" she asked.

"Like I'm drifting away," Elle said.

Dr. Stevens smiled wanly. "Your mind is preparing itself for what is to come."

"My mind is preparing to see my mom?"

"Today is the beginning of a revolution, a new world order, and you're to be the one to lead us all, starting with everyone in the stadium."

There was something ominous in her statement, but Elle could not comprehend it. Sadness gathered in the pit of her stomach. Something awful was going to happen; she could feel that one thing. Dr. Stevens was delivering her into danger.

"I'm afraid," she said.

The truck eased to a stop and the driver spoke to someone outside. Elle looked out the front window and saw that they were at some sort of security checkpoint. Dr. Stevens put a hat on Elle's head and donned one herself.

The door opened and a police officer stepped into the truck. He looked around and stepped off just that quickly.

After a few moments, the truck lurched forward at a snail's pace. Beyond the window, she recognized the Greene Stadium concourse. A guy in a green reflective vest waved his arms vigorously in the spot where he wanted them to park. He disappeared as the truck swung to the right.

The other two moved to the back and began to get ready to open for business. The woman pulled open the serving window and set up a display of potato chips and bags of the cotton candy. The man plugged in a popcorn machine and began to pour in ingredients. Outside, people were already beginning to gather in the impatient way people do.

Elle could smell hot dogs, popcorn, and cotton candy, but like all her senses, they registered with no feeling behind them, as if she were a robot. She sat with Dr. Stevens, and they watched the people for about twenty minutes. The man began to take orders, and Elle could hear the bright, shiny voices of people.

Dr. Stevens opened the black case and carefully removed a box of black metal, completely smooth in that it was seamless. The material it was made of did not seem to reflect or absorb light, as if it existed on its own wavelength.

The woman had stopped her cotton candy hanging to watch.

Dr. Stevens placed the box in a backpack and zipped it up. She looked to the woman as if to give reassurance. The woman returned to her task of adding bags of cotton candy.

"That's enough," Dr. Stevens said. "We don't need to be weighed down or delayed. It just needs to appear legit."

They moved out into the sunshine and the people. It stunned Elle how many people there were, young, old, some were smiling in anticipation of the game that was to come, others looked stauncher in their determination to get to their seats. Dr. Stevens steadied the rack of cotton candy in Elle's hands.

"Hold on tight," she instructed.

The world moved around her in flashes, and sometimes froze on faces and forms as if buffering. She was aware that she was moving through the crowded concourse where people purchased concessions and snapped pictures with their phones. There was a woman in front of a camera, a local anchor reporting on the event.

Elle and Dr. Stevens were stopped by those who wanted to buy cotton candy. She stood by docilely while Dr. Stevens collected money and gave back change when needed. They moved on in between sales. She was certain that they had not escaped Gloaming Hill to come and sell popcorn, but it was hard to hold on to her thoughts.

Then came a thunderous sound shaking the ground beneath them. The crowd parted as the university band marched through led by the dance team in glittering leotards. The bison mascot danced around with members of the crowd.

Dr. Stevens used the distraction to lead Elle away. They approached the two-story press box, part of a three-story structure attached to the south bleachers. Elle had been there before with her mother. She never missed a homecoming game. There were five members of the Metro Police Department gathered at the two ways to get up to the press box—stairs and a small elevator. The cops were relaxed, chatting each other up and barely checking people heading up. She could call out to them.

Elle was sure one of them would recognize her. She wanted to tell them that she was Elle Pharell, the missing daughter of a congresswoman. When she and Dr. Stevens approached, one of them opened the elevator. Another radioed that the cotton candy ladies had arrived.

"What are we doing?" Elle whispered as the doors closed.

Dr. Stevens quickly shushed her.

You drugged me," Elle said, her fear giving way to anger. She was some helpless pawn in an intricate plot to somehow terrorize the homecoming game. She thought back to the meeting with her mother and doctors, the picture of the Gorgon, no, her name was Cass, perhaps. It was hard to know.

Another officer stood there smiling when the door slid open.

"Those sure look good," he said of the bags of cotton candy as he pointed the way. He was young and fresh-faced. Surely, he would know something was amiss—a tall, auburn-haired woman with several nights of sleeplessness under her eyes, and Elle was certain that she looked worse.

Dr. Stevens ushered her across the breezeway that connected the elevator to the press box. A woman wearing a suit and a headset spotted them and breathed a sigh of relief. She directed them to a table prepped with warming pans. Elle knew it was a buffet for the VIP fans like her mother used to enjoy while they watched the game.

The woman with the headset told Dr. Stevens to fit as many bags of the cotton candy as she could into a designated bin at the end of the table. She gave them both a once-over. Her curiosity outweighed by the pomp unfolding outside, she wandered over to the window overlooking the field. Her cell rang and she hastily left the room. On the field, someone began to sing the national anthem. The game would start soon, and no one wanted to miss the kickoff.

When they were alone, Dr. Stevens removed the backpack she wore, and retrieved the strange black box. She picked at the corner with her nails until a layer of clear film came away in her hand. She then stuck the box on the underside of the table. She gave it a jiggle to ensure that it would stick.

"Almost there," she said, looking at Elle with a smile that had once been reassuring.

They returned to the elevator. The friendly cop waited, loyal to his post. She thought that she should warn him about the black box Dr. Stevens had left under the table, but she could no longer interact with the world. She was merely an observer. A ghost tethered to Dr. Stevens who urged her forward to the hooded outdoor suite for VIPs.

Dr. Stevens pressed the button for the second level instead of the ground level. The announcers sat on the top level. Her mom liked to sit on the top level.

Dr. Stevens was once again reaching into the backpack, muttering to herself. Outside, Elle could hear an announcer's voice booming over the gentle roar of the spectators. A children's choir began to sing "This Land is Your Land," their young voices rising on the wings of their innocence. Elle felt chilled at the core as hot tears began to stream down her face.

The elevator doors opened. There were two cops standing in the breezeway, their backs to Elle and Dr. Stevens. They were captivated by the little singers below.

From her peripheral vision, Elle saw a black blur and a flash. There was a loud pop. The cops heard it. One turned around, the other fell. She cowered and covered her ears. Dr. Stevens pulled her along quickly.

No one had heard the commotion over the singing.

Dr. Stevens opened a door revealing the sound booth. Still holding on to Elle, she raised the gun, a silencer on the end, a metallic finger pointing the way to death. She shot four people.

Elle was beyond seeing, or hearing. The world came to her in nonsequential bits between stretches of black. The people in the booth were lined up in front of the window overlooking the stadium one moment, then black, then they were slumped in their rolling chairs, headphones and limbs dangling.

Elle almost choked out a scream. Not finding a proper release, the scream seemed to backfire and ricochet around her brain before exploding. The pain came in a blinding flash of white behind her eyes followed by black. For a moment, she thought Dr. Stevens had shot her.

The world came back to her suddenly. She sat in one of the announcer's chairs; Dr. Stevens stood close by. She held the gun in one hand, a mic in the other.

"It's time now," Dr. Stevens said. "Tell them everything, Elle. This is your moment to change the world."

She stared at the thing not sure if she could form the words to speak. The world was starting to go black again.

"Go on," Dr. Sevens whispered. "I know you can do this."

She heard a rushing in her ears, her vision blurred completely and faded to black. She felt as if she were asleep, yet she was barely conscious of the crowd below and an uneasy tension among them. They were beginning to sense that something had gone wrong in the sound booth. This was her chance to tell them to leave the stadium.

And she did.

Only, the words she spoke were not the ones she formed in her mind. The rushing noise grew louder, the pain in her head worsened.

The darkness clouding her mind gave way, and she could see the blue sky and the buildings of the campus beyond.

"Elle?"

Her father was at the door. An MPD officer slid in behind him and saw the carnage. A look of horror crossed her face and she reached for the gun at her side.

Dr. Stevens was faster. She'd ditched the silencer and aimed her gun at the cop and at Dad.

"This *is* our daughter," he explained as if he could hardly believe his own words. He looked over his shoulder and called for Elle's mother.

"Put the gun down, ma'am," the cop ordered.

Dr. Stevens regarded her for a moment. She looked to Elle, to her father, and back to the cop. Her hands shook as they clutched the gun. Outside, Elle could hear the distinct crackle of static from a police radio. Someone had sounded the alert.

"Please," Dad said. "Let my daughter go. Take me instead and we can talk things over. We can pray if you want."

Typical Dad.

"Elle is free to go," Dr. Stevens said. "Our part in this is done."

"Thank you," he said. "Come on, Elle, baby."

She could not move. She sat there frozen.

"It's okay," Dr. Stevens said. "This is where we say good-bye, Elle."

She touched her shoulder. There were tears in her eyes. "It's been an honor."

An explosion rocked the press box. Everyone cowered, except her father. He sprang into action crossing the space, stepping over bodies to reach her. He grabbed her into his arms and held her close, then retreated.

In the residual thunder of the initial explosion, the cop saw her chance. In a flash, she freed her weapon.

Elle heard the shots as her father pulled her toward the doorway. She looked back and saw Dr. Stevens, her eyes wide, arms at her side. Through the window beyond her, Elle could see a thin column of smoke rising to the sky.

Out in the narrow hall, there was complete chaos. Through the smoke, she could see blue uniforms. At first, her father was half carrying her toward the stairs and elevator, but an officer turned him around.

There were gunshots and everyone started running. She could hear screams and shouting as they went. They took cover in the room across from the announcer's booth, the club house.

She saw her mother, a cell pressed against her ear, her face blanched from shock.

The police barricaded the door with a table. Her father let go of her long enough to inspect her for injuries. There were tears in his eyes. He hugged her close again and called out for Elle's mother. She could smell his aftershave and feel his warmth.

Her eyes focused on her mother. She still had her cell phone to her ear, but she wasn't speaking, she was just listening intently to whoever was on the other end of the call. She put down the phone, her face ashen with fear as she stared at Elle.

"We all need to get out of here now," she announced.

"Congresswoman Pharell, we got fire near the stairs," one of the cops informed her. "Something's happening out in the stands, not sure if it's fire or another explosion."

"We're better off trying," she said.

"Regina, what's going on?" Dad asked.

More gunshots.

Everyone cowered. She could hear the police radio, another cop in a panicked voice.

"She's armed with some kind of weapon. She's coming your way."

"Take cover," one of the officers said.

Her father pulled her to the floor, and they took shelter under a counter along the wall among a few barstools. He grabbed her mother and pushed them both behind him.

The two cops flanked the door, their guns drawn.

A hand reached in and snatched one of them. He struggled for a second, but the attack was too swift, his assailant too strong. He fired his gun once and disappeared.

The remaining cop backed away, his gun trained on the doorway.

Cass appeared in the frame, a mask over her nose and mouth, eyes fierce, her arms up, palms open to show that she was unarmed. Seeing her made Elle doubt the world around them, she felt lightheaded, like water swirling down a drain. For a moment, she was certain that the mist would fill the room and carry them all away.

The cop ordered Cass to kneel.

A strange gust of wind filled the room as if Elle's fears were coming to fruition. The cop flew off his feet backward into the window that looked over the field. The glass cracked, but did not break, and the officer fell to the floor on his side, unconscious.

Cass spotted Elle cowering behind her father and her fierceness faded.

"Are you okay?" she asked.

CHAPTER TWENTY-ONE

Washington, DC

Cass approached the Howard University campus on foot. She was dressed in the school's colors to blend in with the crowd. The fall weather felt unseasonably warm as she walked down the tree-lined street. It was strange to be in the company of so many people. The pulses sang out to her as she followed their tide onto the campus.

The group split off into factions, those waiting for either of two shuttle buses, and the brave souls able and energetic enough to walk to the stadium. She broke off into the latter faction as she was too anxious to wait in line for the ride. The walkers were a joyful group waving playfully at the full shuttle that passed them on the road into the campus.

Cass scanned the area for any signs of Elle and kept alert for her pulse. She made sure that her jacket from Elle's stash in Austin concealed the gun tucked in the waistband of her jeans.

She was aware of one of the revelers suddenly moving close, matching her cadence.

Charybdis.

"What are you doing here?" she asked.

"We're here to help."

"We?" Cass asked.

Charybdis caught hold of her sleeve and pulled her to the side of the walkway.

"Thora is close by," she said and opened the jacket to reveal, hidden in the lining, several gas masks of Thora-esque design compressed in a gray film. "She says we will need these once the cover explosion for the gas release goes off."

"Gas?" Cass asked. She looked around them, for signs of alarm but only saw the rabble of people moving toward the campus.

"Something terrible is going to happen here today," Charybdis told her, handing her two of the masks.

Cass tucked the things into her jacket. "Elle's mother is here."

"Elle is here," Charybdis said.

She stared at her in disbelief. "Has Thora been pulling the strings this entire time?"

"I don't know," Charybdis said.

"Bullshit."

"She claims that today has to happen," she said. "This is Project Songbird."

Cass felt anger swell inside her.

"Thora says that Elle can survive this," Charybdis said. She reached out and touched her shoulder. "After this is all over, you'll need a place to go, you'll need the resources to keep Elle safe."

"Thora is offering us all of this? Forgive me if I'm a little suspicious."

"Even if you don't accept the offer, you won't be able to turn me away." Charybdis spoke with finality, but her eyes pleaded with her not to turn her away.

"What's the plan?" Cass asked.

She passed her a ticket for the game.

Cass took it, grateful she would not be hampered by stopping to make a transaction. As they neared the stadium, she kept a sharp lookout for Elle. She was glad to have Charybdis at her side. They stood in one of the two lines of ticket takers. Cass noticed security guards as they surveyed the groups of people entering the stadium.

Once they were past the gate, Cass motioned that they should split up.

She could hear cheers on the field. An announcer instructed everyone to please rise for the national anthem. She heard singing.

She explored the concourse and found no sign of Elle. She went out into the stands. To any observer she looked to be searching for her seat.

On the field, a children's choir began to sing. She turned to see them on the large screen above the press box. She noticed that the roof was dotted with camera operators filming and photographing the events below.

It occurred to her that if she could find Regina Pharell, Elle would not be far away. She began the climb to the top of the stands.

The sound of the choir cut out and the audience breathed in a stunned gasp. Cass looked over her shoulder. The choir had stopped singing.

A new voice came over the loudspeakers, a gentle whisper, the words unintelligible. A noise came with it, almost like a pulse. Cass looked around at the bewildered crowd.

She knew that Elle was up there in the press box.

She ran up the bleachers to the first level. A police officer noticed her approach. He shouted for a VIP pass. She tried to make up some excuse as to why she did not have one. When she mentioned the congresswoman, he retrieved his radio from his belt.

Just then, one side of the press box exploded, raining glass from the first level onto the crowd below.

Panic ensued. The spectators screamed collectively in a chorus of terror as everyone's worst nightmare began to unfold. It had come to be something people treated as one of those unavoidable possibilities. A madman with a gun or a bomb and armed with a set of warped ideas.

The cop steadied himself, eyes widened in alarm and suspicion. She used the Aegis to push past him and into the first level of the press box. She remembered the mask and removed it from her jacket pocket. She fumbled with it and was able to place it on her face where it self-suctioned itself around her nose and mouth.

People moved in panic as they made their way to the exit. She pushed through them looking for Elle. She found a stairway to the second level.

About three members of the Metro Police were there waiting for her. She used the Aegis to scatter them. She could feel Elle's pulse, as clear and refreshing to her as the children's voices that had filled the stadium earlier.

She passed the announcer's booth and saw that some carnage had transpired, as several bodies crowded the floor of the small room. She recognized one as Dr. Stevens.

Cass went to the next door. She tried to push it open but found resistance. She forced it with a small blast of the Aegis.

She saw Regina first, fear in her eyes. Then she saw who she guessed to be Elle's father and several police officers ready to use deadly force to protect them. They immediately started shouting at her. She ducked behind the frame. Waited. Listened. The cop closest to the door crept closer. She could hear his booted steps. She could feel his pulse broadcasting his fear as a static-filled warble. She reached around the frame and snatched him into the hall. The gun went off. She tried to shake it from his hand, but he held on to it in a vice grip. Their brief struggle ended when she punched him savagely in the throat.

She returned to the Pharells and saw Elle huddled behind her father.

"Are you okay?"

"Yes," she said and glanced toward the field. "What's happening out there? Is it because of me?"

"You're all in danger, a neurotoxin has been released in the stadium."

Cass reached into her jacket and retrieved the other mask. She removed the film and handed it to Elle. She reached out but paused.

"You didn't bring any more?"

Damn Thora.

"I'm sorry," Cass said. "Please put it on."

"Do what she says," her father said.

Elle did so. Cass noticed Regina watching. She hadn't said a word.

"You look like you've seen a ghost."

"The National Guard will be here soon," she said, her tone lethal. "You're not going to make it out of here alive."

"She's a friend, Mom," Elle said.

"Is she?" Regina asked. "This woman is a terrorist. She hurt you." Elle shook her head.

Regina touched her daughter's shoulder. "I know everything is confusing, I can't begin to imagine what's happened to you."

"We have to get out of here," Cass said.

"We're not going anywhere with you," Regina said. "We'll wait here."

At the moment, Elle clung to her father, her fear now concern for him. Mr. Pharell stood still, staring into space. A tall man, he dwarfed his daughter. Like a forgotten child, she shook his arm, but he would not acknowledge her. At first, Cass thought he was in shock, but when she tuned into his pulse, she found something more disturbing.

"Something's wrong," Elle said as she clutched on to him tighter. Her gaze met Cass's imploringly. "What's wrong with him?"

"I don't know," Cass said. "There is someone who can help him."

Regina went to her husband. A look of grief crossed her face, followed by one of outrage.

"This is your fault," she told Cass.

"Is this not what Olympicorp told you in their plans?" Cass asked. "You were foolish to trust them, Regina."

"You're a delusional monster," she countered.

"No, you're the monster," Cass said. "You sold your own daughter out? What did they promise you? The vice presidency? The presidency?"

Regina did not flinch at the accusation.

"Whatever you're involved in it's over," Cass said. "It's obvious you've been double-crossed. Save your daughter."

Cass expected Regina to interject. She looked to her and saw that she too had succumbed to the gas and stood still, staring wide-eyed.

Elle went to her mother and tried to rouse her. When her mother did not respond she let out a grieved whimper muffled by the mask. Cass looked out at the stands opposite where people had stopped whatever they had been doing in those chaotic moments after the explosion and stood statue silent as if they were once again observing the singing of the national anthem. On the field, she saw that some of them had fallen in the true fashion of panic, and they lay still in the state in which they'd landed.

"My God," Elle said, peering out the glass at the people in the stands and on the football field. She looked to Cass, heartbroken. "Did I cause this? Up until now, it's like I've been in a bad dream."

She tore her eyes away from the eerie sight. "None of this is your fault," she said. She touched Elle's forearm. "We have to move."

"We can't leave Mom and Dad," she said.

Cass took a breath. "Do you think you're strong enough to pull your mother along? I can guide your dad."

She nodded and linked her arm with Regina's. The congresswoman moved along docilely but otherwise gave no indication that she was aware of anything that was going on around her.

"The roof access is to the right, at the end of the hall," Elle informed her. "There are more stairs that lead down to the bleachers."

"Let's go."

She grabbed Mr. Pharell's forearm and stepped out into the hallway.

Four gunshots rang out followed by the staccato of an automatic weapon. She judged the shooters to be on the second level, and was grateful that they did not need to go in that direction. She hurried them along to the roof access, left propped open with a piece of cinderblock.

"Go up," she told Elle, giving her Mr. Pharell's hand so she could lead him.

She turned to look down that hall. Charybdis, masked, appeared and ran toward her. Behind her, there came a blindingly bright light that for a few seconds bleached the color from the world. A loud bang like thunder accompanied the phenomenon.

A flash bomb.

Once the light faded, she could see Charybdis's silhouette on her hands and knees, crawling forward. Cass ran forward, just as a half dozen cops appeared equipped for war.

Her intent was to use the Aegis, but she needed to clear Charybdis.

She wasn't fast enough. A spray of bullets tore holes in the wall. She felt a stab of hot pain tear through her upper thigh. She powered through the last few steps to put Charybdis behind her and let the Aegis loose at full force.

The cops bowled into each other in a tangle of limbs.

She limped backward. Charybdis had collected herself.

"I've got Elle," Cass said.

"Good," Charybdis said. "We need to get down to the field."

As they neared the door that led to the narrow staircase, they heard the unmistakable sound of a helicopter. They exchanged a look and rushed up to the roof.

Elle was waiting for her there with her parents, but so was Thora and the Geist device. They were standing close together, and her ex-handler held the cane between them. Elle stood, blank-faced. Her hands reached out and grasped the handle.

A commotion behind her caught her attention for a fraction of a second. Charybdis was busy holding off the relentless DC police that had attacked them in the press box. Cass strode toward Thora and Elle, a fury growing inside her to see them together.

A helicopter zoomed close. It bore the National Guard insignia on the side, but something told Cass that this was not going to be a rescue mission. Elle and Thora seemed oblivious to the chopper and continued to stand both holding on to the Geist device.

Her suspicions were confirmed when a soldier leaned out of the side and began to fire at the roof. A scatter of bullets ricocheted onto the rooftop only feet away from Thora and Elle. Cass ran forward and unleashed the Aegis.

The chopper nearly rocked over onto its side, losing the shooter. Cass saw the gun fall and the panicked face of the pilot as she struggled to right the bird in time. The pilot circled the roof. Another blast of the Aegis interrupted the momentum of the main rotor, and the pilot was not able to recover.

Cass made it to Elle's parents, and as she skirted past them, they collapsed. She paused and felt a shift in the air, much like the Aegis, but dry, suffocating. In the stands, she could view the people in the bleachers on the opposite side of the field fall into heaps and stacks.

She grabbed Thora's shoulder and pushed her to the side. Cass was mortified to see that Elle still held on to the Geist device, her eyes half closed, her face slack as if she were dozing off. She reached out to grab the thing but stopped herself. She called her name, but Elle did not answer.

Cass turned to Thora, who stood there a smug smile tugging her lips. Behind her, Charybdis had finished off the cops. She staggered forward, dragging one leg. She was bloody and broken, her clothes torn, a knife clutched in one hand. She fell on her knees next to Thora who didn't bother to even glance her way.

Sickened, Cass grabbed Thora by her jacket ready to blast her with the Aegis. Charybdis somehow got to her feet to help her, and Cass pushed her aside.

"What did you do to Elle?"

"I didn't do anything that hasn't already been done," she shouted.

"You knew about this all along," she shouted. "You knew all these people would be hurt, that Elle would be involved."

"Yes," she said simply.

Cass shook her. "I never should have trusted you."

Thora's eyes flashed with anger. "Yet you did, because somehow you knew even if my plans were nefarious that I would lead you to her."

Cass shook her again, enraged.

"And I am here, way off my planned course, lured by the idea of spoiling Project Songbird, of wrangling Elle and by proxy, you."

Cass's anger faltered as Thora spoke.

"I suspect that my actions since you and Lyles explored the white room have not been my own. I have been wrangled."

Her words shocked Cass before her brain could fully register them. She let go of Thora.

"Who?" she asked. "Who wrangled you?"

"The one who took you from me the day you met her in Kuwait. Elle."

In the distance, she could hear sirens and more helicopters. They would soon have more than cops to escape if they lingered any longer.

"She was created by a secret faction of the US government, with Olmpicorp technology to make all these people thralls, a controlled version of what happened in Kuwait."

Cass turned away to her, to Elle.

"Of course she's not consciously aware of enlisting us," Thora said and when Cass did not respond she grabbed her arm.

"Listen to their pulses," Thora instructed her.

She did and felt a gentle rhythm coming from them, not like before.

"She is wondrous," Thora said with a dry chuckle, and as she did, Cass could feel the faint hum of a pulse. Still, none of that made anything she said true. Something had gone wrong with Thora, maybe the mask she wore was defective and she'd breathed in some of the gas.

Charybdis was back on her feet, her face a grimace of pain. She and Cass exchanged a knowing glance. She would die defending Thora if needed.

Cass readied the Aegis. The choppers were getting close, and soon the Guard would have assessed the situation below and would be ready to take them out.

"I brought the Geist device here to wrangle her, to put a kink in Olympicorp's plans. I figured that once I succeeded, you would follow," Thora said.

Cass stared at her in disbelief. "How were you planning on getting out of here?"

Thora looked up to the sky. "Liang will land a helicopter on the field."

Cass stared at her for a moment. "That's it?"

"We'll have the nano cloud to cover us," she said.

She felt a sense of dread wash over her. She looked and saw it in the distance like a flock of birds flying south for the winter.

"Don't let that thing get near the ground," Cass told her.

"Not to worry," Thora said.

"Then we should get going," Charybdis said. She moved forward to lead the way.

Thora went to Elle. She removed the Geist device from her hands and returned it to her side as her cane.

Elle did not move for a moment, then her eyes fluttered open and she surveyed the rooftop. Horror struck her face when she noticed her parents. She was on her knees next to them, touching them in an effort to wake them.

Cass lifted her up. "Elle, we have to go."

"What happened here?" she asked.

"You saved them," Thora told her.

"How?" Elle asked.

"With this," Thora said, showing her the Geist device.

"Who are you?" Elle asked.

"We have to go," Cass said gently.

Elle looked down at her parents and back up at them. She nodded. Cass's heart broke for her, she seemed so lost.

"Hey," Cass said softly. "We're going to get you out of here and then we're going to sort everything out."

"Sort things out?" Elle asked in disbelief. "I don't know if I'm in reality or if I'm somewhere on the other side of the mist."

Cass felt heartbroken and helpless at that moment. Thora noticed her hesitation and spoke up.

"I think what Cassandra meant was that we should leave this place and live to fight another day."

Elle nodded and allowed Thora to take her hand. Cass's eyes met her old handler's, and she knew she could not allow her to get on the helicopter.

They made their way to the other side of the roof and made their descent. Cass made sure to keep an eye on the field for any trouble. She saw the eerie stillness of the people below. There was a man on the first landing in a seated position. His legs sprawled through the gaps in the railing and dangled awkwardly over the side. He looked as if he had had a few too many drinks at the game and fallen asleep. It would have been best if the man's day had ended so uneventfully. Thora said the people were fine, but what irreparable damage would the gas yield?

They reached the bleachers. Cass and Charybdis had to physically remove people to clear a path for them. Halfway down, she noticed soldiers coming onto the field from the concourse. They were masked, their guns at the ready.

"Keep them moving to the field," she told Charybdis.

As she moved away, Elle reached out for her.

Cass reached back. Their hands touched.

"Be careful," she said.

She could hardly believe the words she spoke next. "Stick with Thora."

Cass left them. The Guardsmen were fanning out, taking stock of the fallen people, searching for movement.

She made herself known to them.

"Hey," she shouted.

Her heart hammered against her ribs as the chill of the Aegis claimed her brain. Dozens of red dots, the laser sights from the soldier's guns covered her head and torso. She raised her hands slowly.

An explosion bellowed from above. Cass looked over her shoulder to see a fiery storm as the wreckage of a helicopter plummeted from the sky and onto the home team's end zone, wiping out the goal post in a screeching metallic wail. As the fire of the explosion faded from the sky, it left a familiar overcast like the proverbial silver-lined cloud, yet far more sinister; the nano cloud had struck.

In the stands, Charybdis, Thora, and Elle crouched, momentarily frozen by the crash. In her mind, Cass urged them to move.

Someone was yelling for her to get on the ground. The outbreak of red laser points on her body had worsened. She shrank a bit, as if she intended to surrender and then blasted them with the Aegis with everything she had.

Bodies, some the sleeping spectators, some soldiers, were lifted into the air along with guns and other forgotten belongings. They littered the maelstrom created by the Aegis. She did not let up, even as they all crashed into each other head over ass.

She glanced above and saw that there was no more sky, only the nano cloud churning over the stadium.

Something hit her shoulder, hard. She managed to keep her footing. Cass looked and saw a glowing metal rod sticking from her shoulder. Her first thought was of Thora, but movement from the corner of her eye revealed the real culprit: a soldier with what looked to be a rocket launcher on their shoulder.

Her second thought was to reach up and rip the thing off. A sound like synthesized crashing of waves filled her ears. A strange feeling overcame her as if she were in the ocean and being dragged into the pull of a passing wave. The noise echoed inside her head, the continuous roar of breaking surf. She reached for the thing but found her reactions slowed.

Her limbs locked and she fell into the grass. Paralyzed.

Above, the nano cloud parted and a helicopter passed through on the finger of a shaft of sunlight. A missile tried to follow but was shredded into fire. The chopper landed and Cass saw the figures of Thora, Charybdis, and Elle go meet it.

Cass made an attempt to move. Pain wracked her body when she did. She managed to sprawl over onto her stomach toward Thora's chopper. She dragged herself forward a few feet, struggling with the bolts of pain that jolted her body, as every muscle in her body seemed to cramp in revolt to her movement.

Charybdis veered away from Thora and Elle and ran her way. Fire came from the stands, but she was faster. Clods of dirt and grass flew in her wake as if she were making her own running play in the doomed game. She reached Cass and fell to her knees and looked Cass over for what ailed her. She saw the metal rod in her shoulder. She wrapped her hands around it and pulled it away. At the same time, she aimed her gun at someone. Before she could fire, a bullet tore into her throat.

Cass screamed into a spray of blood as Charybdis fell forward over her in a last effort.

More gunshots.

She did not have time to grieve.

Thora's chopper lifted from the ground.

With a roar, Cass pushed Charybdis aside. Mad, and blind with both mental and physical anguish, she aimed the Aegis toward the stands. She did not linger to watch the tumble of bodies and just ran.

The chopper lifted higher, a story high, now.

Running would not be enough.

She did not think after that.

At first, she stumbled back to the ground, her teeth rattling together between her clenched jaws. She kept her footing, kept running. She was right beneath the rising helicopter now. Somehow, her aching legs gained speed. Confident in her momentum, she let the cold feeling take over her brain, and she jumped.

The distance she gained shocked her. She thudded headfirst into the bottom of the chopper. Her flailing hands grabbed the ruts by pure instinct.

She held tight as the helicopter lifted higher. The nano cloud enveloped them in a silvery black cloud.

Hands reached out from above. She reached for them. They pulled her up and she found herself in Elle's arms. Liang and Thora waited behind them.

"Fuck. You flew," Elle said breathlessly.

"Did I?" Cass asked.

"Your shoulder."

"I'm fine," Cass insisted. "How do you feel?"

Elle touched her temple, her eyes soft with sadness. "More like myself, I guess."

She seemed aware of their closeness and moved away shyly. Cass gave her a reassuring smile. She wanted to tell her that she was glad that she was finally safe. She felt extremely tired.

"We're not out of the woods yet," Thora said. "But I think I can handle it from here."

Elle gasped.

"Her body has been through a lot," Thora told her.

She moved in close. Cass did not have to see the syringe or feel its sting; she could taste whatever it was, flowing through her veins.

After that, everything went black.

CHAPTER TWENTY-TWO

A White Room

Elle woke back in her room at Gloaming Hill. She sat up in bed quickly, startled out of her mind. She'd had another nightmare she supposed, or another hallucination of Robert Loera back from the grave. She did not remember either.

Outside, thunder rumbled. She called out for Nurse Grace but got no answer. She called out for Dr. Stevens. Once again, no one answered. She eased herself out of the bed and went to the bathroom. She used the toilet and went to the sink to splash some water on her face. She reached for a towel and dried herself. When she put the towel down, she saw another reflection behind hers in the mirror: an old woman with white hair. When she turned, there was no one there.

She returned to her bed. Something was wrong.

She tried to remember the previous day but could not recollect anything. Had she seen Dr. Branch for a session? That could be one reason why she was so foggy.

She did some deep breathing as instructed by Dr. Stevens, to calm herself.

As she finished the exercise, she noticed that there was someone there with her obscured in a curtain of shadow. Fear struck her and she was sure that it was Rob Loera back from the shadows to torment her.

"Hello?" she called.

The figure stood and approached the bed. The shadow faded revealing the old woman whose reflection she had seen in the mirror. She was dressed smartly in all black, a lovely red-and-white-checkered scarf with an overlapping pattern of vines. She leaned on a cane.

"Who are you?"

"You know who I am, Elle," she said in a cultured drawl.

She paused for a moment.

"Thora."

She smiled. "I've been searching for you for some time."

"I've been lost for a long time," she said, confused. "Is this Gloaming Hill?"

"It certainly looks that way," Thora said and tilted her head. "What do you think?"

The question amused her, but at the same time she realized why the old woman posed the question. There was something off. "I guess it's not, but I can't explain why."

"Gloaming Hill was never a real place," Thora said. "Not in the physical sense."

"In what sense?"

"Come with me, and I will show you."

Elle climbed out of bed, and Thora offered her arm as if they were going on a stroll in the country. Though she was not sure if she should trust her, Elle knew that Thora was not a threat to her.

She felt that she knew many secret things, riddles with solutions that could not solidify in her mind until they were posed.

When Thora opened the door to her room, there was only the mist at once loose and solid, mysterious, yet familiar. This was not Gloaming Hill, at least not the way she knew it.

"What is this? Where is Dr. Branch? Dr. Stevens?"

"They were real people, but they were players," Thora said. "They played their part as they were assigned, like actors in a movie."

Together, they stepped into the mist.

When it cleared, Elle saw that they were in the ruins of the convention center in Johannesburg. From their vantage point they could see the crowd of people like zombies shuffling through the debris.

"The events of Johannesburg never happened," Thora said. "The memory was implanted in your brain."

"By who?" Elle asked. "Why?"

"People who wanted to mold you to fit a narrative," Thora said. "People who wanted to set you up as a sacrifice."

They moved through the chaos to a broken exit door that revealed the mist. Elle peered through, but she could see nothing. She ducked her head and passed through. Once again, the mist dissolved and she was in the refrigerated truck with Leslie, and the bodies on hooks. She sensed Thora close by and turned to see her.

"This never happened either," Elle said.

She gave a wise nod in return.

Elle turned back to the scene. Unlike the mist, things were starting to solidify in her mind. She moved to the door at the back of the truck and grabbed the freezing cold latch. She knew there would not be a road but mist.

The next stop was a place she had long forgotten. She recognized it thanks to the poster which featured an image of a kitten hanging on to a length of rope with its little paws.

"Hang in there," Elle said and laughed. "This is my camp counselor's office."

The door opened and a younger version of herself walked in followed by Dr. Branch, who she remembered then as one of the counselors.

"Tell me of your favorite memory," she said.

Surely her mind had mixed things up. She couldn't be sure anymore, between Gloaming Hill, the so-called memories dredged up by Dr. Branch during her sessions, the strange places between the mist, and the events at the stadium.

She was back at the Luling Bowling Alley. She moved among the lanes until she came across Thora sitting near the snack bar, her cane planted beneath her feet.

"What did you see?" she asked.

Elle came to sit next to her. "I saw my camp counselor. It was Dr. Branch. How could I have forgotten something like that?"

"It's because they wanted you to."

"I didn't let her," she said. "Not this time. I made her show me the truth."

"You've come into your own," Thora said. "That wasn't the plan. The plan was to use you, to make you into a terrorist, to hurt people."

Memories of the homecoming game flooded her mind, a series of images not unlike what she experienced during her sessions with Dr. Branch. The homecoming game, the people standing still in the stands seeming not to see or hear the explosions that rocked the place, or the National Guard marching in, guns drawn. Her parents had been among them.

"My parents, the stadium, all those people"

"They will be treated in various hospitals around the area," Thora said. "The doctors there will do their best to help them."

"And what about Cass?"

"She's not important," Thora said. "She's a powerful weapon, but weapons are not as important as the ones who wield them."

"Cass is important to me," Elle said. "Where is she?"

Thora sighed. "The two of you have a bond that cannot be broken. I'm sure it's wonderful, but from someone who knows how these things work, it's a curse."

"What have you done with her?"

"She's resting."

"Where exactly?" Elle asked.

"Physically, you two are in the same space," Thora said.

Elle walked to the red exit sign. Its ominous glow no longer frightened her. Nothing beyond the mist frightened her. She found it there where the back parking lot of the Luling should have been. Thora was behind her as if she meant to follow.

"I'm going to find Cass," she said. "Don't shadow me any longer. This is my place and you are not welcome here."

Thora sneered at her but took a step backward.

"You'll have to get to her before I do," she said.

Just as Elle suspected, the sage, kind old lady act was just a ruse. She left her there and entered the mist.

Elle did not have to roam for long. She found Cass in the tiny apartment, wherever in the world it was meant to exist, bundled in the bed amongst a tangle of covers. Elle realized that it was all along a safe place where she could keep her memory of Cass while Dr. Branch bombarded her with false memories.

She was beginning to see the truth.

Elle joined Cass on the bed. She looked just as she had the day they'd met. Strong and sexy. Her mind had preserved her memory perfectly, carefully curated from the few soft quiet moments they'd shared with each other.

Cass stirred and opened her eyes. She smiled and immediately wanted to pull Elle in with her. When she found that Elle would not budge, she sat up.

"Can't we just stay here?" Cass pleaded.

It was tempting, but dangerous. The warmth of her seemed so real, Elle could easily slip into this moment and stay forever.

"Thora would have us both," she said.

She watched Cass's expression change as she realized what awaited them.

"I'm sorry," she said. "I had a moment of weakness."

"You don't have anything to be sorry about," Elle said. "Let's go."

She stood and reached for her hand.

"I'll need your help to get me out."

Elle took her hand and together they walked out of the little apartment and into the mist.

EPILOGUE

Cass sat up dripping chunks of the clear, brownish gel. Elle helped to steady her and used her bare hands to wipe the mess from her face so she could open her eyes. When she did, Elle leaned over and kissed her lips. Cass smiled around the kiss. When they parted, she glanced around their surroundings.

"Where's Thora?"

"She's gone," Elle said. She too was damp, her hair slicked back with a towel draped around her bare shoulders.

Groggy from the drugs, Cass inspected the space. In the dimness, she could see that they were in a wooden cabin, the inside paneled with wood and above them handsome beams leaned in like tented fingers. From her vantage point, she could see a small kitchen; beyond, she could see trees and mountains. One of Thora's secret hideaways, no doubt.

"She tried to wrangle me," Cass said. "She tried to wrangle you."

Elle helped her to stand on unsteady legs and guided her to a chair near the fire. She saw the second pod then, the one that had held Elle.

"Who woke you?"

"No one," Elle said. "I did it on my own. When I got my bearings, I climbed out and helped you out too."

She dried Cass with towels and covered her with a heavy blanket. She brought her tea and a plate of cookies. She sat close by on a little low stool.

"Where are we?" Cass asked.

"Arkansas," Elle said in disbelief. "There's a map in the kitchen along with a bag. It has guns. Passports. Cash."

"A gift from Thora," Cass said.

"An offering, maybe," Elle said. "We had a conversation in the mist."

"Yeah?"

"Yes, I told her to leave us alone."

Cass stood and went to the kitchen to see what Thora had left behind. She saw everything laid out on the counter along with a stack of newspapers, national and local.

She read through the headlines.

Neuro-terrorism. The New Threat
Terrorists Destroyed University Surveillance
Victims of Stadium Attack Still Suffer Mass Amnesia
Congresswoman Among Homecoming Attack Victims
Where is Elle Pharell?

According to the dates, it had been several weeks since the stadium. Thora had held them for that long trying to get inside their heads. Had Elle been able to chase her away? Their eyes met. She was smiling a little bit.

"I'm glad to see you back on your feet so soon."

Cass smiled back shyly. She checked out the map and saw that a spot in Arkansas had been marked, as well as the way to the nearest major highway. She moved on to the bag Elle had spoken of. Inside were documents for the both of them and a substantial amount of cash.

"We can trust this stuff?" Elle asked.

"Yes," Cass said. "Thora's not a fool."

"What do we do now?" Elle asked.

"We move," Cass said. "Eventually, we'll have to get rid of everything we take from this place. Get new identities on our own."

Elle nodded in agreement. There were tears in her eyes and her voice quavered. "I want to expose what happened to me. The world needs to know what happened to those people at the stadium. They need to know who has corrupted our government."

Cass's shyness faded and she walked around the counter and pulled her into her arms. Elle hugged her and sobbed into her shoulder.

"Thora said those people may never be the same again. My dad. And Mom. I know that she was corrupt. I know she basically handed me over to them."

"I'm so sorry."

"I'll never be able to go back to my old life."

"I can protect you," Cass said.

She pulled away. "Or we could look out for each other."

"We've done a pretty good job of that so far."

"Thank you," she said. "For saving me."

"You saved me first," Cass said. "I was only returning the favor."

The End

About the Author

Tanai Walker lives in Houston, Texas, with her wife, Janette, and two elderly dogs. When she's not writing, she teaches art to inner city youth.

Books Available from Bold Strokes Books

Curse of the Gorgon by Tanai Walker. Cass will do anything to ensure Elle's safety, but is she willing to embrace the curse of the Gorgon? (978-1-63679-395-5)

Dance with Me by Georgia Beers. Scottie Templeton mixes it up on and off the dance floor with sexy salsa instructor Marisa Reyes. But can Scottie get past Marisa's connection to her ex? (978-1-63679-359-7)

Gin and Bear It by Joy Argento. Opposites really can attract, and as Kelly and Logan work together to create a loving home for rescue cat Bear, they just might find one for themselves as well. (978-1-63679-351-1)

Harvest Dreams by Jacqueline Fein-Zachary. Planting the vineyard of their dreams, Kate Bauer and Sydney Barrett must resist their attraction while battling nature and their families, who oppose both the venture and their relationship. (978-1-63679-380-1)

Outside the Lines by Melissa Sky. If you had the chance to live forever, would you take it? Amara Rodriguez did and it sets her on a journey to find her missing mother and unravel the mystery of her own heart. (978-1-63679-403-7)

The No Kiss Contract by Nan Campbell. Workaholic Davy believes she can get the top spot at her firm if the senior partners think she's settling down and about to start a family, but she needs the delightful yet dubious Anna's help by pretending to be her fiancée. (978-1-63679-372-6)

The Value of Sylver and Gold by Michelle Larkin. When word gets out that former Boston homicide detective Reid Sylver can talk to the dead, the FBI solicits her help on a serial murder case, prompting Reid to assemble forces once again with Detective London Gold. (978-1-63679-093-0)

When It Feels Right by Tagan Shepard. Freshly out of the closet Marlene hasn't been lucky in love, but when it comes to her quirky new roommate Abby, everything just feels right. (978-1-63679-367-2)

Lucky in Lace by Melissa Brayden. Straitlaced stationery store owner Juliette Jennings's predictable life unravels when a sexy lingerie shop and its alluring owner move in next door. (978-1-63679-434-1)

Made for Her by Carsen Taite. Neal Walsh is a newly made member of the Mancuso crime family, but will her undeniable attraction to Anastasia Petrov, the wife of her boss's sworn enemy, be the ultimate test of her loyalty? (978-1-63679-265-1)

Off the Menu by Alaina Erdell. Reality TV sensation *Restaurant Redo* and its gorgeous host Erin Rasmussen will arrive to film in chef Taylor Mobley's kitchen. As the cameras roll, will they make the jump from enemies to lovers? (978-1-63679-295-8)

Pack of Her Own by Elena Abbott. When things heat up in a small town, steamy secrets are revealed between Alpha werewolf Wren Carne and her human mate, Natalie Donovan. (978-1-63679-370-2)

Return to McCall by Patricia Evans. Lily isn't looking for romance—not until she meets Alex, the gorgeous Cuban dance instructor at La Haven, a newly opened lesbian retreat. (978-1-63679-386-3)

So It Went Like This by C. Spencer. A candid and deeply personal exploration of fate, chosen family, and the vulnerability intrinsic in life's uncertainties. (978-1-63555-971-2)

Stolen Kiss by Spencer Greene. Anna and Louise share a stolen kiss, only to discover that Louise is dating Anna's brother. Surely, one kiss can't change everything…Can it? (978-1-63679-364-1)

The Fall Line by Kelly Wacker. When Jordan Burroughs arrives in the Deep South to paint a local endangered aquatic flower, she doesn't expect to become friends with a mischievous gin-drinking ghost who complicates her budding romance and leads her to an awful discovery and danger. (978-1-63679-205-7)

To Meet Again by Kadyan. When the stark reality of WW II separates cabaret singer Evelyn and Australian doctor Joan in Singapore, they must overcome all odds to find one another again. (978-1-63679-398-6)

Before She Was Mine by Emma L McGeown. When Dani and Lucy are thrust together to sort out their children's playground squabble, sparks fly leaving both of them willing to risk it all for each other. 978-1-63679-315-3)

Chasing Cypress by Ana Hartnett Reichardt. Maggie Hyde wants to find a partner to settle down with and help her run the family farm, but instead she ends up chasing Cypress. Olivia Cypress. 978-1-63679-323-8)

Dark Truths by Sandra Barret. When Jade's ex-girlfriend and vampire maker barges back into her life, can Jade satisfy her ex's demands, keep Beth safe, and keep everyone's secrets...secret? 978-1-63679-369-6)

Desires Unleashed by Renee Roman. Kell Murphy and Taylor Simpson didn't go looking for love, but as they explore their desires unleashed, their hearts lead them on an unexpected journey. 978-1-63679-327-6)

Maybe, Probably by Amanda Radley. Set against the backdrop of a viral pandemic, Gina and Eleanor are about to discover that loving another person is complicated when you're desperately searching for yourself. 978-1-63679-284-2)

The One by C.A. Popovich. Jody Acosta doesn't know what makes her more furious, that the wealthy Bergeron family refuses to be held accountable for her father's wrongful death, or that she can't ignore her knee-weakening attraction to Nicole Bergeron. 978-1-63679-318-4)

The Speed of Slow Changes by Sander Santiago. As Al and Lucas navigate the ups and downs of their polyamorous relationship, only one thing is certain: romance has never been so crowded. 978-1-63679-329-0)

Tides of Love by Kimberly Cooper Griffin. Falling in love is the last thing on either of their minds, but when Mikayla and Gem meet, sparks of possibility begin to shine, revealing a future neither expected. 978-1-63679-319-1)

Catch by Kris Bryant. Convincing the wife of the star quarterback to walk away from her family was never in offensive coordinator Sutton McCoy's game plan. But standing on the sidelines when a second chance at true love comes her way proves all but impossible. (978-1-63679-276-7)

Hearts in the Wind by MJ Williamz. Beth and Evelyn seem destined to remain mortal enemies but are about to discover that in matters of the heart, sometimes you must cast your fortunes to the wind. (978-1-63679-288-0)

Hero Complex by Jesse J. Thoma. Bronte, Athena, and their unlikely friends must work together to defeat Bronte's arch nemesis. The fate of love, humanity, and the world might depend on it. No pressure. (978-1-63679-280-4)

Hotel Fantasy by Piper Jordan. Molly Taylor has a fantasy in mind that only Lexi can fulfill. However, convincing her to participate could prove challenging. (978-1-63679-207-1)

Last New Beginning by Krystina Rivers. Can commercial broker Skye Kohl and contractor Bailey Kaczmarek overcome their pride and work together while the tension between them boils over into a love that could soothe both of their hearts? (978-1-63679-261-3)

Love and Lattes by Karis Walsh. Cat café owner Bonnie and wedding planner Taryn join forces to get rescue cats into forever homes—discovering their own forever along the way. (978-1-63679-290-3)

Repatriate by Jaime Maddox. Ally Hamilton's new job as a home health aide takes an unexpected twist when she discovers a fortune in stolen artwork and must repatriate the masterpieces and avoid the wrath of the violent man who stole them. (978-1-63679-303-0)

The Hues of Me and You by Morgan Lee Miller. Arlette Adair and Brooke Dawson almost fell in love in college. Years later, they unexpectedly run into each other and come face-to-face with their unresolved past. (978-1-63679-229-3)

A Haven for the Wanderer by Jenny Frame. When Griffin Harris comes to Rosebrook village, the love she finds with Bronte de Lacey creates a safe haven and she finally finds her place in the world. But will she run again when their love is tested? (978-1-63679-291-0)

A Spark in the Air by Dena Blake. Internet executive Crystal Tucker is sure Wi-Fi could really help small-town residents, even if it means putting an internet café out of business, but her instant attraction to the owner's daughter, Janie Elliott, makes moving ahead with her plans complicated. (978-1-63679-293-4)

Between Takes by CJ Birch. Simone Lavoie is convinced her new job as an intimacy coordinator will give her a fresh perspective. Instead, problems on set and her growing attraction to actress Evelyn Harper only add to her worries. (978-1-63679-309-2)

Camp Lost and Found by Georgia Beers. Nobody knows better than Cassidy and Frankie that life doesn't always give you what you want. But sometimes, if you're lucky, life gives you exactly what you need. (978-1-63679-263-7)

Felix Navidad by 'Nathan Burgoine. After the wedding of a good friend, instead of Felix's Hawaii Christmas treat to himself, ice rain strands him in Ontario with fellow wedding-guest—and handsome ex of said friend—Kevin in a small cabin for the holiday Felix definitely didn't plan on. (978-1-63679-411-2)

Fire, Water, and Rock by Alaina Erdell. As Jess and Clare reveal more about themselves, and their hot summer fling tips over into true love, they must confront their pasts before they can contemplate a future together. (978-1-63679-274-3)

Lines of Love by Brey Willows. When even the Muse of Love doesn't believe in forever, we're all in trouble. (978-1-63555-458-8)

Manny Porter and The Yuletide Murder by D.C. Robeline. Manny only has the holiday season to discover who killed prominent research scientist Phillip Nikolaidis before the judicial system condemns an innocent man to lethal injection. (978-1-63679-313-9)

Only This Summer by Radclyffe. A fling with Lily promises to be exactly what Chase is looking for—short-term, hot as a forest fire, and one Chase can extinguish whenever she wants. After all, it's only one summer. (978-1-63679-390-0)

Picture-Perfect Christmas by Charlotte Greene. Two former rivals compete to capture the essence of their small mountain town at Christmas, all the while fighting old and new feelings. (978-1-63679-311-5)

Playing Love's Refrain by Lesley Davis. Drew Dawes had shied away from the world of music until Wren Banderas gave her a reason to play their love's refrain. (978-1-63679-286-6)

Profile by Jackie D. The scales of justice are weighted against FBI agents Cassidy Wolf and Alex Derby. Loyalty and love may be the only advantage they have. (978-1-63679-282-8)